Her mind plunged.

Abby had woken her up in the dark. Her aunt's hands shook as she handed Maelle a cup of hot chocolate. Startled at being waited on, Maelle sat up, got out of bed, and pulled on the jeans she'd left crumpled on a chair. Asked for her mother.

"I have to tell you. There's been an accident. Your mommy, she's been hurt. Badly." Abby lifted the cup to Maelle's lips, and Maelle saw the lie in her aunt's eyes.

She pushed the cup to the floor, spilling the liquid over the rug, under the bed. She screamed and ran out of the room. After that, a blur. The funeral, some kind of chanting up at Joyous Woods, then just staying there, living in the pagoda house with Johanna and Neil. The reminiscence came to Maelle in flashes of full color, like a dream, but full of gaps in logic.

But she must concentrate. A man was looking at her. This Zachary with a scar.

Kudos for Margaret Ann Spence

Margaret Ann Spence's previous release,
LIPSTICK ON THE STRAWBERRY,
won
the 2015 First Coast Romance Writers Beacon Contest,
and was a finalist in
the 2019 Eric Hoffer Award
and
the 2019 Next Generation Indie Awards.

Joyous Lies

by

Margaret Ann Spence

Joyous Lies

COPYRIGHT © 2021 by Margaret Ann Spence

Cover Art by *Debbie Taylor*

The Wild Rose Press, Inc.
PO Box 708
Adams Basin, NY 14410-0708
Visit us at www.thewildrosepress.com

Publishing History
First Edition, 2021
Trade Paperback ISBN 978-1-5092-3472-1
Digital ISBN 978-1-5092-3473-8

Published in the United States of America

Dedication

To John, whose patience is never-ending

Acknowledgments

Writing is a lonely profession, but no one publishes a book in isolation.

I'm grateful for the insight of my first readers, The Tapestry Writers' Group, the sisterhood of the Women's Fiction Writers Association, and the editing skill of Eilidh MacKenzie at The Wild Rose Press. As she did for my debut novel, *Lipstick on the Strawberry*, Debbie Taylor created a wonderful cover that evokes mystery, inviting the reader in.

Finally, I am so thankful for the support of my family. I would not do any of this without you.

Prologue

A chain-link fence loomed out of the darkness to her right, its outline of steel diamonds a warning. Angela cut the headlights and slowed to a crawl as her car passed the concrete-block building in a wooded area some way out of the city. Her eyes adjusted to the darkness as she inched forward beyond the end of the fence and parked in the shelter of the bordering trees. A lone Volvo sat empty near the entrance. In the darkened laboratory, a few lit windows showed someone was working late.

She stepped out cautiously and headed back toward the lights of the building, zigzagging from shadow to shadow. Gradually, she made out the shapes of trees alongside the road. As she approached the fence, she tripped on a rock and pain tore through her ankle. She suppressed a cry and limped forward. When she reached the chain-link barrier, she leaned against it for a moment, breathing deeply. Then grasping the metal links while leaning backward like a monkey, she scaled the fence. Over the top, she lowered herself down, trying to make no sound.

She was in. No one had seen her.

She tiptoed toward the building. In the silence, twigs crackled under her feet as she skirted the laboratory. The air nipped her hands and face with an early-fall chill. Fear gripped her stomach. The door

1

loomed, black, unlit. She fingered the keycard.

Deep breaths. A sudden trip light would reveal her dark-clad shape, eyes frozen in terror. She must try to get near the building in the gaps between motion sensors. She crept onward, then back a few feet, trying all the while to soften her toe-steps in the scrunchy leaf-fall. It slowed her progress.

Was anyone there? That car parked outside. It meant someone must be inside, working. Him.

Her heart started beating wildly, her breath came fast. How insane to try to talk to him without witnesses. What was she thinking? Maybe she should regard this trip as a trial run, come back when the lab would be completely empty and dark, then release the animals on her own, quietly. She shivered.

She leant against a tree, breathing deeply to slow her thoughts. What she wanted to achieve. The obstacles. The threats. Even if she was arrested, the publicity would be good for the cause of the animals. But her career? She could not be caught. She could not go to jail. What about Maelle? What would happen to her? The girl needed her mother.

Angela must consider this carefully, weigh the moral imperatives. She resisted a violent urge to ping a pebble against the window in frustration.

It came to her. She must face him.

Chapter One

The plants, she hoped, would have something to say.

With the door to the laboratory closed and the sound barriers in place, Maelle fixed acoustic sensors onto two potted plants, situated side by side in a glass dome so even the vibrations of her breath could not disturb them. Above one, she played a recording of the sound of a caterpillar munching leaves. The noise, when magnified so humans could hear it, sounded like the march of eager feet over rough terrain. After twenty minutes, she removed the recording, put on her earphones, and waited.

She heard it, a faint clicking sound.

The plants were talking to one another. She'd have to give another explanation for it, in scientific jargon. Was it the sound of the xylem flowing up through the plant stalks? Was it the sound of electrical signaling? Or was it merely her imagination?

Maelle gripped her white coffee mug so tightly her hands, long-fingered, short-nailed, paled to the color of the mug. On the table in front of her, a laptop held her research notes. Had she proved there was a significant difference between plants exposed to a sound as opposed to those which had grown in complete silence? The trick was providing a sound in isolation. The world was never completely silent, except in an artificial situation like the one she created in her pristine laboratory. She'd added a sound of a predator. She believed the threatened plant signaled its companion that danger was near.

She put down her cup, sat back, and let the thought sink in. Yes, she'd proved plants could hear. And if they could hear, could they talk to one another too?

It sounded preposterous, but when you really thought it through, it made sense. Sound waves traveled through the atmosphere just like magnetic waves or radiation. Why wouldn't plants be sensitive to changes in the atmosphere made by loud noises?

The bigger question was, if plants could hear one another, what were they communicating?

She'd always sensed they could, of course. All those years of seeking peace from the commune by walking into the forest and lying on the ground, feeling the earth underneath her, cool, prickly with twigs, alive. She'd lie there and just listen. The forest was blessedly free from the din of humans, the only sounds birdsong and the rustle of small animals. And after a while the forest itself spoke, full of noises. A regular cacophony of crashes and bangs, squeaks and murmurs. Not just the soughing of the trees in wind, but creakings and tearings. Trees were not passive at all.

She pulled her ponytail into a tighter knot, tensing her temples. She needed to get back to the forest this weekend, get out of the sterile lab environment and back to the farm. Her grandparents, Neil and Johanna, needed her more now they were getting older.

Maelle recorded her findings onto a spreadsheet. She'd repeat her experiments over and over, to try and find a pattern.

She needed another coffee to spark up her mind. She put away the sensors, uncapped the glass domes, returned the seedlings to their sunny place on the bench, and returned the closed laptop to the backpack she carried everywhere.

Outside, the sun shone, the day sparkled, and Maelle marveled at how nature managed to carry on despite the depredations of man. Chernobyl, for example. After that radiation leak which shut down the town in 1986, humans left it alone; the authorities forbade entry. But that didn't stop the plants from invading the place and thriving, and the wild animals and birds of the region had come back.

She shouldn't muse like this, locked in her own world. In the cafeteria, she smiled at a few people she'd seen around but saw none of her colleagues. She bought a coffee, using her own chipped mug (better for the environment!), and added a salad, realizing she'd gone out the door without breakfast. Finding an empty table, she sat down, plumping her backpack next to her. She was unzipping it, about to take out a book, when she sensed a presence beside her.

"Mind if I join you?"

Maelle looked up to a white shirt, then farther up to dark eyes, a long, tanned face with a crooked smile, and curly black hair in need of a cut. The stranger put his foam cup down on the table without waiting for an answer and folded himself into a chair opposite her. Despite the unruly hair, the man was more formally dressed than most at the university. He wore pressed pants, a collared shirt, and a jacket. A visitor, perhaps?

"Zachary Kane," he said, extending his hand. "Here for a conference but had to nip out for a jolt of caffeine to keep myself awake."

She smiled. "Coffee. Me, too. I'm Maelle Woolley. What conference?"

"Psychiatry." He raised his cup. "I'm in psychiatric research. Working on the genetic basis of mental illness. Bipolar disorder, for one."

Maelle froze. Her mother's face flashed before her. Angela, distracted. Angela shouting. Angela excited and waving her hands. Angela lying on the bed, too depressed to speak.

"Is mental illness inherited?" Her voice came out in a squeak.

"Probably. In some cases, anyway. We don't know a lot yet."

Slowly, Maelle let out a breath. She knew this, knew there was some genetic correlation. But that was the case in so many diseases. And anyway, no one had ever actually told her that her mother had been crazy. Perhaps her imagination had gotten the better of her. Even though she monitored her own moods obsessively, anxious for a sign, she felt as fine as an even-keeled boat sailing in smooth waters.

"You don't do clinical work?" She sipped her coffee, looking at Zachary over the rim of the mug. Thinking about Neil, her grandfather, and his up and down moods, which made everyone walk on eggshells around him. Not that she'd bring that up with this stranger.

"No. Research only. Though I do believe talking therapy has its place, especially when there's no clinical diagnosis. You know what they say about sunlight being the best disinfectant. Only by opening up the past and seeing it in the full light of day can you put it finally to rest."

"It gets pretty dirty up at the farm. My grandmother opens all the cupboards and storage bins in the spring, cleans out the cobwebs and insects that nest in there."

"You got the idea." The skin around his eyes crinkled when he smiled.

"I spend a lot of time at ground level. Under it, actually. Studying fungi, roots, and other ways plants connect. I'm a botanist. Doing my PhD."

She twirled her fork in the salad bowl. A piece of radish and a vibrant red beet nestled amongst the arugula under goat cheese and a dusting of nuts. Nature's vibrant colors, created to attract pollinators. The libidinous plants, sluttishly exposing themselves for fertilization by any passing bee. Good grief, what a thought to strike her. How embarrassing. Must make conversation. Make an effort, Maelle, even if small talk is as foreign to you as Chinese.

"Mind if I eat?" She lifted her fork and smiled at her unexpected companion. "I just realized I'm starving."

"Of course. Go ahead."

Did he think she was weird to be eating lunch at ten o'clock in the morning? Living alone, she had become used to doing things on her own schedule. Her lab work sometimes required all-night shifts. She pushed away her self-absorption with a sudden shake of the shoulders. "My grandparents made cheese like this."

"Really? Is it their farm you mentioned just now?"

"Yes. I lived with them a long time. From when I was about ten till I went to college."

"Your parents?" Zachary tipped his head back to drink the dregs of his coffee, twisting slightly so she saw him in profile.

Maelle stared. The man had a white scar running from just above his right jawbone down his neck, disappearing under his collar. Now that she'd noticed it, she had a hard time looking away. He must have lived through some trauma. Suddenly Zachary had her full attention.

"My mother died," she said. "I didn't know my father, actually."

"He didn't look after you when your mother died?"

"No. They separated before I was born."

"Ouch. How does that make you feel?"

"What are you, a psychiatrist or something?" Maelle laughed, knew it sounded a little forced. She rarely shared such personal information, even with friends. But perhaps the fact that he was only a visitor made it safe to tell her story. She'd never see him again. Working alone with plants, she'd been starved of human interaction. Not that she needed it. But this man—it was as if he pressed a button and she'd started purring like a machine being warmed up. A glow started in her stomach and spread upward. How good-looking he was, especially when he smiled.

"Sorry. Didn't mean to intrude. Just curiosity. And sympathy," he added quickly.

"What about you?"

"You mean, my parents? Well, actually, it's funny. You and I have something in common. We both lost a parent when we were young. My mother's still with us. She never remarried. Struggled financially but tried to do the right thing by me."

8

"Mine too, from what I remember. You're lucky still to have her." Her mind plunged, remembering that day.

Abby had woken her up in the dark. Her aunt's hands shook as she handed Maelle a cup of hot chocolate. Startled at being waited on, Maelle sat up, got out of bed, and pulled on the jeans she'd left crumpled on a chair. Asked for her mother.

"I have to tell you. There's been an accident. Your mommy, she's been hurt. Badly." Abby lifted the cup to Maelle's lips, and Maelle saw the lie in her aunt's eyes.

She pushed the cup to the floor, spilling the liquid over the rug, under the bed. She screamed and ran out of the room. After that, a blur. The funeral, some kind of chanting up at Joyous Woods, then just staying there, living in the pagoda house with Johanna and Neil. The reminiscence came to Maelle in flashes of full color, like a dream, but full of gaps in logic.

But she must concentrate. A man was looking at her. This Zachary with a scar.

Wariness made her alert. Who was she to open up like this to a complete stranger? A shrink, too? He'd probably overinterpret her every word and make a judgment. Call her neurotic or something.

But Zachary's eyes telegraphed kindness and curiosity. "Your name," he said. "It's so unusual."

"Yes. Maelle."

"You look pretty female to me. Sorry. That's not a very PC thing to say. Forgive me."

"May-elle." Maelle gave an exaggerated sigh as she pronounced her name slowly. "Means ambitious and goal-oriented. French. From Brittany. Not that I have French ancestry. German actually; my grandmother is Johanna. She was born in Cologne right after World War II. Funny how in English we use a French word for a German city." Why was she running on and on like this? What was the matter with her?

"Are you ambitious and goal-oriented?"

"I guess I am. Want to finish my PhD, get a teaching position. Somewhere where I can get outside and be with trees. Must be all those years on the farm."

Commune. She could not bring herself to say that word to Zachary. He'd think she was a whack job or something. Not that anyone on the farm was the slightest bit weird. Modify that. Not now, anyway. Her mother, of course, possibly. Was.

"What are you finding out about them? Plants, I mean?"

Oh. A subject dear to her heart. He wasn't judging her at all. Suddenly lighthearted, she took a deep breath and dared to say it. "I believe plants talk to one another."

She placed her hands firmly on the table and leaned her back into the chair till only its rear legs were on the floor. "So now you must think I'm crazy."

He shook his head. "Tell me more."

"Talking is the wrong word." Maelle hesitated, then went on in a rush. "But experiments have shown that plants communicate with one another."

"Why not? Communication helps survival."

A sudden warmth energized her. "Yes, take an octopus! People say plants can't hear, because they have no ears. Duh! Of course they don't. Here, I'm an octopus." She flung her arms out, spread her fingers. "I don't have ears. But I have an amazing sense of touch." She closed her eyes and put her hands in front of her, running her fingers over the table. She felt ridges and the coldness of its metal edge.

"You have beautiful hands."

"Oh. Thank you." Maelle opened her eyes and shoved her hands back in her lap, embarrassed. "Octopi sense through every tentacle, not an ear in sight."

"Hmm. Touch is very important to all creatures. Proves we're alive."

Maelle grabbed the table's edge, suddenly unbalanced. "Yeah, but plants. What I'm studying." Caffeine. Please. She took a sip of coffee, grimaced to find it cold, and put her cup down. "What they do is not just instinctual. They can anticipate something, if they've been placed in a controlled environment and given a stimulus that accompanies a light. Plants always move toward light. That's because they need sunlight to make food. Experiments show they can learn, after a lot of repetition, to move toward the light before the light goes on, as soon as they sense the stimulus."

"Sounds like the classic Pavlovian experiment."

"Yes. But with plants, not dogs."

"Makes sense. Plants and animals share many genes. And it's logical from an evolutionary point of view."

"That's what I think. It's a growing area of research, anyway. But the theory is still controversial, not quite proved to the scientific community's satisfaction. I'm trying to think up novel experiments to show learning in plants. But right now, I'm focused on them communicating in real time."

"Amazing. If either of us had mentioned these things a century ago, people would have said we're both crazy. Plants talking to one another, the origin of a person's personality encoded on a tiny thing we cannot see, a combination of genes. Yet here we are. We know so much, and yet we know so little."

"True." She could talk to this man for hours. Hours.

Zachary scrunched his coffee cup and started to rise. "Got to go," he said. "But I'd love to get together again. Want to do something tonight? Catch dinner?"

And so it began. They got on so well. He laughed, she laughed too, though this was new to her. Maelle felt an affinity with her plants in the changes in her own body. Her hair shone now like glossy leaves, her skin glowed like smooth bark, her limbs felt supple yet strong as new branches. And underneath, in the hidden recesses of her body, she felt herself growing toward Zachary Kane like the underground networks of mycorrhizae connecting the trees of the forest.

Chapter Two

Johanna raised the handful of angora to her face and sniffed. Rabbit fur. Good and healthy. She sandwiched the white mound of fluff between the toothed carders, pulling one over the other with a strong, sure hand to straighten the fibers and free them from snags. Later, she'd spin the fur with washed, dyed wool and create a blended yarn.

But now it was time to spin a previously prepared batch. Her gray plait swung as she worked. From time to time, she paused to stretch her gnarled fingers, shifted her seat on the narrow stool. It was becoming slower, this spinning business. She had to stop, stand, and stretch her aching body. Nevertheless, it sustained her, this ancient practice, knowing she was keeping an old craft alive. Knowing that when the yarn had been spun, colored in glowing shades from the dyes her own plants produced, she would turn it into beautiful garments.

Expensive garments, to be sure. The irony of it. Homemade, natural products were now so expensive that only the wealthy could wear them, and her daughter, product of the commune, sold them in her store. Thank goodness. Abby had the sales skill, the charm, the ease with strangers that Johanna lacked. Isolated in the hinterland as she had been for fifty years now, Johanna dreaded going to the city. The farmers' markets were her forays into commerce these days. Even with these friendly markets, she was happy to let Sally be the salesperson. Sally, her friend since girlhood, was good at that. The division of labor let Johanna be the idea person, the person who not only made the garments Abby sold, but the one who stayed behind on the commune, putting together the jams, the jellies, the cakes, quiches, cookies, and breads that brought in cash.

Pocket money.

There was never enough.

She put away the spindle and went into the kitchen. Surveying the remains of last night's meal in the old white refrigerator, she figured she could add a couple of onions to it, maybe a butternut squash, turn it into a vegetable stew. She walked into the newly gleaned garden, and the sharp cold autumn air revived her. She breathed deeply. Frost would come any night now. She spied a few green onion strings flattened on the ground, the bottoms of the bolted lettuces. There! The squash lay fat, nestling in its wide green leaves and furry stalks in its patch under the stripped bean pole.

She made dinner and, as usual, prided herself on her creativity with the little they had. Not that Neil acknowledged this. He was in one of his moods, his eyes far away.

"You're not listening to anything I say," she said, getting up and gathering the dishes, dumping them in the soapy water. She stood at the sink and watched the sun set behind the hill. The rains were late; they'd only had a few showers since September. If this kept up, the harvest could be poor next year. But whenever it rained, another problem presented itself. Their wooden pagoda-shaped house looked like something out of a catalogue for a Chinese vacation. In fact, that was exactly what it was. Neil and his buddies had fashioned the unusually shaped building from plans he'd scoured from somewhere and had made some idiosyncratic additions. He was going through a vaguely Buddhist phase at the time. The building was hexagonal, and each of the bedrooms on the second floor looked out over a balcony onto a view of fields blending into woods. After so many years, the balconies were not safe to walk out on.

In the years since Angela and Abby had grown up and Maelle did not come back much either, she and Neil had moved to separate bedrooms by unspoken agreement. Her part of the house was on the east side, and Johanna welcomed the morning through the wide windows, the first person in the house to feel the warm rays and the soft light of day. At the ground floor, a large stone patio surrounded an enormous tree. It had not been enormous when they built the house, but over the years, unpruned, untended, the tree grew up to the second story and engulfed the balcony of the south side. Rather than cut the tree back, Neil had sawn a circle in the floor of the balcony to allow the tree trunk to grow ever upward. Now it threatened to crack the entire balcony apart. Johanna sighed. She knew Neil would actually let that happen.

He'd lost the knack of carpentry. And of plumbing and of almost everything else. The topmost part of the pagoda, capping it like a hat, now had a leaky roof. Neil refused to pay it any attention. Up till now, they'd made do, patched and repaired everything. But now everything seemed perilous. Age, that's what it was.

For all Neil's unpredictable moods, the high cost of food for the animals, gasoline, electricity, and all the regulations that the dairy had to abide by, age was the big villain. It had attacked Neil and Johanna and the others with a vengeance. Their bodies, as well as their ideals, were cracking up.

Johanna finished drying the dishes and turned to Neil, whapping the dishtowel on the butcher block counter. Not only did he never help, he didn't even listen.

"What are we going to do, Neil?" she said, quietly at first, then louder.

"About what?"

"About this, about you, about us, about everything! It's falling apart, and we're broke. As you know. We're living week to week on the dairy, on the goodies I make and the angora jackets we knit here, the pottery Sally makes. This and that and nothing."

She dropped the towel on the counter and folded her arms, facing him. "Tell me, Neil. What exactly are you doing to contribute?"

He straightened up. "Hey, not fair! I contributed a lot. Me and the Circle, what's left of it. Not my fault that most of the others left, went back to the city. Is that what you wanted, too, Johanna? You want to be trapped in the consumer treadmill?"

Johanna bit back her thought. They were trapped anyway.

"Actually," he said, and a grin slowly spread across his face. "I've had a letter."

"A letter?"

"Yes, from a filmmaker. She wants to do a documentary."

"On what? Subsistence farming?" Johanna could not keep the bitterness out of her voice.

"Not at all. She wants to do a film on what happened to the hippies."

"That's a ridiculous old-fashioned term."

"So? It's what we called ourselves, way back when. When we came out here."

"To escape the draft, Neil."

"Yep. You went along with that, Johanna. Anyway, this woman, Pamela, thinks it's an interesting story. Something that's been nearly forgotten. She wants to make a movie."

"Invade our privacy?" Suspicion flared Johanna's nostrils.

"If you like. But she's offering us a chance, Jo. The publicity for Joyous Woods, for what we make and sell from here, would be great."

Johanna's shoulders slumped. "It will be so disruptive."

Neil gave her one of those looks. Despair mixed with irritation.

"When's she coming?"

"In a couple days."

"Everything's a mess. That balcony is a disgrace."

"Since when did you become all middle-class, Johanna? Pamela doesn't care. That's what she's here for, to get the authentic commune flavor. Back to the seventies."

Instinctively, Johanna put her wizened hands into the folds of her dress. What would this Pamela person see but a frumpy old woman? Her hair hung long down her back, gray streaked with white. Her skirt sagged shapelessly on her ample frame. Gone was the svelte and ardent young rebel who'd shouted with abandon during the antiwar marches at Berkeley. So long ago. This young digital wizard would mock them and their values.

"Why did you agree to let her come? Shouldn't we discuss it as a group?"

"What's the problem, Jo? Why do you always make difficulties? She wants to do a film about us. She's an artist. Same way that Angela wrote stories. Only difference, this will be on film."

An image of a dark-haired, willful young woman flashed before Johanna's eyes. Their daughter, named for the 1960s political activist Angela Davis, could be as single-minded, as strident, as beautiful as her namesake. Johanna shook her head to override the discomforting picture. Angela, at the morgue.

She wiped her eyes with the dishtowel, then started stacking dishes on the open shelf. "What's so interesting about us and our farm?"

"It's lasted since 1971. Not many of the old communes survived that long. Look, we still have some of the original members; we still live in the houses we built ourselves."

"And we still use the composting toilets. You don't think the health department will be after us?"

"Oh, come on! This is California after all. They're used to countercultural."

"Yes, the land of overregulation." She gave a sarcastic laugh.

"Humph." Neil turned away. His jeans fit badly, loose on a body that was still taut and trim from working outdoors all these years. His hair had thinned only a little, though the fair thatch had faded to gray.

"Where are the others tonight? Have you discussed this film business with them?"

"I mentioned it to the guys. Not sure they took it in. Anyway, Sally and Curtis won't be back till tomorrow. Curtis is trying to sell his paintings at a gallery. Hey, maybe I should try again."

"What?"

"Write a new song. Make a recording. I always knew I had it in me."

Johanna knew better than to contradict him. It was too late now. Neil might have had some small songwriting talent, but he'd been too undisciplined to persevere. He'd never understood what seemed to be obvious to her and to the others who'd persisted at Joyous Woods. Only if you plugged at something day in and day out, no matter if you were sick or discouraged or alive with possibility and achievement, only then could you actually succeed.

Neil. He'd been so charismatic when they were young. So handsome. His blue eyes had wooed her, and his persuasive tenor. For a moment, the long years disappeared and Johanna remembered the glow that had shone from Neil at twenty and captured her.

She crossed the kitchen and put her hand gently on his shoulder. Her voice became almost tender as she said, "All right. Tell me when, and I'll prepare something special. Ask the filmmaker to stay for dinner. Show her we are not just a bunch of dope-smoking dropouts. Show her we run a productive farm and have not lost our manners."

Chapter Three

The slim figure slid out of the SUV. High-heeled boots the color of burnt umber encasing shapely calves lowered gently onto the ground, narrowly missing a goat turd on the dirt turnaround in front of the house. Johanna's gaze rose to a face still in the warm bloom of youth, almost but not quite beautiful, the roman nose slightly hooked. It gave the young woman, alarmingly, an air of authority. She wore tight-fitting jeans and a light brown leather jacket. Under a tan corduroy baseball cap, the visitor's tawny hair reared up in a ponytail. She had cheekbones so high they created perfect little hills against the craters of her dark, darting eyes.

Following her, two young men stepped down to unpack camera equipment, tripods, and other gear Johanna couldn't name.

Neil, beaming, shook hands, introducing members of the Circle. One by one, the male members of the commune greeted the camera crew.

Looking her people over as a stranger would, Johanna smiled. Except for their long hair and patched and faded clothes, they looked like elderly members of a homeowners' association. One of them even held a clipboard. She stood at the back of the group, wondering when Neil was going to introduce her to the visitors.

He ignored her for at least five minutes. Wishing she'd combed her hair, she pushed her way forward, her hand out to greet the glamorous woman in charge.

"Welcome to Joyous Woods," she said. "Call me Jo."

"And I'm Pamela Highbury," the newcomer replied. "Joyous, Jo...Is this farm named after you?" She withdrew her hand from Johanna's and sniffed the air. "Fresh and natural."

Johanna inhaled the scent of fresh grass mingled with a waft of woodsmoke and the strong pong of manure. She straightened her back, smoothed her jeans with her hands. "Not at all," she said, "But we started it with joy and hope."

Pamela looked at Johanna, and Johanna felt naked. The young woman's eyes raked over the gray plait of hair, the T-shirt under a faded cardigan, denim pants, and work boots. Johanna, the relic. She lowered her eyes under the filmmaker's gaze. What was this woman's true purpose? Curiosity? Judgment? Would she portray them as freaks?

Well, she would try to make a good impression, show how things had progressed from the nuttiness of the earlier years to a working, organic farm. She'd get in first, before Neil had a chance to say something tactless.

"We're pretty proud of the fact we're still standing," she began. "Most of the intentional communities of the sixties and seventies collapsed under pressure."

Neil cut her off. "Come inside, Pamela, and get comfortable."

He gestured to the Circle to assist the film crew.

Johanna stood with her hands limp at her sides, momentarily at a loss.

Pamela picked her way through the mud. She almost toppled as a heel caught a tree root, and Neil grabbed her arm to steady her. She shot him a grateful look. She rocked back on the too-high heels of her boots and gripped the edge of his sweater to stop herself falling. The camera crew trailed behind.

"Some of our early members couldn't take the rural life." Johanna strode forward quickly, so she walked on Pamela's other side.

"Yes, I can see why," said the filmmaker. "Survival of the fittest, eh?"

Or survival of the stubborn. Johanna swallowed the thought. "How do you want to start?" She made a sweeping gesture with her arm. "What can we show you first?"

"The Circle will meet with Pamela and make the plan." Neil lifted his chin toward the house. "Could you organize something to eat and drink, Jo? These guys have come a long way."

Johanna hurried inside, leaving the others behind. Neil didn't need to direct her like that, like he had the authority he'd once claimed. Oh, yes, Neil had radiated authority in the early days. He was the undisputed leader; the others had rallied round him like he was their salvation. Of course, that was because he could give them, in this unspoiled land, a place to go, a place to hide.

She hustled into the kitchen to find Sally and Linda putting together a tray of coffee and scones fresh from the oven. The warm, delicious aroma permeated the kitchen, welcoming, homey. Where would the commune be without its women? They literally put food on the table. She put her arm around Linda, pulled Sally in by the wrist. She tucked a stray thread of Sally's salt and pepper hair behind her ear and lowered her voice to a whisper.

"I think the guys are about to be bowled over. So let's show them who's really in charge here."

Doubt spread over Linda's broad, freckled face. Sally snorted in suppressed laughter.

"Wait till you see the woman's get-up. Looks like something out of a fashion magazine."

Johanna broke away from her friends' embrace and turned to pull butter and jam from the fridge to put on the tray. She ran water in the sink and scrubbed her hands, trying unsuccessfully to dig the dirt from under her broken nails. As she dried her hands, she eyed her friends with affection. She and Linda and Sally were the survivors of the communal experiment. It was true, as she had told Pamela, that not everyone could take it. The hard work of clearing and plowing and sowing and caring for the animals, the orchards, and the dairy had left little time for leisure, for making oneself attractive.

Yet here was this woman, Pamela, cashing in her feminine wiles in her fashionable clothes, her slim figure, and her long hair, beautifully made up, fully subscribed to the Hollywood values as defined by its powerful men, and making money, too.

A racket at the door announced the group. Neil ushered Pamela and her crew inside.

"Take off your jackets," he said, though the house lacked a coat closet. From the kitchen area, separated from the great room only by a low wall, Johanna could see Pamela looking forlornly at the mud she was tracking in, but Neil waved her through to the great room with a grin.

There, Pamela stood on one leg, then another, obviously uncomfortable.

Johanna nudged Sally, who was also sending irritated vibes to Neil. Let Sally take the heat.

"It must have been a long drive," Sally said on cue. "Let's show you to the facilities. The composting toilets, that is."

To Johanna's satisfaction, the camera crew stifled snickers, while Pamela's face paled.

A little spurt of spite darted through Johanna's mind. Let her sit her pretty little butt in the outhouse. Let's hope a wasp gets in her jeans.

When she returned to the room, Pamela's face was taut, but her nose pointed as high as her last name. She fitted Neil with a tiny microphone on his sweatshirt.

"Now then, Neil," she said, "I'll sit on the sofa, and you take this chair nearest me."

Neil obeyed the pretty stranger without question.

With them both settled, Pamela began. "First, we have to do a camera and audio test. Won't take a minute." That done, she asked Neil, "Ready?"

When he nodded, she addressed the others. "I'm just doing an intro here, for the audience. If you could just hold your comments till I'm done with this."

She spoke into her own mic. "This film is about what became of the Vietnam era protesters. The dropouts, the ones who fled to Canada, and the ones who stayed here. The ones who kept their principles through the years."

This little introductory speech made Johanna smirk. What did this young, smug hipster know?

"We'll walk around, and you can show us Joyous Woods," Pamela went on. "But first, I want to know what led you to this lifestyle." She signaled the cameraman to focus on Neil's face. "You're the son of a wealthy family, I understand."

"Correct." Neil shifted in his seat.

"Tell us about your childhood, then. Why did you become a…farmer?"

"Songwriter, by choice. Farmer, by necessity." Neil waved an arm toward his guitar, propped up by a chair.

From her position on the other side of the room, Johanna, who had not been graced with a mic, saw Pamela cast an eye around the tattered furniture in the great room of the pagoda house. Built of logs, the walls had been plastered inside, but they had not been properly insulated. A water stain ran from the eaves, dribbled alongside the edge of a window, and down to the polished concrete floor, upon which several sheepskin rugs had been thrown. Once white, the rugs were now matted and gray.

The filmmaker perched on the edge of the handmade sofa. Its oiled wooden base bulged with thick, comfortable cushions, contrasting with the rest of the room's shabbiness. As if she felt too warm, Pamela pushed aside the mohair throw that lay across the back of the sofa. She lifted her cap from her head, revealing gold highlights in brown hair shining in the light streaming from the window.

Johanna's gaze darted back and forth from Pamela's unlined eager face to the throw, Johanna's own handiwork, which the visitor had flung aside. Why was this woman here, lounging on these cushions?

What did she want? And why was her very first question to Neil about his family's wealth?

"More coffee?" Johanna crossed to the old wooden table in the middle of the room and raised the french press in Pamela's direction.

The filmmaker barely glanced at her as she waved her hand in a dismissive gesture.

Sleek, city creature. "Her boots will soon get muddy, I'll make sure of that," Johanna muttered under her breath. She poured herself more coffee and retreated to the back of the room. With only half an ear, she listened as Neil told the story she knew by heart.

"How did it happen? The war was in full gear when I turned eighteen. So I hoped I wouldn't get the unlucky number."

"You mean, by that stage of the Vietnam conflict the government had stopped universal conscription and started drawing numbers for eighteen-year-old males?" Pamela paused for a moment, consulting a clipboard hung with notes.

Johanna rolled her eyes at this tedious monologue. She sipped her coffee. Of course, the filmmaker needed to recap history for her audience. This generation could have no idea of the ins and outs of Vietnam-era history.

Neil looked confused. "Uh. That makes it sound logical. It wasn't really."

"Explain, please."

"When the lottery system was introduced, people noticed it wasn't fair. The numbers weren't mixed up enough. People with birthdays later in the year got their numbers placed in the barrel last and drawn first."

"I didn't realize."

"Yeah, well, I don't suppose many people do. The

night the draft was drawn for me was in 1971. We had a keg of beer in the dorm. All of us guys were joking, kind of covering up how scared we were. The system was, birthdates of guys who turned nineteen that year were put into these little blue capsules and mixed up, and then pulled. The lower your number, the more likely you were to go to Vietnam. My birthday's November seventh."

"So you were pretty nervous?"

"You bet."

"And your number was?"

"Seventeen."

"So you were out of luck!" Pamela smiled, encouraging Neil to go on. She motioned the cameraman to scan the room, to show everyone listening raptly while Neil told their story.

"See, in my year, the government suddenly changed the rules. If your number was low, you were only allowed to finish the semester before reporting to the draft board."

"And you chose not to do that?"

"Damn right! Berkeley was in an uproar about the draft, but more importantly about the stupid war itself! It had nothing to do with the United States. People from our country were dying because our idiot government had gotten us in the middle of a civil war on the other side of the world."

He stood up and flexed his muscles. "Story of our times. It's happened over and over again. But anyway, I don't think that's what you're asking."

He looked a little disappointed that Pamela had diverted the camera away from him and over toward his fellow draft resisters, Curtis and Ray. He sat down, slumped in his chair.

"No. Of course. About you. So there you were, in your dorm room, thinking doom awaited. Did you think of going to Canada?"

"Yeah. But you know"—he grinned—"it's cold up there."

"And?"

"My parents had this land. All this land." Neil stretched a hand toward the window. "Hundreds of acres they'd amassed over the years. Pretty worthless land in the beginning, miles from the road, shops, the sewer."

"Still miles from the sewer," Johanna said.

"Yeah. I talked to my parents, and they never actually said what I should do, but they did suggest Jo and I come up here for a weekend and talk it through. What to do, I mean."

"It was so beautiful," Johanna said. "As you'll see."

For the first time, Pamela studied Neil's partner. Johanna shook her hair, as if to prove to Pamela it was still thick, even though a mane like a wet mop had replaced her once dark lustrous tresses.

"We took some friends up with us that weekend, with sleeping bags and propane stoves and tents."

"Lots of dope, too," Curtis added to Neil's tame description.

Johanna saw Pamela's expression change to one of envy, or admiration, perhaps. The young woman looked at Neil with her head on one side, as if imagining how Neil turned a camping trip into a bid for freedom.

"And when we got back to Berkeley," Neil went on, "we planned it. Finish the semester to escape suspicion, then Johanna and I would just disappear. We put the word out that if anyone needed"—Neil made quote signs with his fingers—"a place to stay, then we could accommodate that."

"You persuaded other people to join you. Your parents were okay with this?"

"We didn't tell them at first. Thought it best for them just to think we'd slipped over the border to Alberta or British Columbia."

"No one looked for you here?"

"We pushed pretty far into the woods. Made a track that's now a road, sort of. Not paved or anything."

"What efforts did the government make to find you?"

"I have no idea, Pamela. I guess they went to my parents' house, and they must have told them I'd hightailed it to Canada or something. Same with the other guys here, Ray, Curtis, and the others who were with us at the time."

"So, you're up here, you're scared, and you have to make a life on the lam." Pamela moved her chair closer to Neil, her growing admiration for his insubordination evident on her face. "You have your girlfriends, so it wasn't so bad?" She gave a soft laugh and glanced at Johanna, then looked away quickly and back at Neil.

Johanna could see that Pamela could not imagine that when she was nineteen her hair was rich and long, her figure slim, especially in the long flowing Indian skirts she favored, the tie-dyed T-shirts she wore over unsupported breasts. She tinkled with bangles in those days, flashed with silver from her dangling earrings to the silver threads woven into her skirts.

"And you, Johanna? You weren't in danger of

being drafted. You decided to hitch your life to a man on the run? What was it like for you?"

Johanna's face burned. She'd spent her life questioning her choices, but that was for her to do, not some stranger. Besides, Pamela obviously didn't understand.

But Pamela had turned once again to Neil.

"So how did you live? Smoke a lot of dope? Meditate?"

Neil looked amused. "Yeah, Pamela, we were your classic hippies. We lay around all day, you know, pontificating about life when we weren't stoned."

Embarrassed, Johanna spied some dust bunnies under the table. Itching to get a broom, she fought the urge and sat rooted to her chair.

"That's the image people have of your generation. The draft dodgers."

"Resisters. That's what we called ourselves." Neil's eyes flared at Pamela's use of the insulting word.

This woman needed a history lesson. Where was her respect? Johanna coughed to get Pamela's attention.

"When Neil's ancestors came from Europe a hundred fifty years ago, they had to clear the forest with axes for farmland and school their kids at home if they taught them at all. That's what it was like for us, up here. We were like pioneers. Not everyone could do that."

"We had chainsaws. That was a help." Neil nodded. "We didn't really know what we were doing. We read up on these utopian communities, on groups that lived on the land and made it productive."

Moving nearer the window, Johanna gestured to fields in the distance, the result of their years of work.

"These methods mean you learn to live off the land by letting it nurture itself. You have to leave some of the land forested; you have creeks and beaver dams. Every couple of years, you leave a field fallow or plant it with beans to replenish its nitrogen. We create and use a lot of compost."

The filmmaker glanced at her with little interest.

"We put the beehives in and encouraged flying insects." Johanna opened the window, letting the smell of animal dung infiltrate the room. "They're essential to the project."

"They pollinate," said Neil.

"Guppies in the pond eat the mosquitos. Frogs eat the flies from the latrine. Insects can sting, of course. Nothing like a mad hornet." Johanna glowered at Pamela.

"What about money? You can't grow everything." Pamela crossed her legs, drawing attention to jeans attached to her slender thighs like a second skin. She twirled a foot. The motion seemed to hypnotize Neil, whose blue eyes remained riveted on Pamela's shapely legs.

"My father, with his woodworking skills, really helped," said Johanna. "Neil's parents, they were generous. But really, we did this on our own. Trying to make a better world."

Pamela raised an eyebrow.

"Look," Johanna persisted, "we need to be as self-sufficient as we can be, here. We run an organic farm. We don't take government subsidies. We're not what you seem to think we are."

"Which is?"

"Irresponsible hippies. Taking from the land and

not giving back." Neil laughed and shook his hair, emphasizing its length. He tied it back with a rubber band, eyes twinkling. "Dope fiends!"

"Oh, don't say that, Neil," Johanna blurted. "We weren't like that at all! We had a vision. These woods around us, we tried to leave them as they are. Let nature take care of itself. If humans strip every edible from the woods, there'd be nothing left for animals and insects and the plants themselves."

"That sounds very responsible." Pamela put a hand to her face to hide a smirk. "I can see you're the serious one around here. So you don't like corporate America and you don't want to hunt and forage, so how do you feed yourselves? You become farmers by default?" Pamela consulted her notes before continuing. "You were a hippie colony motivated less by a philosophy than by running from the draft. You were joined by like-minded young people who rejected our government's involvement in the Vietnam civil war, right?"

"Yes, we did!" Neil was on his feet, waving his arms. "They told us that war would protect us from Communism. But some of us thought, what? And for what? For corporations and for consumerism? We were communitarians. Motivated by an ideal, Pamela. A philosophy, you might call it. We wanted to live together and own nothing, or not much, anyway, and to farm and try to be self-sufficient, to avoid buying useless goods, and to not use insecticides and other environmental poisons."

"A group of good guys then?"

"Yeah." Neil sat down again.

"So tell me," said Pamela, "how did things work

out when you had to make decisions? Did you argue?"

"Some people left, or were asked to leave," Johanna said. "Not everyone could take the hardships. It's just the six of us now, Curt and Sally, Ray and Linda. Of course their son, Kevin, he lives here too. So seven. And Maelle, my granddaughter, she lived with us till she grew up. We're committed to organic farming. And everyone's equal here. Still trying to practice love. That's all there is."

Johanna looked at her audience. "Where's Linda?"

"Think she's gone back to work," Ray said, glancing toward the door.

"Why don't we show Pamela around?" Curtis interjected.

"You go. I have to finish this jacket I'm making." Johanna wanted this woman out of her house. "You see, I work to deadlines, just like you do. I'm almost seventy years old, and I'm still working."

But Pamela was out the door, with Neil in tow, and the camera and audio people followed with their equipment. Curtis and Ray shrugged and followed too, with an apologetic glance at Johanna. The half-full coffee pot and the untouched scones sat there, mocking her. Once more, her handiwork dismissed. She started to gather the cups.

Linda rushed in, her face flushed. "There's been an email," she said.

The commune shared one email address on one old computer, using it to conduct farm business. "I was just checking on the cheese order from the Coop in town. An email popped up. It's from Neil's sister," Linda said. "There's been a family emergency."

"I'll get him." Johanna pushed the tray into Sally's

hand. "You'd better show this camera crew the guest quarters. It sounds like Neil will have to go to the city."

Chapter Four

Maelle chewed her lip throughout the service. She did not feel sad, exactly, but her stomach roiled nevertheless. Her great-grandparents lay in their double casket before the congregation.

"A double casket?" Johanna had questioned.

Neil shrugged. "It will all burn up in the crematorium."

Maelle stared ahead at the mahogany coffin. How many trees were killed to make it? All just for show—in an hour or so it, and its contents, would be ash. What a waste. She tried to ignore remarks from people behind her.

"How touching, how good for them to die so close together. They'll never be separated now." The murmurs sounded like bees.

Maelle picked at a nail. She couldn't imagine a partnership so close it would last a lifetime and beyond. But then she'd never been taught such a thing. Neil and Johanna had always denied an afterlife.

What kind of funeral would she like for herself? Best just to be laid down in the forest and covered with dirt and leaves. Just as she'd lain down so often after coming to live with Neil and Johanna as a ten-year-old girl. The trees had swayed in the wind, keening, it seemed to her, joining in her grief.

Maelle kicked the kneeler. How did her great-grandparents manage to have so many friends? Was it because they'd been philanthropists, supporting charities innumerable? Neil's parents had lived conventional lives, prosperous lives, but at the end of the day, the end of a life, what made a person happiest? To go with the flow, to accept conventional wisdom, had certainly led to a very long life for her great-grandparents.

Not that she had known them very well. She'd never been invited to sit astride a knee or to stay overnight in the San Francisco mansion. Her great-grandparents' lives had been so removed from her own they might almost have existed only in the pages of a book. She suspected they viewed their parentless great-granddaughter as an obligation rather than a delight.

How different they were from Johanna's parents, who, though long gone, left memories. The warm lap of her German great-grandmother, the bristly cheek of a man her mother called Opa. How odd that Neil, when he became a grandfather, never let Maelle call him by one of those cuddly terms. As to everyone else, he was always Neil to her.

She had been taught to call his own parents Great-Grandmama and Great-Grandpapa. So formal and old-fashioned. Seemingly immeasurably old by the time Maelle became conscious of them, Neil's parents had cocooned themselves in their hilltop house with its view, protected by their wealth from discomfort. As they aged, secretaries, maids, and nurses tended their every need.

And then, all at once, in their nineties, their infirmities caught up with them. Neil's mother took a fall, broke her hip, and never came out of the hospital.

Having received the email from Neil's sister, Neil and Johanna had driven as quickly as their ancient truck could transport them to San Francisco but were too late. Neil's father, bereft at the loss of his wife of over seventy years, collapsed at home and died before the housekeeper could call an ambulance. To accommodate Neil's brother and sister, who lived in distant states, a double funeral was arranged. Perhaps that accounted for the throng in attendance today.

Maelle knew she owed the old people a debt of gratitude. They'd paid for her college education and were pleased when she'd done well enough to enter graduate school and the PhD program. Since then, she was ashamed to admit, she'd had little time for them, and though they lived just across the Bay, she had not seen them in months.

Sitting here at their funeral, Maelle could summon no grief, just a vague sense of an era ending. All morning she'd been trying to identify why she had butterflies in her stomach. Her habit of analyzing her feelings—just to check she was normal, she told herself daily—paid dividends today. There! That was it. A sense of guilt coupled with a vague sense of foreboding. And yet what was the reason for that? Her great-grandparents had led fortunate and productive lives and had a blessed death.

"You okay, Abbs?" Maelle whispered to her aunt.

"They were lucky. What a great way to go." Abby squeezed Maelle's fingers.

Maelle shivered and thought of her own mother, whose death had come too soon. Best not to think of that. She tilted her head to lay it on Johanna's shoulder. Her grandmother sat rigidly, hands folded in her lap, her eyes on the extra-large casket. Flanking Maelle, Johanna and Abby each wore one of Johanna's angora jackets, dyed in pastel colors and bedecked with ribbons. An odd fashion choice for a funeral. No doubt a not-so-subtle marketing ploy by Abby. Maelle peeked at Neil, tense and awkward in his unaccustomed suit. She squinted. What did he really think? He had taken a path so different from that of his parents.

Years ago, they'd enabled Neil's wish to "live on the land," yet his attitude to his parents' largesse seemed always to have a kind of resentment to it. They'd never held him accountable for his choice of lifestyle. Most of those in the hippie life had eventually accepted the reality of the need for health insurance, for a mortgage. Found work which they'd liked or hated, depending on talent or luck. But not Neil. He'd made a go of farming, such as it was. He'd stuck to his ideals, more or less. The commune operated as a socialist collective. The result of that was material poverty. Neil had not supported his family as he had been supported himself. Had he taken his parents for granted? Or as the youngest child, was he the spoiled, indulged one, the son they loved best? Perhaps, Maelle mused, this set up a complicated dance of guilt and anger in his mind.

Could that explain why he, the only one of the three siblings who still lived in California, had not paid sufficient attention to his parents in their declining years?

"They have plenty of help," he'd growled when Maelle had asked him if they could visit.

To be fair, Neil's more prosperous and conventional siblings had not visited his parents much, either. Robert and Martha lived far away and saw their parents rarely.

Today, Martha wore a black jersey dress and jacket, her stiffly coiffed hair dyed a golden blonde to perfectly complement her suit. In contrast to Johanna's, Martha's skin shone with the effects of dermabrasion and expensive cosmetics. She looked years younger than her age. Neil's older brother Robert, the family spokesperson, gave the eulogy in a gravelly voice, his bald head and thin shoulders confirming his years. This great-aunt and great-uncle were almost strangers to Maelle. A bevy of first cousins once removed and second cousins filled the second and third pews. A pang hit her heart. She might have once wanted the opportunity to get to know these relatives, but it seemed that distance had removed this possibility. In the great American experiment of individualism, families once split were hard to remake. She gripped Abby's hand.

The service ended, and Maelle joined the crush of the reception afterward in her great-grandparents' magnificent home. Enormous sweeps of pale carpet led to floor-to-ceiling windows overlooking the city. Sofas and chairs clad in silk upholstery dotted the drawing room strategically, here taking advantage of the view, there huddled together in a conversation circle, over there taking up a position near the bar.

Maelle wandered, speaking to cousins, nodding to strangers. She circled Neil, who was talking to his brother. He beckoned her over, put his arm over her shoulder, and introduced her to Robert as if she were meeting him for the first time.

"We were just talking about what's going to happen next," Neil said.

"Next?"

"Yes, all the estate matters. Not really a polite subject for today, but with Martha and Robert only staying a few days, we're just making a vague sort of plan. For the land," he added.

"What land?"

"Our land. Joyous Woods, amongst other things. There's a lot of acreage there. You know how Mom and Dad started accumulating parcels in the fifties, when the land wasn't worth much. Took a gamble on the expanding population." A smile lit up Neil's face.

Robert's eyes gleamed. "And now look at it. Worth a fortune." His hands twitched, as though he could barely resist rubbing them together in anticipation.

"Oh." The implication pounded in Maelle's head. "That land is mostly so unspoiled." Her voice rose. "Home to forests and animal habitat. It's magnificent."

"Indeed," Robert said. His brown eyes pinned hers, condescending.

She took her moment. "I hope you'll find some way to keep it all intact. Some things are more important than money, aren't they, Neil? Isn't that the principle you live by?"

"Oh, you're way ahead of the curve, honey." Neil patted her shoulder. "Nothing's been decided yet."

"We'll look into it. Everything takes its time." Robert's voice took on a reassuring tone.

Maelle narrowed her eyes at her great-uncle.

He cleared his throat. "You see, Maelle, that land really is ripe for development. The operating principle of real estate is to turn land to its highest and best use."

"What's that?"

"It means, the use that yields its greatest value."

Maelle's stomach flip-flopped. She reached for her

40

grandfather's hand and pulled. "Can we talk?" she whispered.

"Later." Neil nodded to Robert as Maelle found a tissue and blotted tears that irritatingly started to rise. "She's upset," he said unnecessarily. "Give us a moment, Robert. Sorry."

"Why didn't you plan for this?" Maelle struggled to keep her voice down as Neil propelled her to a quiet corner.

"How could we plan? You mean buy this land from Mom and Dad? Couldn't afford it then, can afford it even less now. Why are you complaining? We've had fifty good years there. We need to retire. I can't raise goats for the rest of my life. Johanna and I, with the money developers will pay, can go live on a tropical island, anywhere we want, and never have to work again."

"But a developer will wreck it! Cut down trees! Drive out the animals. Don't you see?"

Neil put his arms around her and shushed her wail as if she were a child. He took on a soothing tone. "I do see. But I also see that there simply aren't enough houses for the population. That causes a social equity problem. Your grandmother and I, we were idealists. We protested for social justice. Hey, I even got arrested once!"

"What's that got to do with trees?"

"You know as well as I do that if there's less land available, it becomes very expensive. If we free it up, more housing can be built. Then the people who buy it should be able to make a profit on it. It's the capitalist system."

Maelle looked at him sideways. "I thought you

lived your whole life on the idea that you were different; you hated capitalism. I thought you were committed to looking after the earth."

"Honey, you could get other people to argue that agriculture is not taking care of the earth at all. To really look after the earth, you'd have to go back to hunter-gatherer times."

"Yes, but climate change! We have to think really radically, Neil. We just can't keep on doing what we're doing, paving everything in sight. It's ruining everything."

"You have a point, sweetheart. But you're a mature woman now, not in high school. Don't get all sentimental on me. Your grandmother and I have to think of our old age. Besides, we don't have a choice. Your great-aunt and great-uncle want to sell the land, and we can't afford to buy them out."

"I think I need to get some fresh air." Maelle backed away. She pushed through the crowd, opened a french door, and stood on the terrace, drinking in great gulps of the damp San Francisco air. Beyond her, she could see the Golden Gate bridge, stretching north to Marin through a deepening fog.

Something agitated in her brain, a thought trying to work its way through her shocked gray matter. That bridge. And what lay beyond it. Developed, yes, but a National Seashore farther north and west. A home for plants and animals and sea creatures. She'd look into the history of it. That didn't happen by accident. Protection of the land came from people fighting against materialists like Robert.

But fighting was for other people. She couldn't do it. Confrontation, making people angry—it was too awful. She could speak to the trees, ask them what to do. Like her, they preferred to stay still, but they got their way in the end. Strong, powerful, they breathed in and out, oxygenating the air for the rest of the world. If cut down, they just grew back. Their stumps dug deep into the earth, holding on. Trees could be relied on. They didn't just disappear without a trace.

Chapter Five

Johanna and Neil sat silent on the way back to the farm the day after the funeral. He's sad, she told herself, as Neil gripped the steering wheel of the truck, his face grim. She knew so well that tight jaw, tension making his neck cords stand out.

"No matter how old you are, how old your parents, are, it's always a shock when they die." She patted his knee. "Brings you up short. We're next. To face the darkness."

Neil grimaced. Johanna turned to the window. Rain slid down the side of the glass and gathered in rivulets on the window's bottom, and Johanna pulled her long cardigan around her. The windshield wipers whined as Neil crouched forward, trying to see through the fogged glass.

The miles slid by, each one a victory over the weather and Neil's mood.

Johanna tried to put the best spin on things. His parents always indulged him. He never had to grow up. Well, now, the rubber hits the road. He's on his own, we're on our own. Maybe there's some comfort in it. Neil's inheritance could give us some security. All of us, Ray and Curtis, Sally and Linda, we could fix up the farm buildings and the houses, hire more help on the farm, cruise gently into old age. I'll keep up my work— it keeps my mind active as well as my hands.

Though the weather had cleared when they got back to the farm, Johanna's mood clouded when she saw the film crew's SUV in the driveway. She found Sally in the kitchen of the pagoda house, and Johanna, though desperate for a cup of coffee and a chat with her friend, followed Neil out into the yard. There they found Pamela Highbury and her crew treading carefully through the muck. Pamela exclaimed at the portable coops, set in a fallow field. Curtis, beaming, was lecturing Pamela on the benefits of free-range eggs and how they helped the cakes, cookies, muffins, and bread baked by the women of the commune sell out each farmers' market day.

"We couldn't do it without the girls," Curtis said.

Johanna's spirits sank a little lower. He was not referring to the women.

He picked up one of the hens and stroked her feathers. The bird nestled against his beard.

Pamela cringed.

"Gertrude here, she and her sisters get all comfortable at night in the coop." Gertrude gave a strangled cluck, and Curtis set her down. "We pick up their eggs in the morning." He opened a door at the side of a wooden enclosure raised about three feet off the ground and the crew peered in. A row of straw-strewn wooden nesting boxes lined the sides of the coop, while between the sides of the attic-shaped structure, crossbars allowed the chickens to roost.

"See, we raised the coop off the ground to protect it against rats and other critters and also because it's easier for us to reach in and get the eggs if we don't have to bend down so much." He massaged his lower back briefly, as if a spasm had echoed his words.

45

"Rats?" Pamela shuddered.

"It's a farm." Curtis shrugged. He backed away from the little house and beckoned the cameraman to film the coop's exterior, painted in gaudy colors. A chicken-width ridged ramp led from the structure to its yard, the whole thing supported by posts on wheels. Protective chicken wire covered the sides and top of the coop and its enclosure.

"But that's only part of it. Those girls out there"— he pointed to hens farther away, scratching in the dirt outside the fenced yard—"are having a great time out in the field. Electric fencing keeps them from going too far. Keeps out the coyotes, too."

A breeze stirred his shaggy gray hair as Curtis strode down the muddy field faster than Pamela in her fancy boots could keep up. Neil and Johanna kept pace with her.

"The brilliant thing about the movable coop is that this system cuts out a lot of the cleaning," Curtis shouted over the wind. "Out here in the field, the birds do double duty." He laughed at his own joke. "They eat the weeds and bugs, leave their poop behind to rot in the field. Next year it's mixed with compost and plowed under so we can plant vegetables."

"That's what we mean by being an organic farm," Neil added. "No pesticides. Natural fertilizers. Compost and manure enrich the fields. We plant closely to prevent weeds."

"Fantastic stuff." Pamela glanced furtively at the grass around her shoes, then raised her face and smiled. "I can see why you're all so fit and healthy. Good food, hard work."

"All we have to do is haul the darn chicken tractor

every week." Curtis rolled his eyes.

"How do you move it?"

Pamela signaled the crew for a wide shot of the chickens, the coop, and the wired run. She tried to lift one of the supporting posts and failed to raise it more than a few inches. It thudded to the ground.

"We pull it. But I'm thinking of training a couple of young goats as pack animals. They can do the hard work. I'm getting too old to be the draft horse here." Curtis winced as he twisted to face Pamela.

She tipped her head to one side. "You have goats?"

"A dairy. We make cheese. Linda manages that. Artisan cheese they call it. That's Ray and Linda's department. Linda's probably in there now. Talk to her."

Curtis excused himself, saying he had work to do, and Neil took Pamela's arm to direct her and her crew to a cluster of dairy buildings. Inside the galvanized iron structure, milking stands stood on a bare concrete floor. The next room held a big refrigerator, counters, and sinks. The creamery, a separate building, housed an old vat. Though clean, the creamery looked old-fashioned.

"Where's Linda?" Pamela gazed around.

"She's very shy." Johanna clasped her hands behind her back. "She's proud of her cheese, but she'd hate to be filmed."

"I've heard of Joyous Woods' cheese," Pamela said. "But all that artisan cheese is so darned expensive. I don't know how you compete."

Neil agreed. "It is a problem. But goats actually provide our greatest income stream. We use the Nubian and the LaMancha breeds for milking and cheese-making. We mate the does, and they kid every year. Have to keep the bucks separate from the does. Not only because the billies—that's the bucks—are aggressive and horny"—Neil cast a sly glance at Pamela—"but because they have another use."

"Really, what's that?" Pamela directed a shot of the milking stanchions.

"Our Spanish goats are great weed eaters, so we hire them out to clear hillsides. Pedro, our shepherd— he's from Peru—transports them in a trailer and watches them eat their way across a hillside. They eat everything in sight. Weeds, brush, poison oak, and ivy. Makes them popular as a fire-prevention service up here."

"Can I see some goats?" Pamela said.

"Sure. We breed them to keep up the supply, but we don't keep bucks. Or rather, when the bucklings are born, we sell them or wether them."

The film crew snickered uncomfortably. Pamela looked blank.

"Castrate them," Neil explained. "Wethers make the best animals to work with if you're not just running a dairy. They're good-natured and don't smell like bucks. They also have the best fleece for shearing."

"Where are they?"

"We put them in the far fields, because they like to eat things growing on trees, the trees themselves, actually. That's why we have to keep them away from the vegetable gardens and the orchards."

"Sounds like you need that shepherd. A goatherd."

"Guard dogs help. Ray and Linda's son, Kevin, helps Pedro. He works here at the farm, while Pedro takes on the off-site jobs. Kevin's a good kid. Didn't do so well at school, never wanted to leave home."

"Does he get paid? Oops. That's none of my business, but it just came out." Pamela put her hand over her mouth. "This is a bit medieval. A bit feudal. A goatherd. Out in all weathers. I never thought of money being exchanged in the business of goatherding."

Neil dug his foot into the ground, creating a divot. He pushed the earth back into it forcefully. "On a farm, since we're all in this together, none of us gets paid what you people outside would call a fair wage. We just split the profits."

"Equally?"

"Pam, you're here to make a film. I don't have to discuss our finances with you. You certainly aren't free to put that in your movie. Would you make a film about anyone else and ask about their profits?"

"Sorry to pry. I didn't mean that. It's just that you had this ethos of sharing and communality and not working for money." Pamela scribbled something, then looked up at Neil expectantly. "But reality intrudes. I'm just curious how it all works."

He waved an arm expansively. "We made it work. But you can see it's not about making a fortune. Ask any farmer, he'll tell you. This is about organic farming, trying to make a light footprint on the earth, as they say."

Johanna's voice rose from the back of the group. "We've shown you that it's hard labor and it never ends. Why don't you put that in your movie?"

She didn't have time for any of this film nonsense. And nor did any of the others. There was work to be done!

"I'll help Sally make the lunch." She turned her

back to them and walked quickly to the house. The aroma of freshly baked bread coming from the kitchen made her mouth water. It had been a long time since that early breakfast in San Francisco.

"Oh, you're back! I'm glad." Sally stirred a huge cauldron of vegetable soup. "All these people here—reminds me of the old days with people dropping in, staying for meals."

Johanna laughed. "The dropouts who dropped in. Some of us never left." She pulled out a colorful home-dyed tablecloth and spread it on the big great-room table.

She saw it now, how she'd always protected Neil. In the early days, ever wary of losing his interest, Johanna had seen that after some time of living away from the city Neil's mood dampened. He missed the excitement of student activism, the threat of expulsion. Once or twice, spooned against him on the sleeping bag, damp despite the wooden pallet he'd built to protect them from worms and ants and the occasional scorpion, she'd asked him, "Would you consider going back?"

"They'd arrest me for draft dodging."

"Or maybe just send you to Vietnam. You could go, serve your tour, and come back."

"Or not come back. Or come back wounded. Or come back filled with shame that I participated in an immoral war. Isn't that what your parents were ashamed about? Isn't that why they came to the US after Hitler was defeated?"

"You're right. This is the price we pay for resisting. But it's not easy up here, Neil."

"Nope. But fun, too, isn't it? This land—all this

land, from my parents—we have an opportunity to do something with it, Jo."

"Then lead us. Please."

He tried. Or rather, he made long speeches. He told them they were making a political statement as much as hiding from the authorities. He made it all bearable by his singing, by talking about love and how they were making a new world.

A new world. It was always a new world, decade after decade.

But it seemed to be happening outside the confines of Joyous Woods.

Johanna pulled jelly glasses from a shelf, placing a chipped one at Neil's accustomed place.

"You know, Sally, I never thought I'd say this, but at Neil's parents' funeral, I got the sense he was really shell-shocked. Like he looked at the past fifty years and wondered what happened."

"Everyone feels that at some time or other, don't you think?"

"I don't know. This Pamela woman. Making a film. Neil set that up without telling any of us. Maybe he's thinking this will be some kind of legacy. Make some meaning out of all the struggle we had here."

"The ideas we had, you mean? They were radical then. Coming back into fashion now. Organic farming? Trying to reclaim the earth, that kind of thing?"

"I suppose. I'm not sure I know, anymore. How things have changed since we were kids. All that digital media, the endless recording of one's own life. It's egotistical, Sally, that's what it is!"

"Calm down, Jo. It's okay. Lots of people try to record their lives when they come near the end. Think of this film as a kind of memoir of us."

"A memoir of us!" Johanna slapped down silverware on the table with such violence that spoons skittered on the floor. On her knees on the floorboards to collect the cutlery, sound amplified, and she stood up, startled. The door slammed.

She saw, through the screen door, Sally running toward one of the film crew. He zigzagged toward the house, shouting, his hands batting at his face.

A swarm of furiously buzzing bees followed him like a phalanx of warplanes. Ray ran behind, his white beekeeper's suit hampering him.

"He got too close to the hive," he panted. "Tried to film it before I got the smoker going."

Johanna hauled open the freezer and dumped ice-cubes from a metal tray on the counter. She wrapped the inadequate ice in a cloth and ran outside.

"Hold this to your face."

She rushed back inside and poured apple cider vinegar in a dishpan and grabbed a table napkin, sloshing it into the vinegar. Ray and Sally supported the victim in and sat him at the table. He moaned.

"Rub your arms with it. It'll soothe the sting. The bees are outside. They can't come in."

Johanna eyed the broken edge of the screen and quickly hung up a dishcloth over it, securing it with thumbtacks she found in a drawer.

Sally set to work to make a paste of baking soda and water and applied this to the young man's neck. "When you're ready, I'll smear this onto your face as well. It will help take the sting away."

The cameraman, now literally white-faced, thanked them and told them he'd skip lunch. Ray took his elbow to show him to a bedroom.

Sally and Johanna had finished lunch preparation when Pamela and the others trudged in.

Pamela tried to make a joke of the cameraman's stings. "I told him to stay out of the way of the bees."

No one responded. Johanna exchanged glances with Sally, their astonishment at Pamela's lack of concern unspoken. Over lunch, as Ray answered Pamela's questions about beekeeping and Pamela's second young assistant just picked at his food, Neil tried to lighten the atmosphere.

"I'm glad you didn't ask the commune to sign an insurance waiver."

With that, Pamela finally went to check on her colleague and came back to report he was feeling better.

"Maybe you should keep an eye on him," Johanna said. "It's a thirty-mile drive to the nearest hospital."

"He's fine. He's not allergic," Pamela replied tartly. "You'll be relieved to know that we'll call it a day for now, though. I've reserved rooms for us in town at a B and B."

Johanna could not keep her face from softening with relief. Then she frowned. For years she'd welcomed the strays and the idealists who'd dropped into the commune and stayed, worked or lazed, then moved on. There'd been shared laughter and shared disasters. But this seemed different, more invasive. The sooner this filmmaking was over, the better. Pamela had better show the success of this unlikely farm. Not that she trusted Pamela for one second.

Accuracy, for Pamela Highbury, seemed to be all about documenting human failings. Failings that were all too familiar.

Chapter Six

"Uncle Robert wants to sell the land, Zach."
Maelle snuggled close to Zachary. His long body
seeped its warmth into hers as they lay side by side. She
rubbed her toes along his, felt the arch of his bony foot.

"Who is Uncle Robert, and what land is that?"
Zachary nibbled her ear.

"My great-uncle. And my grandparents' place. The
commune. I told you about it. I spent so much of my
childhood there. It's an organic farm. It was just all
woods and streams and untouched pasture when my
grandparents and their friends went up there. Because
it's way up north, no one wanted to settle there then,
but now there seems to be a market for it."

"Hmm. That's good, isn't it? Sounds like it was a
good investment."

Maelle pulled her feet away from their footsie
game and looped them up under her knees protectively.

"That's not what I think. You're talking just like
Uncle Robert! I'm worried about what will happen to
the farm, the animals. And the trees."

"You mean it's your grandparents' farm, but they
don't actually own it?"

She sat up, her naked shoulders chilly. "That's
right. And I'm worried. My grandfather, Neil, is okay
with the land being sold to a developer. Along with his
brother and sister, he'll get a big fat paycheck because

54

the land belonged to their parents. No one else has any stake in it.

"And there's another problem. He hasn't said what he'll do to compensate the others, Ray and Curtis, Linda and Sally, who stuck it out with them over the years. The commune's their way of life, *and* their livelihood."

"Maybe he can give them some of the money?"

"Or he may not be inclined to."

"Oh. Then that would be bad. Very bad." Zachary lay back on the pillows, arms behind his head. "Why do you say that?"

"Neil's difficult. Can be super charming, and I've been told he was a leading antiwar activist back in the day. Charismatic. When they came up here—evading the draft, it seems—the land wasn't worth much, but now it's been cleared, it's a working organic farm. Neil—he always wanted me to call him that—relied on the others to do most of the work. The way I see it, the people who stuck it out with Neil are his partners, but being hippies, they never made any formal arrangement. As far as I know, those few left on the farm haven't offered to buy it from the estate and they couldn't afford to anyway."

"Surely they'll appeal to his reason. If they had sweat equity, they can work something out."

"Any suggestions?"

"It's none of my business, Maelle." Zachary sat up and swung his legs over the side of the bed. "Right now, making coffee is."

Suddenly, astonishingly, the bed was lonely. How quickly it had all happened, this intimacy, and how surprising. To find someone safe, with whom she could confide her hopes and fears. Someone who could understand her science, or at least didn't dismiss her theory of plant intelligence. So far as she'd told him about it, anyway. Someone who'd also lost a parent when young. Still, she remained wary. A little afraid. Over the sound of the coffee grinder, Maelle wondered if she'd said too much.

Her childhood home still pulled at her, but she had other priorities. She needed to focus on her own life and career, let her perfectly intelligent grandparents work out answers to their problems. She shouldn't involve Zach in this at all. She really didn't know him well enough to dump all these issues on him, and it must bore him to death.

Zachary came back to hand her a steaming mug. He sat on the edge of the bed.

"Sounds like these friends of your grandparents stuck it out through good times and bad. Did the farm employ them, or were they unpaid workers? What documentation is there? Some plan they made to face this kind of scenario? They must have anticipated something like this."

"They might have embraced voluntary poverty by rejecting materialism."

"That was the ethos of the times. So I have been told."

"Yum. This coffee's great." She bent over her cup to breathe the aroma. "You're right, though. It's for them to work out with Neil and his family. Thanks for caring, Zach. But I'm most worried about what's going to happen to the land itself. Become golf courses and condos?"

"You'd hate that, of course." Zachary grinned.

"My golf game isn't as good as it should be. My God! Condos and clubhouses and swimming pools and pavement. Concrete! The trees!"

"They'll be cut down."

"Zach, what am I going to do?" A sudden jerk of her hand splashed him with hot coffee.

"Ouch." Zachary dabbed his thigh with a corner of the sheet. "I'm not sure you can do anything. Or should. I know you're attached to this old farm, but farms are going by the wayside everywhere. It's not an economically viable way of making a living anymore. If it ever was."

"That's not the point. If you saw Joyous Woods, you'd understand."

"No? Weren't you just wondering how your grandparents will get by?" He winced as he pressed the stained sheet to his leg.

"Sorry about the coffee. Clumsy. Let me get ice." Carefully, she pushed the bedclothes aside, ran to the kitchen, and came back with a plastic baggie filled with ice cubes. She laid the bag gently on Zachary's scalded limb, then bent and kissed his thigh. She climbed back into bed.

"I am really, really concerned about the trees. And the animals. And all the natural world. I study plants, Zachary, don't you remember? I'm a molecular biologist. The forest is part of my laboratory."

"I thought you worked in a lab on campus."

"Yes. Trying to understand exactly what plants do. If they can learn, if they can think."

"Hmm. Learning's different from figuring things out. Thinking? You might be ahead of the curve on that one, Maelle. What's your colleagues' opinion of your theory?"

"My theory's about plant communication. I guess I never explained exactly what I'm trying to prove." She sat up, waved a hand excitedly. "I told you about a couple of experiments, but no details. I didn't think you'd be interested. You haven't burdened me with your own research, have you?"

"Okay. Fair enough. I do care, though. So what, exactly, do you intend to do?"

"About my work or the farm?"

"What's most pressing, in your mind?"

"Good question. The land sale is just an idea at the moment, but I need to start thinking about what I can do to help, if anything. Maybe start a petition to stop the development."

"Suppose you do that. What will your grandparents live on in their old age without money from the land sale? Can they keep farming till they're ninety? They're almost seventy now, aren't they?"

"How did farmers in the old days survive?"

"They moved in with their grandchildren." His eyes twinkled.

Maelle laughed. "Don't you dare suggest that!" She almost punched his arm in answer to the tease, but a glimpse at the coffee-ruined bedclothes stopped her just in time.

Zachary hadn't finished his thought. "The children took the brunt, usually, to give the grandchildren a few years of grace. But your mother, she's gone, isn't she? What about your aunt? Would she help?"

"Abby's store sells beautiful jackets my grandmother makes. But JoJo's getting arthritis. Maybe she could help Abby in the store, part-time, just to get out and be with people."

"There! One solution anyway."

"Sorry, Zach." Maelle kicked the covers away. "I shouldn't involve you in this."

"Not at all. Just don't leap ahead so fast. The people directly involved can work out a compromise, using lawyers and real estate people. This is not really your problem to solve, at least not yet."

"What's my problem, then?"

"You need to concentrate on your work, not worry about other people quite so much. Finish your dissertation. Get a job—preferably near me. Teach, have a life."

"Hmm." Maelle sipped her cooling coffee. He'd made a statement of intention to be with her. But maybe not quite as forcefully as she'd hoped.

He stroked her arm. "If you are so worried about your grandparents, don't follow their example. Get a job with a pension and benefits. Be stable."

"How uninspiring." She made a mock-bored face. "Staid. Dull."

"I mean it, Maelle. You see what can happen when you get old if you don't abide by the rules."

"I didn't realize you were so conventional, Zachary."

"Am I? I think I'm pragmatic."

She set her mug on the bedside table and reached up to run a finger along Zachary's scar, a white uneven line down the side of his neck. "What happened to your face?"

He twisted away from her hand. "We all have our moments of decision."

"What do you mean?"

"I went into research because of something that happened to me."

"You're being very mysterious. Tell me, please."

"I was in psychiatric residency at a hospital. I wanted to go into private practice."

"Your father was a doctor, was he?"

"Yes. He was also in medical research. Research, as you may already realize, doesn't pay as much as clinical work. Anyway, I told you my father died when I was in high school. My mother had to struggle. I borrowed money, worked all the jobs I could to pay my own way. I really wanted to go to medical school. More loans. No wealthy relatives for me."

"Ouch."

"Never mind. Anyway, I was really interested in mental illness so I chose psychiatry as my specialty."

"And what happened?"

"One day, my last patient—he'd been waiting a long time, I suppose, and was impatient—sorry, bad pun. Where was I? I'd just closed the door after he stepped into my office when he lunged at me with a knife. Cut my face and neck. Not my jugular, which he'd aimed for. The nurses heard the racket and rushed in, saved me."

"What a horrible shock! Why did he attack you?"

"Nothing rational I know of. He was crazy. That's why he became a patient. The man was just acting out his delusion. Anyway, that decided it for me."

"What do you mean?"

"I chose not to be a clinician. I didn't want to be attacked again. But the other reason is that I genuinely wanted to understand what causes delusional behavior. What would make someone act irrationally?"

"So we should all be totally rational?"

"Most of the time, yes."

"People should not be swayed by their emotions?"

"If the emotions have negative effects, we should try to control them."

"If we all acted totally rationally, we'd be robots."

"We might see that keeping an old farm which is falling to bits isn't a good idea."

"Whoa!" Maelle stared. "That's a leap in logic. How do you know it's falling to bits? You've never seen it!"

Zachary waved a dismissive hand. "I saw communes like it when I was a kid. Before my dad died, we'd go up to the country every now and again. He showed Mom and me where he grew up on a vineyard, the school he went to. He said there were communes around. They looked pretty run down and decrepit, even then. Seemed like a weird lifestyle choice to me."

Maelle blushed. Zachary was like all the others, then, all the people she'd met over the years who disdained the old hippies. Yet the hippie values— sharing, equality, anti-consumerism—seemed right to her. She scooted away from Zachary to the side of the bed, laid her head on her knees, and looked up at him sideways.

What would life be like with this man, long-term? Could she stand such judgmental comments?

Zachary tried to mollify. "You know, I'd like to meet your grandparents. Particularly your grandmother. That is, if you want me to. You've talked about her so much, about the farm. She seems to have had a great influence on your life."

"She'd want to meet you, too." Maelle's voice rose in enthusiasm, then suddenly dampened in anxiety. "Not to check you out or anything medieval like that. That'd be embarrassing."

Zachary smiled.

"It's a good idea, though. She needs to meet new people. We'll stay overnight. You'll see how my life was…"

She stopped. She mustn't jump ahead about her relationship with Zachary. "I'll tell her we just need a weekend in the country."

"Anything to please you, my Maelle. I want to know everything about you and your family."

Maelle gave him a delighted grin and pulled him to her under the bedclothes.

Chapter Seven

Johanna knew she should tamp down her annoyance. Pamela was temporary. Although she seemed to be taking a long time making her film, coming back, day after day. Sitting at the table now, eyeing the filmmaker's sleek figure, her shiny chestnut hair, her immaculately pressed shirts, her boots shined to a polish, Johanna had to push away a niggling sense of regret. For the years gone, for Neil's irritating childishness, for her own clinging to the dream. The grizzled man before her kept tangling in her mind with his golden youth.

In those early days—that heady time—she'd first seen Neil as he stood on a podium, megaphone in hand, denouncing the government that sent its young men to war on the other side of the world.

"It's a lie," he'd shouted, and the crowd roared. His blond hair caught the sunlight, his curls illuminated like an angel's. His unlined face looked triumphant. He had the sheen of righteousness on him, and the crowd clapped.

"Resist! Resist!" People pumped their arms into the air. At the stage's end, the eucalyptus trees shuddered in a light breeze, dropping brown leaves.

Johanna pushed her way through the crowd, hoping he'd notice her. He didn't at first, so she moved closer to the podium steps. She couldn't believe she was acting so boldly—after all, she'd been a shy little immigrant girl who'd had to learn English in first grade, and still spoke with a hint of an accent. But to her, schooled in guilt by her parents, his message sounded right. She climbed up the five steps to the stage. Her shoes thudded on the wood, but only she heard them in the roar of the crowd. She approached Neil, stood beside him, and raised her clenched fist too.

"I'm with you! My parents are German, and they wished they'd stood up to evil. Never again. Let it never happen again!"

Then, to her own astonishment, she pulled Neil's face to hers and kissed him.

As the crowd roared even louder, another student took Neil's place. He, shocked and pleased by Johanna's embrace, took her hand and bounded down the steps with her. On the ground, he held her at arm's length for a moment, then grinned, and folded her into a long, probing, passionate kiss. She could feel his heart beating under his shirt, her mind a little apart, astonished that such a powerful student activist would want her.

So Johanna and Neil, the couple, began. After they'd bedded each other in her dorm, fortunately empty at midday, Neil invited her to a meeting that night to plan a march. She went and sat mesmerized at his knee, staring raptly at his beautiful face. When he spoke, she wanted to lap his words like honey. When he stood again, she marveled at his slim strong body, shirt taut over muscles that had seen many workouts, leg muscles outlined through his jeans, evidence of his running addiction.

As for herself, Johanna experienced a brief period

of narcissism, enjoying Neil's pleasure in her. Oh, the bliss she felt when people flocked to hear Neil talk. Later, when the boom fell and his draft number was called, she felt empowered, emboldened, by his invitation to join him far away in the hills. Curtis and Sally had been there from the very beginning. Curtis and Neil were best friends at Berkeley, determined to avoid the draft together. A little later, Ray, then Linda, came to the experiment in communal living.

She pulled herself back to the present. They all still sat at the table, the members of the commune riveted by Pamela's interest in them and yet embarrassed by the attention.

Pamela pushed her baked apple dessert aside and took out a notebook.

"So there's six of you here—seven if you count Linda and Ray's son—and you all live together amicably?"

Plates clanged as dishes were passed, and the people of Joyous Woods looked from one to another.

Sally sat stiffly, scowling. "We have our moments, of course, but here we are, after all these years."

"What about decision-making? Who did that?"

"Consensus means you agree." Neil locked eyes with Pamela, and Johanna saw that Pamela already knew the answer to her question.

For a second, she identified with Pamela, remembered her own wilt under Neil's charisma. Not only had she done Neil's bidding, she'd wanted to. Until later, when she'd learned to work around him, while letting him think he was the leader. Only now, that charade had led them into a cul-de-sac. He still had the power.

Curtis and Ray looked at each other.

Neil evaded Johanna's gaze as he said, "It was a process. At first it was like a big summer camp—except that the first rainstorm convinced us we needed better shelter." He laughed. "People pooled their finances. Some had savings, some were still on their parents' allowances." He looked at the floor.

Curtis rescued the awkward moment. "We tried different ways to make a living locally. We became laborers and fruit pickers. And yes, some of the guys just wanted the free food and shelter and didn't contribute. That became a problem after a while, so we had to figure out a system."

Neil broke in. "After a few years we instituted the Circle. A group that rotated every year, back when we had a lot of people living here. We even had ballots to elect them, until that seemed too city-council, so we dropped the idea. The Circle is who you see here—me, Curtis, Ray."

That comment hung over their heads for a few moments. Pamela said nothing. Linda looked at her hands; Sally got up to bustle. Johanna felt her face flame. To her own fury, she heard herself defend Neil.

"Personalities sometimes jarred. It was difficult to get any efficiency or order without a central authority." Her eyes drilled into Neil's.

He looked away. As if daring her to tell him to stop, he spoke loudly to make sure it was recorded. "So to loosen things up a bit, get people mellow, we smoked a lot of dope. We grew it, back there in the woods, in little plots. Not too big a patch because the feds had helicopters buzzing around up here, looking for marijuana farms. Ours was just here and there, in sunny patches so it looked like a weed." He laughed. "Which of course it is."

The tension in the room eased. Neil went on. "The problem was, a lot of the men who came to Joyous Woods were useless. Dropouts too stoned or too lazy to pull their weight. And there was a lot of work to do, hard physical work like plowing and building. You had to at least know how to dig a posthole. Some of these guys couldn't even put up a tent."

Johanna could see Neil flex his arm muscles. He was still taking credit for the farm's survival. But the women had done the day-in, day-out work.

She spoke up. "I think it was Sally who made her pottery kiln herself, from an old oil drum, soldering equipment, and a propane burner. Her pottery is beautiful." Johanna lifted a mug to demonstrate. "We sell that, and our knitted items at craft fairs and through my daughter's clothing store in Berkeley. All avenues for revenue."

As if Neil focused on that! For some time now, Neil had zoned out when she suggested a tactic to increase profitability. Last year they'd grown a bumper crop of beautiful chrysanthemums. He'd ignored her suggestion to raise the price to twelve dollars a bunch, so she, Sally, and Linda raised the price anyway and sold out the crop. Oblivious to this effort, the men toked it up in the evenings, saying their sore backs and aching muscles needed to relax.

Self-mockery curdled her voice. "The outdoor work was the most demanding physically, you know, digging the wells, putting in the solar system and the windmills. So we reverted to what you'd call traditional roles. We women ran the laundry, the kitchen, the dairy, and did plenty of work in the garden and orchard, too. Must seem old-fashioned to you."

"But it was supposed to be an equal partnership, right?"

"It was. It is. Of course it is," Neil said.

"I wouldn't say that." Johanna bit her lip.

"Partnership isn't the right term, actually, Pamela," Curtis interjected. "Hey, I can see where you're going here. What happened to feminism in the Age of Aquarius?"

"Yeah." Pamela traced the weave on the handwoven tablecloth. "Sounds quite nineteenth century."

Johanna explained. "We didn't know about feminism. Stuck up here in the woods, we had very little contact with the outside world. All this talk of men helping women run the household and women aspiring to run corporations, it would have been irrelevant at Joyous Woods."

"Any partnerships, as you call them, dissolved and reconnected pretty freely up here," Neil said.

Johanna flinched. Why couldn't Neil let it alone? He was encouraging Pamela in her intrusive interest in their intimate life.

Pamela directed a shot at Neil's craggy face. "Are we talking about sharing sex partners? Were you like that commune in San Francisco, the one its members considered a group marriage?"

Silence descended and stayed.

Ray shot Linda a worried look. Curtis feigned shock, lowering his head too late to hide a snicker. A chair scraped as Linda rose to go help Sally clear the dessert dishes from the table.

"No coffee, thank you," Pamela said to the room, her eyes on Johanna. "I had to ask. Let's get a visual on the question."

She led them from the room, a gleeful Neil right behind.

The nerve! Johanna wanted to wallop both of them.

Upstairs, they set up in Neil's bedroom. Its headboard-less mattress was covered, seventies style, with a faded Indian bedspread. Johanna's heart twinged at the recollection of intimacy—she'd bought that bedcover years ago at a street fair. She took a seat on an old trunk on the other side of the room, pushing aside old books to make space for herself. She picked up a book, opened the flyleaf, and noted its library due date was years past. Typical Neil.

"We shared everything. Yes, it's true." Neil took a dive onto the bed and lay there, grinning at Pamela provocatively. "See, we thought we could run a community where everyone was tolerant, everyone loved everyone else. Sex was separate from that, but it could be free-flowing too. Relationships were fairly loose."

The cameraman took a moment to turn his lens toward the balcony, where the unpruned tree spread its branches over the parapet, making the room dusky, though the sun still shone outside.

"I can see this room's just made for a tryst." Pamela laughed, her back to Johanna. Johanna peered at Neil, watching his reaction. The filmmaker must have sent Neil a come-hither look, because Neil's eyes glinted, full of humorous invitation as he returned Pamela's gaze.

He hadn't given Johanna a look like that in a long

time. Acid rose in her throat.

"What was your attitude to children? To having children, I mean?" Pamela said.

Neil ran a hand slowly over the bedspread. Johanna's throat tightened at his provocation. She couldn't believe it. Pamela was going to ask about the predictable result of all this amorous pairing.

But Neil had a different take on the question. "You mean, what did the kids think about all the partner sharing?"

"Yes, among other things. Weren't you worried about that?"

"I think we were just a microcosm of the larger society." Neil locked his hands behind his head as he lay supine on the bed, legs splayed apart, looking directly at Pamela. "I mean, families were breaking up all over in the seventies and eighties. It was a thing."

"My parents divorced." Pamela spoke so softly you could hardly hear it under the clatter of camera equipment.

As if he had not heard her, Neil continued, "One thing about having a polyamorous philosophy is that the kids don't have to worry about their parents separating. It's not an issue."

Johanna felt like a fly pinned to a specimen tray. Pamela was prying. Asking no one's permission, Neil allowed this Pamela to get in their faces and quiz them on their past relationships—and soon she'd broadcast them to the world.

"That's over now, of course," she said firmly.

"I kind of enjoyed it at the time." Neil sat up and stuck his chin out defiantly, avoiding Johanna's eyes.

But the aftereffects of those long-ago days had

unsettled Johanna's stomach. Joyous Woods wasn't exceptional in its group infidelities. Some of the other communes nearby (and there were several—this was California after all) had broken apart when unscrupulous leaders demanded sexual dominance of submissive women. But that had not happened at Joyous Woods.

Neil was charismatic but not a bully. The women had gone to him willingly, and if it made him happy, Johanna reluctantly accepted it. Up here in the hinterlands, away from the ferment that was Berkeley and the big cities, they'd seen the sexual revolution only in terms of men being free to tell women to get over it if they had to share. And the women, thinking they were modern, postmodern even, sucked it up. For a while, anyway.

Why had she accepted it? She studied her spotted hands. At the time, she'd racked her brain thinking how to get Neil to stop his open trysts with the other women. She tried to find something to prevent him from just dismissing her the way he'd dismissed the bra-less feminists. Not that she wore a bra herself.

She could have left Neil to his commune. The thing was, she loved it over and above Neil. The idea of living communally, sharing everything, never being alone, sustained her. She accepted his behavior as she accepted him because it had lasted. Neil always came back to her.

She'd had enough for today. Johanna tossed her gray plait, stood up and moved to the door, leaving Pamela and Neil to their mutual admiration. As she left with her head high, she couldn't help thinking that Neil, his long hair escaping its ponytail as he lay on the bed, reminded her of one of the goats.

"Bucks," she'd read in a manual, "should be chosen for body conformation and fine hair." Autumn was breeding season. Perhaps Neil had been among the animals so long he identified with them. A satyr in the hills of California?

She could cry. But she started to laugh.

Chapter Eight

"I've met someone, JoJo." A smile played around Maelle's mouth, till she covered it with her hand. She scarfed the last piece of cornbread, wiped the fallen crumbs from her shirt, and scooped them up off the table onto a yellow cloth napkin.

"Tell me." Johanna wiped her brow. The cast-iron stove let out a prodigious amount of heat in the autumn air.

"Can we open the door? It's stifling in here."

"The flies will be all over the pies and the cornbread." Johanna's eyes went to the loaves set out on the counter. "Neil hasn't fixed the screen on the door."

"Can't someone else do it then? Ray or Curtis? Or me? I'll just go get a staple gun, and it will be done in a sec. If you want something, you have to do it yourself."

"I guess." Johanna patted her granddaughter's shoulder. "I suppose you've learned that, living alone. Tell me about this friend of yours."

"He's a doctor. I met him when he was visiting on a conference. We've hung out a bit, but he lives a couple hours away. So there's probably not much in it. Geographic impossibility."

"Do you like him, this doctor? Well, obviously."

"I do. I wouldn't mention it otherwise. But you know me, nothing ever works long-term. When it gets intense, I can't concentrate on my work. And I want to do that, most of all the things in the world."

Johanna raised her eyebrows. "Takes two to tango. No doubt he has a career to attend to as well. He comes to see you, does he?"

"Yeah." Maelle's voice brightened. "We clicked, JoJo. Instantly. It's good. For now, anyway."

"Maybe I need to meet this young man." Johanna waved her dishtowel over the cooling baked goods, stirring up air in the close room. "What kind of medicine does he do?"

"Psychiatric research." Maelle went to the sink to rinse her coffee cup. Running water masked the gulp of her words. "Into the genetic causes of bipolar disease and schizophrenia, he says."

Johanna froze, her hearing still acute. "Does he do clinical work?"

"No. Not anymore. Prefers research, like me. We're alike that way. Rather not get up close and personal, if you know what I mean."

"Maybe he knows someone. Can get Neil to see someone. He's…well, you know what he's like."

"Moody."

"You could say that."

Maelle turned off the water, returned to the cooling cakes, placed a plate over a hot loaf pan, and turned it over. The cake slid out onto the plate, joining the others cooling on the counters. She tossed the loaf pan into the sink.

Johanna turned toward the window. "Maybe I'm the one who's down in the dumps. Neil should be, of course; he's just lost his parents."

"I was going to say something about that. Robert

said he wants…" Maelle couldn't finish the sentence.

Johanna spun around and burst out in a flurry of agitated words. "Your grandfather…I'm really worried."

"What about?"

"He seems to have lost his senses. He's acting overexcited. He says crazy things. First, he said that they're going to sell this land, he and Robert and Martha. Joyous Woods, all of it!"

Maelle took a deep breath. "Yes. What I was saying. Robert mentioned that at the funeral. It's not crazy. At least not to them. But it would be a disaster, JoJo. What can you do?"

"I don't know!" Johanna's voice rose to a wail. "I didn't believe him. Thought he was hallucinating."

"No, sadly, I think it's real. It's Martha and Robert, not Neil. They're behind it."

"Well, he seems enthusiastic about the idea. Talks about going to live in Hawaii, spending his days drinking piña coladas. Can you try to talk sense into him, dear?"

"I'm not sure I can! There's money to be made, and where there is money, Robert makes it. I don't like the idea, but maybe that's selfish. Maybe you'll be better off than you could ever imagine. Zachary says so, anyway."

"Zachary? You mentioned this to someone else?"

"Zachary's my friend. The one I just told you about." Maelle pushed the cooling loaves together, trying to make them tidy.

"Don't do that." Her grandmother lifted Maelle's hands gently away. "Let the air circulate between them."

"It's good, because he doesn't have an emotional interest in the situation one way or another. So when I talked to him, he had a few ideas that made sense. He said everyone directly involved should be able to work it out. That means you, JoJo."

"Maybe. But there's another problem, Maelle." Johanna turned away as she wiped her eyes with a dishtowel. "There's a woman came here, a filmmaker. She and Neil…they've formed a connection."

"What kind of connection? She wants to make a film of the farm? There's a lot of interest in back to the land, organic farming now. Could be good for our cause, JoJo!"

"What do you mean?"

Maelle put her arm around Johanna's shoulders. "It's clear you've never worked in the world of filthy commerce, but if she makes a film, this could be good publicity."

"How?"

"First of all, if she makes a film and Joyous Woods becomes famous, then people will want to buy our goods. The sales, JoJo, think of the increased sales of the cheese, or the clothes!"

"But what if the land is sold?"

"More people than you realize don't want to see land overrun by developers. Maybe I could talk to this filmmaker and tell her what is going on, how Uncle Robert wants to sell for top dollar."

"Don't do that. Please."

"Why not? Wouldn't it help?"

"I think you should stay out of it. This is between Neil and me. He's up to his old tricks again."

Johanna went to the sink and ran water, wastefully,

over the loaf pans. Maelle itched to turn it off, but she could see a faraway look in Johanna's eyes.

"What tricks?"

"That Pamela woman, the one making the film. She and Neil, well, for some reason she's captivated by him. The silly man's flattered."

"Oh, JoJo. I'm so sorry. It's probably just an old man's fantasy."

Johanna's eyes narrowed. "A lot of old people, as you call them, are still capable in the sack. I know, you don't want to hear it." She switched off the water and turned to Maelle. "But I agree with you, at his age it's crazy to get all excited about a woman in her thirties."

Maelle put her arm around her grandmother. "Just act normal. Like nothing has happened. It will pass, JoJo."

Her grandmother gave her a grateful look. "I know, dear. I'm sure it will."

Maelle started moving toward the door. Childish it might be, but she didn't want her grandmother to confide in her like this. Suddenly, a wave of anger washed over her. She'd come to tell Johanna about her new boyfriend. She'd wanted her grandmother to be pleased for her. And Johanna had turned the conversation to herself. And then, she'd tried to make out Neil was nuts. Well, maybe he was. That was the problem with these self-righteous people who claimed to live by principle. They couldn't see they were as much at fault as everyone else.

"I think I'll just go outside for a bit," she said, and let the door slam behind her.

So Johanna was more worried about Neil's peccadillos than the fact that the land they'd lived on for half a century would be snatched from beneath them. Neil and Johanna needed to cooperate if they were to stop the sale, and they needed to get the other communards' help.

Maelle walked quickly along the dirt path to the woods. She passed the dairy, the pottery studio with its kiln, the chicken coops. Her heart pounded. Why assume that Neil held all the power? He was only one of the remaining adults on the farm. A commune meant communal decisions.

She probably shouldn't have confided in Johanna today. She'd wanted to share her happiness about Zachary, however temporary it might prove to be. (She didn't dare hope, at this early stage.) But then her grandmother had begun to talk about her own problems, acted like Zachary was a professional she could consult! She hadn't even asked his last name!

She strode toward the rise on the hill where the fields ended and the woods began. She walked faster, into the familiar woods, where her beloved trees spread their branching arms to embrace her.

Always, the trees soothed Maelle. Tall, strong, their tops rustled and stirred, communicating in their way to the girl, though she knew they were unfazed by human sorrow. After her mother died, the trees provided her greatest solace. Their predictability saved her. Their presence. Their actuality. Their leafing out each spring reassured her. If they were evergreen like the oaks and the pines, they made her feel even better. They weren't going anywhere.

So Maelle began to take notice of life at the base of the trees. She dug and examined the roots. She observed how some trees grew taller, and how groups of species clustered, as if the parent tree protected the offspring, crowding out rivals for sunshine and water.

She explored, going farther and farther as she got older. She loved the peace of it. The fragrant air beyond the stinking barnyard, the sound of the trees soughing in a strong wind. Up in the woods she'd go, by herself. Johanna forbade her to go too far, told her to stop when the forest thickened. She could lie down and listen to the earth and all the creatures in it burrowing and squeaking, but only on the path—all right, only a few feet off it. The grown-ups told her that she must never ever go into the deep woods by herself, where mountain lions might lurk. So she never dared.

Amazingly, Johanna knew where all the flowers grew. That was one reason Maelle didn't stray. If she pulled wildflowers from the woods and brought them home, Johanna knew exactly where she'd picked them. She'd thank Maelle and tell her to be careful to leave more than she pulled so the plants could return next year.

One day, JoJo said, "What you're learning about nature on your own is a terrific education." At that, Maelle's heart swelled. But then JoJo said that when Maelle's mother and Aunt Abby were young, kids on the commune had "learned by doing" and had to grow their own food.

"All of it?" The thought scared Maelle. Curtis and Ray worked in the fields, all day long. Linda ran the dairy; that was a full-time job. And in the kitchen, a never-ending list of tasks loomed. Like facing a mound of potatoes. String beans to be trimmed. A lump of bread dough, needing to be kneaded, left to rise, and shaped before it could bake.

"Did they have playtime?" Maelle had asked her grandmother. "There's sheds I found. Old falling-down sheds. Like you could play house in them."

Dilapidated structures dotted the farm, usually used for storage. An old chicken coop had been converted to living quarters in the commune's crowded early days. When it was no longer needed, the wood had been salvaged for another purpose. The building Maelle had found was farther away, and larger, and rather than being stripped for reuse, it simply looked abandoned.

"That was a school," Johanna said curtly. "There were sleeping rooms, too, for the kids."

"A cubby house?"

Johanna had handed Maelle a scrubbing brush and peeler. She did not smile but went on cutting potatoes.

The memory made Maelle uneasy. What happened to that building? She supposed she could find it again. But she didn't have time.

She looked around her, seeing the landscape as if for the first time. The pagoda house stood in the distance, tilting gently, its solar panels threatening to fall off. Smoke rose from its chimney, curling toward the clear sky. It wasn't cold, but the old range remained lit, the women of Joyous Woods cooking throughout the day. Buildings appeared here and there haphazardly, all wooden, modest, blending into the soft browns and greens of the vegetation. The bucolic scene looked like something out of a painting. Old-fashioned, stuck in time.

What would the other members of the commune think about selling the land? After all, they all had this problem in common. They'd never planned for a future when they were too old to work the farm. Maybe, if

Neil would divide up his share of the money from the sale of the land with the others, it would be a payout for all those years of work. A way for them to retire gracefully. But would there be enough money for all of that? And would he be gracious and kind? After all, Neil had held them all in a kind of feudal power.

"It's my land," he would say whenever someone protested about unfairness or the fact that he seemed to do little while the others worked hard. Oh, Maelle had noticed, once she was old enough to become conscious of fairness, when she came back to live at Joyous Woods at the age of ten.

And if it was feudal, why was the present arrangement at Joyous Woods worth saving?

Maelle stopped short as an idea hit her. In front of her stood a majestic redwood. Its immense height cast deep shadow around her, amplified by dozens of other trees just like it in the grove. At the foot of the trees, shade lovers like sword fern, redwood sorrel, and redwood violet nestled. They seemed happy not taking any of the glory from the big trees. If this was the political system of the forest, it worked. The taller trees spread their leaves like an umbrella to photosynthesize while getting water and minerals through their roots, the combination providing the sugars that fueled the forest. The redwoods used red light in the spectrum more efficiently, while plants below them in the shade evolved to love the far-red light which reached all the way through the canopy's leaves down to the ground.

At the forest floor, the smaller shade-loving plants reveled in the wealth of nutrients supplied by the ecosystem underground. Living next to these peons of the plant world, the lords above took from the richness of the underground network's supply chain. It worked because the plants below expressed their own joy of living in the shelter of the overstory, nourished by the carbohydrates sent down from above. Every plant adapted to its own niche, each productive in its own way. What connected them was a web of roots. Cut the roots out and the whole system would collapse.

What a metaphor for the way the human world should work. Individuals were much less important than the whole. Individuals could not survive without the whole community working for survival together. There must be a way to save the farm and the trees, while also allowing those who wanted to retire to do so.

Neil and Johanna had chosen this life and kept at it for all these years. And for all its poverty, it had given Maelle an appreciation of nature and a vocation. She never once dreaded going to work with her beloved plants.

Maelle quickened her walk. She must get on the road soon, back to her work. She'd see Zachary tomorrow.

She pictured herself tending her plants in the laboratory and Zachary too, poring over his research, utterly absorbed. Two people who valued intellect over the simmering feelings deep underground. She sensed this in Zachary just as she knew it about herself. He was holding back the true expression of his feelings. Just as she always had, and did so, even today. But still, something inside herself uncurled like a leaf in spring. She'd been touched by rain and sunlight. Happiness. JoJo's problems with Neil were not hers to solve. Or even to know about. The main thing was the farm with its fields and its woods, its productivity and its pastoral peace. If she could help save Joyous Woods from the bulldozer, everything would be perfect.

Chapter Nine

"Sit still, will you? I'm trying to count stitches."
Johanna sat on the sofa, knitting, in Abby's apartment.
A light breeze fluttered through an open window. The
sounds of children shouting in the afternoon air, the
distant roar of traffic, and the occasional racket of a
lawnmower filtered in, stirring little waves of
discomfort.

Abby paced back and forth across the room. She
swung her arms, then scrabbled her hand in her long,
wavy hair, its natural tawny tones colored today with
streaks of pink. She halted in front of a mirror over her
fireplace, ran her fingers along the mantel.

Johanna, seeing her daughter's reflection, noticed
the tiny pleats around the eyes, now deepened into
seams. Had it really been twenty years since Abby had
first sold her mother's clothing creations? She sighed.
Abby had done well. She could afford to live in one of
the sought-after old-fashioned Berkeley apartments,
drafty but with loads of style. On the mantel, she
displayed a row of Rookwood pottery. Now that was
expensive! Johanna could never have afforded the
luxury of art. How beautifully the cool green glaze
shone with its incised patterns in the Arts & Crafts
manner. The color complemented the green of a gauzy
patterned curtain that swung from the window.

Abby picked up a vase and cradled it in her arms

for a moment, moved her hand up and down its cool rounded surface.

"I remember when you first bought that." Johanna turned another row of stitches.

"The Rookwood? One of my first finds. Learned about it when I worked at the antiques store. I found some at a flea market. My boss told me I had a real eye."

Her mother laughed. "You must have learned to scrounge at my knee. You had better taste, though. I remember all those scarves you turned into floaty dresses and the old paintings you found at flea markets. You bought them for the frames."

"I did. Sometimes Curtis would give me paintings he'd done, and I'd put them in those old frames and sell them at the store. I found other good stuff, too. Silver and ceramics. I studied it. You know why the Rookwood appealed so much, don't you? It was the first manufacturing company founded in this country by a woman."

Johanna scowled. "Commerce."

"What do you think Woolley's is, if not commerce? A store that sells clothing, including the cashmere and angora items you make! My store! And it has to make money to stay in business."

"Oh, I wouldn't worry about that. You have a loyal customer base. Berkeley's that kind of town. The people here like sandals and handmade clothes. Clothes fashioned from nature, as you keep telling me."

"That's what we need to talk about." Abby pressed her hand to her forehead, frowning. "I've been thinking. The store needs a new look. The city's changing. People want better quality. I want to move upscale."

"Upscale? Meaning what?"

"I mean the clothes I sell must be the height of fashion, fabulous and original."

"They are original, Abby. Handmade! Look at this?" She raised her knitting, a crimson sleeve. "Stop fidgeting. What on earth's the matter with you?" Johanna stuffed an errant spool of yarn back in the cloth workbag that rarely left her side.

Abby turned away, smoothing the tunic she wore over leggings. "I'll make us some tea."

"Fine. I should have brought us some cake." Johanna settled her knitting back in her lap. "I'm experimenting. Chocolate cake with orange. It's different. People seem to like it."

"Next time, thank you. Tea's enough for me." Abby went into her kitchen.

"You should eat more. You're much too thin."

"It's yoga, plus standing all day in the store." Abby clattered dishes, setting up a tray.

"Yoga doesn't seem to be making you all that calm."

"Maybe not today."

Abby lifted cups and saucers from a cabinet, taking a long time to select two of each. The electric kettle began to bubble.

"Don't fuss." The needles clacked. "I'd get up and help, but I'm in the middle of a row."

Abby prepared a lacquered tray, placed two pretty flowered cups over saucers, and added a spray of grapes on another flowered plate. She poured hot water over teabags in a teapot and slowly carried the tray toward her mother.

"What's wrong, dear? You look worried."

"I'm not sure how to tell you this without upsetting you." Abby placed the tray carefully on the coffee table, poured tea into two cups, and stood up. She took a deep breath. "I need to make a change in the business. Stock more sophisticated items, more dresses, fewer hand-knit sweaters."

"Oh, dear." Johanna leant forward as if to take a cup but, instead of putting her bamboo needles aside, tightened her grip on them. "I thought hand-knit was the latest thing. Shows craft and love. Expensive, but isn't that the point?"

"Yes, Mother. But I need to grow my clientele, and therefore I need more product. Joyous Woods originals and other one-of-a-kind items aren't sufficient. I just can't keep up the supply I need fast enough."

A skein of scarlet dribbled down the side of Johanna's workbag and gathered on the floor. Johanna stared at it blankly for a second, then gathered the yarn up and shoved it back in the bag.

"What about us? What will happen to Joyous Woods if we can't sell what I make to Woolley's? All that effort to raise the goats for cashmere, to comb the fleeces by hand, the shearing too, the dyeing and spinning, the knitting…" The needles pointed at Abby. "And the rabbits. Same thing. Combing the angora wool, all that."

"That's partly the point. The production method you have going at Joyous Woods is not efficient." Abby sat down again and took up her cup.

"What on earth are you talking about?"

"You have to feed and care for the goats and rabbits, harvest their wool by shearing and hand-combing. You have to clean it, then spin it into yarn. It all takes so much time, and time is money."

"I like doing all that."

"I know. And it all sold. But lately people have been showing resistance to the folk-art style." Abby reached over to pat her mother's arm. "Maybe you could sell the yarn before it's knitted or woven. That would save you a lot of time. Most cashmere and angora producers sell the wool on, once it's been harvested and cleaned. There must be other outlets for your yarn. Other stores. You could get online and research them."

"Online. You know I'm not good at that."

"There's a computer up on the farm. Maybe I could buy you a new one, just for the yarn business. Would you like that?"

"I suppose I could ask Linda to help me."

"Yes. You know she'd do it."

"What about you? How will you find suppliers for your clothes? Find designers?" Johanna had not touched her tea.

"They're around."

"You're not going to stock that cheap stuff from China? You know they harvest angora there in ways we'd find really questionable. You'll lose your clients."

"It's a matter of design. Lately, customers want materials that swing when they walk. Designs with careful, clever stitching that make the wearer look slimmer. With climate change, we need cooler, breathable materials, less wool, more cotton." She shook her head. "No, not even cotton! I've heard that growing enough cotton to make a single pair of jeans uses two thousand gallons of water. And a billion pairs of jeans are sold every year."

Johanna had set down her knitting, rubbing one hand with the other. "You don't stock jeans! And I don't make them. Anyway, those natural materials are your trademark. My trademark."

Abby heaved a sigh. "What I'm trying to say, not very well, is that one-off article creation just doesn't pay. And I have to keep up with market trends to stay in business. I'm exploring different ways of doing that."

She finished her tea and held the cup at a distance, examined its flower pattern. The cup's pretty scalloped rim and almost translucent glaze showed its age. An antique, it had been passed from hand to hand. "Recycling's where it's at, Ma."

Johanna scoffed. "That's nothing new. Remember how I used to cut up old quilts to make clothes? I used to sew our clothes from remnants we found at yard sales."

"Yeah." Abby grimaced. "But I'm talking upmarket. When I say recycling, I mean what's happening is amazing. They even make fabric from recycled plastic. I've seen polyester boiled so it melted. Then it can be molded over pebble-like forms to make a bubbly fabric. That can be turned into ruffs and collars that look like tiny gathered balloons."

"I couldn't do that. We don't use plastic on the farm if we can help it."

"No. Of course not."

As silence settled in the room, the muted sounds of outside life sharpened, became louder. Johanna defiantly turned a row. Her gray plait swung as she purled.

Abby pushed the plate forward. "Have some grapes. It's natural sugar. Good for you."

Johanna waved it away.

"Mother, you need to think about slowing down. About retirement."

"Retiring?" Johanna snorted. "I work. I come from German stock, after all."

"I know. But eventually, you'll have to stop."

"Why?"

"You can still make money from the goats and the rabbit fleeces. For now, anyway. As I've said, you could sell it wholesale before you turn it into clothes. You could sell to craft fairs. Your yarn is beautiful, as you know."

"Not beautiful enough for you, though. You have to understand, Abby. The clothes—they're like my babies."

Abby pulled herself up to her full height and looked her mother straight in the eye. "Well, then," she said, "like your babies, you can just let them go. Let other people make them into what they want."

"I don't know what you're talking about." Johanna's head bent to her work. Hurt flared from her brain to her fingers, sharp as a wasp's sting. She dropped several stitches. Doggedly, she retrieved them, knitted to the end of the row, stuck her needles forcefully into the unfinished sweater, and shoved it into her bag. The thanks she got. For doing her best.

Chapter Ten

"Would it be all right, dear, if I stayed with you tonight?"

Johanna's call startled Maelle, stuck in her laboratory, absorbed in her plants. Her grandmother hardly ever picked up the phone or sent an email, and she couldn't text. Last Christmas, Abby had given her a cell phone—for safety reasons, she said—and Johanna spent several frustrated hours trying to master it, finally grasping the function of the button that allowed conversation. Now, her voice sounded anxious, so Maelle, glad to get away from her plant puzzle, agreed to pick up her grandmother in downtown Berkeley.

Maelle found the older woman staring disconsolately at the window display of a clothing boutique. So rarely did Johanna shop that Maelle wondered what had come over her.

"Just trying to get some ideas. I guess I'm way behind the times," Johanna said as she got into the car. She pulled on her seatbelt roughly, shoving it into the buckle, averting her eyes from Maelle's.

"Tell me." Maelle patted her grandmother's arm.

"Abby wants to go upscale, and our Joyous Woods clothing couldn't be more down to earth."

Maelle tossed her hair to hide a smile. Johanna wore sneakers, which looked incongruous with her dark skirt and multi-colored knitted cardigan, and her bun had come loose, spilling gray hair with ragged ends. She looked every year of her age.

And so forlorn.

In all the years Maelle had known her, Johanna had never once tried to change her style. Had Johanna made such a point of "being herself" all those years ago, that now the psychic cost of sticking to her principles prevented her from modifying them?

Maelle sat at the wheel, letting the thought sink in. She turned to her grandmother and wrapped her arms around her. "I'm so sorry, JoJo. Is there anything I can do to help? I'll talk to Abby, if you like."

Johanna smiled, and Maelle gulped and smiled back. Abby lived in a different world—the real world, of profit and loss. More in tune with Robert and Martha than with the ideals of the commune. What had really happened between Johanna and her daughter today? Maelle would have to coax it out of Johanna in the evening, when they were comfortable.

They stopped at the market, allowing Johanna to choose supplies for their dinner. Maelle paid and would not let the older woman carry even one of the heavy paper bags up the stairs to her apartment. But Johanna's hands could not be idle, and she eagerly opened the bags, organizing things in order of preparation. Maelle marveled at her competence.

A living room, bedroom, small kitchen, and doll-size bathroom completed Maelle's dwelling. Since the weather had cooled and Maelle had brought them inside from her balcony, potted plants made passage through the rooms a gauntlet through greenery.

She spritzed the plants with water. "You take my bedroom," she insisted between squirts. "I'm happy with the sofa."

Abby had more room! Why hadn't she offered to host Johanna as she usually did? Maybe Abby had romantic plans or had to get up for an early meeting. Maelle had taken in what Johanna had told her about Abby's need to change her store's vendors but couldn't believe this could strain the mother-daughter relationship to the extent that Johanna felt unwelcome at Abby's.

That night she tossed and turned on the lumpy couch and pulled a pillow over her head to cover the snores coming from the bedroom. Was it really possible that old people moved in with their grandchildren when they aged? God forbid. That was even more reason to save Joyous Woods.

"Will you be all right, going back on the bus, JoJo?" she said next morning when Johanna emerged from the bathroom.

"No problem. Sally will pick me up at the station."

"Good. Sit. I have croissants. I bought them just for you." Maelle passed her grandmother a cup of steaming herbal tea.

"How nice, dear." Johanna bit into a croissant. The flakes scattered down the front of her shirt. "Maelle, tell me. What am I going to do about Neil? I'll have to deal with him somehow." She shook her head. "Maybe it's all my fault. I let everything slide. We didn't think what would happen when we got older."

"Oh, JoJo. I hope you haven't lain awake all night worrying."

The lined face sagged. "Our lifestyle turned out to be so hard. We had such fantasies about it."

"Here's some of your own jam, JoJo. Put it on the

croissant." Maelle opened the jar. "Are you thinking maybe it's okay to sell the land so you and Neil can sit pretty for the rest of your lives?"

"That's just it!" Agitated, Johanna almost knocked over her tea.

"What is?"

"I told you about Neil and this Pamela person. She's disrupting everything! What if Neil does side with his brother and sister and sell the land. Where am I?"

"But JoJo, you've complained before that Neil has these little affairs. He always comes back." A ball of nausea gathered in Maelle's throat. She hated talking about this with Johanna, forced to take sides.

"It's because of the sale. If he goes off with Pamela, or if he just abandons me anyway, then I'm left out in the cold. Literally. I have no claim on any of Neil's assets."

"Why not? I thought California was a community property state."

"It is. But it doesn't recognize common-law marriage. Neil and I never got legally married. Resisted conformity. We were proud of our stance. Of course, my parents were disappointed, but that's the way it was then. For our generation, marriage was very uncool. Very bourgeois. So we never did." Johanna stroked her hair, not yet braided into her customary plait.

"But all those years together! They must count for something."

"They don't. Apparently. I've looked into it. In order to get what they call 'palimony' in California, the plaintiff—that would be me—would have to prove that I actually thought we were married. And I didn't. I was

94

an active participant in opposing that little mark of convention."

Maelle crossed to the other side of the table and nestled her cheek next to her grandmother's dry and papery face. They did not speak for a few moments. Suddenly, Maelle pulled away and stood straight. "I guess that means Abby and Mom were illegitimate, like me."

"What an awful word! Last time I looked, having a baby isn't illegal, and nor is the child. Anyway, it's done you no harm, has it? Or Abby?"

"Guess not. But you, JoJo. What are we going to do about you?"

"Anyone with half a brain can see this Pamela is just after Neil's money, now she knows his parents are dead. Any woman of thirty-five who goes after a man of seventy has to have an ulterior motive."

"It's not a mental illness, JoJo, what Neil's doing. If that were the case, half the older men in America would be certified."

Johanna shook her head. "Really? They're not like Neil. He turned it to a fine art. And we all—I mean the women—bought into it."

"How so?"

Johanna put an arm on the table to prop up her forehead. "I can't believe it now. Neil was pretty attractive back in the day. It didn't take much. He'd just give some of the new girls a look, and they'd come to him."

"New girls?"

"Back in the seventies, dear, a lot of people came. They thought it would be all drugs and free love. Oh, a few were serious. The ones who were willing to work stayed. But Neil got away with a lot."

"Did you say anything to him, JoJo? Why didn't you leave him then?"

"That's a good question. You know, though, I got my own back."

Maelle frowned. "With another man?"

"Actually, yes. But I didn't care for him. It was just to pay Neil back, make him wake up to what he was doing."

"Hmm. Okay. Was this before you had Mom and Abby?"

"Oh, yes. It was back in the early days."

"I bet you were very pretty, JoJo. You could have had anyone."

"But I loved Neil. I still do, even though he's a fool."

Maellè started to sweat under her shirt. The room was stifling and smelled of an unmade bed, dirty breakfast dishes. The notion of septuagenarian sex was unnerving. How could a much younger woman be captivated by a wizened oldster like her grandfather? She gripped the edge of a chair and forced her face into a bland but sympathetic mask.

"He's a bit past that, isn't he? You must be imagining it."

Johanna turned away, crumpling a napkin in her hand.

Her grandmother, incapable of competing with the charms of a much younger rival. But wanting to. That the older woman could feel jealous had never occurred to Maelle. Johanna had never been one to belie her age with makeup and Botox. But a man's age kind of slid around. Neil's trim fitness and full head of salt and pepper hair made him look younger.

So unfair. Older men could attract younger women, but the opposite rarely happened. In the reality of mammal biology, females were attractive to males as long as they had an egg supply. When that ran out, they were evolutionarily of no use. Plants had no such prejudices. Of course, as a plant biologist she'd known of very weird practices in the world of flora. But with trees, age had the advantage. As she'd always thought, they were superior beings in every way.

JoJo might not be mistaken about Neil's infatuation with the filmmaker, but surely Pamela could not be infatuated with him. It had to be a flirtation, nothing more. Something to brighten the day. Something to tease the communards about. She was only trying to amuse herself as she filmed them, showing the poverty of their chosen way of life.

Flirtation or not, Johanna had raised a serious question. What were her rights?

"The question is, JoJo, what are you going to do? Do you want to stay up there on that land if Neil goes off with Pamela? We both know the farm buildings are pretty much falling apart. Anyway, the land's going to be sold."

"I'm having a hard time taking it all in, Maelle. It's hard to change at my age."

"Look, I really think the best thing is to try to reason with Neil. Tell him you two have too much history to throw away."

"So much." Johanna's eyes filled with tears. "Maybe your friend Zachary could talk sense into Neil. Isn't he a psychiatrist?"

"JoJo, I have to get to work," Maelle said,

caressing Johanna's hand. "You need a lawyer. I'll ask around. Let's get you ready, and I'll take you to the bus."

And I'm going to arrange a sit-down with Abby, Maelle determined. Soon as I can.

Chapter Eleven

Sally was waiting in the truck when Johanna arrived at the bus station.

"What's happening at the farm? That film woman still at it?"

"Yep. Right now she seems focused on the goats."

"How are Ray and Linda handling that?"

"Ray's dealing with it. Linda's being protective of Kevin. You know they're both so shy and quiet. And Pedro doesn't speak much English."

"She came at the wrong season. We're going into winter. No shearing going on now, but we'll breed the goats. Maybe she'll be really interested in that!"

Sally grinned. She gunned the accelerator, passed a slow car, making the truck rattle.

"Is Neil behaving like an old goat?"

Sally leaned over to pat Johanna's knee. "Maybe you're reading too much into it, Jo. He just seems much more lively at the moment."

"Probably going into one of his up phases. He's been in a downer for quite a while. It's so exhausting, Sally."

"I know. How did we all put up with it? How do we?"

"How old do you think this Pamela person is?"

"Thirties, maybe. Hard to tell with all that makeup she wears. Why do you ask?"

"Just wondering. She acts so naïve and so cunning at the same time. She seems so ignorant of history. She says she wants to do a documentary on us, as if we're really countercultural still. We've moved on from that. We're just organic farmers."

"I wonder what her agenda really is." Sally glanced at her passenger. "What point is she trying to make?"

"She's so focused on all the negative stuff. People today are so down on us baby-boomers. We weren't always old and grumpy. We wanted to make a better world, didn't we?" Johanna snorted. "Yeah, that really happened. We have to face reality, Sal. Neil and his brother and sister want to sell the land. Joyous Woods won't last. Maelle is upset about it."

"He hasn't said anything to us." Sally swerved to avoid a boulder on the road. They were climbing into the scree-covered hills, an area prone to landslides.

"That's typical."

"You know, Jo, how long can we keep on farming?"

"I hadn't planned to stop."

"Yes. But Curtis and I, we're old and we're tired."

"Farmers don't retire."

"Why not?"

"Because it's the only life we know. It keeps us physically active too. Can you imagine us in an assisted living place?"

Sally hooted with a laugh that turned to a cough. "That'll be the day."

She slowed the accelerator, and the truck chugged round a bend. "Though really, Curtis and I will have to make some kind of plan. To be fair, since we shared everything equally, expecting to do the same with the

100

profits, maybe when the land is sold Neil can simply give us our share?"

"You think he actually would?" Johanna shook her head.

"Curtis will talk to him. They understand each other."

"Curtis is a prince compared to Neil at the moment."

"God, you're a cynic, Jo!"

Johanna stared out the window, remembering. How she'd met Neil, captivated by his enthusiasm, his gorgeous, sculpted face, strong straight nose, glittering blue eyes, and the untamed, tumbling hair she'd ached to run her fingers through. Talking to Maelle last night had brought it all back.

Neil's magnetism kept the commune going because the women kept coming. Was it those curls, the timbre of his voice, his ready laughter? He made the whole enterprise a lark. Whatever it was, the women who heard about him—and the other good-looking, fit young men at Joyous Woods—streamed up here in the late seventies and eighties, providing a work crew for the fields and the kitchens, to sow and harvest, to make the breads and jams and cakes they could sell at farmers' markets.

No question that the men who visited were often drifters and dreamers, but the women came to stay, motivated by idealism, the pungent perfume of pot, or the sweaty, sexy scent of Neil. They came for the chance to be his lover for a time, even for a night. And Johanna stood by and saw it happen. And let it happen because the women worked.

"Unreconstructed, that's what they call Neil and

the others, Sally. That's the word Maelle used the other day. As in men expecting to lord it over us."

"Up here in the backwoods, we missed all that." Sally laughed. "The Women's Movement, I mean."

"I don't know why we put up with it, Sal. The idea that we had to share. The men telling us to get over it."

"Do you regret that?"

"Hmm. It's so hard to know, now, what was the right thing to do, then." A sharp pain hit Johanna's chest at the memory of the humiliations she'd suffered.

She hadn't been able to stop his relationships with other women, especially the long-haired sylphs with pretty singing voices, soft hands as yet unhardened by toil. Jealous fury had roiled her stomach, made her helpless with tamped-down rage. When a new couple applied to the commune, Neil sized up the female partner. He let in the ones with the long wispy hair and the soft voices, rejected the political polemicists. Especially the feminists who emerged toward the end of the seventies. Especially the earnest ones with horn-rimmed glasses who lectured him about social justice. Neil just shrugged, implied that the commune already had its full complement of workers.

And then one day a particularly handsome new man arrived. Like a movie star he was, clean-shaven, played a mean guitar. The women found themselves washing their hair more than every few days, slathering their skin with coconut oil. Skirts were sewn that gave an extra sashay to the walk, blouses created out of gauzy material and worn without the usual covering shawls.

You could almost smell the testosterone as the two bucks, Neil and Edward, locked horns, so to speak, in a battle for possession of the women of Joyous Woods. But it wasn't until Johanna herself gave in to Edward's charms that the final break came. Despite his looks, Johanna had not wanted Edward at all, not really, but her simmering anger at Neil's infidelity made her beautify herself to attract the rival. When she bedded Edward in one of the outer cabins she hadn't enjoyed it in the least, kept her mind off what she was doing by silently planning dinner as Edward rocked back and forth. But afterward she'd been sure to walk past Neil with her head held high, wafting her scent like a bitch in heat. Just to annoy Neil. It worked. Neil came back to her. His rival moved on, taking some of his concubines, as Johanna liked to call them.

For a time afterward, she'd been reinstated as the queen bee. She, Johanna, who had never aspired to such a role. The workers surrounded her, Neil acting as the drone. It would have made her laugh, if she weren't so irritated by it. She sighed.

"Do you think we enabled it, Jo?" Sally shook her head. "All the sex with whomever came along?"

"Do you? It was confusing. I remember that."

"Kind of fun, too, though, wasn't it? Curt and I always thought of it as a test. If we still wanted each other after all the sexperiments…" She laughed at her own joke.

Johanna clutched the door handle. "I can't…I can't relive those days, those decisions. It's what we are today, what we've become." She winced as the truck jolted over a bump.

"This truck. It's on its last legs." Sally shifted gears to third as the engine strained up a steep hill. They rode in silence till they reached the farm and unloaded the bags of rice and beans Sally had bought in town.

The comforting solidity of the pagoda house's old wooden cabinets, the sight of onions piled in netted bags in the pantry and the scent of rosemary, thyme, and bay leaves hanging in long strips by the door sent a wave of relaxation over Johanna. She eased into a chair, unlaced her boots, stretched her back. Sally, at the stove, put on the kettle, but Johanna didn't get up to help.

She raised her eyes to a high shelf. A hand-woven basket sat there, knitting needles poking out of it from a skein of wool the color of honey. Her work, her comfort, her joy. A stab of pain hit her heart.

"Another thing," she said. "Abby's more or less kicked us out of the store. Says she wants to carry a more fashionable product. Taken a sudden dislike to the angora sweaters."

Sally had started sorting the staples into their big glass jars. She stopped. "Oh, Jo! How awful. How insulting! Why didn't you tell me before?"

"Couldn't face it, I guess. Tried to put it out of my mind. But Sal, I've been sewing since I was thirteen years old! Remember I brought that sewing machine with me when we came up here? And that trunk of fabrics. I was so scared of what we were doing, and sewing always soothed me. My stress reliever when exams were coming. Didn't help my grades, but I always got something useful out of it. And all the time I spent sewing and knitting here when we started? That gave us the idea of getting rabbits and goats in the first place, so we could use their fleeces and spin it into yarn." She picked at her cardigan, removing the fuzz.

"Oh yes. But Abby wouldn't know all that. What

do you think's behind this decision?"

"I can't figure out if she thinks I'm losing my touch, or if she really does want to sell different things. I mean, surely there's a way she could do both."

"Maybe. I don't know."

Johanna's mantra of never leaving her hands idle returned. "Let me wash up, and I'll help you start dinner." She hauled herself up, scrubbed her hands at the sink, and dried them on a dishtowel.

"Let's have some tea, first, Jo. Linda made a cake today."

"Where is she?"

"I think she's demonstrating cheese making to the film crew."

"Humph!" Johanna suddenly lost her balance. She held on to the side of the old hutch, then to the tops of the chairs as she made her way to the worktable in the middle of the kitchen.

Sally eyed her, frowning, as Johanna pulled out a chair and sat down carefully. "Jo, you feeling okay?"

"Just dizzy. Get these spells every now and then. It's nothing. Nothing at all."

Sally cut her a piece of lemon cake and set a cup of steaming tea before her. Johanna smiled and thanked her. She drew the sugar bowl toward her cup and raised the spoon, hesitating. She gave a little laugh and put it back.

"Think I'll go lie down," she said, holding onto the side of the table as she stood. The kitchen twirled around her, and she stumbled out of the room.

A few minutes later, it seemed, she heard voices downstairs. Late afternoon shadows darkened her bedroom. She brushed her teeth and hair and, holding onto the banister, made her way downstairs one step at a time. As she drew closer to the kitchen, she recognized the tinkling laughter as Pamela's.

Boots lined up on a bristle mat at the door—several pairs of utilitarian men's work boots, and a tall woman's pair polished to a chocolate glaze. A chatty group gathered around the table, and Sally handed the film crew thick white cups and chipped saucers, encouraging them to help themselves to cake. They all looked perfectly at home. Not surprising, given their shyness, was the absence of Linda and Ray.

Johanna's gaze drew toward Neil. She couldn't believe it. His hair, normally long and fastened in a ponytail, had been cut and shone with a recent wash. His jeans were unstained, his shirt the brilliant white that only a line-dry in the sun could achieve. She could smell it from across the room. He'd drenched himself in the lavender water she used to spritz the sheets.

"Hello, Jo. How'd it go in Berkeley? See Abby and Maelle?" As she drew nearer, Johanna could see Neil's fingers slip apart from Pamela's.

Johanna's muscles tightened, her spine went rigid. "They're fine," she managed to say. The kitchen filled with bodies suddenly stifled her, the voices buzzed in her ears.

"Excuse me, I'll just go and nip some parsley, pick something for salad." She stumbled as she reached for the door handle, desperate for oxygen.

Outside, she gulped deep breaths of air. It had cooled to a chill, bringing with it the lingering smells of a farm's day—manure to fertilize the winter fields, the drenched scent of grass absorbing an afternoon shower, the nose-tickle of chaff wafting from the chicken coop where the hens muttered. The sudden change of temperature made her cough. Johanna hugged her cardigan close around her and walked quickly to the cabin where Ray and Linda lived with Kevin.

The boy—not a boy, but they always thought of him as a not-yet-adult—came to the door. He limped slightly, and the brown iris of one eye wandered toward his nose. Linda and Ray should have patched that when he was young. A momentary regret surged through her, as Kevin ushered her in, tripping over the doormat as he did so.

"Mom's in the dairy," he said, recovering. "Dad's talking to Pedro. The goats are going out tomorrow to a grazing job."

"Oh. I'll wait," Johanna said. They sat down on the sofa—packing cases covered with homemade cushions. Even sparer than the pagoda house, or Curtis and Sally's wooden structure, which was filled with her pottery and his paintings, Linda and Ray's home had the air of student digs, fifty years after they'd been students together. An old door laid over two large oak barrels served as the table, while boards and bricks formed a bookshelf against the wall. Two bedrooms flanked each side of this main room, Johanna knew. The commune members ate most meals at the bigger pagoda house, so Kevin and his parents made do with a simple sink sunk into cabinetry carved by Ray, a kettle, and a toaster oven. A bare bulb hung from the ceiling. In an alcove, partially hidden by a cloth curtain, an old bathtub sat on clawed feet next to a low wooden stool. Johanna remembered how Linda sat on this to bathe Kevin in the bathtub years after the other children had graduated to showers, shoving his head under the water to his protests, lathering his hair with a bar of homemade, scentless soap.

"What do you think of this movie they're making on Joyous Woods, Kev?"

"Good! We're actors. We could be in the magazines!"

"I don't think so. It's a documentary, dear. They usually don't make the headlines or fill the movie theatres."

"Oh."

"Are they interfering with your work?"

"No. I like it when they ask questions. I like their big car, too. Wish we could have one of those."

"Do you wish you and your parents could leave Joyous Woods and live in another house, somewhere else?"

Kevin looked confused at this question. "Somewhere else?"

"You know, like the other kids did when they left. Like Abby. Or Maelle. Jasper and the others. They live in town."

"Oh."

She should have known better than to ask him that. Kevin had rarely been to town. Once or twice to Sacramento, once or twice to Berkeley and San Francisco. He could barely read. Here at Joyous Woods that had been a simmering worry with Linda and Ray. They'd homeschooled him, along with the other children when they were elementary school age. But he didn't progress very far. There were special education classes available to him, but the long bus ride proved too much for his limited stamina. When Linda and Ray told the authorities they'd prefer to continue to teach him at home, the school's special education director seemed relieved. Johanna frowned. Hadn't the commune saved the school district thousands and thousands of dollars? That must be why it didn't push harder for him to be enrolled.

But now, he had no marketable skills. Where was Linda and Ray's responsibility in this, and where was the commune's?

She looked at her empty hands. She'd meant to go to the kitchen garden for parsley and instead had gone to look for Linda and Ray. She'd wanted them to agree not to talk about Kevin's birth, in case Pamela started quizzing them. But she'd have to leave that for another day. She got up, kissed Kevin on the forehead, and stepped outside.

In the distance, Pamela, Neil, Curtis, and the film crew were peering into an abandoned building. She hurried over, a prickle of uneasiness making the hairs on her arms stand up. She arrived just as Pamela had once again fitted Neil with a microphone. The sky gave barely enough light to see.

"What's this place?" Pamela said. The cameraman swept a wide shot of a concrete block building. Unoccupied and desolate, it looked even more so in the lengthening shadows.

The camera crew tramped down weeds to edge through a splintery door. Johanna followed, despite Neil's discouraging glare. The inside, a house of sorts, had clearly been unlived in for a very long time. A kitchen held a dirty stove and a rusty sink, with a refrigerator-wide gap between open shelves. Three long bedrooms held a few cots, rust eating the wire frames. In one of these rooms, a long table took up space.

Underneath the waist-high tabletop, two hampers stood, empty, their canvas liners dirty and torn. In the single bathroom a long, low steel sink and a half-dozen faucets lined one wall. A ripped plastic shower curtain, pale blue with a pattern of cavorting gray elephants, hung sadly from the rail of a communal shower.

"What was this, a school or a dormitory?"

Neil smiled lopsidedly. "Both, sort of. Yes, the children were taught in here. They had other lessons too. We believed in outdoor education. Learning about farm life. A different sort of education, if you like." His foot pushed the droppings of some animal into a corner.

"Take the camera outside," he said roughly. "It's getting dark. There might be enough light to see the fields the children worked." He led them all out, slamming the door.

The group stood uncertainly, facing a smaller, wooden building. They entered one by one, through a low door into a room holding a long, low box carved at intervals with holes. The wood of the seat was splintered and stained. Fly-screened windows let in weak light. An outhouse, apparently made for midgets.

Curtis said, "See, this was clever. The toilet block could be dismantled and moved to another part of the field every year or so."

"You mean this latrine fertilized these fields?" Pamela's face expressed dismay.

"Not as raw sewage. Look, manure, animal or human, mixed with straw, composts down nicely over time."

"Oh. You're lucky no one got sick. And what was this?" She directed the film crew to shoot a scene of muddy fields, darkening rapidly. "Their own mini-farm?"

"Learning by doing, it's the only way!" Johanna pushed forward. "The kids were taught to plant and dig their own potatoes, to grow beans and squash around the corn, like the Native Americans did. They learned history as well as agricultural lessons by actually doing the work."

The filmmaker looked dubious. "Did they all want to do this work?"

Johanna turned away, hiding her face, which had inexplicably crumpled. Of course there had been some problems. Some of the communards left around the time their kids got old enough to be commanded into the fields. Said it reminded them of slave labor or something silly like that. Sally and Curtis's boys, too, they'd been difficult. Jasper was willing enough, when he was given a talking to, but Kyle, he was such a problem. He had to be disciplined. She pulled her cardigan around her tightly, hugging her arms to her chest.

"I'm a little chilled," she said. "I need to go back and help with dinner."

In the herb garden, she picked parsley, loads of it, and cut a big bunch of basil. And garlic, too. She pulled a few potatoes for good measure and went back to the kitchen. Sally was at the worktable, chopping onions.

"Sal, I'm afraid." Johanna dumped the vegetables on the wooden counter and reached for a cutting board and knife. "Not just about Pamela and Neil. But about her making us look like reckless idiots." The knife thunked again and again on the wooden board.

"What will happen to Kevin when the land is sold? Where would he go and what could he do?"

"I suppose he'd live with Linda and Ray—with us, like he always has, Jo."

"Poor Kevin. We should have known better than to try that home birth. We nearly lost them both. I'm glad Neil's parents insisted we go to a hospital for each of the girls."

"That was Ray and Linda's decision. Anyway, none of us had health insurance, remember? You were lucky Neil's parents were always a backup."

A sharp pain gripped her heart. Was Sally being judgmental? Was it true that she and Neil had played at the hippie philosophy, getting others to work for them while they always knew they could return to civilization at any time?

No. It had been her backbone, her grit, that had encouraged the others to keep at it, to develop an actual working farm, not a lazy man's paradise.

Instead of being a passive victim of Neil's shenanigans, she could confront him in front of everybody, in front of witnesses, in front of the camera—and ask him what he intended to do. What would be the fate of the commune and its dependent members?

She chopped the garlic, blanched the basil, and dumped it into ice water, then squeezed the water out to preserve its bright color. With pine nuts from their trees, and parmesan Linda made, she'd pound it all up to make a pesto to serve over spaghetti. She fell into a familiar rhythm, her hands working automatically, their competence calming her anxiety.

She'd show this Pamela that her world was worth saving.

She chopped, and a pesto appeared, deep green,

flecked with white and gold. She scraped it into a large bowl. As she opened the old refrigerator to shove the bowl inside, a smell of stale food escaped. Greasy stains marred the shelves. She pulled out a pitcher of rancid milk. Her nose rebelled. Couldn't one of the others have turned this into buttermilk for scones or pancakes before it soured beyond hope?

Sally, obliviously sliding chopped onions into a bowl, wiped her eyes with the corner of her sleeve. No, not Sally. The neglect was not Sally's fault. The kitchen was not her domain. Sally's kiln churned out art pottery that helped support the commune. And Linda, quiet, gentle Linda, ran the dairy that made cheese people overpaid for. She, Johanna, was the cook. And merely an organizer, just an everyday knitter and weaver.

Obviously not a very good one at that. The milk had turned while she'd been away. Abby probably took her jackets and sweaters on as a charity. She had to face reality. She had done nothing of any importance. She'd assumed charge of the kitchen, and Neil acted as though that's where she belonged. She could never stand up to him. The world spun, and she pushed a hand onto the table to steady herself.

Chapter Twelve

"My door's always open for you, Maelle," Abby said on the phone. "Come over after work."

Questions had bubbled up in Maelle's mind since her evening with Johanna. She thought she'd known everything about her family, but obviously she'd made a lot of assumptions.

Abby greeted her in one of her subtly patterned kimonos. The peach-colored flowers on a light blue background brought out the tints of her hair and eyes and played up the sheen of her skin. Maelle marveled, as she always did, at Abby's unstudied beauty. Maelle drew a hand through her hair, pulling at tangles. She could take a few pointers from her elegant aunt.

Fortunately, Abby didn't seem to notice and gestured to a chair while she poured wine. "What's on your mind, Maelle?"

"This land sale Uncle Robert wants. It's a disaster!"

"Poor Mother. Everything seems to be coming at her at once. Neil can't afford to buy Martha and Robert out. He'll get money from the sale, of course."

Abby switched on a lamp next to her, creating a halo around her face. She looked like one of those Madonnas in the paintings in art books. Maelle glanced at her own stained jeans and scuffed sneakers. She'd rushed straight from the lab, had to hustle to put her experimental tomato plants to bed without her usual tender crooning to them. She so wanted Abby's support in the battle for Joyous Woods.

But Abby didn't seem concerned. Maelle drummed her fingers on the bowl of the wineglass.

"True, but everything will be ruined! The farm, the life they've all lived. Their livelihood."

"I don't know. It could be great if the farm could be sold—not just the farm, but all the surrounding acres too. You could build a whole town there. Relieve the relentless pressure on house prices and rents in the Bay Area. Roads and sewers and water mains, it all would have to be built. And think of the money that would come from that. To Martha and Robert and Neil, and eventually to you and me, Maelle."

"And the others?"

"Oh, I'm sure they'll be all right. Curtis and Sally are artists. Ray and Linda—well, I don't know, but they'll think of something."

Maelle took a deep breath. "Abby, did you know JoJo and Neil never married?"

"No one ever said. Why does it matter?"

"Because apparently Neil's fallen in love with a younger woman."

"Oh. That's sad." Abby set down her glass so hard the wine trembled in the bowl. "It's not the first time, of course. It usually blows over. When did she tell you this?"

"The other day. If Neil leaves JoJo, what does she have left?"

"Aren't there laws about that?"

"I don't know. Are there?" Maelle bit a fingernail.

"Probably. But surely he'd share with Mother.

Aren't you jumping way ahead, Maelle? Why do you assume Neil would be so mean?" Abby rose and went to the refrigerator, peered inside. "Something to eat?"

"I'm not very hungry, thank you."

"Anyway, what did Mother tell you?"

"She claims Neil's making a move on this young filmmaker, Pamela."

Abby's eyes opened wide. "A filmmaker? What film?"

"She's doing a documentary on what became of the hippies. Our family lost their hipness a long time ago. Maybe Neil's trying to make up for it." Smiling, Maelle poked a strand of her hair behind an ear, glad of its soft, youthful texture.

"Hah!" Abby laughed, tossing her own hair. "This filmmaker came just in time, then. Don't you see the commune's on its last legs? I think my dad's fed up with the whole thing. Mother loves what she does. He doesn't. The physical labor of farm work is tough on the body. What Mom does is hard work too, but it's creative. Maybe he feels left out, or that he got the raw end of the deal."

"Don't take his side, Abby! He chose it." Maelle eyed the wine bottle, itching to pour herself another glass.

"Oh, this has been a lifetime problem for them. He just does more or less what he wants with women. In the old days, he was sort of king of the commune. Women came and went. Mom just seemed helpless about it. When I realized and asked her about it—I was about twelve at the time, I suppose—she said that the commune believed jealousy was wrong."

Abby arranged a platter with hummus and carrot

sticks and celery, put them on the high counter separating kitchen from living room. Her long hands, their slender, buffed fingernails aglow with a soft pink polish, were so different from Johanna's gnarled fingers. Her kimono enveloped her, her body so thin within its folds. She carried the platter into the living room and put it on the coffee table, next to the wine bottle.

Maelle held out a glass so Abby could pour. "So, no jealousy. I remember that, too. All those lectures about sharing and equality and being kind to the earth. Still, JoJo must have repressed something to believe all that."

"Maybe. She just went along with all Neil's ideas. The faux-progressive ones, like not calling our parents Mommy and Daddy—though Johanna didn't fuss about that. Other stuff, like letting all the little kids run naked. But she had some of her own ideas too. Some really out-there beliefs."

"Such as?"

Abby refilled Maelle's glass. "Oh, you know, everything loosey-goosey yet rigid at the same time. I'm not doing a very good job of explaining. But what I'm saying is, they were in this together. It's why Johanna never left Neil. He gave her this creative life, a life she really loves."

Her face tensed. "The point is, now, how will those old people up there ever afford to retire, if they don't get the money from the land sale? They may have held everything equally, but they never had 401Ks and IRAs. They never saved a cent because there was never a cent left over to save." She went to her fireplace, lifted and nursed one of the Rookwood vases.

"Look, Abby, you seem to be smarter than your parents about money. You've invested and saved and even your hobbies, like that vintage pottery, can be lucrative. But JoJo said that if they sell the land, she'll never see any of that money. She believes it will all go to Robert and Martha and Neil."

Her aunt sat down on the sofa, and the kimono relaxed around her. She gestured toward the food.

Maelle hesitated. She should eat. She had nothing much in the fridge at home. She shook her head.

"You know, Maelle, let's just drop this." Abby ran a hand under her hair and down her neck. "We're talking hypotheticals, here. First, the land isn't even on the market. I can talk to Neil and see what he really has in mind. You can research lawyers. There has to be some way out of this. But don't hire anybody yet because nothing's happened yet. This Pamela thing will probably blow over like all the others did." She bit delicately into a stick of celery.

Maelle sipped her wine, taking a moment. Aunt and niece had never talked so frankly before. Since Maelle had gone away to study, then devoted herself to graduate school, she'd stopped working weekends in Abby's store, and while she'd missed the camaraderie, she'd been so busy she'd just pushed the thought out of her mind. It felt good to talk, though a little jarring to recognize Abby's hard edges.

"I do wish she'd told me, though." Abby paused, another piece of celery on its way to her mouth. "The other day—I might have waited to give my little speech about her needing to find a different market for the fleeces if I'd known about this latest problem."

"You know, I will. Thank you." Maelle took a

carrot stick and ran it through the hummus, creating a messy streak. Abby and Johanna had often been at odds. "Maybe she thinks you're closer to Neil than to her?"

"Well, that's sort of true. Often happens in families, don't you think? Girls love their daddies. Freud and all that."

"I wouldn't know." Maelle avoided choking as she swallowed a carrot stick.

"I'm sorry. That was tactless of me. Your father, he disappeared. Poor Angela. Not that she was the only one who made a bad choice of partner."

Maelle's head shot up at the sudden change of topic. "You never married, Abby."

"No. Have you wondered about that?" Abby hunched over. Sharp shoulder blades, so noticeable through the thin kimono, made her look vulnerable.

"Did anything bad happen to you, Abby?"

Abby twisted in her chair toward Maelle, her face full of anger. "I'm with my parents on the institution of marriage. It's an artificial construct. It has nothing necessarily to do with love. And love, how long does that last?"

Maelle's heart raced. Abby had a point. You couldn't trust love. It would always be withdrawn from you just when you needed it most. Like her mother. Just gone.

Abby leaned over to pat her hand. "This infatuation could pass. Just like all the others. Let's wait and see. It'll be months before the estate's sorted out."

Maelle's throat hurt. "Joyous Woods turned me into a botanist. I—we—are learning so much about trees now, and it all comes from observation."

"Yes, I can see that. You have a professional interest."

"We have to save this land, Abby!"

"So that's what this is about, really? The land. Joyous Woods. Yes, it's beautiful. But it's just land. And it's not yours to worry about. You can buy your own place someday."

Maelle sat still. Was that true? Did she have a right to a secure future, like other people?

She swallowed. "I guess Joyous Woods means more to me than it does to you. It's my home, too, Abby, just as much as it was yours. It saved me when Mommy died. You have a mother and a father—I don't have either. You don't know what it's like to have everything ripped away from you, the one person you relied on, just gone, disappeared!"

"Don't I?"

"Of course you don't. I was trying to help JoJo, and you just defend Neil. I don't understand!" Maelle slapped a hand on her thigh in frustration. "Why are you taking his side? Why aren't you defending your mother against this terrible thing?"

"There's more to it than this, Maelle. Maybe I could have timed my announcement better, but Mother needs to retire. They all do. Everything they make is beautiful and sells. I should amend that. Sold. The whole raising-animals thing, spinning, dying, knitting, is too labor-intensive. I've seen Johanna popping aspirins. I think arthritis affects her more than she lets on. They're simply getting too old to do it all, up there."

"But she wants to work! It's what she does. This prospect of her losing everything, everything she cares about, terrifies her!"

Suddenly, Abby's eyes turned cold. They were as blue as ice, and yet they burned into Maelle's own. "Everything she cares about," she mocked. "Maybe she should have thought about that, all those years ago."

"What are you talking about?"

"I'm talking about how we were brought up. In that hippie lifestyle. Oh, I'll tell you sometime."

"All I know is that Neil's acting weird. Hurting JoJo. You want to cut off her source of income, and without it the farm will go under. And all the others on the farm will have to leave."

She stood up abruptly. She should go. "I need to get back to work," she said. "Thank you for the wine, but my plants, they need me."

Chapter Thirteen

"Hello, my favorite great-niece! Nice to hear from you." Robert's baritone boomed from the phone.

"Uncle Robert, may I talk to you about what's going to happen to Joyous Woods?"

"My, my. And how are you, too, my dear? Everything going well?"

Maelle pressed her nails into her left hand. Tact was never her strong suit. She wasn't brought up to make small talk like conventional people. She took a deep breath.

"Sorry, Uncle. I didn't mean to blurt it out like that. But I can't get it out of my mind. Everyone's on edge. I'm worried."

"Neil's had a shock, like all of us, our parents dying so suddenly. It's natural for things to feel strange for a while. Why don't you ask your grandfather how he's doing?"

"That's my problem, Uncle. Neil's acting weird. At the funeral, I thought you said the three of you plan to sell the farm and all the acreage around it. Are you really going to sell *all* the land your parents accumulated over the years? I have to tell you this doesn't really seem to be making Neil happy."

Maelle could hear Robert stifle his exasperation.

"That's a bit premature, Maelle. There are other factors to consider. Taxes, for instance. We're looking into other options."

"Such as?"

"I know parts of California are pretty anti-development, so we may have a revolt by the county on our hands. Of course, if they want to dictate how we can use our own land, we may demand concessions from them in return."

Her voice brightened. "You mean it's not a foregone conclusion?"

"Not yet. But it would help, Maelle, if we could get a more or less independent investigation from someone like yourself, who is not directly involved."

She let the words settle for a minute. Not directly involved. That threw her. Then she understood that Robert was just referring to the fact that she was now an independent adult with her own self-supporting career. Like so many others, including Zachary, Uncle Robert did not seem to understand the depth of her attachment to this particular piece of planet Earth.

The dirt road she could traverse like a trained rat, the trees that had always comforted her, the animals whose bleats, barks, clucks, and squeaks had woken her with the birdsong of dawn. The earth itself, whose smell she sensed even in her dreams. How wonderful it all was.

To have it all go away was unimaginable.

"Do you think it would be possible, Uncle Robert, if the land were sold, that it could be kept as a farm? Could the county require that?"

"Probably not. It could be sympathetic to its preservation. But it is private property. The owners have every right to develop it in the most profitable way. Property rights are the basis of our law."

She huffed. "Profit. That's what Neil and his friends protested against."

"And look where it's got them. None of them have two beans to rub together. From my point of view, selling the land and allowing Neil to take his share relieves me and Martha of a massive burden. Without his inheritance being cashed, we'd have to support him and Johanna and probably the whole lot of them up there at Joyous Woods."

"You mean that?"

"Well, if you don't save and you don't pay into Social Security and you don't have health insurance, what are you left with? Not even the government can help you."

"I see your point. But there's Medicaid, food stamps."

He barreled on as if he hadn't heard her. "Of course, it's not all that bad. Neil and Johanna have made a go of it. They are getting by with their various gigs. The goats and the pottery sales and the clothing store and all the rest of it. But without an influx of younger people to keep it going and to look after the older ones, it will all fall apart. It's already happening. They're all getting on. Anyone can see that."

"So maybe they can advertise for younger people to come and live on the commune?"

"Not a bad idea. But maybe it's too late. I don't think Neil wants his authority toppled, do you?"

Maelle had to bite her tongue to avoid answering rudely. That was a snide remark for Robert to make about his own brother. But making an enemy of Robert wouldn't help.

"I hadn't thought of it that way. Maybe you're

right. There are only six people—seven, counting Kevin—on the property at the moment. But Neil did have an idea. Right now, there's a filmmaker doing a movie about Joyous Woods. Could give it a boost of publicity."

"Oh? I didn't know about that. How's it going? Seen any of the takes?"

"Not yet. It's a work in progress. Pamela's interviewing everyone."

"A filmmaker? Probably independent, not well known. I can look into it…"

As Robert rambled, Maelle reflected that Pamela had not interviewed her. Of course, she was irrelevant to the commune experiment. Just an offshoot. But maybe she should ask to be interviewed, state her views on the importance of the farm to everyone who had created it. Use Pamela as a mouthpiece for her argument.

Doing so would mean cutting across JoJo's obvious disdain for the woman. It would mean siding with Neil to a certain extent. Her heart started hammering at the familiar conflict of competing loyalties. Her once-adored grandfather versus her commanding but loving grandmother. Was Johanna being fair to hate Pamela so much? Was Pamela really interested in Neil, as JoJo claimed? What were Abby's views on the matter? Well, of course, she knew that. Abby sided with Neil. Poor Johanna. Cast aside, the older woman unable to compete with a younger rival's charms, an older woman unable to keep up with fashion, her lovingly created handwork no longer desired by customers and thence by her employer, her own daughter. And perhaps JoJo was not well. Tired often, sometimes lost in thought, sometimes aching with arthritis. But also perhaps, too angry at the filmmaking enterprise to think clearly. Unable to see it as a way to help the commune. What happened on the commune that Johanna was trying to hide? All those long-ago shenanigans when the commune members were young, the casual sex, it surely wasn't so shocking now, was it? Times had changed. No need for Robert to know any of this, of course.

She drew a breath. Robert was asking a question.

"Do you think this film could be useful to us? See if you can make sure the camera shows the landscape to advantage. We could use it as a sales tool."

"I was thinking of it as a demonstration of how to make an organic farm. That's actually a really useful thing to create, Uncle Robert. Organic's popular now, and it's going to get more popular. There's so much interest in it today. As a plant scientist, I could talk to you about the damage to crops done by GMO plants and all that. But I don't think you have time for that."

"No. I'm thinking that any kind of farming is a waste of time on that land."

Maelle shoved a swear word back in her throat. She swallowed hard. "All I know is that JoJo is worried about what will happen to her. To everyone on the farm. Neil hasn't said a word. And I think that means he's ambivalent."

"Then maybe you should ask your friends up there to raise the question. My impression is that Neil needs a little push."

That was true. Maelle did not confirm Robert's supposition—that Neil was happy to bask in attention from Pamela, maid service from Johanna, the built-in audience for his guitar-playing. Sure, he'd like comfort in his old age. But he'd already got it, without doing a thing. He had no incentive to change. Everyone else worried. Neil didn't need to.

"Change is hard, Uncle. But if it's two against one, you and Aunt Martha against Neil, then whatever happens to the land is your decision. I guess all we can do is to try to minimize the damage."

"Oh, it's not that bad, my dear. Think of the financial reward to the family."

"Yes, but what's a family, when it comes to the commune? That's the question, Uncle Robert."

"Oh, nonsense, dear. As I see it, our parents tolerated all these hippies living on their land, or I should say, living off their land, for all these years. Fifty years ago, that land was just a speculative investment. But now California has a real housing shortage. It's selfish of these hippies, don't you think, to want to stay, sponging off Neil and Martha and me? Not for our sake, of course." Robert coughed. "I mean, naturally the family will benefit financially if the land is sold. But it's selfish not to let others use it. To prevent houses and apartments and shops being built. Roads. Sewerage. Hospitals. Schools. All the rest of it. This is the twenty-first century. Get with the program."

The familiar, hateful feeling rose up in her. Soon the farm could be paved over and made into housing developments, shopping malls. The redwoods would groan as they fell, sending the squirrels and bobcats, deer, coyotes, wild turkeys, snakes, and newts to scatter, slithering, running, sneaking away to the ever-shrinking forest. Bulldozers, power lines, sewer pipes would churn up the earth, killing the earthworms that gave it fertility. Houses, shops, roads, schools, would spring up, held together by a retail strip of brand-name clothiers, all discounted, with a hideous flashing neon sign visually assaulting drivers on the highway. *Joyous Woods Outlet Mall*. She shuddered.

Who would defend Joyous Woods? The farm that had become part of her own being, the roots of its plants and trees entwined in her own sense of self. Her mother, dead. Her father, unknown. The commune a part-family. A false family. A family consisting entirely of people her grandparents' age. And they were innocents, babes in the woods against the wiles of people like Robert. People whose minds were spinning tops of financial figures.

And she was an academic. Immersed in the world of plants, the only money she had to manage was trying to do her work within the grant budget.

Maelle mumbled a goodbye to her great-uncle and hung up with relief.

Chapter Fourteen

The wind shook the blackened treetops as Zachary drove them through a fire-ravaged landscape near the wine country, till finally, the green hills of a northern California November soothed Maelle's anxiety, as it always did. In a distant field, a few sheep grazed. Nearer, goats nosed a tree, scarfing up ivy under the supervision of a shepherd.

Closer to the farmstead, the car bucked on rutted tire tracks. Mud squished under the wheels with every depression in the road. Ahead, the pagoda house loomed. It looked more dilapidated than ever since the latest earthquake had left it listing to one side. As they drove up, Johanna waved from the garden. She arched her back, rubbing her spine, then straightened.

Zachary parked under a tree and unfolded himself from the car, helping Maelle do the same.

"We need a stretch too," Maelle said. "It's a long drive."

"I'm glad you came." Johanna held out a grubby hand. "Welcome to the farm."

Zachary smiled broadly, thanked her for inviting him to stay. Maelle gave her grandmother a hug.

Johanna rotated her head to see if they were alone, then spoke in an undertone. "Maelle tells me you're a shrink. Are you coming to give a diagnostic on Neil? He's still acting—like I told Maelle—up and down like a yo-yo."

Maelle cringed. "We're just staying overnight, JoJo," she said quickly. "We both have work to do tomorrow."

"You don't take a weekend off?"

"Not all of it, no." Zachary reached into the car for the bottles of wine they'd bought. "That's why we want to make the most of our time here."

"I'm not sure where Neil's got to," Johanna said, looking around. "Probably in a huddle with that Pamela woman."

Zachary held out his offering, then hauled their overnight bags from the trunk. He said, "So, the videographer Maelle told me about? You'll be famous."

"Not sure we want that. But come inside. I was just pulling some lettuce for a salad." Johanna indicated a basket at her feet. "And we have a great crop of apples. I'll make a pie."

Maelle grabbed the basket. "Let me take this inside and show Zach our humble abode." She started toward the house.

Johanna shot Maelle a disapproving look. "Humble it is, I guess, to some." She smoothed down her jeans. "Come on, then." She strode onward. "I think it's beautiful," she said over her shoulder to Zachary, who had spun on his heels, taking in the view.

When his eyes came back to Maelle's, they were slightly unfocused, as if he'd been seeing some other picture in his mind than this bucolic scene. He took her hand.

The bedroom Maelle always used at Joyous Woods held a double mattress over a wooden platform. It had been freshly made up with a blue cotton duvet. Maelle thought she'd seen a dress in Abby's store in the same brightly colored fabric. She smiled at the thought that Johanna had made an effort to welcome her friend. However, the two pillows topping the bed were thin and frayed. Why had she never noticed before how shabby this room looked? It must be because Zach was the first man she'd brought up to Joyous Woods. She watched hesitantly for his reaction.

He drew her close and crushed her to him, kissing her ear. "It's good to know where you come from," he whispered. She kissed him back. This had been a good idea, to bring Zachary to see her family.

They went downstairs, and Maelle opened one of the bottles of wine they'd brought. She led Zachary and Johanna, holding their glasses, out to the weed-bristled, uneven stone patio facing the hills. The moment of peace settled over her. Quiet at this time of day, the farm radiated calm. They raised a toast, the chilly air nipping at their throats, until Johanna said they must get back inside to prepare dinner.

The communards gradually wandered into the great room. Maelle brought Neil over to introduce him to Zachary. Zachary started back suddenly, eyebrows raised, when Neil spoke in his distinct melodic tenor. At dinner, Zachary joked and chatted amiably with the communards, looking now and then across the table at Neil with a concerned expression.

Neil seemed lost in thought and contributed little to the conversation.

Johanna tried to engage him. "Have Pamela and the film crew left for the day?"

He merely nodded, pushed his plate away, and left the table. Johanna hid her embarrassment by rising to take away the plates till Maelle stood up too and gently pushed on her grandmother's shoulders to force her to sit down again.

"He seems to spark up only when she's here," Johanna said to the emptying room.

The others sidled away, one by one, making excuses to get on with their evening. Probably mortified by Johanna's obsession. Maelle twisted her cloth napkin between her fingers, over and over.

"It's just the novelty of it, Jo," Sally said, as she rose. "She's giving him a lot of attention, and he doesn't get that from the rest of us at the farm. Now you enjoy your company."

Maelle took a sip of water. She needed to lighten up, not involve Zachary in these family anxieties. "He might feel only the dogs appreciate him," she said, lifting the pie plate toward Zachary, offering him another slice. "Maybe that's because the guard dogs see the goats more than they see Neil. Absence making the heart fonder and all that."

Johanna allowed herself a little giggle, and Zachary smiled.

As the others left, he visibly relaxed. "I'm not a therapist. I only do research." He propped his elbows on the table. "So take what I say just as friendly advice. When a family member dies, there's a lot of stress. Maybe Neil's acting out simply because he lost both his parents at once. Do you think that's it?"

Johanna fingered the tablecloth's hem. "He's definitely been affected. Sometimes I wonder if he's rethinking his whole life and wished he could do it over."

He nodded. "A lot of people go through that. It's a

stage of grieving."

Johanna refilled Zachary's wine glass, then Maelle's, and her own. "Grieving for everything, maybe. We all have a sense of things coming to an end."

Zachary's brown eyes softened with empathy.

"Robert and Martha—that's Neil's brother and sister—want to sell the land." Johanna gulped down a long drink. Her hand shook as she placed the glass back on the table.

Maelle laced her fingers with her lover's. "Yes, it's terrible, isn't it? The land paved over, made into shopping malls and look-alike houses."

"Does it all have to be sold?" Zachary sounded reasoned, calm. "There are three heirs. Why can't you and Neil and the commune take a third?"

Johanna smiled brightly. "Never thought of that. It's a good idea."

As she got up to put on the coffee pot, her step seemed lighter. "Let's look at some photo albums," she said. "Show Zachary your family."

The young people cleared the plates, then came back to sit. They all found places on the sofa, and Johanna dug in a wooden box beside it to bring up a photo album. When she opened the book and placed it on Maelle's lap, it smelled musty.

Johanna took up the subject of her nemesis again. "Pamela seems interested in the pictures. She wants to talk about Joyous Woods as it used to be. That seems to be mostly what she cares about." She rolled her eyes. "At least in public."

The album had thick, cardboard pages, slit to hold colored photographs by their corners. Maelle's fingers trembled as she opened the book. The pictures of her mother as a child, as a teenager, and as a young woman always tore at her. The photos, evidence of her loss, suddenly hit her with a pain that knifed through her as if she'd been stabbed. She was twenty-five already. Would she too, die at the age of twenty-eight?

She pushed the superstitious thought away as she nestled on the sofa under Zachary's arm. His warm nearness comforted her as he held the book in his other hand, flipping through.

Glossy photographs of a great many characters populated the album's pages. Zachary's fingers lingered on a group shot of young people around a campfire. It appeared to be late afternoon; shadows sloped through the trees onto the ragged grass of a clearing. Beards and long hair predominated among the men. Women wore long flowing Indian skirts shimmering with shiny disks. Everyone looked very thin. Running through the group were children in various stages of undress. Their hair was matted, their bodies dirty, their clothes, if they wore any, torn.

"That's my mother." Maelle pointed farther down the page to a photo of a girl who looked to be about eight or nine. She held a rabbit up to her face, kissing it. So much lustrous fur covered the animal's face that it hid one of the little girl's eyes and melded with her own hair, forming a patchwork of white and brown.

"Yes, Angela loved the animals." Johanna peered at the album over Maelle's shoulder. "Especially the rabbits. She fed them and cleaned their cages."

Maelle gently turned pages, searching for more photographs of her mother. Here and there her image was captured, sometimes with Abby, sometimes on her own. Farther along in the book, they came to pictures of people she didn't know, photos of dilapidated structures, and some of Maelle herself as a child. She'd inherited her mother's dark curls, though she tried to straighten them, wearing her hair away from her face, the better to peer at her plants.

"You look like your mother," Zachary pointed out. "Genetics at work."

"Yeah," said Johanna wryly. Maelle wondered if anyone ever thought of the genetic contribution of her father. He'd been one of the wandering young men who'd come to the commune for a short time, then disappeared. He had a name, but Maelle had been told it was probably fabricated.

For as long as the commune had been in existence, it had been a haven for the lost and those on the lam. Few questions were asked. Shelter and food were available as long as the visitors did their share of the work. A rumbling discomfort roiled Maelle's belly as she sat next to Zachary and realized he must be taking in the implication of the parade of nameless young men who posed for the camera at Joyous Woods. For two generations they'd done this, and it was hard to tell the years in which the photos were taken, so similar did all the young men look, despite their differences in height and hair. All were skinny, all stared at the camera with intensity.

What must it be like to have a father who was a steady presence in one's life? Zachary of course had had that, and then he lost him in that accident. Just as she'd lost her mother.

Until now, the absence of a father in her life had seemed muted. In part, no doubt, because Neil had been such a large presence. For her whole life, he had been there, moody or not moody, letting her trot beside him as he worked, holding her on his knee as he read her a story at night. Even when Angela had taken her daughter to Berkeley and rented an apartment there, they saw Neil often enough on the weekends. But to have as a father one of those haunted guys in the photographs, that was a bit unnerving. She stiffened under Zachary's arm, and he looked at her with concern in his eyes.

"I'm a little tired," she said. "Can we call it a night?"

Back in her childhood bed, Maelle lay stiff and still. When she didn't respond to Zachary's caresses, he asked her what was wrong.

She laughed, embarrassed. "The fact is, Zach, I'm pretty much an outlier in the hippie world. The casual sex is just not me. Even though I'm the result of a hook-up here."

The warmth in his eyes told her he understood. "It's fine, Maelle. You're you, that's what matters to me."

"It makes me feel weird when JoJo talks about Neil getting interested in this filmmaker. I can't really see what she sees in him."

He nodded, lying undressed and relaxed beside her. "That's because he's your grandfather. Just think of it as an old goat farmer acting in sympathy with his bucks. Usually, they're kept away from the young does because they smell and make the milk rank. Maybe he's just seizing this rare chance when he has it. On the other hand, maybe your grandmother's imagining the whole thing."

Maelle giggled, smug with the confidence of youth, squelched sympathy for Johanna, and kissed Zachary's chest, absorbing the warmth of his body so intensely she felt like a tree, inhaling his presence through every pore.

****

In the morning, Zach said he'd like to look at the farm, and Maelle said she'd be happy to take him around as long as she could show him her favorite place, the woods beyond. That was where she'd found her solace, she told him. After her mother died she'd spent many hours alone in those woods and learned to listen to its never-silence, its continual susurration.

She took him on a tour, stopping by the ceramics studio and pottery kiln, the dairy, the goat pens, the shearing shed, and the chicken coops, gesturing toward the dilapidated buildings in the distance. She explained that the commune harvested water in great tanks, used solar and wind power. They tramped the woods, holding hands.

"I'm impressed with all this ingenuity," he said, after an hour or so. "Can you show me the rabbit hutches?"

They descended to the valley, walked toward the cluster of buildings near the pagoda house, and Maelle led him into a shed containing wire mesh cages. White balls of fur peeked up at them, button noses and beady eyes. Maelle reached in and patted one or two of the animals.

"Is that all?" he said.

"What do you mean, is that all?"

"The rabbits. There were more rabbits here."

"How do you know?" Maelle stared at him,

astonished.

"Up on the hill. In the far woods. I've been here before, I know it."

Her mouth fell open. "What? How come? And why didn't you mention it last night at dinner? JoJo and Neil would have loved to know that."

He shrugged. "I don't know. It just came to me now when we went into the woods. There was a rabbitry up there."

"Maybe some of the drifters raised them for food?"

"Maelle, it was a real building, like a commercial business. Hidden in the trees."

"No. I don't think so. Not on this farm. I lived here. I know what was here."

"Okay. If you say so." Zachary's face closed. "Look," he said. "I've got a lot of work to do. Let's go back to the city."

"It's only eleven o'clock!"

"Yeah. I know. But let's just pack up and say goodbye."

They said little on the long drive back to Berkeley. The atmosphere chilled as if an icebox sat on the seat between them. She turned up the heat, but it didn't help.

"Zach, you're being very strange. What's going on? Why do you think you know all about Joyous Woods? Up there you acted like you'd seen it before."

"It all came back to me."

"What did? There were a number of alternate communities up here. How do you know it wasn't another farm? Another commune?"

"I went to Joyous Woods when I was a kid," he said. "With my dad."

"You did? But Neil and Johanna didn't say

anything when they met you."

Zachary laughed sardonically. "I guess I've changed since I was thirteen or so."

"Were they friends with your father?"

"I doubt it. It was more of a business transaction, I think."

"Oh." Maelle fiddled with the radio dial, searching for music. "That's not surprising. They sold everything from vegetables to goats."

"Rabbits." Zachary kept his eyes on the road.

"Did you want a bunny as a pet, Zach? You were a bit old for that, weren't you?"

"No. I didn't want a bunny, as you call them, as a pet. And neither did my dad."

He reached a hand out to the dial on the car radio and turned it very loud.

Maelle could see he didn't want to continue the conversation, so she dropped it and tapped her fingers on the glove compartment in tune with the music.

They didn't speak for the rest of the way home. And when he dropped her off, she didn't ask him in.

Chapter Fifteen

Johanna waved to the receding car as Zachary and Maelle drove back down the rutted road. They seemed anxious to get away. Maybe they were embarrassed at Neil's lack of welcome. He'd been distant again, probably pining for the filmmaker. Pamela, taking a few days off, would no doubt be back before long to ask more questions, once again arousing Neil.

It galled Johanna, this undefinable quality that drew women to him like a moth to a flame. He'd long since switched off the warmth toward her. Oh, it wasn't like that in the early days, not at all. It was hard to say when the change began.

Maybe it had started when she tired of Neil's childish ways and took charge. Evenings, the guys sat around, passed the bong, picked at the guitar, and stoned, giggled. Johanna, on the other hand, always had a project. She spun and wove and knitted, her hands never still.

Then Curtis started painting seriously, and Sally worked her magic with clay, and Ray and Linda tended Kevin away from the other children. Maybe Neil needed something to occupy his mind, and he turned to other women.

She shook her head to dispel the image of Neil and Pamela in bed. Had it happened, or not? She couldn't tell, and that too, worried her. She'd lost that sure sense of smell, both psychological and physical.

Back in the kitchen, she stretched up to a high shelf, pulled down white paper and crayons, and began to sketch a blue mandarin-collared jacket. Despite what Abby said, she wasn't going to let her dictate how she did her work or what she made. She had a proven market, didn't she?

Linda wandered into the room. She looked weary. She put a batch of curds into the refrigerator and a glass bottle of yellowish whey on the counter.

"Thanks. I'm making bread later, so I'll use that." Johanna swept her crayon across the paper.

"I read the other day that whey's good on your hair, too. Makes it shine when you rinse with it. Or put it on your skin as a moisturizer."

Johanna rolled her eyes. "Since when did we care about beauty products?"

"I don't know, Jo. What's wrong with keeping your skin moist and your hair shiny? We both need all the help we can get these days." Linda held out callused thumbs. "It's from milking. Twice a day. I need gloves."

"Now there, I agree. Put them on the shopping list. Soon, I'm going to dye a new batch of yarn with woad. I'll be blue as a Celtic warrior if I don't use gloves."

A vat sat out in the dyeing shed, full of leaves fermented for months, enriched by the men pissing into the bucket to raise the pH of the mixture. An old-fashioned method, used to make the blue uniforms of the French army in Napoleon's day. Still worked. And the hillsides would burst into bloom with the yellow-flowered weed come spring, all to be gathered and made into new dye.

Linda dawdled, coming over to inspect Johanna's sketch.

"Do you need some paper? Here, take this." Johanna handed Linda a scrap scrawled with a discarded drawing.

"Thanks. Nice to see Maelle bring a boyfriend up to the farm." Linda picked up a pencil hanging from a string attached to the wall. "That's never happened before, has it?"

"You're right. They must be getting serious. I'm glad. Everyone needs a partner." Johanna cleared her throat. "A partner you can rely on."

Linda scribbled a shopping list. "I've seen that Pamela flirt with Neil, Jo. Don't worry about it. All the guys here need a little excitement now and then. We don't get out much. It doesn't mean anything."

"Excitement? I've had enough. I need peace and quiet." Johanna put her crayon down, picked up her picture, and held it toward the light from the window.

"Neil's probably just acting out because he's grieving. Let it go, Jo."

"I hope Maelle's not in for a rough ride. But it's good to see her at that magical early stage of a relationship."

"He seems like a match for her intelligence. That's good."

"She's a loner, my granddaughter. Even though she spent so much time with so many people." The sketch back on the worktable, Johanna resumed drawing. Even living in a close community like Joyous Woods, loneliness was possible. Group living really did dull individual relationships, stopped them flowering into fruition.

Linda patted Johanna on the shoulder. "That jacket will be beautiful." She let the captive pencil swing back toward the wall and left Johanna to her paper and crayons.

Johanna shook her head. She'd lost her train of thought. Her drawing was not at all satisfactory. She ripped out another piece of paper and started again.

Where was the Neil she'd fallen in love with? Who can remember after so many years that youthful idealism and that falling-off-a-cliff feeling of being deliriously in love? Johanna could. Maybe she had to, because falling in love with Neil meant such a drastic change in the course of the life she thought she'd have. Her parents, her dear, hardworking, immigrant parents, wanted their daughter to be happy, yes, but they also wanted her to continue her studies, maybe take up a profession. She'd dropped out to follow Neil up into the woods. But she'd never stopped learning, had she? She read avidly, books about philosophy and psychology mostly, about utopian communities, including about the kibbutz experiment in Israel.

Maybe that was a mistake.

Maybe it had all been a mistake, her whole adult life one big mistake. Looking at the photos last night with Zachary and Maelle, she saw the commune with the eyes of a stranger.

There was so little food, then; that was the thing. Feeling almost overfull after the dinner she'd cooked last night, Johanna found the pictures from the early days unsettling. Those long-haired youths looked wasted, and the children had such thin arms and legs. But didn't most children have thin arms and legs? It came from running around outdoors all day. When they were hungry, they sometimes sneaked into the fields and orchards and picked beans or tomatoes or fruit. That was all right, she supposed; they needed the vitamins.

But with a commune to feed, you couldn't have people taking things whenever they felt like it. Everything had to be shared, but also allotted according to need, according to what they deserved, too. She'd had to devise a system. You couldn't ask the men to do it. They were too busy railing against the industrial-military complex or getting high. Figuring out the practicalities always seemed to fall to her.

It was she, Johanna, who hitched into town and using her name, not Neil's, obtained a library card and brought back book after book—on living in the backwoods, on how to establish a farm without pesticides or large mechanical equipment. Not that they could afford herbicides anyway. Couldn't even afford a tractor. So they were forced to use the no-till method. Which turned out now to be the latest thing in organic farming; it didn't ruin the soil. Johanna and Sally and Linda and all the other women read books on home canning, raising sheep, cows, and goats, and on dyeing cloth with the plants around them. Her work formed the backbone of her life; the rhythms of the farm ruled her days.

For Linda and Sally, it was the same. Up with the dawn to milk the goats, make the cheese, work the vegetable gardens, cook the meals, comb the rabbits for their fur. That was what they did, the women of Joyous Woods. Made something beautiful out of unpromising beginnings.

What did the men do? A lot, they would say. They

seared the baby goats' heads so their horns couldn't grow, castrated the bucklings, brought buck to doe to mate, goats and rabbits alike. Curtis had charge of the hens, Ray the fields, Pedro and, when he grew up, Kevin, looked after the goats and helped in the dairy. All the broken-down bits of the buildings were likewise the responsibility of the men. You'd think they worked harder than the women did. When Pamela asked her, Johanna told her the way it was, sure her explanation would make the filmmaker laugh.

"The men did the heavy lifting, and then we women did the detail work. We ran the laundry, the kitchen, the dairy and garden and orchard."

She was right. Pamela did laugh. The radicals who'd become so old-fashioned.

But even with this traditional division of labor, there was something they could not do.

In order to feed themselves, the children had to work. And their parents did not have time to take care of them. School was a solution they hit upon, and it was fortunate that early on, one of the communards was a trained teacher. They started classes in a little shed. The curriculum may have been haphazard, but it was practical. The vegetable patch and fruit trees offered valuable lessons in basic science. The kids learned animal husbandry. They collected eggs from the chickens and learned to bake, how to double and halve measurements for bread, cakes, and pies. They all, except for Kevin, learned to read and write, and managed to get by when they went to middle school.

Just ask Maelle. She'd tell you happily what she'd learned from working alongside the adults when she went up to live at Joyous Woods. Neil taught Maelle about photosynthesis, and she'd marveled at how the seeds she'd been given to plant poked up green shoots above the ground. That's how it had been for her.

Johanna sat back in her chair as a pain hit her chest. In the early days, people streamed to the commune. More people, more work. Not all pulled their weight, and there was really not enough food to go around, not enough hours in the day. Especially with toddlers around, it was impossible for the adults to have eyes in the back of their heads to supervise the little ones.

They had to think of something else. Johanna did a lot of reading and came up with an idea. The Children's House.

A long blue mark smeared itself over her new design. Why had her hand slipped? Arthritis had troubled her lately. She tore yet another page from her sketchbook and began again, carefully transcribing her ideas to paper, concentrating hard to crowd out her thoughts.

Chapter Sixteen

Though it was only midafternoon when they got back to town, Maelle could not face going into her lab. The photos of her mother had made her mood plummet. Then Zachary claimed he'd visited Joyous Woods as a kid, seemed grim about it, and mentioned rabbits. What the hell did rabbits have to do with anything? Everyone loved rabbits, and the angoras at Joyous Woods were lovingly combed. The rabbits needed to lose the hair, it molted anyway. JoJo would card it, dye it, spin it, and ply it so a little ball of yarn would result, its circumference haloed in the softest colored wool you'd ever seen.

Maelle sat at her home desk, still as a tree trunk. Outside her window, a Japanese maple stood bare branched and isolated under a gray sky. She needed to banish her worries about the sale of Joyous Woods, about her grandmother's obsession with Neil's supposed infidelity, about Zachary's strange comments about rabbits. But she could not concentrate on her work. Truth be told, she hadn't been able to concentrate very well since Zachary had come into her life. Twenty-five years old and an aspiring academic, she'd met him and been ambushed, struck by the force of emotion.

Since then, she'd behaved like a sixteen-year-old. He was her boyfriend, but given her track record with men, she should really cool it, take it a whole lot more slowly. After all, none of her previous relationships had worked out, so why should this one? She was odd, she knew it. Focusing her mind on nonsentient beings like plants, how could she switch so easily to the complicated emotions of humans? Of course, plants *were* sentient. That's what she was trying to prove, anyway. Sentient, maybe, but they couldn't share her feelings. The houseplants' lack of empathy annoyed her. The spider plants and philodendrons seemed to mock her, sprawling unconcerned over her low wooden credenza.

She sent Zachary a text to say she'd come over in a few days. He answered with a short message, asking her to call. To hell with that. She needed to see him face to face. But she was way, way behind at work. She needed the week to catch up.

The work week was not productive. She found herself avoiding her colleagues and her supervisor. By Thursday, she could stand it no longer. She'd have to find out what had happened to make Zachary act so rudely to her. She rang again that evening and left a message saying she was on her way. It would be a test, she told herself as she began the two-hour drive south. If he evaded her questions, it was over.

****

He greeted her with a guarded warmth, a smile but no kiss. Dark stubble lined his tense face. From the front door, her line of sight led through to his kitchen, where two glasses and a wine bottle waited on the counter. She followed him in, depositing her purse on a hall table, and stood several feet apart from him as he poured the pinot noir. He set out a dish of cashews, then invited her to sit. She perched on a stool. It felt

148

uncomfortable, as though she might fall off. She settled herself and drank.

It only took her a glass and a half of wine to get to the point.

"Zachary," she said, gripping the goblet so firmly she could feel her fingers almost dent the glass, "what's going on?"

He drummed his fingers on the counter, then flexed and straightened them, one by one. "All right. I'll tell you. I remembered it all when I went to your farm. I went there with my father. When I was a kid. There were rabbits up there in the woods, a little set-up there, a building just for rabbits. Seemed to be hidden."

Goosebumps tingled Maelle's arms. "The rabbits were near the main house. I looked after them. Fed them and helped comb their fleeces. JoJo said my mother used to love to do that too."

"Well, this was another lot of rabbits. Your grandfather, I recognized him last week." His eyes were gauging her reaction. "He showed my dad the rabbits."

"So? Maybe there were more rabbits then. So what? I don't know what you're trying to say." She took a large sip of wine.

"I'm saying that your family knew my father."

"That's strange. My grandparents never mentioned that. But I don't see why they should." She glared at him. "Kane is a common name."

"Well, of course, your mother is dead. Which is the point." His eyes pinned hers.

"What?" She drew back from him. "What point?"

"Was your mother a vegetarian?"

"Yes. Quite a determined one, as I recall. Or I think I recall. I was only ten when she died, but we always ate a pretty strict diet."

"Did she get into squabbles with your grandparents about this?"

"How would I know? I was just little."

"That's true."

"For God's sake, Zach, are you going to tell me what's going on?"

"That day I went up with my father to see Joyous Woods—it's all coming back to me now—Neil showed us this small building, hidden and very secure up there in the woods."

"Hmm. I thought they grew pot deep in the woods."

A corner of his mouth drew up, a half smile. "Maybe they should have given it to the rabbits. Neil was breeding them separately from the angoras, and he was selling them."

"So?"

"They were meat rabbits. Not that there is anything wrong with that. But your mother probably objected, if she was a vegetarian."

"Okay. Go on." She picked up cashews, nibbled them one by one, licked the salt off her lips. She hadn't eaten but didn't want to ask him for anything. Not that he usually had much in his fridge.

"My father was a doctor, but a doctor who did medical research. He used rabbits as subjects in his lab."

"Oh."

"Yes. Rabbit eyes and testicles are greatly valued in the field. They command top dollar. Researchers can't get enough of them."

Maelle pushed away the nut bowl, sickened. She

used to nestle the angoras to her breast, kiss their fur, groom them. "So you're saying my mother objected to that? I get that she would, as a vegetarian. I would too, I guess."

"What did your mother do? What was her profession?"

"She was a journalist."

"Figures." He folded his arms across his chest. His light blue shirt was wrinkled, as if he'd been wearing it since he'd dropped her off last Sunday.

"What do you mean?" Her heart beat fast.

She pictured their old Berkeley apartment. Her mother had typed on the clunky word processor on a desk covered with a bright green cloth. The carpet's wavy pattern and a big doll's house placed strategically on it hid a stain from a cup of coffee Angela had spilled when she was dancing around in one of her up moods. She spent hours tapping away at that computer.

"That first day we met—" Zachary stood up and went to the window as if the view of the courtyard suddenly consumed his attention. He turned back. "We found out that we'd both lost our parents when we were young. You were ten. I was fourteen. But neither of us said how they'd died."

"You just went into psychiatrist mode."

He frowned. "What?"

"Asked me how I felt about it. Not what happened."

"My father died in an accident. Yours?"

Something in Zachary's tone warned her to be careful. "I don't know...An accident?" Her voice turned up at the end, as doubt fogged her brain.

"Coincidence, don't you think?"

"What are you getting at?"

"Well, it turns out, our parents died together."

Maelle dropped her wine glass. Wine splattered on the pale wood floor, a pattern of spilled red. It looked like blood.

"My father was David Kane. He died in an accident at his lab. The newspaper account identified the woman who was found dead with him. Angela Becker."

"Oh, my God." Maelle slipped off the stool, her legs wobbly. She stepped over the broken glass, edging to the opposite side of the room, as far away from him as possible. She gripped the back of an armchair, her fingernails scratching the fabric of its arm. "What do you mean, they died together?"

"I recognized Angela from the photos you showed us. There was a picture of the same woman in the paper. I kept the clipping."

"Clippings? I didn't know anything about that." Her knees shook. "No one said how Mom died. I thought she was hit by a car. She was so badly hurt they wouldn't let me see her." A memory flared up, another memory tamping it down. Perhaps she'd believed her mother had died in a car accident because children were drilled about looking to the left and to the right when crossing the road. Abby, and then her grandparents, had let her believe that. The funeral had been a blur, and for the rest of her childhood the past had been bundled up, muffled.

Zachary stood across the room, looking at her steadily.

"My father was a medical researcher. Using animals to test drugs and so on. Some people object to

152

that. I don't, of course. So many medical advances have only happened because of this work with animal subjects."

"Oh." Maelle's brain scrambled, trying to take it in. "Our parents died in your father's lab? Why did they die? People, I mean, not the animals."

"The animals died too. There was a fire."

"What does it mean? Mom visited your father for some reason, and there was an accident in the lab?"

"It seems that's what happened. But *why* is the mystery."

"There must be police records."

"Yeah. But they're limited. They said 'accidental death.' Caused by a fire."

Maelle choked. "But you think that's suspicious?"

"Something's off. It's weird. The accident happened at night." He went back to the window and pulled down the blind, shutting out the neighbors' lights.

"My mother was a journalist. Maybe she was writing an article about your father's experiments."

"Well, why interview him at night? She must have had another reason." Zachary spun around to face her, his voice rising.

She wasn't getting it, and he was annoyed. Why should she make it easy for him, whatever he was trying to say?

"He could have told her to come then," she said. That was reasonable, wasn't it? "He could have said he was too busy during the day. Invited her to see the lab." Her vision was dimming, a buzzing sounded in her ears as Zachary came near.

"Possibly." He paused, looked at her with concern.

"Listen, you look so pale. I think you need to sit down. The chair's right there. Let me help."

She flinched. "I'm fine, Zachary." She folded a leg over the chair and sat on its arm, her brain scrambling. She couldn't keep up with what he was saying.

"What kind of article would a committed vegetarian write about a lab that uses animals? You have to admit she probably wasn't going to write something flattering. So why would my father have agreed to the interview?"

Maelle's mind raced. Was her mother some kind of activist? If so, she was very different from her daughter. Maelle cringed at the idea of confrontation. A weakness in herself, she knew, but she couldn't help it.

Zachary sat down on the sofa, facing her, and explained, as if to a child. "Some people object to animal research. If your mother did, she was ill-informed. Experimentation on mammals is how scientists learn how medicines work, or how a particular surgery improves outcomes. Almost all the medical advances of the past century have come from these controlled—"

Maelle interrupted, angry. "Don't lecture me! I'm a scientist, too. I chose to work with plants because I didn't want to hurt animals. Lots of people think animal experimentation is cruel. Especially vegetarians. They won't eat meat because they think killing animals for any reason is cruel. They think that animals' lives are as precious as human life."

"All right." Zachary put his head in his hands. "I get that. But sometimes people who think like that can become fanatics."

"A fanatic? No. That's not how I remember my

mother. Not at all. People make choices, get all fired up, preachy maybe. But fanatical? What's your definition?"

"I'd say a fanatic is a person who'll sacrifice something important for the cause."

He had a point. Only fanatics assassinated their enemies, kidnapped and decapitated their victims, flung them in prison. Fanatics on each side of the political divide caused disruption, started wars. On the other hand, obsessives produced all the fine things in the world, its art, music, and literature. You had to be obsessed to become excellent at what you chose to do in life.

She picked at the fabric on the chair. "Maybe my mother just became obsessed with the belief that cruelty isn't justified. She wanted to persuade your father of that."

"I think when obsession becomes more than a personal quirk, it's fanaticism. When it involves other people, when you try to change them. When the obsessed person can only associate with like-minded people. When they think that others are wrong, that only they know the truth."

"I don't like people like that."

"No? Think about it carefully, Maelle. Isn't your family like that? Your grandparents took a stand back in the seventies, threw over comfortable lifestyles for a commune in the woods. Wanted to live off the land, not take part in conventional American life. So they devoted everything to their goal."

"Yes, but Neil was also escaping. Escaping the draft. Escaping going into the army and getting killed or maimed in a war he thought was wrong. They were idealistic. Don't be so judgmental!"

"Not judging, saying. To me, it's obsession of a sort."

"Or maybe it's just survival."

"Okay." He spoke slowly and deliberately. "Then I'm the one who's obsessed, Maelle. It's haunted me since my father died. How did he die? Why did he die? What were the circumstances?"

Pain crossed his face. He put a hand over his brow, and spoke slowly, looking at the floor. "Let's go over it again. This accident was at night, after hours. It's possible your mother came to the lab to interview Dad. On the other hand, maybe she had another reason. I think it's because she was a fanatical anti-vivisectionist."

"She never mentioned one word about that. Just because she was a vegetarian doesn't mean she was a terrorist, if that's what you're suggesting. Maybe she was just trying to free the animals?" Why was this going so badly? Zachary had never met her mother and now he was implying…She waited, not wanting to finish her own thought.

"And she just happened to kill them all. And my father. And herself." He looked up at her, his eyes hard, his voice bitter.

He'd said it. Unbelievable. "You just accused my mother of something horrible! First you said our parents died in a fire and it was an accident. Then you said my mother killed your father. That's shocking. How could you? I don't believe you."

Her throat clogged, and she could hardly see. She wiped her eyes with her sleeve, and, getting up, grabbed her purse and keys from the entry's table before he could stop her.

"I have to leave now. I have to think." At the door she turned, her voice rising to a wail. "Oh, Zachary, this is so hard to take in."

She slipped out and ran to her car. She gunned it up the driveway and out onto the road, breaking the speed limit all the way to Berkeley.

Chapter Seventeen

It hurt. It hurt so much more than previous relationships gone sour. She'd believed she was falling in love with this intelligent, attractive man. They'd laughed together, eaten together, slept together, and as far as she knew, been true to each other in the weeks they'd known each other. That feeling, the connection she sensed with Zachary, was all new. Never before had she experienced it, and she put it down to her own naivety.

Focused on her beloved trees, Maelle had been slow to the dating game. Unlike her acquaintances, she'd never looked online for a partner. The parties she went to were mostly with colleagues, who were either unavailable or held no romantic interest. With men she'd been wary. Not that Zachary was her first lover, but the others didn't count. Love had not entered into it. Now it did.

And before Zachary, she'd taken this state of affairs for granted. From the age of thirteen, she knew her career path would have something to do with plants, that she would keep people at arm's length. She always knew her destiny would not allow a good relationship with any man. Perhaps it was hereditary. Her own mother had never sustained a relationship and nor had Abby. And as for her grandparents, according to Johanna, they'd been unhappy for years.

Open yourself to love, and you will regret that emotional investment because one day it will disappear. An excess of feeling, both positive and negative, had poisoned her mother's life, maybe even caused her death—according to Zachary.

And he was a psychiatrist. Supposedly he knew more about human behavior than most. He had insulted her mother.

She hoped he was ashamed.

She parked her car, went inside her tiny apartment, flung her coat on the sofa, and collapsed onto it. Her mother could not be a murderer! Why did Zachary make that assumption? His father might have been the killer. A man who tortured animals could be capable of anything. She shivered, covered herself with her coat, and shoved a cushion under her throbbing head.

Of course her mother would have tried to stop David Kane from hurting rabbits. Maelle would have done the same. But she knew her mother wouldn't want to hurt anyone. She certainly wouldn't commit a violent act. No one had ever suggested such a thing.

She couldn't cry. Her stomach clenched in pain, and she curled up in the fetal position on her side. Missing her mother as never before. No mother, no father either. An accident of conception, a fetus who should never have been born. Who didn't deserve life, let alone a mother's love.

The phone rang, shrieking through her wall of self-pity.

Maelle didn't want to answer, especially if it was Zachary. But just in time she checked the number.

Her supervising professor sounded worried. "What's going on, Maelle? You haven't been in to work for a few days. Everything all right?"

Maelle garbled a few words of excuse. Said she hadn't been feeling well but would be in tomorrow.

****

The meeting did not go well. The professor asked if she'd made progress on proving that plants communicate through sound.

She told him about the clicking noise. How one little potted tomato plant, isolated in its separate container and exposed to the sound of a munching caterpillar, communicated with its fellow.

"How many times have you observed this? You'll have to replicate this result. And back it up with reference to other research about plants acting in a cooperative way."

"Yes, I know."

"Bioacoustic research in plants is controversial, as you know. It's one thing to theorize that plants hear, another to prove it. We know that plants give out chemical signals to deter predators when those predators threaten them and their neighbors. This means that they do sense danger to their companions. But *how* do they do that? We have to prove that somehow plants use sound waves to detect peril and communicate the threat to another plant."

Maelle slumped in her chair. "Hearing is just sensing sound vibrations. But you're right, I need another experiment. Not just a repeat of this one. I'll have to come up with another which shows the same thing."

"Go on."

"What if I cover the container holding the threatened plant and see if it still responds to the sound stimulus? Cover it with black cloth. If it responds, that would show that changes in light and shadow are not the cause. Then cover the unthreatened plant's container too. If it responds to the warning from the other plant, we'll know it's not a response to light—that the threatened plant actually warned its neighbor."

"Good. How about another control? Eliminate smell as well. We know plants have an olfactory sense; they respond to volatile chemicals in the air. If your plant can't smell the chemicals being emitted as a warning about the predator, but responds anyway, then you're on the way to proving that sound is the medium of communication."

The conference over, a deep exhaustion settled over Maelle. The scientific method. Comparing effects by eliminating one cause after another, working with each in isolation. It was as if her mind was peering down a long funnel at a far-off object, while the bodily world, the world of emotion and accusation, love, and rejection, battered her from the outside.

What she really wanted to prove was a step beyond the idea that plants can hear, even that they communicate. She wanted to show that they could learn. That they could *remember* the sound of a caterpillar, so that if it failed to actually nibble the stalk, they took note. When she repeated her experiment over and over again, they stopped responding. She didn't quite dare to state this aloud. Were the plants playing with her? Teasing her? Or had they stopped responding because the threat to their well-being had not actually happened? If so, this meant they could anticipate.

She was treading on thin ice, scientifically. She'd told Zachary plants could learn, but few experiments proved it. Calling a plant blasé would not go down well. She'd lose her fellowship, be thrown off the study. Her career would be shot.

She dragged herself back to the lab. Heather, a fellow researcher, waved a cheery greeting. The colleagues were friendly but did not socialize. With her long blonde hair, Heather looked like a model rather than an academic. Tall, but shy, in the nerdy company of other scientists, Heather might be compared to a giraffe munching the treetops while around her zebras chewed grass, heads down, oblivious to other animals. Heather noticed things. Usually, Maelle smiled at her but did not make more than small talk. Today, Heather spoke first. "You all right, Maelle? You look pale."

"I can't concentrate. My work's not going well. And my boyfriend and I have had a disagreement. Our first." To her own astonishment, tears welled up.

"Oh, that sucks!" Heather jumped up and enveloped Maelle in a hug. "I'm so sorry!"

It felt good, this unexpected concern. After a moment, Maelle stepped out of their circled arms. "I'm out on a limb here, with work. Trying to prove plants communicate. That seems so obvious when you see them in the wild, but we're so arrogant we don't recognize the signs."

"Well, good luck. Plants compete, Maelle, for water and sunlight." Heather sat down and resumed her position at her microscope.

"All creatures on earth compete. But some also cooperate. Isn't that the important message? Those who survive get to pass on their genes to further generations, each generation protecting the next. Plants of the same species do protect each other. They even recognize their own offspring. Try to give them space and light to grow."

"All right. So prove it."

Talking about work calmed Maelle, brought her to a mental space she could navigate. "Trying to understand another life form is so fiendishly difficult. Our brains simply can't fathom what a plant feels. I know we're not supposed to use that word, feel. But plants *are* connected. Much more connected than animals. Their roots form a web with each other and with other life forms of the forest. How does isolating one thing from another in their world prove anything?"

Heather looked up. "Kind of like a fish saying humans who can't breathe underwater or use sonar to navigate aren't very bright?"

"Even fish swim in groups. Schools. Creatures need each other."

"What's worrying you, Maelle? Really." Heather swiveled her stool to face Maelle.

"I want to know that communication is more effective than ruthlessness."

"Wow! Where did that come from?"

"I want to know that my mother wanted to protect me more than an oak tree protects its acorn."

"Oh, Maelle." Heather frowned in sympathy.

"My mother abandoned me."

"Did she? How did she do that?"

"She died."

"Well then, she couldn't help it, could she? She didn't mean to leave you." Heather swiveled again. "For now, though, let's get back to work. We can go out later for a drink, if you like."

On the wall, a diagram of a plant's vascular system

made it as plain as could be. Blood ties. Shocking human arrogance, to suppose that life forms other than mammals and birds don't care for their young. Was it male dominance in science that declared the maternal instinct did not truly exist? If it did, where was her own mother's? If Angela took on the task of resisting animal experimentation, she risked her life and, in doing so, abandoned her daughter.

What right did a mother have to engage in activity that could lead to her death? Police report notwithstanding, Angela's death was not really an accident, was it? Her mother must have sought some kind of confrontation. And by doing so, she risked everything. Her mother died for her beliefs.

The room turned icy, her whole body chilled. Wasn't a child more important than an idea?

Maelle turned to her microscope, hiding her face from her colleague. The lens of her microscope swam with tears, obscuring her view.

She couldn't concentrate. Finding out what happened to her mother had to take priority over trying to prove if a tomato plant had a mind of its own.

"Could we take a rain check on a night out?" she said. "I think tonight I just need time to myself."

Chapter Eighteen

Hot milk had not helped. Nor had a second cup laced with whiskey. Sleep refused to come. Maelle curled up on her lonely sheets, pulled up her heaviest quilt, and tried vainly to remember the names of all the goats at Joyous Woods. They kept slipping away, so she'd have to start again.

And then, instead of goats, rabbits made their infuriating way into her mind. So many she couldn't count. She imagined their soft white fur, long ears, and black noses, their bodies strapped down on an operating table, a scalpel poised above them.

Zachary had said, if not in so many words, that Joyous Woods' noble experiment in peace and love had been jettisoned for few extra dollars. But he wasn't angry at Neil. Instead, he'd accused her own mother of causing his father's death.

This, for now, was between herself and Zachary. Their relationship seemed to be at a standstill, but who had dumped whom? Should she call him? She checked her watch. No, too late. She turned from one side of the bed to another, trying to work it out.

Zachary said Neil had sold his father rabbits for medical experiments. Somehow, Angela knew about this and, trying to save the animals, set out to stop it. Was this true? How could anyone prove it one way or the other?

Maelle tossed, put a pillow over her face, then flung it on the floor. Perhaps one of the reasons she'd repressed so much was because just before her mother's death she'd been acting strangely.

Angela's moods swung wildly, that was for sure. Maybe she was really ill. All Maelle could remember was that her mother seemed to change from a loving mommy to someone often anxious and angry, at other times distant and almost comatose. One day she was up, up, twirling Maelle in the air, buying her presents on a whim, filling the refrigerator with a child's delights, ice cream and sweets and sodas.

Then, suddenly, she'd sort of collapse. Sometimes Maelle could not wake her up in the mornings. She'd had to leave for school after fixing her own bowl of cereal, her hair brushed hastily, her clothes not always clean. Weekends, she struggled to wield the vacuum cleaner, learned to work the washer and dryer. Whenever the money ran out, she'd walk over to her aunt Abby's house or her shop and hang around till Abby took notice and fed her.

One thing Maelle couldn't deny was that Angela never earned a great deal. After they'd moved to Berkeley so Maelle could start at public kindergarten, mother and daughter lived in a rented apartment in a seedier part of town. They stayed there for years. What was the name of the company Angela worked for? Maelle had no idea. It was a writing job, that's how her mother described it.

She did recall her mother's cluttered desk in the corner of the living room, the papers and files that threatened to spill off it, and the computer monitor. Sometimes Maelle used it to look up items for school.

What had happened to her mother's own papers, her own research, that computer?

Did the police know? They must have investigated the accident.

Maelle sat up in bed, gripped by an idea. How did one go to the police to ask for information about a fifteen-year-old case? Her upbringing made her wary of police. People of the commune had an uneasy relationship with the law. The marijuana patch, the lack of building permits, the truck with an expired registration all made the communards wary of the authorities. Surely Zachary, who had been fourteen at the time to Maelle's ten, had more information about the accident than she did. What about his mother? Hadn't Zachary pressed his mother for information?

What could she do now? She should confront her grandparents about what they knew and why they had hidden the reality from her. She'd have to ask Neil, that was it. He was the only one who knew the truth about the rabbit scheme—unless the other men at Joyous Woods did, too. But Neil was her grandfather. He owed her an explanation.

Maelle shivered. The blankets puddled on the floor in a heap, and she pulled them up to wrap around her shoulders. She didn't want to confront Neil. She thumped her knees with blanket-bundled hands. Yes, she was afraid. Afraid of his anger, afraid he'd withdraw his love. She'd seen that happen repeatedly to people at Joyous Woods.

She threw off the blanket, got up, and went to get a drink of water. The faucet gurgled. Water dripped over the side of the glass, running over her hands. Why had she repressed everything till now? It should not take such a huge psychological effort to tackle Neil on his behavior, on his ideas of fairness. She shut off the water and drank as if parched. But if she did confront Neil, what good would that do? She guessed how it would go. He would hug her, his beloved granddaughter. He would croon and mollify, show a sweeter side of himself. She'd be drawn in, captivated by his charm, just like all the women over the years.

Not that he'd been sweet and charming last weekend, when she and Zachary had visited. Then, he'd showed the side Johanna complained about. He was like a Janus—one side sunny, one side dark.

Did the realization that Neil was manipulative, difficult, and not to be trusted come to her mother as well? If so, how was it relevant?

She must focus. The point was to find out what her mother thought about animal experimentation, if she had any opinions about it at all.

She pulled a sweater over her pajamas, went to her desk, and powered on the laptop.

She lost track of time.

****

The dawn seeped through the windows. It greened the houseplants, sent a prism of light through the abandoned water glass on the kitchen counter, illuminated Maelle's sparse furniture, touched on her tousled bed, and lit up the screen of the computer. She turned off the desk lamp.

So far, the digital leads on her mother had proven elusive. Becker, Woolley, Kane. All dead ends. It was hardly earth-shattering news, two people dying in a fire. The obituaries were hard to search as well, even if narrowed to the month and year of their deaths.

Alternating waves of hot and cold flushed through her body. She needed to find out what her mother believed and why. To do that, she must read everything Angela wrote. So far, the search for her writings had uncovered little with Angela's byline. A few articles, here and there. But her mother had made a living, had she not, as a journalist? She must have left a longer paper trail.

What a lesson in humility. Her mother was not a household name. It appeared she'd hardly been noticed. What was the result of all that tapping away at the computer in the corner? How did journalists start out? Most began with their local paper. She'd heard it took years to make it to the big time, if they ever did.

Maelle hugged herself. She'd become chilled, working at the computer in the night. She took a shower and made a cup of coffee. Saturday stretched before her, minus Zachary, who'd so filled previous weekends she'd almost come to believe their relationship was steady and sure. But a dateless Saturday was also an opportunity. She could take a drive, a long drive, to visit the county library, where copies of the local weekly must be stored.

****

It took three hours of steady driving. A light rain fell, slowing traffic, then stopped, and the clouds cleared as she drove farther north and inland. As she sighted the exit at last, Maelle understood why she had not made the effort earlier to find copies of her mother's work. Effort it certainly required.

She'd forgotten how the town almost took one by surprise, suddenly appearing off the freeway behind a stand of poplars. It exuded a funky charm. Streets fronted with shops selling vintage clothes, spices, marijuana, and hardware intersected Main Street, which was book-ended by a supermarket and an enormous emporium devoted to off-grid living.

Maelle found the library at the town's far end. Stumbling, cramped and stiff, from the car, she faced a low wooden building surrounded by a native-plant garden. It radiated a sense of calm. Butterflies flitted in the soft autumn sun as it emerged from the clouds, glancing off trees and flowers that glittered with recent raindrops. A black cat with matted fur lounged on a wooden seat under an arbor. A sign announced a seed exchange in the library grounds the following week. Maelle pushed open the library door.

There were few patrons inside on this early Saturday afternoon, some students on the computers, a couple of older people reading magazines. At the desk, a kind-faced older woman with long silver hair greeted Maelle with a smile. "Welcome. Are you new in town?"

"Not exactly. I grew up close by, and I've come to research articles in the local paper from the first years of this century. My mother's articles, she was a reporter."

"Would I know your mother? I've been here quite some time."

"Angela was her name. Angela Becker."

The librarian gasped. "My goodness, you're Angela Becker's daughter? I remember she used to haunt the library as a teenager. She'd come after school and catch a late bus home. I followed her career as she started writing for our local weekly. I always hoped she'd make it as a full-time salaried journalist on a major paper." The librarian shook her hair, which was tied loosely at the back with a white ribbon. She wore a faded blue chamois shirt and had clipped, sensible nails on hands which moved constantly.

"Maelle Woolley." Maelle held out her hand.

"I'm Samantha Hughes. Sad that she died so young, your mother. An accident, wasn't it? Do sit." She gestured toward the chair in front of the help desk. "I'm so sorry. You must have been quite young." Her face brightened. "As it happens, the local paper—the original copies—are in the back room, stacks and stacks of them. Should be a good resource. It still doesn't offer a digital version. Sadly, we don't have the staff to do the digitizing or even microfiche; we're years behind." She lowered her voice. "To be honest, the local paper is on its last legs."

Maelle groaned inwardly. She'd never find anything.

But Samantha clasped her hands together. "Yet it's such an important historical record. That's why I've taken it upon myself to preserve all those stacks. You'll find every single copy in there."

She smiled at Maelle, her eyes begging for affirmation. "Some people would say local news isn't important. I disagree. Local newspapers are the lifeblood of small communities. And for future historians, if we rely on digital versions, it will all be gone, just like smoke. No one reads compact discs any more. Soon thumb drives will be irrelevant. I hate to think what will happen if some war or calamity destroys the cloud. What will happen to our records then?"

"How true! That's why I'm here. I couldn't find

much at home." Maelle shifted her backpack. "I'm hoping to read the actual papers, maybe make some copies."

"So go in the back there, and take your time." Samantha Hughes pointed to a door.

Surrounded by papers, Maelle soon found Angela's byline. She read her mother's words with a strange sense of disconnection and recognition. Alive, her mother had thought these thoughts and written these words. The news Angela reported was both perennial and long past. Problems looming large then had been solved or forgotten, yet the issues were timeless. Angela wrote about committees and meetings, efforts to save local creeks, bookstore events, movie reviews. As a cub reporter, she'd hopped around, covering this and that.

Eventually, rising from the stacks without finding anything of interest, Maelle realized that her mother's job on this paper offered no clues to her death.

But a report on her death itself? She found it. The funeral notice in the local paper verified the date in black and white. From there, she tracked backward through a week's worth of old newspapers until finally, she saw it. An accident at a medical laboratory, under police investigation. The two people killed in what looked to be a fire were Angela Becker and David Kane.

Becker and Kane.

Zachary had said that he realized Maelle was Angela Becker's daughter only after he recognized Joyous Woods. How was that possible? Very possible, she supposed. Maelle and her mother did not share a last name. It was a little unusual in her case, but not so strange for a woman to use a different professional name. Did he put two and two together when he met Johanna, who went by her maiden name, Becker? She thought back. Zachary and Johanna had never actually been introduced using surnames. Still, it was weird. Had Zach been stalking her all along? For what purpose? She shivered.

In the short time she'd known Zachary, he'd always been courteous, never hot-tempered. He'd been considerate and kind. What was his father like? After Zachary said rabbits were used widely in medical research, she'd looked into it and found they provided antibodies and were useful in testing cardiovascular therapies.

Who knew that rabbits and humans shared so much anatomy? As a scientist, she should have guessed. Even plants shared a surprising number of genetic similarities with the animal kingdom. Research in the name of medicine was a good thing. Why then, had Neil and his cronies gone to so much trouble to hide this rabbit house in the woods? Did he assume Angela would object to it, and did she object to other animals being milked or sold for meat?

Then too, how did Angela know about Joyous Woods' role in the rabbit supply chain, if it was all so secret?

So why had Angela died? Her question differed from Zachary's. He wanted to know why Angela had gone to the lab at night. He'd more or less accused her mother of being a terrorist. He could not know that. And so far there was no proof. Anyway, he assumed motivation, when the first question should be, what actually happened at the lab that killed two people?

Maelle struggled to remember the commune's reaction to her mother's death. No one ever, ever talked about it.

But they must have known if Angela felt so passionate about animals she'd do anything to save them. That would have caused conflict on the commune, a working farm by the time Angela grew up. Was she fanatical about her beliefs? Or were her actions beyond her control because of her wildly fluctuating moods?

Her mother had changed in the months before she died. Or was it simply that Maelle was growing old enough to notice? Angela had been sometimes sharp, sometimes loving, sometimes efficient, sometimes disheveled, her manner sometimes distracted, sometimes focused. Was this because of her brain chemistry, or was it something she was investigating? Had she been threatened? Or was she truly crazy? If she'd been an animal rights terrorist, surely the newspaper would have reported that the police were investigating that link. And if he had been obsessed by his father's death, why had Zachary not interviewed the police himself and asked them to pursue the eco-terrorists, even after all these years? There was no statute of limitations on murder.

Maelle made copies of the articles with Angela's byline. Thanking Samantha Hughes, she left with her stack of paper clutched to her breast, a thin and unsatisfactory link to her mother's thoughts. What next? Her mind went blank, her blood sugar low. She retreated to the library's café to eat, drink, and think.

Her sandwich tasted dry, and her coffee stale. It had not been a very successful day. She'd come away with a pile of photocopied articles, none of which were relevant. She'd found the obituary of her mother. That was pretty much it. She felt so alone. Zachary seemed to have withdrawn his love, yet she'd done nothing to cause that.

"May I join you?"

A shape appeared in Maelle's watery vision. With her sleeve, she wiped her eyes, so irritatingly beyond her control, and looked up at Samantha Hughes.

"Hello there. Join me?"

"Thank you, it's my break time." Samantha sat down, placing a china cup crayoned with her name on it in front of her. "I'm so pleased you came to the library today. I'd love to know anyone connected with Angela Becker. I was so fond of her. I remember you as a tiny girl. Your mother used to bring you here sometimes. I was the children's librarian then, and she'd park you in the front row of the kids for story hour, so I could keep an eye on you while she worked."

"Oh." Maelle smiled. "That must have been before we moved away. It's much quieter here. You'd always be pulled in to do a task at the farm."

"That's what Angela told me. Growing up on a farm sounds romantic, but it's really hard work." Samantha dunked her teabag, removed it to her saucer, and leaned close as if sharing a confidence. "You know, I'm really interested in history, as I mentioned earlier. Your commune, it's pretty unusual because it lasted so long."

"Only a few people are left now."

"I suppose that's inevitable. Even by the time you were born, the commune had been going at least twenty-five years. That's a long time. Admirable. I always wanted Angela to write about it, but she wouldn't. Of course, when you're young, you never realize you're living through an historic time. It's just your life, what you're used to."

"Someone's writing about it now. Well, making a documentary film."

"Is that so? That's wonderful! When it's done, I'd love a copy for our film library."

"Really?" Maelle broke into an amazed smile. "There's some disagreement at Joyous Woods about whether it's a good idea. Something about respecting privacy. That's my grandmother's view, anyway. My grandfather, though, it was his idea. So it's happening."

"Well, I'm delighted to hear it. Oral history is so important. It's an era that was quite influential, so many attitudes changed in society from that time. I'm glad it's being memorialized."

As long as all of it is not. Maelle examined the table's edge, running her fingers along the metallic grooves. Suddenly she slapped her hand flat, sloshing the remains of her coffee.

"Samantha, will you help me? If the commune really has some historical importance, shouldn't it be preserved? The organic farm that came out of it was instrumental in pushing the farm-to-table ethos along."

She dabbed the spill with a paper napkin. "Here's the problem. My great-uncle—my grandfather's brother—wants to sell the land now his parents have died. He suggested there might be grants or trusts or something that could be used to save the land from development. I got the impression that the owners got money in return for keeping the land in trust or something. But I don't know how it works."

Samantha beamed. "What a great idea! Let me put together a list of resources for you, Maelle. I'd love to help." She stood, holding her cup and saucer in one hand. "Break time's up. But leave me your contact details, and I'll be in touch."

Maelle thanked her, wrote her number and email address on another paper napkin, and handed it over. She drained the last dregs of her cup, picked up her backpack, and drove to Joyous Woods to stay the night.

Chapter Nineteen

The farm lay still, serene on the cusp of the evening, when Maelle parked her car under the red-barked madrone a little way from the main house. Seeing nobody, she took her backpack and walked to the kitchen. Deep shadows cloaked the corners, so her eyes took time to adjust. Heading to the sink, she ran a glass of water, drinking deep.

"Don't bother to rinse the glass. I'll use that one, but could you bring me some water too, dear?" Johanna's voice startled Maelle. Usually, her grandmother would be outside this time of day.

Peering, Maelle saw a figure sitting by a window in the fading afternoon, knitting, colored yarns in neat piles at her side. Johanna switched on a hurricane lamp nearby, and in the halo of light, her gray hair twinkled with gold and her wrinkles softened.

Maelle brought the glass to her grandmother and placed it on top of the little side table over an old copy of an organic farming magazine, its cover marred with countless ring-stains.

"It's a lovely surprise to have you here, dear. Are you all right? You look worried."

Maelle picked up a stool and scooted it close, sitting so her shoulder almost touched Johanna's.

"JoJo, I just can't stop thinking about Mom. I've been at the county library, reading her old newspaper pieces. It makes me feel a little closer to her, you know. Like her thoughts are here in this room."

Johanna held her work in progress to the light. The green mohair scarf shimmered like a sunlit meadow after a light rain.

"Yes. She's always here with us in spirit, dear."

"I didn't exactly mean that. I want to know everything about her. What she believed. How she died."

Johanna set down her knitting. "Oh, Maelle, what a thing to ask, out of the blue. Don't upset yourself. You've got your own young life to lead. Your work to do. Get a good job, dear. Get that PhD."

"That's what Zachary says."

"Nice young man. How's that going?"

"Oh, JoJo!" A lump choked Maelle's throat. "I don't know. He's been really weird since we left here. I've hardly seen him! He swears he came here as a boy."

"Really? I don't remember that." Johanna lowered her head to count her stitches.

"Well, as he says, he looks a bit different now. He said something strange. Like he didn't know you were Johanna Becker or Angela Becker was your daughter. He said, if she was my mother, why do I have a different last name?"

"Not so unusual. Most children take their father's name. Some don't."

"Ouch, JoJo! You know I don't have a father!"

"You certainly do. It's just that we didn't know him very well."

"What was his name?"

"We don't actually know, dear. Angie tried to trace

him, but no luck. So your mother gave you Neil's surname."

"That's weird. Because Mom used yours."

The needles clicked, the mohair scarf tumbled over Johanna's lap. "When Angela was born, I decided not to give her Neil's name." She quickened her pace till she came to the end of a row.

Maelle narrowed her eyes. "Was this when you were angry with Neil about all his girlfriends?"

Johanna shifted her shoulders, a noncommittal shrug hampered by her lapful of scarf. "It was a thing, then. A little stand against patriarchy. Anyway, as I told you, we weren't married. Not that we cared about that kind of semantic quibbling up here in Joyous Woods. I mean, it was not a feminist thing. It was more practical.

"First, you know Neil's last name is Woolley. Please! Do you really think saddling a little girl with that name is fair? Especially since Angie had dark curly hair. We named her for Angela Davis, that Black activist who had a wild Afro. She led the war protesters at Berkeley back in the day, and we all admired her."

"But Abby's name is Woolley!"

"We'd settled down by then. When Abby came along, I gave in, so she's Tabitha Woolley."

"So why is my last name Woolley if Mom was Becker?"

"Oh, Angie just adored her father. She had to pick a last name for you, since we didn't know your actual father's. She chose Neil's. I was persona non grata with her for some reason. She was just at that rebellious age, if you ask me."

Maelle listened silently. Curious how both Abby and her mother had seemed to hold something against

Johanna. This JoJo, so loving and kind.

The needles flew, and Johanna turned another row. "Abby, though, hated being named after a cat. The kids at the high school teased her. Called her Catfur. So she started calling herself Abby. Actually, the last name worked out for her, though, don't you think? Her shop in Berkeley sells handmade angora and wool jackets, hand-knitted sweaters, baby clothes, all those lovely things. She just called it Woolley's—so appropriate."

"I guess." Maelle bit her lip, willing herself not to interrupt.

Johanna paused the needles, so that the one in her right hand pointed upward, a green thread snaking downward from its row of stitches. "And now Abby wants to stop selling our products. I can't keep up with all the changes around here." She shook her head. "Why these questions, all of a sudden, Maelle?"

Maelle put her arm around Johanna's shoulders. "You've meant everything to me, all of you at Joyous Woods. But think how I must feel now I'm old enough to want to have my own kids. Didn't anyone try to track my father down? Especially after Mom died."

Johanna turned, gave Maelle a sharp look. "You're not...? What about your studies?"

"No. Not pregnant. Don't even think it. I don't know what's happening with Zachary at the moment. But truly, it's only normal to want to know about your parents. And Mom! No one talks about her. I'm just trying to figure out who my mother was, what made her tick. See, I can't remember what she looked like anymore. Her face is blurry. Last week, when you showed Zachary the photos, it brought it all back. I miss her!"

"That's natural, I suppose." Johanna took a long sip of water.

"Will you tell me more about her? About my father?"

"Your father left before Angie knew she was pregnant. You're right, we had a different attitude to sex. It was more fluid, less serious. Had to be, I suppose."

"If casual sex was the norm up here, why are you so angry at Neil?"

To Maelle's amazement, Johanna blushed. She bent her head to her knitting.

"I tried not to be resentful and possessive. Neil and I had so much history; we started this experiment together. Your mother and her...well, not boyfriend, he just happened to be here for a few weeks. After the kids became teenagers, it would have been hypocritical of us to try to control them."

"It makes me feel like only half a person, knowing so little about my parents."

"Oh, sweetheart." Johanna laid her hand on Maelle's. "You were such a beautiful baby. We all fell in love with you. Especially your grandfather and I. We told ourselves we'd do better with you than we did with our own kids. It's a grandparent thing. One day you'll understand."

"What do you mean, do better than with your own kids?"

"Oh, it's complicated. But let me say this. Angela was different, always touchy as a child. Difficult. Had fears. Protective of Abby."

"Sounds like she was a good sister. Protective of Abby, how?"

Johanna's face took on a faraway look. "All the kids on the farm, when they got to be about twelve, we sent them to public school near the vineyards. It was miles away, took so much time on the bus. But we had no choice. There was no school nearby."

"You tried to give your kids the best."

Johanna's voice dropped, sounded sad. "Angie had a really hard time at that school."

"How?"

"Ganged up on, bullied. All the commune children wore handmade clothes. It was all we could afford. Couldn't afford the cafeteria either. The kids had to bring their own lunch. Smelly homemade cheese, they complained. They were laughed at."

Smelly cheese—a person could turn into a vegan, right there. Maelle raised her eyes questioningly at her grandmother. Johanna had always been so nurturing to her. It was hard to imagine her ignoring the needs of a daughter. But maybe the shock of losing that daughter made her change.

"You sent me to that school, too, JoJo. I didn't mind it."

"You were a good student. Angela had some academic trouble. She had a hard time concentrating. The school said she had attention deficit or something. They called it ADHD and said we should get some pills for it. Well, we had plenty of pills; we weren't averse to drugs at Joyous Woods. So she was put on some kind of attention pill, and that helped. But really, both girls found it so hard."

Johanna sipped her water thoughtfully. "No one had smart phones in those days, but the kids were encouraged to use a word processor. We couldn't afford that, either. So they struggled. Eventually, Neil's parents took pity on us and bought a computer and monitor for the farm. That's when Angie took up writing. She could do that at least, even though she was terrible at anything to do with numbers. Abby was more practical. She worked and sewed and sold her clothes. She's done well."

"She has. I learned a lot from her."

"Your mother, it was hard. She was just eighteen when you came along, and that was that."

"You make it sound like a death sentence."

"Certainly not."

"Jeez, JoJo!" Maelle hugged herself. "This is so disturbing. All this stuff, coming out now!"

"You never asked before. Goodness knows, we would have told you. Water under the bridge, Maelle. You don't have to bring up painful memories."

"Sometimes not knowing is more painful than knowing."

"Animals, that was Angie's thing. She loved all the animals here on the farm. The goats, the sheep, the dogs, the rabbits. She chose the rabbits as her special chore. Changed their water and cleaned their cages." Johanna ran her fingers over the soft tufts of her work. "She loved to comb their fur. She groomed them and saved the wool for me to knit."

"That sounds nice. I liked the animals, too." Maelle pushed her fingernails into her palm, willing JoJo to tell her about her mother and her views without being prompted.

"Yes. We all became attached to them. Angela became a vegetarian, too. Got on a bit of a soapbox about it. She probably made herself unpopular at school, taking up a cause like that."

"Lots of people are vegetarians, even vegan, and no one judges them for it."

"This was long before those ideas came into the mainstream. Anyway, Angie became a writer, as you know. Worked on the local paper, did some feature articles for newspapers, some farming magazines, that kind of thing. Hard way to make a living. She waitressed too. Used to get Abby to watch you, sometimes, when she couldn't get a sitter. It was always a scramble."

"I don't remember that." Maelle bristled in defense of her mother.

"It's not a criticism," Johanna said, as if she'd read Maelle's mind. "It's just that it was a hard life. If you'd lived up here, we could have helped to take care of you. But Neil and I lived too far away to pitch in."

"Oh, I wouldn't say that." Maelle squeezed her grandmother's shoulder. "But I do remember Abby being with us a lot in Berkeley. In fact, she was there the day Mom…" She stopped, then began again. "The night Mom didn't come home." She stood and faced her grandmother. "JoJo, I need to know what happened that night. You never told me. You just said it was an accident, so I always assumed a car accident."

"Hoping to save you heartache, dear. And ourselves, of course."

"Okay, so what happened?"

"Since she was a journalist, she might have been working on a story about the lab."

Bingo. "What lab?"

"Your mother died when she was visiting a medical research lab. I don't know what kind of research. Anyway, there was a fire, and two people died, Angela and the lab researcher. I'm afraid I can't remember his name."

Johanna's eyes fluttered. She cast them down and resumed knitting. For an instant, Maelle doubted the thought that darted into her mind. Her grandmother was the soul of honesty. She wouldn't lie, would she?

She could, though. Anyone could. Everyone tells lies in their lifetime, little or big.

Johanna stowed her knitting and stood, stretching her back. "I need to get on with dinner. You can help me if you like, or just go and freshen up. You must be beat after that drive."

Johanna was dismissing her. Maelle hesitated, then hefted her backpack. On the way to her bedroom, she realized she'd done it without thinking, as always. She'd obeyed her grandmother.

Her bedroom in the pagoda house looked as plain and clean as a nun's cell. The floorboards were swept, the walls unadorned. It was nuts to bring Zachary up here. Suddenly, she hated the commune and everything it represented. She swung her bag on the bed and went outside.

Chapter Twenty

"Hi, honey. Nice surprise!" A deep voice boomed out, scaring up a flurry of birds settling for the night. Curtis and Ray, coming toward Maelle as she picked her way carefully by the fields, grinned at her with avuncular fondness. Mud squelched under their feet. "We're just knocking off for the day. Staying for dinner? Come in."

They'd arrived at a low sprawling building to which Curtis had made many additions over the years. Inside, Curtis heeled off his boots, tossing them on a mat. Ray did the same.

In the large open room, anchored by a huge wall of brick enclosing a hand-made pizza oven, Curtis switched on the space heater which helped solar panels warm the house and waved his guests toward the wooden table and chairs he'd made himself.

As a child, Maelle had spent plenty of time in this house, enjoying Curtis and Sally's convivial natures and their artistic streak. She noted at the back of her mind the shabbiness of the pagoda house compared to this demonstration of its owners' house pride.

The large room had been freshly painted, and Curtis's glowing canvases hung on every wall. In one corner of the room stood an easel, with paint cans and brushes resting on a shelf nearby.

"Art sales going well, Curtis?" Maelle asked.

"You bet. The street festivals are over for the season, but a gallery in the city contacted me about an exhibition. Just last week." He headed toward the refrigerator. "Can't believe it, after all these years."

"Power of persistence." Ray nodded.

Curtis pulled out two beers from the fridge, passed one each to Ray and Maelle, who had sat down at the table, and reached in for another. He lifted the can's tab with his pinky, showing hands dark with grime and paint stains. He took a swig, and beer dribbled down his grizzled beard.

Maelle drank. The fizz unsettled her stomach. "That's great, Curtis. Of course, if Joyous Woods is sold and paved over with roads and shops, you'll be able to sell your work right here." Maelle could hear sarcasm sour her voice.

"Hey, hey. What's going on? Why so angry all of a sudden?"

Maelle batted away a fly. It buzzed off, annoyed, then circled her again. Perspiration dampened her underarms and her forehead. Probably the fly could smell her sweat. "Surely you've heard the news. This land's going to be sold. Neil doesn't really own it, and his sister and brother want to unload it."

Ray raised his eyebrows, questioning. Curtis shook his head. "Just a rumor, sweetheart."

"I was at the funeral when they discussed it."

"Drink your beer, Maelle. It's not your concern. We're a team here. The Circle."

Maelle kicked her chair rail. These guys. So radical they thought they were, but so old-fashioned, too. Like the Circle was some kind of corporate structure. That was it! If the Circle was the decision-making body, then they were responsible, all of them, for the rabbit scheme. She studied their faces. They revealed nothing.

"Ray, Curtis. I have to ask you something." She softened her tone. "I want to know more about my mom. She was a journalist, so I've been trying to find what she wrote about. Did she write anything about the treatment of animals?"

"I suppose so. This is farm country. She wrote for the local paper and other publications. Why do you ask?"

"Have you ever read what she wrote?"

"Nah. Too busy." Curtis took another swig and another and tossed the empty container into a bin next to the sink.

Ray swiped his hand down his can, making tracks in the condensation. "She was a bit of an agitator, Angie. Did she write about those stinking feedlots where the cattle stand in muck waiting to go to the slaughterhouse? She might have. Angie didn't like eating meat. But she knew that we raised our animals with love."

"Love?" Maelle's head jerked back. "The animals here are a commercial product."

"True. But we treat them right. Look at how Kevin cherishes those goats. You can love the animals and use them, too. If you run a farm, being a vegan's just not realistic. You see animals in a different light. You can't be sentimental." He curled and uncurled his fingers, as if making sure they still worked.

"You all right, Ray?"

"Touch of arthritis. Just keeping the hands flexible."

He formed his fingers into a lattice, palms facing

out. It signaled a barrier. Maelle changed tack. She turned to Curtis.

"You know what I'm talking about. The hidden rabbit house."

He reared up. "How do you know about that?"

"You can't keep things secret forever. I've been looking into how my mother died, and I think she was trying to stop animals being hurt in a research lab."

Ray gave a nervous laugh. "Is this being recorded? Are we on camera?"

"Stop it." She glared. "Is this funny?"

"Oh, Maelle. Always were a serious little thing. Look, what happened was years ago." Ray bent down to scratch an ankle, revealing a darned and grubby sock. "Toss me another, will you, Curtis?"

Curtis loped over to the fridge and mouthed, "Another?" to Maelle, who shook her head.

"You better tell her, Curtis." Ray looked resigned.

"Okay. Neil, Ray, and I, we were all very worried about the finances of the farm. I know, we pretended to be nonchalant about it. We were against capitalism, all that. But we needed to support the farm and ourselves, and you kids."

"Nice of you."

"The dairy, the goats, the crops, the eggs and the jams and jellies, Johanna's clothes, they weren't sufficient to keep Joyous Woods going."

Curtis untabbed another beer. "This stuff is better than what we made. Remember, Ray? Our own beer. Not bad, but not commercially viable. Point is, we had to find something profitable."

Ray gulped the beer, as if he hadn't had a drink in days.

"It was a struggle. That's when a lot of the people here left. Couldn't take the poverty. But we were committed. Didn't want to work for the man. Anyway, Linda really loved the dairy, and she was getting a name for the cheese we produced here. It's persistence, like with Curtis's painting. You're about to give up, then you get a breakthrough. We really needed one."

"I thought you grew marijuana."

"Everyone around here grows weed. Remember how it used to be illegal? Heavy prison time if you got caught. But we found a place higher up in the hills, and it supported us for a while. We'd sneak up there in the middle of the night to cut the harvest, carry it out in garbage bags, dry it.

"But the whole industry became more and more difficult. Helicopters circling, looking for the hidden crop. It got worse. Once they found the marijuana fields, the feds would bring in these infrared cameras that work at night, hide them, and film the people who worked the field. So we had to think of something else to make more money."

Curtis said, sitting down again, "Had to be legit, too. We were getting too old to deal drugs."

"Did Neil tell you what should be done, or did you decide together?" Maelle twisted in her chair to face Curtis.

"Mutual decision." He looked huffy. "If you're trying to pin this all on Neil, that's not fair. We agreed."

"Who agreed? You didn't tell the women."

"No. That was because your mother—even though she wasn't living here, she would have had a fit."

"Well, she did. Have a fit, I'm guessing. What happened was worse."

"Yes."

Both men looked uncomfortably at their feet.

"Go on." Maelle sipped her beer.

"Neil found out about a medical research community near here. Used rabbits to test drugs."

Ray interjected. "I told Neil, I'm not sure I feel good about that. But Neil said, we're years away from hating the establishment. We have to work with it. Making cures for disease is good, not bad, don't you agree?

" 'Course, I told him. But it's the way they do it in these labs. Don't they hurt the animals? But Neil said they took precautions to minimize the pain."

"See, the problem was—" Curtis paused and placed his can on the table, looking away from Maelle, toward Ray. "—the rabbits were Johanna's department. She thinks of them as her babies. We decided we'd have to keep the operation secret from the women."

Beer spewed from Maelle's mouth. "That's ridiculous," she shouted. "You guys, you're so patriarchal, acting like we're the squeamish ones."

Curtis ducked his head. "The thing is, your mother started lecturing us about not being kind to the animals. She wasn't the only one with a bee in her bonnet, either. Jasper and Kyle, well, they took off. Kyle, you know, he…" He gripped the beer can.

Maelle strained to remember Curtis and Sally's sons. Many years had passed since they left. Jasper was a chef, she'd heard, in Seattle. Rumor was that Kyle had serious relationship problems, but that, too, had been brushed off, never discussed.

Ray picked up the conversation as if Curtis had not spoken.

"Linda doesn't eat red meat either, but she's no vegan. She's not squeamish, running the dairy. She's in there with the goat teats and the goat shit, their parasites and worms. Helps get the shearers in, ties the goats' feet so they won't kick free. I'm sure sometimes she wouldn't mind killing a mean goat or two."

Curtis leaned forward. "Neil said the payback would be good. This research doctor told Neil that his lab would pay good money for rabbit eyes, their kidneys and testicles, too."

"Jesus. That was a bit confronting at the time." Ray clasped his hands over his crotch. "But we treated those rabbits so well. We had to deliver the rabbits in healthy condition, use a different stock from the angoras. We set up a separate rabbit-breeding operation. You know we have these goat shelters, far up on the hill, a long way from the house? Johanna and the girls are too busy to go way up there. Only Pedro goes there, keeping watch on the goats at night. So we built another shelter, for the rabbits. Very nice it was, too. Had to be a proper building, concrete walls and floors, with its own electric generator. We bought four New Zealand whites and had a litter in no time."

Curtis wiped up a spill with his sleeve. "We had to make the rabbit house really secure. Not only that, it had to be sterile. Not that we weren't used to that, with the dairy. We had to dig a well, put in lines for water, made a field around it to grow feed for the rabbits. It was a lot of work."

"I'm sure." Maelle tried to visualize the hutches. How had they escaped her notice in all her hillside wanderings? "Can I see these rabbit houses? They must be well hidden, because I never found them, all the years I lived here."

"Yeah, but you were only a little kid at the time. Anyway, about the rabbits," Curtis said. "Neil was adamant. Said he wanted to keep it from the girls, particularly Johanna. He was afraid it would remind her of the Nazis. Her parents were German, hated what went down in their country in the war, came here to try to forget it."

"Not the same thing, surely!" Maelle crushed her can between her hands, feeling the metal bite into her fingers. "Rabbits aren't people."

"That's what we said. We argued, Neil, what's the difference between using rabbits for their fur, or eating them, or selling them to a lab? But he said he owed it to Johanna. Said when she learned what the Nazis had done, she empathized with the Jewish people. Then, after Angie...went, we tore the whole thing down. It seemed only fair to her memory, if she hated it."

"I guess your plan to prevent the women knowing about this rabbitry didn't last long."

"I really don't know. I don't know how Angela knew. Johanna and Sally and Linda still don't." Ray thunked his beer can hard on the table, as if wanting the conversation to end.

Maelle raised her eyebrows at the two old men. Incredible that they believed that they could run a little side operation with impunity and without anyone knowing. Maybe it was because of their history. They'd fled the draft, all those years ago, hidden in the hills, and no one found them. Living under the radar, it was just what they did.

"I can see my mother's point. Not wanting to hurt animals. How long did this go on for? This rabbit thing?"

"A few years," Curtis said. "It paid well. Kept the farm going."

"It cost my mother her life." Maelle's throat hurt. She struggled to keep back tears.

Curtis reached over to put his hand over hers. "Honey, we lived by our beliefs. We taught our kids to do that too. For better or worse. You can't blame your mother for trying to stop animal killing if that's what she believed in."

"You mean she tried to stop it forcibly?"

"I thought you knew. I thought this is what you're saying."

"I'm asking, not saying."

Curtis picked up the beer cans and walked them to the bin, his back to Maelle. Ray seemed to find a sudden interest in a splinter in the wooden tabletop.

"I know she went to the lab. I just don't understand why she went in the middle of the night. It doesn't make sense!" She sprang up, clutching the table for support. "And why would *rabbits* be more important than looking after me? I was her only child!"

That sucked all the air out of the room. Maelle stared at both men, who stared back at her, their faces blank.

Finally, Ray said, "I'm starving, aren't you?" and Curtis sighed in relief.

All the fight had slipped away from her, and mechanically, Maelle followed Ray and Curtis to the pagoda house, her stomach hollow, but not from hunger.

On the way back to the pagoda house, Maelle stopped at the rabbit shed near the house, where

Johanna kept her angoras. Reaching into a cage, she brought out its furry inhabitant, and nestled him under her arm. She took the dark-haired English Angora into the great room and sat on a chair to groom him. Johanna had set aside an armchair for grooming, a towel folded in a basket next to it, with comb and hair dryer inside. As she stroked out the rabbit's fur, Maelle crooned to him. She placed her left hand on his back, and with the right, she switched on the hair dryer to cool, and its breeze lifted the hair. She combed it, first with her fingers, then with the comb. The warmth of his skin, the long soft hair, and the action of grooming calmed her, calmed the rabbit. She'd loved doing this as a kid.

How could the men of Joyous Woods even think of selling rabbits, knowing they'd be hurt? No matter how beneficial the results for human health might ultimately prove to be. In the bustle of the kitchen, Maelle's courage returned. She'd take Neil aside and ask him about the rabbit scheme. She would! But she couldn't find him before the gong sounded its call to the communal dinner, and she returned the rabbit to his place with a reward of lettuce.

Neil shambled in late, his face dazed. Pamela was nowhere in sight, had left only a trace of her scent in the bathroom.

Perhaps that was why Johanna seemed more relaxed. Over their lentil and mushroom burgers, she and Sally and Linda chatted about what they would do with the last of the squash. They'd put the potatoes under hay in the root cellar tomorrow and ask Curtis and Ray to check the ventilation pipe in there, to make sure it wasn't blocked. Maybe send the cat down to the cellar, to clear it of mice.

Neil said little at dinner. Maelle found him hard to read. His moods were so labile, ranging from charming to churlish. He soared or sank. Observing him covertly, Maelle found herself unable to speak. Why had she come today? She'd wasted her time when she should have been working. Even if she'd pulled the truth, at least part of it, from Curtis and Ray, Neil knew more. Maybe he knew all of it.

After dinner, Neil plucked at his guitar, composing a new song. He could have been a rock star, he was fond of reminding them, if he lived in the city. You might have chosen to go back there to test that theory, Maelle had often thought, but like everyone else in the commune, she'd never argued with him. The song went on and on, something about love lost, and Neil's voice cracked at the high notes, croaked at the low.

If he would only stop, she could take him aside and quiz him. But he didn't look at anyone or raise his head from his guitar. She fidgeted in her seat. She shoved her hands under her thighs to stop them jiggling, then drew them out and looked at her fingernails. What did she want from him? It pushed at her from deep inside. She wanted remorse.

Lassitude crept over her, exhaustion, deep in her bones. It was no use. What good would confronting Neil in front of Johanna do? What would be the point of his regret? It wouldn't bring back Angela. And if Johanna knew nothing about the rabbit sales, then to go down that path would not add to anyone's knowledge. Besides, to bring it up now would just poison Johanna further against Neil.

****

In the morning, Johanna fussed. As Maelle prepared to drive back to the city, Johanna loaded the back seat of the car with knitted goods for Abby to sell, despite Abby's reluctance to carry them, and filled the trunk with bags full of baked goods and winter vegetables.

"Oh, JoJo. You didn't have to. But thanks. I'll take the cakes and muffins to work to share." The largesse baffled Maelle. She'd have to find a use for Johanna's greens; she had no one in particular to cook for. Few friends and no Zachary. She stomped her way to the car, kicking stones along the way, sending scurries of dust into the air.

Chapter Twenty One

Another week of work. Maelle's mind wandered. After she brought Johanna's German apple cake into the lab, her coworkers' appreciation cloaked her low mood. She dropped off her grandmother's handmade items at Abby's store and decided not to comment when Abby pursed her lips at the sight of the autumn-colored shawls and capes that were Johanna's latest creations.

Instead, she invited her aunt for dinner. "JoJo gave me all these lovely vegetables. And I know you love seafood. Why don't I make something special—just for the two of us? Come next weekend."

Maelle spent Saturday afternoon preparing the ingredients for paella, bought a bottle of wine she knew Abby liked, fussed around the plants, spritzing them with water so they shone, plumped her cushions, opened the windows to freshen the air, and then closed them against the late fall chill. She streamed soothing music through the apartment, lowering it when Abby came to the door.

"Flowers—how beautiful. Thank you." Maelle buried her nose in the bouquet. A hostess gift? Unnecessary, especially since she dreaded the conversation they needed to have. Best to start on a neutral topic. She hunted for a vase, put it on the table, and cut the bottoms off the flower stems so the water could replenish them before gently arranging them.

"Tell me about the plans to change the shop, make it more modern."

Abby's eyes lit up. "I'll start slowly, bring in a few designer items. There are people who are actually making a leather-like fabric from mushrooms, can you imagine? And another leather from genetically engineered yeast. I'd like to get them into the store, but at the moment it's still experimental."

"Those cardigans JoJo gave me for you to put in the store are so pretty."

Abby gave an exasperated sigh.

Wrong topic. Shouldn't have brought that up. She pulled two glasses from a cabinet and poured wine into them, splashing a little.

"Well, other than JoJo getting older and not producing her jackets as quickly as you like, why change Woolley's image? Aren't natural, non-engineered products your trademark?"

"Until now. But it's not sustainable. Old methods of production are actually destroying the environment. People understand that now."

"That's a turnaround from how we were brought up, isn't it? How ironic."

"Each generation has its own take on the problems previous generations caused."

"Hmm." Maelle's mind wandered. Clothes and their manufacture did not hold her interest. She bustled around, busying herself.

"Nice wine, by the way," Abby said. "You and I, we're only fifteen years apart, but you'll probably dream up different solutions to mine."

"Oh, Abby! I need to talk to you about that."

"About what?"

Maelle hesitated, then leaned on the counter to face her aunt. "Mom. Your sister."

Abby raised her head sharply. "Why do you ask? Now, all of a sudden."

"Because everything about her has been shrouded in secrecy." Maelle straightened, turned away.

"You were a child, and everyone wanted to protect you."

"From what?" Maelle opened the refrigerator to retrieve a dish of marinated chicken and chopped onion. The smell lingered in her nose as she backed out and laid it on the counter next to the stove. She dived into the fridge again, bringing out chopped herbs and a little bowl of lemon zest, glad of the opportunity to avoid looking at Abby. Music murmured softly in the background.

"Looks good," Abby said. "What are we having?" She sounded subdued.

"Paella." Maelle rearranged the dishes. So Abby wasn't ready to tell her. She should try a more indirect tack. "It's seafood. But it also has chicken and chorizo sausage in it. I know you're not a vegetarian like Mom was." There! She'd said it, an opening for Abby to pick up on.

"Yes, she was. Do you remember that?"

"Absolutely! I always wanted to go to McDonald's like the other kids, and my mother wouldn't let me."

"Hah! I never even saw a fast-food place till I grew up!" Abby smiled. "Probably a good thing, in retrospect."

Maelle chopped garlic, shook some red pepper flakes from a jar, splashed olive oil in a big wide pan, heated it all, then poured in a cup of rice. "I had to halve the recipe, just for the two of us, but I hope it will be good. I'm not much of a cook."

"I'm sure it'll be delicious. Can I help?"

Abby came forward, and Maelle stepped aside, allowing her aunt to stir the rice expertly, and to add a few threads of saffron Maelle had bought especially for tonight, together with a bay leaf, chopped parsley, and lemon zest. A splash sounded through the kitchen as she covered it all with chicken stock.

"I don't remember if Mom ate fish. Was it that she wouldn't eat anything with eyes?"

"Could be. I don't exactly remember her reasoning. But Angie was pretty determined about the no-meat thing. No one else on the farm was a total vegetarian, though we rarely ate red meat. Too expensive. Isn't it funny how being vegan's much more popular now?"

"Yeah, but as a botanist, I see that argument going nowhere. Plants have senses too. Not nervous systems like animals, but a kind of intelligence. That's what I'm trying to prove in my work, anyway. The point being, everything eats everything else. It's life."

Abby laughed. "You and your trees! Let that cook gently for twenty minutes or so. Could I have another glass of wine?"

Maelle leapt to the bottle, glad of Abby's change of mood. She poured large top-ups for both of them and waved her aunt to the sofa.

Abby drank hers quickly, held out her glass for more. "Okay, get to the point, Maelle. What do you want to know?"

Maelle held her glass up to her face, observed Abby through it. The amber liquid distorted the shape of the bowl slightly. It seemed a metaphor for her memory of her mother. "What was going on with Mom when she died?"

"Why that particular question?"

"Because I just found out something strange was going on at Joyous Woods all those years ago. It's connected with what happened to my mother."

"How so?" Abby's lips tightened. She put her glass down on the coffee table.

"No one ever told me exactly what happened to her. Not even you, just now, when I brought it up. You're just asking me questions, not giving me answers." Maelle stood up abruptly.

"Don't be angry. I'm trying to help." Abby's voice sounded thick, and she stood up too, almost stumbling. "Angie died in an accident. She was a journalist, maybe on a story. No one knows. She was just at the wrong place at the wrong time." Tears welled in Abby's eyes. "She was so young. You were so young. Come here." She enveloped Maelle in her arms.

Maelle's face snuffled against the soft material of her aunt's dress, its damp wool smell infused with the scent of orange blossoms, Abby's signature perfume. How often had she snuggled like this against Abby's bosom, seeking comfort when her mother was in one of her strange moods. She breathed in deeply.

Abby's arms had engulfed her that morning fifteen years ago, when she'd been wakened early, the day her mother died. Inhaling Abby's scent now and resting against her shoulder, she remembered the soothing she'd received from Johanna and Neil, the love and the warmth, the safety of Joyous Woods, the farm, and the woods that received her sorrow and asked nothing of her but that she simply be. How that relief had differed from her mother's uneven care. Was that, possibly, why she'd held back crucial questions?

She drew away. "I always believed Mommy died in car accident, but that's not true, is it?"

"No." Abby's voice caught.

"What happened, then?"

"I don't know myself. Exactly." Abby moved away from Maelle and sat down again on the sofa. She picked up her glass again, sipped slowly.

"I keep asking you, why didn't anyone tell me?"

"Why now, Maelle? It's been years."

"Because of Zachary. What he said."

Abby's eyes widened, startled. "Zachary? That guy you're dating? What's he got to do with this?"

"His name is Zachary Kane. And I just found out it was his father who died when Mom did. David Kane. He was a doctor too." She took a deep breath, and another. "He used animals he bought from Joyous Woods for his horrible medical experiments."

Abby blanched. Her throat opened and closed as if she had difficulty swallowing. Then she leaned forward, her voice coming out in a croak. "Be careful, Maelle!"

"Why?"

"Why did Zachary say this? How does he know?"

"I took him up there to meet the family a couple of weeks ago. He said he'd been there before. Recognized it. Said Neil was raising rabbits secretly in a building in the woods to supply the research lab. Now he knows who I am, we're both going to look into the circumstances of the accident to see if we can make sense of it."

"What do you mean, now he knows who you are?"

"He says he was confused by my name—Maelle Woolley. Had no idea Angela Becker might be my mother. You can see why."

"Hmm." Abby crossed her ankles, stretched her feet. "How long has he known you were Neil Woolley's granddaughter and Angela's daughter?"

Maelle, still standing, gripped the edge of the table with one hand to support herself. She'd asked herself the same question when Zachary told her he'd gone to the farm as a kid. She'd wondered again, later, when he confessed he'd been obsessed about the accident that killed his father, had read everything he could find about the incident.

"JoJo didn't recognize him when we went up to the farm together. Nor did Neil. But that's because Zach was only about thirteen when he came to Joyous Woods with his father. Anyway, I don't think I introduced him as Zachary Kane, just told them his first name."

Abby kept her eyes on Maelle, sipping wine. "That really doesn't mean he didn't know who you were."

"You think he has an ulterior motive? I can't imagine what that would be." Maelle stumbled to the kitchen side of the island separating it from the dining area. She came back with a handful of silverware.

"Your words, not mine. But no. I'm not saying that. Give him the benefit of the doubt if you like. Even if he was stalking you in the beginning."

"Stalking me?" Maelle dropped the forks and knives on the table so hard they scattered across the surface. "What the hell are you talking about? Zachary loves me." She picked up each fork and placed it carefully. "He said so, anyway." Her voice dropped to a whisper.

Abby just sat, not saying a word.

"You're being very strange, Abby." Maelle set salt and pepper shakers on the table. "You don't know Zachary. Or at least you didn't say you did, even though we've been dating for weeks now." She whipped around to face Abby, anger stoking her voice. "I totally understand he'd want to know everything about his father's death, just like I want to know about my mom's. I told you, he didn't know I was Angela's daughter because we have different last names. How could he know we were connected just from reading newspaper accounts?"

"I can see you've thought this all through, Maelle."

"I guess I have. I was completely stunned when Zachary told me he'd been obsessed about his father's death, how distressed he was to learn—he believes—that my mother killed his father." Maelle paced up and down the narrow space between dining table and kitchen island. "Imagine how that shocked *me*."

"Or the other way around."

Maelle halted in midstride. "You better explain that."

"You tell me what Zachary told you." Abby took another gulp of wine.

"Zachary said his father was doing medical research using animals. I confirmed it. Asked Ray and Curtis and they told me."

"Uh huh." Abby's face contorted. "The Circle. It's true. They thought they could keep it from the women. Mother's feelings about her own rabbits were the main reason Neil and his cronies kept their operation secret. From Angie, too. She was so soft-hearted."

"Zachary said she broke into his father's lab to try to stop the experiments. Mom was a vegetarian. So she objected. I get that."

"Objected? A lot of people are vegetarians and live peaceful lives."

"Do you think my mother was fanatical about her beliefs?"

"She did have strong opinions."

"When we lived in a little apartment in Berkeley, Mom wrote stuff. Sometimes it seemed to make her angry. She even threw a cup across the room once, and it smashed."

"She did?"

"Yep. She was moody, Abby. You know that."

"True. She could be."

"What do *you* think happened? Maybe my mother was there for an interview, maybe she was applying for a night job looking after the animals."

"She wouldn't have wanted a night job. She had you to look after."

"Did she write about what David Kane was doing?"

"I don't know. I wasn't into reading her articles, any more than she asked me about the nitty-gritty of working in a store." Abby got up, looked toward the kitchen. "That smells good. Should I check the stove?"

"Sure. I'm a little distracted right now. Stir it or whatever." Maelle leaned against the island, hands gripping it, not looking at the dinner bubbling in its pan. "I guess I'll have to figure this out myself. But I want you to help me. You were closest to Mom, Abbs. You know what she thought, maybe even what she was working on when she died.

"I've been asking the same question Zachary did. What was my mother doing at a remote lab in the middle of the night? If she wanted to expose David Kane's work, she could have done that by writing about it."

Abby grabbed a spatula from a ceramic jar by the stove and slowly stirred the rice. "Yes, but how would she get material for it? You think if she just interviewed David he would tell her the nefarious goings on at the lab? If they were nefarious. I'm just speculating, you know. Medical experiments on animals have a long history. Not everyone thinks they're wrong." She put down the spatula. She tugged at the belt of her dress, looking at the buckle as she did so, so her face was hidden. "I better put on an apron. Do you have one?"

"In the drawer. Top right. You don't want to wreck that pretty dress."

"Okay, thanks." Protected from spills, Abby's voice calmed. "Let me put these chicken pieces in. Do you have another skillet?"

"In the lazy Susan. Here, I'll get it."

Aunt and niece stood side by side at the stove. Maelle heated more olive oil in the second pan and tipped into it the bowl of marinated chicken, stirring till it became slightly brown, then threw in sausage, red pepper, and parsley. Five minutes later, in went the shrimp, and she tossed it till it turned blush pink.

"Looks perfect," Abby said. "What say you?"

"I'd say it looks so good it needs my big, beautiful dish." Maelle reached above their heads to a wrought iron grille. Straining, she brought down a brightly glazed Italian platter. It was so heavy she avoided braining Abby only by stepping aside at the last minute.

"I must find a better place to store that," she said, placing it on the counter.

"It is crowded in here." Abby spooned the risotto onto the platter. "Are you and Zachary thinking of moving in together? If so"—Maelle detected something hard in her voice—"you'll need something bigger than this."

Maelle lifted the skillet of chicken, sausage, and shrimp and heaved it on top of the rice on the big plate. Her hands had trouble holding the heavy pan without trembling.

With surprising strength, Abby took the platter from her and set it on the table. "Although here it is Saturday night, and you're not together. Where is he?"

Maelle noted the dig, let it pass. "I think he's angry. Hard for us to be together after he told me my mother killed his father. Meanwhile, I'm trying to find out the truth. For my sake as well as his."

"Has it occurred to you that the opposite might be true?"

"What do you mean?"

"Let's sit." Abby pulled out a chair and poured more wine in both glasses She held out her plate to Maelle, who had the paella in front of her, playing hostess.

Maelle spooned a helping of the paella into Abby's plate. The head of a shrimp gleamed at her, its antennae still intact, its lower body shorn of its shell. It looked vulnerable, like a white shriveled penis amongst the remains of the chopped-up animals on the plate. She felt sick. Why had she not made Abby a simple salad or an omelet? She couldn't get over the picture in her head of her mother, deliberately targeting David Kane as an animal torturer, murdering him.

Before she even lifted her fork, Abby leaned across the table. Her face tightened. "Isn't it possible that David Kane might have killed her?"

Iced water slid through Maelle's veins. "What did you say?" she whispered.

"They did know each other, you know."

"Why? How did she know him?"

Abby's face went pink. "I knew him. It was through me that Angie met him."

Chapter Twenty Two

"What?" Maelle's eyes riveted on Abby's.

"I met David Kane when he came to Joyous Woods." Abby set her glass carefully on the table, as if she had to resist smashing it.

Maelle held her breath.

"A man came to visit the farm one day. I was outside and happened to greet him. He was tall and good-looking. He radiated that confidence professional men have. I think Neil might have been intimidated by him, thinking if he hadn't run away to the woods he might be as suave as this man. Anyway, they talked, they walked the property, then he left. I thought maybe he wanted to buy the farm, but not, as it turned out. He came back again, this man, again and again."

Abby had eaten nothing but a few pieces of french bread. Now she dabbed at the saucy rice with its end. She reached for the wine bottle and poured herself another glass.

Maelle pushed her plate away. The smell of the shrimp and the chorizo sausage together made her nauseous. She dabbed her lips with a napkin and brought its corner to her nose. She raised her eyes to Abby's and saw in them unconcealed guilt.

"To see me. David kept coming back to see me."

Maelle's mouth dropped open. "You had an affair with him? He was married."

"Yes. David Kane was my lover." Abby jutted her chin forward, eyes gleaming defiantly, then tipped her head back and drained her glass.

Maelle had been holding herself tense, hoping Abby would deny it. Delayed shock ran down her body. "He must have been much older than you!"

"So? When did that stop anyone? He was forty, I was about twenty."

"Abbs, how could you?"

Abby managed a wry smile. "You never heard of a married man involved with a young woman? Oh, I forgot, you're a botanist. Not used to human behavior."

Maelle winced. "Uncalled for. I'm stunned, that's all. Because I care about Zachary. How do you think this feels? His mother was being deceived by his father—and by you."

"Don't judge. Please. I was young. The commune had no concept of exclusivity."

"Zach. And his mother. I wonder how they felt about exclusivity." A stab hit Maelle's chest. Did Zachary know?

"Look," Abby said. "You've planned this lovely meal. I think we'd better eat some." Her voice turned wobbly. "I've drunk so much wine."

"I've lost my appetite. You go ahead." Maelle picked up her own glass and drank. "So how did it begin?"

Abby turned over bits of chorizo and chicken, picking.

"He was with Neil, discussing the rabbits. He was charming. He liked me, and I liked him. One day he cornered me in one of the sheds and kissed me. So it started. Our affair. Of course I didn't know he was married, at first."

She picked up another piece of baguette and stabbed it into the paella.

"Pretty soon, he asked me to come to live in Berkeley. Not with him, though, because he said I needed to keep my independence. But we kept on with our relationship."

"Did my mother know about this?"

"Of course I told Angie." Abby pushed back her hair with her hand. "Not at the beginning. Later."

"Why later?"

A shadow came over Abby's face. "Neil guessed. He told me not to tell Johanna or Sally or Linda. If they knew, they'd realize about the rabbit sales. I don't think he gave a thought as to what I'd tell my sister. I didn't want to tell her at first. I wanted to keep it—David, I mean—just for me. Special, you know?"

"But you and my mom were close, weren't you?"

"Very. She always looked after me. Protected me from the bullies at school, at the commune."

"Bullies at Joyous Woods?"

"You know how kids are, Maelle."

"I suppose."

But maybe not. Maelle had come to live at the commune when its children had grown and gone, everyone else edging into middle age and beyond. You wouldn't find any photos of kids with long tangled hair floating on inner tubes in the creek, sticking marshmallows into a campfire, or running naked through the woods if you looked into albums of her time at Joyous Woods. She'd been the only kid there. And at school, she'd never been bullied.

"When I moved to Berkeley, at first I lived with

Angela and you, Maelle. Do you remember? In that funky old house? I worked in retail, sewed at night because I learned that at home, and started modeling the clothes in the shop where I worked. It was an antique and gift shop, kind of charming the way the owner laid everything out. I got hooked on beautiful things and wanted them for myself. I knew I could do it. I had an eye. I knew how to turn junk into something that sparkled. I started making jewelry too and sold that as well.

"But I was more ambitious. I wanted to be a commercial success—all the things the commune disapproved of." She laid her knife and fork on the plate. "Then David told me I needed my own place. I couldn't afford Berkeley rents on my own, so he set me up in a little apartment. He helped me buy my own store, too, gave me the seed money for Woolley's."

"You mean you were a kept woman?" Maelle knew she sounded ridiculous.

Abby gave a sharp laugh. "You guessed? Yep. David didn't live in the apartment with me because he was married."

"Oh. Oh, Abby, I'm sorry. I can tell this did not end well."

"No. I am afraid it did not. But you don't know the half of it."

Maelle dabbed a piece of bread in the sauce, pushing aside the chorizo, chicken, and shrimp. "Are you going to tell me?"

Abby lowered her head. Sympathy flooded Maelle. She put her hand over Abby's, gently stroking it.

"It's complicated, Maelle. Our childhood, it was different. I was closer to Neil than to our mother. I'm

214

Abby Woolley! She was Angela Becker, Mother's favorite. Though Angie preferred Neil when she was little."

Not this again. For some reason, Abby really had it in for Johanna. Maelle rose and took the plates to the sink, scraped the remains of the dinner into the disposal, and ground it noisily. The crunch of chicken bones blocked Abby's voice. Breaking bones—a grim reminder of the topic at hand. Becoming a vegan wasn't such a bad idea, under the circumstances. She let the dishes soak and came back to the table, feeling slightly sick.

"How did Mom find out why David came to the farm in the first place? Did you tell her?"

"About the rabbits? I guess I couldn't keep it from her forever."

"And she got angry? I get that. She wanted to stop it. But why? She was a vegetarian, but our farm wasn't. She knew that. If she didn't like medical research on animals, why not just write an article to get her point across? I mean vegetarians don't usually creep into facilities at night to do damage." Maelle slumped back in her chair, shoving her feet forward, like a defiant teenager. "Anyway, if she confronted David Kane, it would ruin your relationship with him, wouldn't it? You were close, so why would she do that?"

"She might have had her reasons." Abby turned her head away, avoiding Maelle's gaze. "Maybe she just wanted to talk to him."

"And you're saying he attacked her, not the other way round?"

"I don't know. I still think it was an accident." Abby ran her hand down the wine bottle, as if seeking comfort in its round solidity. "You mustn't take Zachary's word for what happened. If you really want to know, we'll have to dig a little."

"You mean you'll help me?" Maelle sat straighter.

Silence. Abby frowned, then sighed. Furrowed her brow again, as if a battle was going on in her mind.

Finally, Abby said, "I can see you need me to. I've never seen you distressed like this."

Maelle came around the table to kiss her aunt's cheek. "Oh, Abby! It would mean a lot if you'd help." She sat down next to her and gripped her hand. "Here's what I really don't understand. If she knew, why didn't Mom try to stop this animal trade at its source? Confront Neil and tell him to stop selling his rabbits to someone who tormented them!"

"Maybe she did. She might have asked all of them in the Circle. I don't know. But you can see that from their point of view raising animals for slaughter was business as usual. Joyous Woods sold lots of animal products. It wasn't their primary business, but the farm always butchered hens too old for laying and sold the male kids, too.

"The rabbit house was hidden because Johanna had a sentimental attachment to the angoras. She wouldn't want them to suffer. You could say Neil was just sparing her feelings."

"Okay. So Mom could have left this rabbit trade alone. But she didn't. I still think she could have stopped it by becoming an advocate for animals. You know, through her writing."

Abby sighed. "Angela wouldn't get very far trying to expose our farm because that's what farms do—exploit animals one way or another for human consumption. It's hardly earth-shattering and certainly not newsworthy."

"So was she was an animal-rights activist? Or just someone who wanted to have a private word with David Kane? Make sense, Abby. You're not telling me everything."

Abby just stared ahead, her blue-green eyes expressionless. "I do know that Angie wasn't thinking all that clearly at the time. She was erratic. But yes, I think she hated what David was doing and wanted to stop him. I won't believe she meant for anyone to get killed."

Maelle heaved a great sigh. "If only there was a clue! Some writing about animal rights. Then we'd know what she thought about this. The county library has some articles she wrote, but not much and nothing about animals."

"The police did go through your apartment after the deaths. I assume they found nothing there."

"They went through our stuff?" Maelle's hands flew to her face, embarrassed to think strangers had combed through their messy home, upturning everything from the glass jelly jar of rubber bands kept on Angela's desk to the boots and coats jumbled in the hall closet, to her own treasure box, which she shoved under her bed every night so her mother wouldn't peek inside.

"Well, naturally. A fire in a remote laboratory. Two people killed. Of course it was suspicious. But the police didn't find anything in the apartment. Or nothing they told us about." Abby got up from the table. "I need a coffee to drive home. I'll get it. Want one?"

Maelle ignored her. "My treasure box," she

whispered. "I packed that up when JoJo and Neil came to get me to take me to the farm. I had a diary, Abby. Sometimes I'd read it, after Mom died. But it made me so sad I stopped. I wonder where it is now?"

"Did you leave it up at Joyous Woods when you went to college?"

"Oh no. I wouldn't do that. You know what happens to personal possessions up there. They don't believe in them. So I had to hide it there, too. I think I had it in the back of my suitcase, under my clothes. When I got too big for them, I wouldn't let JoJo throw out the clothes I wore the morning Mom died. I wouldn't let her cut them up and sew them into quilts, either.

"You know, I never went back to that apartment after that, and if I took the diary with me when I grew up and moved away, it must be right here, with those old clothes in that little suitcase."

She went into the bedroom and rummaged. Her closet bulged not with clothes, because she had little interest in those, but with boxes of old files, a suitcase on wheels, an old laptop. She hauled everything out and dumped it on the floor. At last, at the very back of the closet, she spotted a child-sized suitcase, the old-fashioned kind, with a handle. It seemed almost weightless as she lifted it and brought it back to the living room.

Abby had busied herself putting the plates in the dishwasher while she made coffee. "No luck?" she said, not turning around from the sink.

Maelle daren't hope that the contents of her luggage would provide the answer to the puzzle. That would be too easy. With a sigh, she placed the suitcase on the table and flicked open the fasteners, releasing a musty odor. She put her hands under a pair of child-sized jeans, a stained yellow sweater, underwear, and sneakers which still exuded a slight smell of sweat. She lifted everything out gently, felt the hard edges of a book at the very bottom. She brought it up from under a protective layer of socks, a lined composition book. The cover title, in capital letters in blue ink, spelled DAIRY. The handwriting was unrecognizable, childish, but Maelle knew it was her own.

"Looks like the moths haven't eaten through the pages. That's good."

"Hold off," Abby said. "Let's have coffee first. A fifteen-year-old diary can wait."

"Maybe for you. I need to see this." Maelle waved away the coffee and opened the shabby little book.

Scrawls in ten-year-old cursive spread across the page. About her classmates, mostly, about slights and triumphs. It went on for page after boring page. Who was this child? Adult Maelle could have been reading a document written by another person altogether. Over time, Maelle noticed, the handwriting improved. But here was something about her mother. She read aloud.

"Mom talked about far last night. I said how far. She said it was an akro something. That means a word made up from capitals, the beginning letters of the words in the name. She made a joke about it and said she was going to see far and it was going far. I don't get it but she laughed and laughed. She's weird sometimes. I think she's going into her crazy time."

Abby turned from the sink to face Maelle, a dishcloth in her hand lifted in midair in front of her, frozen. "Far. She means FAR. It stands for For Animal

Rights. That's an extremist organization. There's a branch here in Berkeley. They keep a fairly low profile. But we can find them, if you like, start the investigation there."

"Oh, Abby. Oh my God. Of course."

"Be warned, they're pretty extreme. If Angela was involved with them, it's not good, that's all I can say."

"But you'll come with me, won't you?" Maelle gripped the exercise book, held it in front of her. "You're the one who knew David Kane."

"And be tarred by association?"

"Oh, I don't know. Am I tarred by association with David Kane's son? People who make assumptions like that are not to be trusted. Anyway, they don't know we know the Kanes. We're related to the woman who was killed with him."

"They're fanatics."

That word again. Angela, political assassin. The unspoken words chilled her. Maelle closed the suitcase with a click, locking away the diary, noting the date of the entry her childish person had made. It was for the month before her mother died.

Chapter Twenty-Three

It took Maelle and Abby a while to find the FAR office, almost hidden on the second floor of a clapboard Victorian on Telegraph Avenue, sandwiched between a liquor store and an aromatherapy-massage salon. As they climbed creaky stairs and rang a bell, Maelle smiled. This serious-minded organization rented space between two businesses devoted to escapism.

Her amusement lasted for only a few seconds.

Footsteps clacked closer at the bell's ring, and a young woman with pink and purple hair opened the door. Scowling, she held a tattooed arm across it, blocking entry. A dusty window behind her shed weak light on a gray industrial carpet, a cluttered desk supporting an elderly computer monitor, bookshelves crammed with ring binders. Beyond the desk, a wall of black and white photos provided the room's only decoration. Peering beyond the barrier of the arm, Maelle gasped. The photos showed vivisected animals.

"Madison." The greeter's voice could not be colder. "What can I do for you?"

Maelle nudged her aunt, wordlessly appointing her spokesperson.

"I'm Abby, and this is my niece, Maelle. Could we come in and chat please? We're trying to get information on an incident about fifteen years ago that involved my sister, Angela Becker. She was Maelle's mother. We understand she may have been trying to free animals at a laboratory."

"Umm…That's a long time ago." The arm holding the door ajar dropped, implicitly inviting them in. Abby and Maelle stepped forward. Madison indicated two chairs in front of the desk and positioned herself in a chair behind it, swinging her legs onto the desktop. The move looked insolent.

Maelle ignored the shiver mounting her spine.

"You're right, it was a while ago. But we'd like to speak to one of your older staff members, please, someone who was there at the time."

"You trying to pin something on FAR?"

"Look, my sister was a journalist." Abby gripped the sides of her chair. "We believe she was trying to document some of the animal abuses that went on at that lab."

"What did you say your name was?" The girl looked at Abby with cold eyes.

"Tabitha Woolley. I go by Abby."

"Woolley!" The legs came off the desk. Madison twisted her body toward the visitors. "You're the one who runs the shop selling fur!"

"Not fur. Clothes. Some of which are made with angora fleeces, collected humanely from our own rabbits, yes."

"You know the sale of fur is banned in Berkeley." Madison slammed a fist on the desk, rattling a jam jar of pencils.

"Certainly. My store is located outside the Berkeley jurisdiction. As you must realize if you know the store."

"You're lucky we haven't picketed it!"

"Well, wouldn't that be great publicity for Woolley's! People who come to the store know how we raise our rabbits and harvest the fleece. Our rabbits are happy."

"Really? Pulling out rabbits' fur is not humane."

Protective fury sparked Maelle to respond. "No, not pulled. It's combed out. Like combing your own hair and getting out the tangles."

"Oh, yeah?" Madison ran a hand through her own jagged, multi-hued mop. She crooked her forefinger. "Come around to this side of the desk. I want to show you something."

Abby and Maelle got up warily, crossed the room, and bent to peer at the computer screen. Madison had switched on a video. Of rabbits. They bled and screamed as uniformed workers tore off their fur. The workers' faces were partly hidden behind masks.

"Look, see how these animals are tortured?" Madison said.

"That video is shot in China." Abby backed away. "Look at the hair and the eyes above the masks. We despise those cruel practices."

"That's what you say."

"If we're so vile, why would we come here to face you? We're opposed to hurting animals. As we told you, we're here to investigate what happened to our relative. Angela cared so much about rabbits she wanted to expose what went on in that lab. We think she was probably trying to save them. The thing is, we just don't know."

"And for the sake of closure, to use that cliché, we'd like to know," Maelle broke in. "She was my mother."

"Hmm."

Maelle tried another tack. "Do you have anything in your files—news clippings about the incident?"

"We have numerous clippings. FAR's always in the news." Madison's mouth curled in a smug smile.

"Well, I'm surprised you don't have more information on this. It's not every day that your volunteers get killed in the line of duty."

"Did you say killed?" Madison blinked, and gripped the edge of the desk.

"Yes. Killed in action, if you like. Maybe you're so used to that phrase applied to animals that you miss it when it comes to humans." Maelle's words caught in her throat. "The fact is that my mother died in this incident, along with the lab director, David Kane."

Madison swiveled her chair and turned away from her interrogators. "Collateral damage, you might say."

"I lost my mother when I was ten years old!" Tears spouted from Maelle's eyes. "How can you talk like that?"

"Did she actually succeed in freeing these animals?"

"No. Something went wrong. That's why we're asking you for help." Abby put her arm around Maelle's shoulders and held out a hand toward Madison, palm up. "Please. Can you put aside the politics? My sister was one of yours. Or one of your sympathizers. She put her life on the line for animals, and she lost it in the cause."

She moved closer to the desk, forced a smile. "Can't you help us find any actual details of that event? Was it FAR-sponsored or not? Maybe she acted on her own, maybe she was doing a story, or maybe it was about something else altogether. All we're asking is to be allowed to speak to someone from that era who might remember Angela Becker."

"All right." Madison picked up a pen, poised it over a scratch pad. "What date did you say this happened, again?"

Maelle told her. As if she'd ever forget.

The tattooed girl rose from her desk haughtily, went to a filing cabinet, and with her back turned to the visitors, hunted through drawers. She fished out a hanging file and pulled from it a manila folder.

"I'm only doing this because you say your relative was one of our supporters. And by the way, we're proud of what we've done to save animals. Look through this. Take a seat over there, and give it back when you're done."

With a singular lack of grace, she handed Abby the folder, then returned to her desk and slumped back in her chair. Abby and Maelle retreated to a couch near the door.

They sat close enough to read the file together, Abby's warm breath on Maelle's cheek. The documents listed actions FAR had undertaken in the months around Angela's death. A fund-raising drive, letters to the newspaper, but no clippings of an accident in an animal lab. No listing of organization members at the time.

Maelle's skin started to crawl. Raiding animal labs was what FAR prided itself on. Why no mention of the accident that killed Angela, if it was an accident?

Abby stood without warning, and the folder slid onto the floor, spilling papers. "I'm sure you have a list of volunteers and staff people?" she said.

Madison stifled a curse. "Sh—That's not public information!"

"But we're not the public!" Abby said. Her voice shook. "We have a personal interest. My sister died, probably trying to rescue animals. If she volunteered for a FAR operation, we deserve to know!"

"Now look here." Madison stared at her for a few moments, as if considering whether to answer. Finally, she turned to her computer and scrolled. Abby moved closer, trying to peer at the screen, but Madison angled herself away so no one else could see what she was reading.

"Nosy!" she muttered. She narrowed her eyes at Abby. "Lots of people hate FAR and what we do. How do I know you're not just spying on us?"

Maelle knelt on the floor and gathered the spilled papers. She shoved the useless information back into the folder. "Well, then, it's spies meeting spies, isn't it? Everyone knows FAR infiltrates groups to get information." She almost spat the words.

"How do you know that?" Madison focused a laser stare at Maelle, a glimpse of fear on her face.

Bingo! Maelle had only guessed that FAR used covert methods to find vivisectionists. It gave her an idea, half formed. She needed time to think.

"I think we'd better go," she said, rising. She dumped the manila folder on Madison's desk and took Abby's elbow, steering her to the door. "We'd hoped you'd be more cooperative and help us. So we'll come back when it's a better time."

"Hold on," said Madison, her green eyes glinting as she rubbed a hand through her spiky neon hair. "We keep records of who visits us. Names and addresses here, please."

Abby hesitated. Maelle nudged her, and Abby took a pen from Madison, wrote down their information, and shoved the paper back into the girl's hands.

They didn't speak as they tramped down the stairs. Once out of Madison's hearing, Abby squeezed Maelle's arm. "I just gave my work address. I don't trust those people."

Maelle inhaled gratefully as they exited the building. Outside the air felt fresh, a brisk wind bringing with it a smell of the sea. They found Abby's car and escaped their narrow parking bay, a cacophony of peak-hour traffic assaulting their ears as they inched into the middle lane. Abby accelerated, switched on the car radio to the news, and, if Maelle hadn't put her arm out to stop her, would have run a red light.

Chapter Twenty-Four

Maelle looked at her experiment, dispirited. She couldn't be sure that the plants weren't laughing at her pathetic efforts to break through their wall of otherness.

Beside her, the phone sang out its irritating jingle. Perhaps she should change the ring tone. Who knew what the plants thought about the one she'd chosen. She hit the button.

Abby's words tumbled over themselves, panicked. "Please, Maelle, can you come over? They're picketing the store!"

"What's happened?"

"A crowd's gathering outside. I saw them as I was coming in, and I tried to sneak around to the back entrance. A man stopped me. He recognized me. The other protesters started to chant, 'Murderer, Satan, hypocrite!' I'm scared, Maelle."

"It has to be FAR. It's only been three days since we went there."

"Yes. That young man has a sign that says 'Fur F's Sake.' "

"Shouldn't you call the police?"

"They'd probably tell me picketing is not a crime. Oh God, someone has a megaphone. They're standing on the street, shouting."

"All right, I'm coming. But I biked to work today, so it could take a while."

Breathless after her fifteen-minute ride to Woolley's, Maelle approached the back of the store and wheeled her bicycle inside for safety. As she entered, she could see the seething crowd through the store windows.

"Why are they doing this, Abby?" Maelle's breath came in short gasps. "I came as fast as I could. Oh, God, Abbs, are you all right? You look so pale."

A young man, his face ugly with rage, lifted a brush dripping with white paint and wrote an insult across the glass.

Abby pulled some tissue paper from under the counter, and Maelle helped her unfold it. Grabbing a black marker, trying not to tear the delicate paper in her agitation, Abby wrote, *I'm calling the police!* She held it up as she walked to the window to tape it up with the message facing out. She brandished her phone to the demonstrators and dialed a number as they watched.

At the back of the crowd, someone raised a pickaxe. Abby's eyes went wide with terror.

Just then a rock came through a window, knocking down a mannequin in a multi-colored jacket. Glass spilled over the floor. The mannequin's bald head thudded onto the floor and the rock nestled into the jacket's flattened shoulder.

The violent gesture changed the mood of the crowd. The jeers became quieter, and several picketers pointed to the sign saying the police had been called. Peeking, in turn, from behind the sales counter where they'd taken refuge, Abby and Maelle spotted some in the crowd turning on one another, arguing and shoving. A few started to sidle away.

Maelle stood up, cautiously. "Thank goodness

someone took the axe off that guy. You think it's over, now, Abbs?"

"Looks like they got it out of their system with the rock." When Abby laid her phone on the counter, Maelle saw it glistened with sweat.

The protestors were losing interest, drifting off. As a parting gesture, one young man taped a poster board sign to a parking meter in front of the building.

"Did you actually call the police?"

"Um, I was about to. I dialed but didn't actually press the button to connect. They stopped, though, didn't they?"

Maelle gave a half smile. Raised on the commune, she and Abby both had negative views of law enforcement. Memories of police raids on neighboring pot farms lay close to the surface, and neither needed to speak of them aloud.

"Whew." Abby sat down on a stool behind the counter and rested her head in her hands.

"Pretty scary, wouldn't you say? I thought they were going to come in through the window and rip our merchandise to threads."

"Who are these people?" Maelle walked around the headless mannequin, assessing the damage.

"It's our fault." Abby wiped her face with a sleeve. "We never should have gone to FAR looking for information. You know that video Madison showed us the other day? She must have sent these people on a mission."

"Yes, it can't be a coincidence."

"Look, could I have a glass of water, please? I feel a bit shaky. You'll find the glasses next to the mugs and electric kettle in the break room."

"I'll get it." Maelle made her way through the debris to a small room at the back of the store. She hunted through cabinets. "Do you have any turpentine in here? We'll have to get that graffiti off the windows."

"I don't have any. It might come off with a flat razor or a paint scraper. Maybe you could run to the hardware store later? I have to keep an eye on everything here."

Maelle returned to where Abby sat and handed her the glass of water. "They're crazy. Our animals, our angora rabbits, are treated well. Very well. They're part of the family. The goats, too. They're shorn in the late spring. It cools them off. The mohair JoJo spins is beautiful."

"Yes. But these people don't like it. Just as well I'm trying to get out of that business."

"Maybe you should tell them that."

"No, I'm going to steer clear. I was stupid to tell them who we are. We made a mistake going down to their offices the other day, telling them as much as we did. They're too scary."

"But if Mom was on their side, surely that should make them sympathetic to us?"

"Look, Maelle, they're extremists. Illogical. If Angie wanted to free animals, she probably wouldn't have acted alone. They're involved somehow in that incident. How could she know how to get into that lab unless she had inside information? Maybe they don't want anyone to look into an action that caused a death. They're trying to intimidate us to stay away from them."

Maelle's back stiffened. "They're the ones who

have made a strategic mistake. It makes me want to get down there and talk to that staff member."

"Are you nuts? Why would you agitate them further?"

"Because they must know something we don't. Because all I want to do is learn about why my mother got herself killed, accidentally or not." Maelle bit her lip, not wanting to agree out loud that the demonstration was a warning. "I'll go get the turps." Abby needed help in the moment.

But Abby, picking up toppled clothes, shaking them off, searching for a coat-hanger, brushed off bits of glass stuck to her jersey dress and stood straight.

She said, her eyes wide with surprised admiration, "If you think it will do any good, go ahead then. Tell FAR to stop picketing my store to punish me. And when you go out, please take that stupid sign off the parking meter."

****

Maelle rode her bike across town to the animal-rights organization's office on Telegraph. Anxiety about taking an afternoon off work made her pedal faster. This could not wait.

The shoddy building's door sprang open to her touch, and Maelle wondered why the organization was not worried about picketers. Their violent philosophy turned off more people than it attracted.

She trudged upstairs, pushed open an unlocked door, and found Madison hunched over her office computer.

"What's going on?" Maelle demanded. "Why are you attacking my aunt's store?"

Tattoo Girl didn't even look up. "She exploits

animals for her own gain."

"Please just stop. Call off the vigilantes; don't do this again. She's not exploiting them. The animals are not harmed. Our farm doesn't treat them like they do in that video from China."

The girl did look up now. "That's a lie! I know what you people do. I got to thinking after you left the other day and went through some of our old files. I found some articles on animal experimentation."

"Yes, Mom was working on that, I think, when she died. That's what motivated her to go to the medical research lab." She gripped the back of a chair in front of Madison's desk.

Hostility gave way to a smirk. "Do you have any idea where that lab got its animals?"

"Hmm." Bile rose in Maelle's throat. "Why would Angela Becker know anything about that?"

"Because she didn't have to look very far. They came from a farm north of here. A farm called Joyous Woods."

"How do you know?" Maelle let go of the chair back and clenched her fists by her sides.

"You know that farm?"

Maelle said nothing.

Madison continued. "That farm belonged to a family called Woolley. A man named Neil Woolley sold rabbits to the lab."

Maelle needed air. She gulped. "Well…" She exhaled. "Even if that's true, it has nothing to do with my aunt's store. Just a naming coincidence," she lied. "Don't go blaming Abby. She sells clothes made by her mother at home from natural materials. Including from the angora rabbits who are loved and cherished. Exactly like the goats who make the mohair she knits."

"You're disgusting." Madison's face knotted with rage. "I know who you are, and I don't understand why you're defending Woolley's. Your mother was trying to get the entire operation shut down. And you object?"

"What are you talking about?" Maelle could hardly speak.

"Rabbits hurt for their fur, rabbits hurt for their body parts. There's no difference."

"People use animals for all sorts of things. FAR members are fanatics. Most people don't agree with your point of view."

"So you disagree with your mother?"

"My mother is dead, and I don't understand exactly what she was trying to do."

"Is that so?"

"I was ten years old when she died. What child understands a parent's motivation?"

Dial it down, Maelle muttered inwardly. Madison doesn't look like much older than a child herself, an angry teenager. Keep calm.

She lowered her voice and took a friendlier tone. "Look, Madison, I'm asking for your help. You don't have to act so hostile. Please listen to me."

Madison slumped sulkily in her chair. She picked up a pencil from a jar on her desk and twirled it between her fingers. Maelle sat down opposite the girl and took a deep breath.

"If Neil Woolley did sell rabbits for medical research, it has nothing at all to do with my aunt's clothing store. My mother never objected to her sister's business. You're connecting the two things just because of the name. Please see sense."

"So why now? Why poke your nose into it, after all these years?"

"Asking about my mother isn't 'poking.' Not long ago, I saw some old photos of her. They made me so sad, and I need to put this to rest. I loved her, and she loved me."

"Don't you care about animals?"

"I do. But plants, too. I study plants. Everyone and everything eats plants. Why not object to that?"

"Because they don't have feelings."

"How do you know? I'm studying just that, actually. Research shows they do have senses, even if they don't have a brain."

"They do? What kind of senses?" The pencil stilled.

"They see, even if they don't have eyes. They must see light because they eat it. Their roots sense water and seek it, and in the forest all their roots are interconnected. Like the internet."

She had the girl's attention now. She pressed her point. "I've been able to show that one plant sensing danger can even warn another. There's no question they communicate."

"Wow." Madison's green eyes looked troubled. "Is that true? They look out for each other?"

Maelle smiled. Maybe she wouldn't be a terrible teacher after all, if she could ever get her doctorate.

Madison's gaze turned to a fading bunch of mums on the desk. Petals had dropped, the stems needed their water freshened. In an anxious voice, she said, "You mean plants feel pain? They hate it when we cut them?"

Whoa. That's a logical stretch. Maybe an explanation for Madison's attitude. Someone hurt her,

235

badly. Poor kid. An opportunity, though, to turn the conversation in a positive direction.

"I wouldn't go that far. In fact, plants are so clever they've evolved to spread their seed through being eaten by other creatures."

Madison sat back, eyes aglitter with interest and amazement.

"But we need to treat them with respect," Maelle said. "What I do know is that every creature on earth needs to be treated with respect. I agree with you there." Maelle reached out her hand. "May I have a copy of that article you've printed out? It would really help."

"I guess so." Madison spun around to the printer. The printout lay in the tray, as if FAR had anticipated this visit.

Maelle thanked her, took it, and paused at the door. "I hope the rest of your day is great, Madison," she said and left, her step light on the stairs.

On her way back to Woolley's, Maelle stopped at the hardware store to buy a can of turpentine, a razor, and some rags. It was quite a long ride back to Solano and Abby's store, and she had time to think. Madison's personality was so spiky, so defensive, she must have had some childhood trauma. Perhaps she was even jealous that Maelle so obviously cared for her mother.

The love of a child for its mother was universal, or should be. Come to think of it, Abby's recent remarks about Johanna were troubling. She'd said her childhood was complicated and unhappy. But for Maelle, Joyous Woods, unconventional as it was, had offered a haven.

There was more to this than met the eye. Something about the sisters' bond didn't add up. Abby had said that she and Angela were close. But Abby seemed fearful, somehow, about Angela's work. Did Angela know something Abby didn't? Or did Abby know something that she didn't want Angela to act on? Strange. It was almost as if Abby wanted to protect Maelle from the reality, whatever that might be.

****

Maelle returned to find Abby trying to scrub graffiti off the store windows. She'd changed into jeans and a T-shirt.

"I bought a scraper, hope it works. Let's not talk out here." Following Abby, she wheeled her bike inside again. After she dumped her backpack by the cash register, she reached in to retrieve her purchase. "Sorry to take so long. I've been to see Madison at FAR."

"Brave you. What did she say? Did she set this mob on us?"

"Wouldn't say." Maelle unwrapped the scraper's packaging. "She's convinced that selling clothes made from animal fur equals vivisection. Party line all the way. And she says she's found articles exposing David Kane's work."

"Angie published articles about David?"

"Just drafts, no byline. I don't know who actually wrote them. Madison gave me a copy of one."

"Let me see." Abby thrust a hand out impatiently.

"In my backpack." She leaned down. "Hang on."

The instant Maelle brought out the copy, Abby grabbed it, skimmed it, and handed it back, exasperated. "The usual diatribe. It's wrong to test cosmetics on animals. There I agree. And humans shouldn't use other species to test cures for disease. Nothing earth-shaking here."

"She knows more. Madison said Joyous Woods supplied the animals to David Kane's lab."

"That's not in the article."

"No, it's not. Listen, though, Abbs. I may have made a little progress with her."

"Let's take a break." Abby shoved a rag into a bucket and took it to a sink in the back of the store. She returned with two cans of orange soda she'd retrieved from a small fridge.

Maelle pulled two stools forward next to the sales counter, and they sat and sipped in silence. The icy soda prickled, and every swallow brought her fresh energy. But Abby just stared into space. Maelle played for time, telling her about Madison's friendlier attitude, asking about insurance, about how many days Woolley's would have to be closed, and if the store should respond to the violence by a letter to the newspaper.

Abby nixed the last idea vehemently. "The less press the better," she said. "Why call attention to what happened?"

"Well, will you still change the focus of the store as planned?"

"Sure, but it'll take time. I don't have much money set aside to cover an event like this. The sooner insurance gets here the better. Meanwhile, I'll just keep on with business as usual and implement the new plan on the schedule I set up."

"JoJo's devastated she won't be able to sell to you."

"I know!" Abby crushed her soda can and tossed it into a wastebasket. "I can't deal with her feelings right now. This is my own crisis, right here, and I have to fix it."

Maelle threw her own can after the other, picked up a broom, and started sweeping splinters of glass and debris. A mannequin, still standing, dripped egg yolk down its dress, bits of shell stuck to the yellow mess. Gazing at it, Maelle identified with the plastic model. Her whole being had been stripped of protection. The humiliation of it. She'd been duped for so long.

Now Abby was in crisis, too, her visit to FAR had provided more questions than answers, and she had not dealt with her own crisis with Zachary. She must get to the truth, no matter what.

She stopped sweeping, stood straight with her hand on her hip. "Abbs, I think there's something you're not telling me."

"Why do you say that?" Abby stood and stretched, arching her back.

"If you loved David, you must have been devastated when he died."

"I did, and I was. And my sister died, too, don't forget."

"At the same place, same time. "

"Yes."

"What do you think that means?"

"Maybe she wanted to confront David about giving me the short end of the stick. But if I go down that route, I'm so conflicted and feel so guilty. I don't want to believe she put herself in danger for me."

"But why was it a dangerous situation? And why on your account? Why would she interfere in your affair? Abby, wasn't it about the animals?"

"Angie and I were always so close, we looked after each other. She always protected me. At school. On the farm."

Abby passed a hand over her pale face. She reached for a tissue sitting in a box on the counter. She dabbed her eyes, the edge of the tissue drawing attention to the age lines etched on her face.

Compassion flooded Maelle. She dropped the broom and circled Abby with her arms. Abby's body sagged, and her bony ribs jutted into Maelle's own.

"I'm sorry, Abby. I've been so focused on myself, on becoming an orphan that night. But you lost your sister and your lover. A double loss."

"It was more than that, Maelle." Abby's voice sounded strangled.

"Then whatever it is, you have to tell me. Can we sit more comfortably? Let's leave this mess for a bit."

Maelle led her aunt out of the chaos of the shop and into the back room, which held a small refrigerator and a table and two chairs. She coaxed Abby into one of the chairs and searched the refrigerator for a sustaining snack. It didn't hold much, but she found a chocolate bar and a half-eaten tub of cottage cheese with a white plastic spoon. She placed the pathetic offering before her aunt, mimed eating, and poured two plastic cups of water.

Head down, Abby rubbed her arms over and over, as if assuaging a deep bruise. The food sat untouched.

"All right." She looked up, lips pursed. She drew a long breath. "Let's try and understand Angela's motivation. I said she wanted to protect me, but maybe that's a bit self-absorbed. Maybe I had nothing to do with it. On the other hand, Angie was my big sister and I always looked up to her."

"Go on."

"Let's assume she wanted to stop the animal

experiments, believed what David was doing to the rabbits was evil. Even though she grew up on a farm and looked after the rabbits we bred for their fur. Even though she knew what goes on in a farm isn't always pretty. That the whole purpose of a dairy operation, or a rabbit fur operation, is for humans to use animals for profit. That's what farms do."

"She wouldn't object to selling the rabbits for medical research?"

"Oh, I think she did. But to the extent she'd risk her life? If so, then you could say I caused her death! You could say I encouraged David from the very beginning because he kept coming up to the farm for the rabbits—and for me."

Maelle had to contain her shock. Her cool, collected aunt had harbored guilt all these years. "You can't blame yourself, Abby. Mom could have asked Neil to stop selling the rabbits. Maybe she did, and he didn't."

"Possibly. And she got so frustrated that she tried to get help. From like-minded people."

"So…you're saying that FAR does have something to do with it. That Mom became involved with them, and they pushed her to do something radical."

"Well, if they knew our farm supplied the rabbits, then Angie must have told them."

"That seems so disloyal. I can't believe my mother would do that." She got up, filled the kettle with water, and plugged it in. "Tea?"

"Okay." Abby took a bite of the stale chocolate and made a face. "You may be right about going to the press. I could draft a statement about Woolley's new direction."

Maelle set out two plain white mugs and placed teabags in them. The kettle gurgled to a boil.

Abby spat the chocolate into a paper napkin and crushed that into a ball. "I definitely need to get away from selling those handmade clothes—it's time the whole hippie experiment folded."

Maelle pursed her lips. "I see it now. You're on Neil's side, aren't you? Let the developers have this land, give up all the ideals we were brought up with."

"I was brought up with. You escaped."

"A generation removed. But not escaped. I didn't want to escape. I loved Joyous Woods."

"You're not going to like this." Abby's voice turned harsh.

Maelle waited.

"You said it was disloyal to tell FAR about the rabbit scheme. Maybe Angie had her reasons. I told you she protected me." Abby looked at her hands, avoiding Maelle's eyes. "Go on, pour. I need the caffeine."

"So you said. You want to tell me why, don't you, Abby?"

Steam rose from the mugs as water hit the teabags.

"It's because, when we were kids, our parents didn't."

"Didn't what?"

"Protect us."

"You all lived together in love and harmony, I thought. That was the message anyway."

"It's total bullshit."

"Huh?"

"Well, I'll tell you. Johanna, your grandmother, she's all lovey-dovey now. So warm and loving, right?"

"Always. So kind."

"Well, she let us go when we were kids."

"What do you mean?"

"They had this theory. Or Neil did, or some of the others. That exclusive love was wrong. People shouldn't form exclusive attachments."

"You mean, free love?"

"Right. But the worst of it was, they had this idea that parents should not be exclusive in their love for their children."

"Meaning what, exactly?"

"It screwed us up. We kids lived in a dormitory. Under the supervision of a baby-nurse called Melody. She's long gone, of course."

"You saw your parents, didn't you?"

Abby rapped her fingers on the table, tap, tap, tap. "Up to a point. It was like living in an orphanage, except our parents lived close by. You weren't allowed to run to them when you fell and cut your knee, or when another kid bullied you."

"How awful!"

"There's more. I'm telling this sort of backward. Before that, when Angie and I were little, lots of people lived on the commune. They lived in yurts, converted chicken coops, sheds. People built shacks all over the place. The only rule was you had to build it yourself, out of sight of the other houses. The idea was to allow each family enough land for a little vegetable plot to feed themselves."

"Sounds cool. A collective."

"Yeah, well, sounds idealistic. The thing was, they couldn't feed themselves. Some were lazy, most were incompetent. Mother was the one who figured out when and what to plant and harvest. Your grandmother's really into work, as you know."

"The men weren't?"

"Not in the same way. A lot of the guys who came to live at the commune didn't really cut it. Stoned much of the time, didn't do much work. Came for the girls, that free love thing, with the predictable consequence. Quite a few babies were born to our cohort, as I think the psychologists call it."

"Cohort." Maelle spooned teabags out of both mugs and set them on a plate.

"It means people born about the same time. Anyway, with all the partner sharing, sometimes the kids didn't really know who their fathers were. Sometimes they didn't know who their real mothers were."

"Didn't know their mothers? You're kidding."

"I am not. But while all this went on, the grown-ups discovered that in order to survive, they actually had to make Joyous Woods a productive farm, and all hands were needed on deck."

"So how did it work? I thought you said some of the people who came to live at Joyous Woods loafed about."

"Hah! You got it. A conundrum. How to feed everybody and yet let everybody live out their dreams. So they came up with a plan. Or Mom did. Childcare."

Maelle nodded. "Sounds sensible. I can see you'd need that."

Abby looked at her with disdain. "You have no idea. They decided to bring up all the babies and toddlers and the little kids in a special house, away from their parents. That way the parents could work full time."

"A special house?" The mug stopped, halfway to Maelle's mouth. "I think I may have come across this house at the farm years ago. Johanna wouldn't talk about it."

Abby rolled her eyes. "Hah! So they appointed Melody as a chief nurse and gave her a couple of assistants—they weren't more than teenagers themselves. When a baby was born, it was sent over to the Children's House and settled in a row of baby cribs. The caretakers were overwhelmed and couldn't attend to so many babies at once. The mothers were only allowed to come in at set times of the day to nurse the babies, otherwise it got too chaotic, I'm told."

"You don't remember?"

"I don't remember being a baby. But Angie was about three at the time, and she remembered being made to go live in the Children's House and she hated it. Hated being away from our mother. See, Melody could give us only minimal attention. The assistants had no experience of babies or toddlers. They got bored, couldn't take the day-in, day-out care. The commune attracted people who wanted to escape responsibility, or at least wanted to avoid growing up. It's not that they were abusive. Not really, anyway. Oh, a little slapping here and there. Nothing serious."

"Sounds terrible." Maelle brought her hands to her cheeks.

"You always had someone to play with. But there was no one to kiss you, to comfort you. And the older kids could be bullies."

"Did they bully you?"

Abby warmed both hands on her mug. "Angela protected me as much as she could. After we got to a certain age, we went to the bigger kids' house. In there, it was like *Lord of the Flies*. No overnight supervision."

"What if you had a nightmare?"

"Cried on your own. That wasn't the worst of it, either."

"Why?"

"Because the bullies got rougher and made the gentler ones feel they deserved the bullying."

Maelle stared at her aunt, horrified.

"That's what got Angela and me into trouble, later."

"What?"

Abby took a sip of tea. "This tea helps. Thank you."

Maelle stood up, afraid her stomach would rebel. "I know what you're going to say. Some of the boys got into bed with the girls, forced them."

"Angela tried to reason with them. But the whole atmosphere of the place encouraged that kind of experimentation. Interfering was considered bourgeois. Sexual experimentation—it was supposed to be healthy and normal."

"At nine and ten years old, is that what you're saying?"

"I am. Saying that. And no one stopped it. Angie tried, she tried!"

Maelle wanted to vomit, held it in. "Where are those kids now?"

"Over time, their parents got disillusioned. Either with the ethos or the hard work and the poverty. They left. Which made it easier in a way. With fewer kids, we got more attention. But our parents didn't want to know. Angie tried to tell Mom what was happening, and she just wouldn't listen."

Abby pushed her mug aside. "So she became a teenager, and eventually some passer-through got her pregnant, and you were born. You were so sweet and fragile, I think it shocked our parents and the other adults. They realized what they'd put their own babies through. And Angie never let you out of her sight. She was a good mother, Maelle."

"Oh." Words like honey. "Thank you for saying that. I remember her being a good mommy to me, most of the time."

"But what happened to me, in the Children's House, with the bigger boys just telling the little girls they had to put out—that damaged me, Maelle. It made me think I deserved it, that I had no power over my own body. That I had no power to resist. It made me weak, weak as dishwater!" Tears pooled in Abby's eyes.

Maelle stroked the back of her head, smoothing her hair. "You're anything but weak, Abby."

"No. I am. I am. Or I was. I thought anyone had a right to do anything to me."

"That's all in the past. It really is all over. No one's going to hurt you, now, Abby."

Abby took her niece's hand gently away from the top of her hair, kissed it, and pushed away from the little table.

"I wish. But it left scars, Maelle, invisible scars." She stood and straightened her cardigan over her T-shirt, now smeared with dirt. "This trashing by FAR has been a shock. Brought it all back. Like I deserve…" Abby swept her hand over the trash on the table, threw it out, and rinsed the mugs. "Thanks for all your help today. Don't know what I would have done without you. But right now, I need a hot bath."

"We could talk tomorrow?" Maelle couldn't think of another way to be supportive.

"Maybe. But maybe not. Let's not talk about what happened up at Joyous Woods any more. I'm over it. Let it be our little secret, Maelle, okay?"

Chapter Twenty-Five

Maelle pedaled away from her conversation with Abby feeling grubby. Sweat clung to her jeans, her shirt, even her boots. Back home she ran a shower, soaping every particle of dirt off her body and hair. Yet toweled off and dry, eating a bowl of cereal and a few slices of toast at the counter of her apartment, a typical dinner for her, she still felt soiled.

The picture of a little girl, helpless as big boys climbed into her bed and made her do things that were far too advanced for her tender years, made her want to cry. Worse, they conflicted with Maelle's image of her grandmother. JoJo had allowed this! For love of Neil, or for love of her lifestyle, she'd allowed her own children to become neglected. Stupid, stupid, stupid.

Yet with her, Johanna had always been so kind. She had nothing but tender memories of her JoJo. Neil too. Her earliest memories.

Only when Maelle was five did Angela move them both to an apartment in Berkeley, so Maelle could go to school. Her mother must have wanted to protect her own daughter from what had happened to her.

She remembered how distressed Johanna had been about the move. Angela had become angry, too, shouted at her mother, and bundled a frightened Maelle into the car and sped off. They lived in an old wooden apartment with a yard so small you'd break a window throwing a ball. But Maelle had liked the views of the city on a clear day—tall buildings stretching to the sky over the Bay's blue water, and the bright orange bridge leading to Marin where, at Point Reyes, you could see the green fields and the sea, and it reminded her of the farm.

At first it was lonely without the others—Ray and Linda and Kevin, Curtis and Sally, and a few other members still living at Joyous Woods. Angela let Maelle sleep in her bed every night, curled up in her mother's protective arms. Later, she had her own room with a bed with a green patterned coverlet and her stuffed animals lined up on the pillow. The apartment had a "bonus room" with a window overlooking a small garden. At first, Maelle had used this as a playroom, till Abby began to visit. They'd moved Maelle's toys to a corner and installed a day bed. That was a couch, her mother explained, which turned into a bed at night. "So," she said, "there's room for everyone."

Who was everyone? Not her grandparents, who rarely came. Angela had not encouraged visitors. She worked on her writing and needed space and privacy above all.

Angela bought an old wooden desk, placed it in the big open living area, and typed away at all hours. A computer monitor took up the left side, and on the right, piles of papers and books and manuscripts. Often her mother took her camera with her when she went out (Abby did a lot of babysitting), and when she came home, she slid it into the right-hand bottom drawer of the desk.

Later on, though, people started coming to the apartment for meetings. Her mom said they reminded her of the ones at Joyous Woods, when people talked all at once. They brought casseroles and bags of potato chips and beer. They laughed and shouted, and sometimes her mother shushed them and talked to them in low tones. Maelle never wanted to go to bed in the middle of the festivities, but her mother bribed her with an extra helping of ice cream. If she was too busy with her guests, she'd forget to remind Maelle to brush her teeth.

In bed, through her half-closed door, Maelle could hear the meeting's buzz. One time she peeked to see what her mother used to call "a show of hands." Arms shot into the air and then lowered. That meant a vote—Maelle's teacher had explained what voting was. You could do it with your hands, or you could do it by writing on slips of paper.

Now she wondered, chomping on a piece of toast, what they'd been voting on. She tried to remember the people's faces. If she could remember the name of just one person at these meetings, then she and Abby might have a clue what they were about.

Could they have been meetings of FAR? Not impossible. The question was motivation. Maelle picked at a crust, crumbling it to bits. Was Angela as fanatical as the others who lived by FAR's beliefs? Was she cunning, or was she crazy?

Maelle sat there, ruminating. Maybe she was neither. Was it possible her mother wanted to punish her parents for what they'd allowed to happen to their children? Stop a source of the commune's livelihood and call it by another name. Principle. Had Angela acted out of principle, a belief that animals' lives were as precious as those of human beings?

It should not be surprising. Growing up at Joyous Woods, among people who'd given up a comfortable life for the sake of a principle, the hatred of war, her mother had only behaved as she'd been taught.

But there was something she'd apparently not anticipated. Someone had suffered the consequences, and that had been her only child.

Even though Maelle knew that her family—all the people of Joyous Woods—did love her, her mother's love meant the most. And now she was gone.

Her mother could have exposed David Kane's operation by writing an article. She chose another way and died. So the fundamental question was, what was so important that her mother needed to meet David Kane secretly and at night? Why was it so important? And who, if it was FAR, had led her on?

She'd read somewhere that deep quiet helped hidden memories surface. She'd try it. She cleaned her dishes, to clear her mind. She lay on the sofa with a pen in her hand and her notebook resting by her right side. After several long breaths, in and out, she relaxed.

Voices, coffee, and the yeasty smell of beer flooded her memory. The crunch of taco chips and a tub of guacamole resting on the table, its light, bright lime green harmonizing with the brown wood and the deeper green of the rug below the table. Her mother must really have liked the color green.

A woman with coppery, shoulder-length hair dug a chip into the guacamole and brought it to her mouth. Someone said something which made her laugh. The woman sputtered and covered her mouth with her hand. Suddenly she started squirming, kicking, her face turned bright pink, her eyes bulged and went panicky.

A young man in a check shirt and lanky ponytail banged her on the back. He said, "All right, Rebecca?" and a green mess of guacamole came out of the woman's mouth and onto a paper napkin someone had thrust at her. She looked embarrassed and ran to the bathroom.

Rebecca. A woman named Rebecca had been in that apartment that evening. She'd choked on a taco chip but had recovered.

Now, if she could only find a photo of Rebecca to link her memory to facts. If she and Abby could get back to that office on Telegraph Avenue to talk to Madison again, they could discover if a Rebecca was a FAR volunteer at time Angela died. If they found Rebecca, then she might tell them what had happened that night and, what exactly, David Kane was doing to the animals in his care.

Chapter Twenty-Six

"We're almost done here," Pamela said.

Johanna, sitting bolt upright on a chair in the pagoda house's great room, relaxed.

"I just have a few more questions. From my research, I've seen that not one of the early communes survived to the second generation. It's not like you were a religious cult. But you did have some ideas you believed in. Ideas you were willing to give up almost everything for. Yet you were like the other communes—after a while, people left. What happened?" Pamela surveyed her listeners with apparent empathy.

Sally raised her hand. "Maybe the material forces around us were too strong to fight against."

"Think about it." Neil smiled at their questioner. "We were just a tiny group. We had the whole government against us! The Man! The CIA, the FBI, the banks, agri-business, the whole military-industrial complex."

"So you were a brave little countercultural outpost, fighting for your spiritual values?"

He grinned, enjoying the limelight. "Centuries ago, religions or cults that pulled away from society formed when people could isolate themselves completely. I doubt groups like ours could survive today—there's too much communication with the outside world."

He paused for effect. "But spiritual! That's a stretch. Give me a little dope though, a little trip, and I'll talk spiritual." He laughed. "No. We made a stand back there in the seventies, and then we didn't want to come back. Things were hard in some ways, but they were good, too."

Johanna leaned in front of the camera. "As you've seen here, we made a successful organic farming business."

Pamela consulted her notes. "So, what we've got here is a story of men who had the bad luck to be drafted but got a lucky out because you could all go and live on this beautiful piece of land. Brought your women with you. You had some wacky countercultural ideas, but actually you turned this wilderness into a thriving farm. I have to hand it to you. The organic food thing was an idea waiting to be reinvented."

Johanna let out a sigh. She must have misjudged Pamela. Seems she was finally getting it.

Curtis inclined his head toward Johanna. "We wouldn't have been able to do that, except for Jo here. She was the one who got us reading about it, who researched old ways of doing things. New ways too."

"I don't doubt for a minute," Pamela said, "that all of you worked hard, especially you men."

The Circle—Neil, Curtis, and Ray—beamed. Irritation itched Johanna's arms.

"But before organic food became more mainstream, how did you support yourselves, exactly?"

"Ma'am…" Curtis waved the roll-up he was passing around. "Can I tempt you with some really excellent weed? Home grown. Organic. The finest quality." He stretched his feet out in front of him, relaxing. He wiggled his toes so they looked like little puppets under his socks.

"All the hippies grew weed. Some got really rich. In the early years, it kept us fed. We camouflaged our profits by sinking them into the farm, bought the goats and built the dairy. Here's the irony—now that marijuana's legal, the profit margin's shrunk. If the government had figured that out forty years ago, the pot business would be just another way for farmers to lose their shirts."

"Another example of our great government keeping their eye on the wrong ball." Neil put his hands behind his head and stuck his feet out in front of him, imitating Curtis.

"You're saying, then, that you were not a typical commune. You planned to succeed."

"There's nothing typical about any of this, or any of us. We just tried to live a different life," Neil said.

"Creativity is as important as putting bread on the table," Sally added. "Look, Curtis is actually quite well known as an artist. He shows in galleries. I do my pottery. Linda's made a name for herself as an artisan cheese-maker. And Jo here makes beautiful clothing."

"I can see that. Any advice for future generations?" Pamela trained the camera once again on Neil's craggy face.

He smiled and looked a little abashed. "If you're going to be creative, maybe don't choose poetry as a profession."

"I didn't realize you wrote poetry."

"Songs, really. Had a few gigs with a band earlier on. Dried up years ago. I put my energies into leading this group."

Johanna put her hand to her mouth, resisting a snort of laughter. She went into the kitchen and started rummaging.

Linda beamed at Neil. "You made some lovely pieces of furniture. See, Pamela, this wood table we're sitting at? Neil made that. Chairs and beds, too. He's quite talented."

"Self-taught. Rustic chic, if you like." Neil grunted. "Lost the touch lately."

"Which brings me to the obvious question." Pamela directed the cameraman to take a shot of the group together. "You're all getting on in years. Like all of us," she added quickly. "Neil, now your parents have died, will you sell your share of this land?"

His face registered surprise. "How did you know about that?"

"Oh, a little bird told me." Pamela lowered her head.

Ray blushed. Curtis looked irritated. The others looked at their hands.

"Hasn't been decided yet. It's between my brother and sister and me. I'll let you know." Neil rose stiffly, caressed a knee with a calloused hand.

"Oh, sit down, Neil." Pamela patted the chair next to hers. "I understand it's painful, knowing you're reaching the end of the road. Goes back to my point about communes being unable to survive till the next generation. Farming's hard work, however you do it. And without a real family to be loyal to, you can't expect the next generation to stay on without the promise of land ownership."

A shocked silence settled on the room as Pamela's curt summation sank in.

"So tell me about the children." Pamela's voice purred.

Johanna, who'd come back into the room, stiffened, sensing there was a trick question coming. Sally's gaze met hers. "You explain, Sal," she said. "I'm starting a cake." She headed back to the kitchen.

Pamela asked, "Do you have any of the children's school reports?"

Sally took a breath. "Reports? Why is that your business?"

"It would help me get a fuller picture."

Sally shot a murderous look at Pamela. "Sorry, that's a no. Our children are adults now. You can't go poking into their personal business. You're interviewing us, but we can't give you confidential information on other people."

"I didn't realize you and Curtis had children. I mean, I know about Johanna and Neil's, and Kevin, but yours, where are they?"

"My children? Two sons." Her voice became wary. "All the commune children except Kev moved away, normal life process. Most kids don't come back after college, though some visit from time to time."

"But the children did actually go to school?"

For once, toking up hadn't mellowed Curtis out. "Our kids went to middle and high school. Got brainwashed there about capitalism being the best system, American exceptionalism, all that neo-colonialist garbage. We countered it here."

Neil, who had sat down as Pamela commanded, went on. "When we started out, we never thought about children. Then a couple brought two little kids. We saw the world didn't stop when kids were around. Anyway, the women here started to get pregnant—it was like someone put something in the water, it was that sudden."

"Then, the thing was, we still had to work the farm, so we came up with the plan of the Children's House." Sally tapped a foot on the floor.

"The Children's House? Sounds like it could be fun for the kids." Pamela turned pages in her notebook, hunting for something.

"Johanna's idea, that one." Neil glanced over the half wall to the kitchen, where Johanna was cracking eggs into a bowl on the worktable. "See, she's a great reader. Original thinker. She'd been reading about the kibbutz experiment in Israel. Being German, she's obsessed about how the Jewish people survived, what they did after the war. So she read books about how those displaced people founded farms in the desert. It was such hard work, and they made it succeed by working as a community in a kibbutz, they called it—everybody sharing everything."

Sally interrupted. "Get to the point, Neil. We had to work so hard to survive, we needed child care from infancy. So Johanna set it up. Worked well. Everybody happy." She bent to tie a shoelace.

"Hmm." Pamela frowned. "That sounds very different from your normal commune. I've seen films and read books about kids wandering around picking daisies, one big party all the time, that kind of thing."

"Not." Johanna's firm voice sounded from the kitchen. She marched into the center of the room, folding floured hands in a dishtowel. "Pamela, we're an intentional community. We decided to make a farm to support ourselves. We did what we had to do to live the life we wanted. Which was nonconsumerist and nonconformist."

Pamela tilted her head. "What do you think was the psychological effect of this unconventional life on the kids?"

Johanna turned her back and stomped back into the kitchen, abandoning the others to Pamela's interrogation.

Sally shot daggers at her retreating back. "As I said, my own children aren't here now to ask. But there's Abby, Neil and Johanna's daughter. She at least honors our way of life. She stocks the clothes Johanna makes in her store."

A crash sounded from the kitchen. Then the tinkle of broken glass being brushed up and tossed into a trash can.

"So it wasn't a nuclear-family type of thing up here. I get that." Pamela motioned for another close-up of Neil's face. "But if there was sexual sharing, how do you know whose child she really is?"

Neil picked up his guitar from its spot by his chair. He looked exasperated. "Oh, not that again, Pamela!" He started to strum. "We did believe in sexual freedom. Still do. We shared partners, it's true. Everybody lived together, did everything together."

"I still raise the question," Pamela persisted. "I meant, when they were little. That Children's House. I know it takes a village, as they say. But these kids were kept separate from the adults. I remember now, you showed me the dorm. How did you know whose kid was whose?"

"Of course we knew our own babies. Don't be ridiculous!" Sally stamped her foot.

The others in the room shifted in their seats. Neil started picking out tunes on his guitar.

Johanna, listening as she mixed batter for a cake, couldn't tell if he were bored or uncomfortable with the questions.

"I'm not talking about your commune specifically," Pamela said. "I understand this group child-raising went on in other communes, too, and I've heard that the kids grew up very confused about who their real parents were."

Sally got to her feet, hands on hips. "That's only if you think that people should grow up in the tiny little nuclear family of mother, father, and two kids. Didn't happen throughout most of human history. But people knew their parentage." She stalked off and joined Johanna in the kitchen.

"Yeah, you could talk to Abby, my daughter," Neil said, half-heartedly. "Here, take her number."

Johanna, listening as she plunged a wooden spoon into a bowl, rocked back on her heels. She was so out of date, this woman with her negative assumptions about the hippies. The thing was, they had all moved on from those early years and those mistaken ideas. Bringing up kids communally was one of them, probably. Though the Israeli kids seemed to have survived. Her kids too. Well, Angela had been a problem, and then she'd died. But that was entirely unconnected with this Children's House business.

"Let it go, Jo." Sally read her mind.

"I can't." She lowered her voice. "She's poison, snaking her way into our lives, asking nosy questions. Judging us."

Johanna had beaten the eggs with the sugar into

such a froth it threatened to spill over the sides of the bowl. She had to hunt for another, larger one, to mix in the flour, baking powder, and soda. Automatically, she tossed in grated lemon zest along with lemon juice and milk, half a cup of the liquids, then another half cup of flour, rhythmically mixing till all was smooth batter, and poured it all into two pans.

"Yeah, well, we should all be proud of Abby," Sally said. "Proof that our system worked. A successful businesswoman, employing her own mother to supply those gorgeous jackets."

Johanna slid the pans into the oven, slammed shut the door. It reminded her. Why had Abby slammed the door shut on her, all of a sudden. What was behind it all? She had a terrible feeling about this film. It was as if everything would come crashing down on them at once.

She stood for a moment, her back to the stove. Its warmth made her uncomfortably hot. Why didn't she want Pamela to talk to Abby? What possible harm could it do? Abby had survived with flying colors. Wasn't a nut like her sister.

There, she'd admitted it. Angela, like Neil, had moods. Manic-depression. That was an old-fashioned term. They called it something else now. Neil always refused to go to the doctor, and they'd all lived with his moods. So maybe Angie had inherited something. From her father. There had been none, none at all, no madness in her family. She, Johanna, was not at fault.

Chapter Twenty-Seven

"Neil." Johanna had tracked him down to speak to him alone. "Abby wants to stop stocking my angora jackets."

These days catching him alone was a challenge, with Pamela so often there, distracting him. Yet here he was, holding a two-by-four, ready to work on the barn door, a hammer in the pocket of his jeans, a couple of nails hanging from his lips.

"Give me a hand here. Hold this steady while I get these nails in."

She did as he asked, just as she always had. Held the board in place while he positioned a nail and raised the hammer.

"Yeah. She mentioned it. Things have to change, Jo. Robert and Martha are coming up here soon, and we can talk about what to do about the farm." He whacked the board, once, twice, three times to make sure it was secure.

"Why must anything change? Why can't Robert and Martha just sell their portion of the land and leave us this bit? Or take their inheritance from the rest of the money your parents left? Why disrupt everything? Don't they realize that the livelihood of everyone here depends on the farm?"

The rest of the nails lay in a box on the ground, half buried in weeds. Typical of Neil to work in such a disorganized way. Johanna picked up the box and held it behind her back.

"Look, Jo, don't jump to conclusions. Martha and Robert are coming here to discuss everything. They haven't been here in years. The first step is to get the land appraised before we make a decision."

"You mean before *you* will make a decision, with them, about what concerns you and me. We've been together fifty years, and you're acting like I'm not important."

He slid the hammer back in his pocket and faced her. "You're important, Johanna. Of course you're important. But you can't stop change. It's inevitable."

"Change! Change happened everywhere around us and passed us by. We opted out of change. Now it's come back to haunt us."

"Exactly. Look, I need to stop farming. We're all getting older. Curtis has back trouble. Linda can't be expected to milk goats forever. You've just told me our daughter doesn't even want to stock the clothes you make."

Johanna looked down to hide the tears pricking her eyes. A terrible pain squeezed her heart. The box of nails fell as she bunched the top of her shirt with her hands. "Oh, Neil, we were partners in all this, yet you're treating me like the enemy. There's a lifetime of history here, and you're acting like I have no say in the decision."

"No. But it is a decision I have to make with Robert and Martha. As you've known all along. As everyone's known all along."

The pain felt like a knife now, cutting through muscle and tendon, right into the center of her body.

She forced herself to stay upright. "Well, what will happen to me and all the others on the farm if you and Robert and Martha sell the land and take the money?"

"Who said we would take all the money?" Neil wouldn't look at her. He reached down to pick up the nails, shoving the box awkwardly under one arm as he held down a piece of wood on the door.

She planted her feet, somewhat recovered. "You've never talked about this with any of us! You've known for weeks that something will happen with the land, and you've never proposed a plan. At the very least, you owe Curtis and Sally something."

He raised his eyebrows, questioning.

"Sally was left some money by her parents. I know that for a fact. That's how they have a nicer house than we do. They put those thousands into fixing up their shack with solar panels and new appliances. That money bought a real kiln for her pottery, not that oil drum she started out with. Whatever money she and Curtis make from their art, they just plow back into Joyous Woods. To improve the crops. Or fix the barn."

"I'm fixing the barn." Neil waved the hammer.

"Oh, stop it!" She flung her arms wide. "You know what I mean."

She wouldn't say anything about Pamela. If it came to a choice between them, he'd have to spell out what he wanted.

"I suppose you're saying I need to call a meeting of the Circle so we can vote on what to do."

The Circle! Could Neil never think through anything on his own? He'd always been intellectually indolent. She'd realized that years ago. He spouted slogans, played guitar, strutted around, lorded it over them. The only ones who rebelled had pulled out and disappeared.

He had a gift for keeping them guessing and catering to his moods. Well, that could work two ways. Neil's laziness could help her. Johanna certainly wouldn't point out that legally she, Johanna, his helpmate since their student days, had no rights to his inheritance.

She folded her arms under her ample bosom—a defiant gesture, but it acted like instant aspirin. The chest pain subsided.

"I think you need to call a meeting of *everyone* to decide what to do. You just can't try to preserve your authority by telling everyone it's your land so it's your decision."

"You think I acted like that? Like I had the authority?"

"Don't you?"

"I thought we all acted however we wanted. Everyone has freedom to stay or go."

"My way or the highway, is that it? You're holding an economic weapon over our heads. Money as authority. Not who has the most ideas, or who works the hardest. Neil, you know this is a very weird set-up."

Neil hammered a nail into the board, and another, so the reinforcement stayed.

Johanna moved so she could see his face. "Think of Joyous Woods as a corporation."

He made a face.

"I know you hate that word, Neil. But you provided the start-up money. That is, the land. But we others worked it; we worked so hard and so long and gave it our everything. You have to consider us equal partners."

He looked baffled.

"More than that." Johanna heard words come out that she never thought she could say. "Curtis and Sally put actual money into the venture, so they need a pay-out. What they put in, plus interest, for what we've made of the land. Me too. I gave up my youth, my working years, all without a salary, and I worked every single day. Those jackets and sweaters I make—do I take the money and use it at a hair salon? No, it goes back into the communal fund."

Neil sounded scornful. "Your choice. I didn't stop you saving anything for yourself."

Johanna shook her head, astonished. "No, Neil. That's not what we agreed. Everything we earned was supposed to be put into the common fund."

"Hah!" Neil aimed so hard at the next nail that he missed and banged his thumb. "Goddammit! Jesus. Look what you made me do!" He kicked the door. "You're not helping. Why don't you help here?"

"Get one of the others. I have too much to do." She turned and walked away. Behind her, the barn was no better off than it had been twenty minutes ago. Before her, the pagoda house looked as flimsy as a cardboard cutout. The top story leaned slightly to the left. Another quake would collapse the whole structure.

What was she fighting? Let the siblings sell the land. She'd demand her share and find a little house somewhere, maybe with Ray and Linda and Kevin. They'd support each other.

She surprised herself when she shouted at him. "If you're dead set on selling, Neil, make sure Robert and Martha understand this is not just raw land. Demand a return on the investment!"

"Johanna Becker, capitalist."

She stopped, turned to face him, hands on hips. "Johanna Becker, standing up for her rights. Neil, I'm warning you. If you and your brother and sister are not fair to me, or to the others, you'll be hearing from a lawyer."

"Save it, Johanna." His voice sounded subdued, almost conciliatory. "Wait till at least we talk it out with Martha and Robert."

"Well, when are they coming?"

"I invited them for Thanksgiving."

Johanna stopped short. "Thanksgiving? That's two weeks away!" She stumbled on a stone. She kicked it, her toes smarting. "And when were you going to tell me?"

"Today," he mumbled. "But what difference does it make? There's always a crowd here for every meal."

"Robert and Martha have families. Are they coming too?"

"Nah. I checked. Robert's kids are busy with in-laws. I think Martha's happy to leave old tortoise-face with their girls. It's a long trip from Florida and cold here in the winter. I think her family's glad to stay home. They know it's a trip to discuss the will."

"But where will they stay? Don't tell me you're trying to get that barn fixed up into a bedroom."

"Wrong again, Jo. They'll stay in town. Pamela said Martha and Robert can take over the place she's renting for the film crew, while they're gone for the holiday. It'll work out fine."

Pamela again. He discussed this with her first! At least Neil hadn't invited her for Thanksgiving, that was a small mercy.

"Ah." A retort escaped her. She didn't know if she was more irritated at Neil's high-handedness, or relieved that she'd be free of Pamela for a long weekend at least.

One or two more people for Thanksgiving dinner would not make any difference. Sally and Curtis's kids never came home. Pedro would be with his extended family. Abby and Maelle would come. She'd do the usual barter with the local turkey farmer. Swap some of the best cheeses, some pies, a cake as well, for a twenty-pounder. She'd arrange it today.

Once again, why was everything up to her? In the confusion of the past weeks, with Neil besotted with Pamela, and Abby rejecting her work, she'd forgotten the date. The others had seemed dispirited too and had not reminded her. This Pamela and her filmic intrusion was getting to all of them except Neil.

"Martha and Robert will just have to take us as they find us." She harrumphed, as she left Neil to his hammering.

Chapter Twenty-Eight

"Sure you won't have a coffee, too, Rebecca? It's very good here." Maelle hoped she sounded friendly.

"Thanks, but no. A cup of water is fine."

After they'd collected their drinks and chosen comfortable armchairs, Maelle cradled her latte in her lap. Across from her, the flame-haired woman took a sip and set her plastic cup on the floor. Her lined face looked older than the forty she must be now, fifteen years after Maelle had last seen her.

"I'm so glad you agreed to meet with me," Maelle told Rebecca. Already Maelle regretted that she'd asked the informant to meet at this upscale coffee shop. Encumbered by her drink and deep in a chair softened by countless backsides, she'd set herself up at a disadvantage. She should have chosen a more private meeting place.

Rebecca's foot jiggled nervously as she sat.

Maelle took a leisurely sip of her latte, raising her eyes above the cup to Rebecca's. "So, I remember you coming to our apartment. My mother, Angela Becker, was researching animal rights violations for a magazine article. She found you through FAR."

"Hmm." Rebecca twirled her glass. Its contents slipped around, creating an eddy, mesmerizing Maelle.

"If you were her friend, anything you will know may help. You see, my family never told me what really happened to my mother. Now I think I'm entitled to know. Apparently, my grandparents accepted what the police told them—that my mother died in a laboratory accident."

Rebecca listened in silence.

"I know that this lab was run by a Dr. David Kane, and he used animals in medical research." Maelle took another sip. "My mother was a journalist. So I have to assume she wanted to interview him. But why go to the lab at night? Why didn't she just interview Dr. Kane during normal business hours? If she was writing an article, that's what she should have done. Got his side of the story."

"Maybe she did interview him to get his side of the story. Such as it was."

"Well, I haven't been able to find any notes. And Madison over at FAR doesn't seem willing to share whatever she has." Maelle put the coffee cup on the low table between them and took out a notepad and pen.

At the sight of the notebook, Rebecca sat farther back in her chair, gripped her blue-jeaned knees together.

Maelle held her pen with her teeth, flipping to a clean page. When she raised her eyes, she saw fear in Rebecca's. She put the pen down and waited. Rebecca had risked something to meet her; Maelle needed to give her time.

She hadn't wanted to alarm the older woman by telling her it had been easier to locate her than she'd anticipated. After she went back to her childhood diary, she read every word obsessively. She found a reference to Rebecca, had even noted the gagging incident. Her last name included. She'd simply had to look her up;

she still lived at the same address.

"You're not going to write a book or anything are you?" Rebecca said.

"I'm a botanist." Maelle took up her cup again, warming her hands around it. "I care about plants the way you must care about animals. There's a lot on my mind at the moment, and writing a book about animal rights is not one of them. I have to finish my thesis and get a post-doc somewhere and eventually teach young people about the importance of the natural environment. I'm sure you can relate to that."

For the first time, Rebecca appeared to relax, giving Maelle a half smile.

"Okay," she said. She ran a hand through her long, frizzy hair. "Angela came to FAR for help with her project. She told us that a guy she knew was experimenting on animals, doing weird stuff."

"Weird like what?"

Rebecca crossed one leg over the other. "I'll get to that. At first she said he was testing rabbits for resistance to various germs, reaction to new antibiotics, things like that."

"Doesn't sound out of line to me. Science is all about testing, over and over."

"We don't believe in it. Animals should never substitute for human beings in clinical trials."

"The FDA won't allow that. Products have to be tested on animals before humans." Maelle wasn't sure about this but tried to look convinced.

"Their idea being that humans are superior to animals. FAR doesn't agree."

"I don't either, philosophically. Animals, including humans, aren't superior to plants, either. And we prune, trim, weed, and eat plants every single day. Please go on."

"Yeah. Well, we had reason to believe this Dr. Kane was doing something more unusual, something worse."

"How come?"

"Angie told us. After a while." She took a long swallow of water, finishing it.

"My mother? How did *she* know?"

Rebecca gazed long and hard at Maelle. "I know you were a kid at the time. But some things…it's better not to tell. I'll just say that Angela got her information from a very close, very credible source."

Maelle picked up her notepad. She hadn't written anything down at all. Rebecca kept glancing at the page.

"Well, Rebecca, this is as much a mystery as it always was. Why was Mom there in the middle of the night?"

"What she told us was so huge, that we decided—FAR decided—to put a watch on the lab. We had to investigate the place first, verify what she told us, then work out a strategy. That's why we met at your Mom's apartment." Rebecca laughed suddenly. "I remember you, now! Cute little kid. Looked like Pippi Longstocking with your braids."

"Mom was raised by hippies. I don't think I ever saw a hairdresser till I grew up."

"So, anyway, this is the strategy we figured out. I'd get hired as a lab assistant and would report back to them. It worked. Though it took all I had not to vomit every morning when I got inside the lab. Because I saw what was going on."

"Which was?" Pen poised, Maelle waited.

"Just listen, first." Rebecca scooted forward and whispered so softly that Maelle could not hear her, then sat back, clasped hands in her lap, legs crossed at the ankles, features blank.

"Sorry," Maelle whispered too. "I couldn't hear. And if I couldn't, no one else can either." She turned around to verify no one was within listening distance. "I need to know, Rebecca. I deserve to."

"All right. He's been dead so long I guess it's okay to tell you. He had a contract with the army. I sneaked a look at his files when he was in another room. David Kane had a contract to test chemical weapons."

Maelle gasped. The coffee surged back up in her throat. She set her cup on the floor so she couldn't see or smell it. "What? What did you say? What did he do, exactly?"

"Kane would shave the fur off the animals' backs and measure how far into the skin various chemicals penetrated. Rabbits, mice, and pigs, too. Oh, it was a picnic in there!"

Thick fog smothered Maelle's mind. It took her a while to process Rebecca's words. Finally, she managed to say, "Did he use anesthesia on the animals?"

"Most of the time. Well, sedation to keep them still while the chemicals were administered. You can imagine the pain when they woke up."

Maelle still struggled to take it in. "I thought chemical weapons were banned by international treaties."

"Don't make me laugh." Rebecca squashed her plastic cup between her hands. "Academics are so

274

naïve! So are the people who sold him the animals."

"You think they didn't know?" Maelle could hear the hopeful note in her voice.

"I don't see how they would. It was all top secret."

"Was he using neurotoxins or corrosive chemicals like mustard gas and lye?"

"Why, am I destroying your faith in your country?"

"Just trying to find out how my mother died, Rebecca."

"Oh, yes. I'm sorry. This is your mom we're talking about. Well, FAR was planning a rescue to free the animals. It would make a big splash in the headlines, and we hoped the uproar would stop the research. But Angie said she wanted to have a chance to talk to Kane first. So she could write an article that was fact-based, not polemical."

"But she never got the chance to do that?"

"Apparently not. See, one night, I took her with me to the lab and showed her the entrance and exits. I'd made a map of the building, the cages, the different places the animals were kept, the operating room, the recovery area.

"She told me she needed it to research her article. She wasn't supposed to be in on the FAR operation. She told us a press person needed to be independent, shouldn't take sides. Or at least, shouldn't appear to take sides. If she'd been caught in the animal rescue, she'd lose credibility as a journalist, she said."

Maelle nodded. "All right. So she knew the plan. She still could have interviewed Kane during the day and arranged to have other members of FAR take photographs on the night of the rescue. She'd need photos, as proof."

"Oh, I had photos, all right. Took them secretly with my digital camera. After a while, Kane trusted me and didn't have me searched when I came to work and when I left."

"There were security guards?"

"Daytimes there was a doorman. But no night guards. That was his big mistake, in retrospect." An edge crept into Rebecca's tone. "I didn't know she was going to steal my key!"

"She had a key?"

"One of those plastic cards you wave in at a sensor. We had a meeting the night before my day off, and that's when she took it from my purse. At first I didn't notice, but then I got mad. I accused her, and she told me she'd give it back the next day. She needed it that night, she said. She was going to go and see Kane."

"Did she say why?"

"First she said that she had to go to the lab to see for herself what Kane was doing. To verify my photos. Couldn't write an article on secondhand information."

"Fair enough. I understand that. We researchers in the sciences have to get our results verified, too. You have to see things with your own eyes and make sure others see them too—"

Rebecca cut her off. "Yes, I told her, but why would she need my key, if he'd invited her for an interview? So we argued about that. I couldn't understand it. I said sneaking in undercut her argument that she needed to appear to stay neutral. She already knew that we'd set up an organized action to free the animals."

"And? I've waited so long to hear this, Rebecca. Please go on."

Rebecca thrust her head forward and lowered her voice to a mutter. "She said she wanted to talk to Dr. Kane about something else. I think she had a bit of a flair for the dramatic. Maybe she was going to bribe him—tell him she wouldn't write about the chemical weapons if he would agree to something she had in mind. But that's speculation. I don't know what it was. But it's like she needed to surprise him."

"You think she was afraid of what Kane would do when he found out she knew about the chemical-weapons research? Maybe she wanted to protect you, Rebecca. You were the one who betrayed your employer."

"We tried to make her see sense. Our raid would have blown everything apart. There would have been a huge political uproar. It would have put FAR on the front page. Not as a group of crazies, like some people think we are, but as a group of concerned citizens who uncovered a scheme that discredited this country."

"So you're annoyed at my mother for spoiling your party?"

Rebecca looked abashed. She looked at the floor. "That's not fair."

"I lost my mother," Maelle said, quietly. "That trumps your loss of publicity."

"Yes, and I'm so sorry." Rebecca reached for Maelle's hand. Her tone softened. "I don't exactly know what happened in there, that night. Maybe she confronted David Kane and he got angry and tried to chase her out. My guess is that she made it into the treatment room where the chemicals were stored and poured them on the floor. Maybe she slipped. The chemicals were flammable, and the whole thing blew up."

Maelle leaned back to stare at the ceiling. Her mother, a saint or a murderer? Who could say? For long moments, words escaped her, while the coffee shop filled with lunchtime customers and the hum of conversation. People, coffee cups in hand, circled the brown leather chairs she and Rebecca had occupied for some time.

Finally, she spoke. "I suppose it could have happened the way you describe. If he was testing chemical weapons for a top-secret government agency, I guess that explains why the police report was so inadequate. They were pressured not to ask too many questions."

"I hope I've helped." Rebecca was getting to her feet. "To give you some closure."

Maelle stood up too. "Don't you hate that word?" Maelle almost spat it. "So trite. No. There's no closure. No end to missing my mother. And I can't imagine what she had to talk to David Kane about that was not about his work. Or how she knew he was testing chemical weapons. I'm sure that's not something the animal suppliers signed on for."

"I really can't help you there," said Rebecca. "You'll have to find out on your own." Rebecca held out her hand, her face pale but her eyes looking relieved the interview was over. "I'm glad I've seen Pippi Longstocking all grown up." They shook hands and walked out together.

Rebecca blended into the lunchtime crowd. Staring after the receding figure, Maelle stood still, feet unable to move. A voice drummed into her head. Your mother was not a political fanatic. She just wanted the truth.

That comforted her. But then, another voice said, But my mother went to confront David Kane alone, and at night. Did she mean to kill him?

Chapter Twenty-Nine

Chemical weapons. Horrifying.

Did Zachary know about this aspect of his father's research?

Exhaustion made her legs weak as she trudged down the street to her parking space. Everybody in her life had nasty secrets. They'd tried to keep it all from her. Did Johanna and Neil know about Abby's liaison with David Kane? Did Neil, Curtis, and Ray know about the chemical weapons tests? And if they knew, how could they continue to claim their life at Joyous Woods rejected the American values of dominance and military might? Wasn't that why they'd fled to the wilderness to make a life on their own terms?

She opened the car door, slid in, and faced the steering wheel. She should drive. She should go to work. The plants she was training to learn would fall far behind in their studies. She banged her head against the leather circle of the steering wheel. How ridiculous her experiment seemed now. She was ascribing human motives to plants, instead of letting them revel in their plant-ness. Depriving them of light, smell, or other natural stimuli just to satisfy her scientific curiosity. Wasn't that as bad as testing done on animals?

She reached for her phone and called Zachary.

He sounded cool and formal.

"We need to meet," she said without preamble. "I

have some information I'd like you to help verify."

"Uh huh." He sounded wary.

"Can't do this on the phone. Don't worry, I'm not angling for a date. This is a business meeting. I'm not trying to blackmail you into seeing me. But I did find out something. Can you come to town tomorrow night?"

Silence at first, then finally, he said, "I'm just trying to process what you said, Maelle. It's pretty hostile—like I think you'd blackmail anyone. You wouldn't hurt a fly. You see everything as good in the world."

She did. Not now. "That's kind. Oh, Zach, I'm sorry." A little spark of hope surged. "How about that Italian place we both like?"

The décor-challenged, inexpensive eatery wouldn't suggest she was trying to win him back. Still, she washed her hair, put on slightly dressy leggings and a top that shaped her figure. Boots made her appear taller, and she wore a scarf draped over her head, which gave her a demure look but actually heightened the part of her above the shoulders, the thinking part. She hoped Zachary would get the subliminal message.

She arrived early, sat facing the door. When he strode in, she couldn't take her eyes off him. Black hair wet and tousled from a wind that had by now intensified to scudding rain. As he sat, his shirt cuffs spurted water drops onto the paper-covered tabletop. She drank in the reality of him. How she'd missed his arms around her, the timbre of his voice, the challenge of his conversation.

"Is it good news or bad news?" He raked his hair off his damp forehead. His voice sounded deliberately neutral, and Maelle recalled his accusatory tone the last time they'd met.

She swallowed. "Good to see you, too." She looked around for a server, her throat parched. "Maybe we should order first."

"The news must not be too bad."

When Zachary half smiled, Maelle regretted suggesting a restaurant at all. Would he choke over his food when he learned the truth? But it was too late. The waitress arrived, set out glasses of water before them. He ordered wine, and Maelle, who usually drank little, eagerly agreed to a glass of house red.

Maelle pointed to her choice on the menu, and the server disappeared.

She took a sip of water to calm her fiery throat. "You first. What did you find out?"

"Mother is losing it, I'm afraid. It's not exactly Alzheimer's, but she's forgetful."

"I'm sorry," she said, and knew it sounded trite.

"She's young, too, to have this, under sixty. I'll have to work out a plan for her future. It's been preoccupying me, and I'm trying to do my research as well. It's a lot to deal with, so I don't have much to tell you. What about you?"

"Well, first"—she clasped her hands on the tabletop—"I discovered Neil and the men of Joyous Woods did have a money-making operation selling rabbits to your father. All kept hush-hush from the women. Not cool, huh?"

"So I'm right. I did recognize Joyous Woods when I saw it that day with you."

She cleared her throat. "I'm truly sorry to hear about your mother. That'll be very hard as things move forward. But maybe it's an opportunity for you to ask her more questions. She may be more uninhibited now."

"Uninhibited? Why is that relevant?"

"Because older people aren't so guarded in their speech if they're forgetful. What I have to tell you..." Maelle stopped, took her napkin, and unfolded it in her lap, slowly.

"Go on."

"Your father was doing more than the usual medical experiments on animals. He was very, very cruel."

Zachary's head reared back in shock. "Maelle, immunization hurts. But it's necessary. Stops later suffering. Sometimes medical research can seem cruel, but the result is good."

How could she go on, without hurting him? Zachary always defended medical research; it was his job. Compassion made her reach her hand out to him, then anger pulled it back.

The server arrived with drinks and a basket of bread. She pulled the proffered wineglass close, drank, and wished they'd ordered a whole bottle.

"Look, I'm just trying to tell my side of the story. What I found out. You remember, Zach, neither of us was satisfied with the police report. Accidental death, a fire. Did you get anything beyond that? I couldn't make myself ask the police. Growing up at Joyous Woods, I was taught not to draw their attention."

"Yeah, I get that," he said. "Not a problem for me. I went to the police station and asked to speak to someone who'd covered the case. He's still there, fortunately. Retiring next year, he said. I got the feeling he didn't have much interest."

"What did he tell you?" She waited. Her hands began to sweat.

"Nothing. Nada. No more information. Maybe the guy was stalling. He just said there had been a fire in this medical lab, and forensics showed a chemical had been spilled. The lab researcher, that was my dad, had been killed, and so had Angela Becker. The detective didn't know why Angela Becker was there at the time. Was she an employee? The lab's records were all burnt, so there was no way to tell, but—you won't want to hear this, Maelle—he said she might have been from that animal-rights group. For Animals Rights, FAR is the acronym.

"But FAR denied responsibility, and they couldn't prove anything. Angela Becker wasn't a dues-paying member of FAR—they'd checked on that—and they couldn't find anything about FAR or the lab on her computer, which they took in as evidence afterward."

"Abby said they went through everything at our house. I've been wondering about her computer."

"Abby? Your aunt?"

"She was living with us, more or less." Maelle folded her napkin over her fork, making a tight little bundle. No way she'd reveal Abby's involvement in David Kane's life. "The thing is," she went on, "my mother did know the people at FAR. She was writing an article on what your father was doing. I did some research and found someone who worked for your dad as a lab assistant. She also knew Mom."

Zachary's eyebrows arched. "Tell me."

"Abby and I went to the FAR office with questions, and the next week a bunch of activists picketed her store. They're against her selling clothes which include fur and wool from our rabbits and goats."

"Those people! Humans have used animals like this for millennia."

"Correct. Well, after the picketing I went back to the FAR office to complain, and the person there said she knew all about Joyous Woods supplying rabbits for research at your father's lab." Maelle gripped the napkin and the tines of the fork bit her hand through the paper. "So that confirmed it. It was probably a mistake to go see them in the first place. They remembered the whole thing, and they decided to take it out on Abby and her store."

"That's a shame." Zachary swirled the wine in his glass. "She's not to blame."

"You could say that. Abby's pretty devastated." Maelle gulped more water. "I needed more proof, though. Then I remembered that FAR had meetings in our apartment, Mom's and mine. I remembered a woman I saw there, Rebecca. I tracked her down, and we met the other day."

"Good. What did she tell you?"

"She'd been a FAR plant, sent to the lab to spy on your father. She managed to get herself hired as an assistant, cleaning the animals' cages and so on. Rebecca reported back to FAR about the horrible experiments. The organization planned a big exposé and intended to free the animals. But my mother, for some reason, got in there first and destroyed that opportunity."

"Why would she do that?"

"That's the question, isn't it?" She paused.

Zachary swallowed, nodded, and she went on.

"I suppose we can accept the police report that a chemical spill started a fire. That's because Rebecca learned that chemicals were used in the experiments, and she told FAR that David Kane—your father—was doing more than just testing rabbits for medical research purposes."

Zachary took a piece of bread, but instead of eating it, squashed it in his hand. "More what? I hope you're not making this up."

"The experiments sounded awful. He shaved the rabbits and painted chemicals on the skin."

"Testing antibiotics? Burn treatments?" Zachary's voice croaked, barely controlled.

Maelle took a sip of water. Maybe he hoped to turn what she'd said into some relatively benign procedure—not that hurting animals could ever be good.

"Yes? Was that it?" Zachary drummed his fingers on the tabletop.

At that moment the server arrived with their food—a bowl of penne marinara in front of Zachary, a calzone at Maelle's place. Not her usual fare, but she needed the pastry to settle her stomach. Steam rose from their plates. Hopefully it would obscure her face.

"No. It's not all. While Rebecca was working at the lab, she sneaked into your father's filing system and found something that really scared her."

"She read his confidential files? Hey, that's bad, Maelle."

"Listen. Just listen. Your dad was testing chemical weapons on contract with the government. Rebecca reported he did the most terrible things to animals to show what these weapons would do to humans."

Zachary cratered forward over the table, catching his head with his hands before it hit his pasta bowl. Maelle put her own hand out to touch his. He raised his head. Sweat glistened on his temples. Her hand dropped.

"How can you prove this?" he said.

"I can't. But maybe the fact the police didn't do more than a cursory investigation is a clue. Maybe they were advised—pressured—to stop investigating, by the CIA or DOD or whoever it is who makes these weapons."

"The US doesn't make chemical weapons."

"Hah! Don't be ridiculous! Don't you know history? Our country may have signed international agreements and object when other countries use chemical weapons, but what would you call napalm? That's a weapon that burns off people's skin. They used it in Vietnam."

Maelle could see Zachary struggling to grasp it.

He took a long swig of wine. "After that war, though, the US promised to destroy those weapons." Doubt crept into his voice. "That process may not be complete, but new chemical weapons research?"

"Look, I don't know. I'm telling you what Rebecca told me. Why not ask your mother?"

"She's moved a couple times since Dad's death. But she may have some of his papers. But if she'd found something incriminating, surely she would have shared it with the police?"

Maelle cut into her calzone. "Maybe she knew it was a top-secret matter." She took a bite and burned her tongue. "Maybe she was too scared to investigate further. Maybe the police had been warned off investigating. I wouldn't put it past them. My grandparents called police the *pigs*. Horrible term. But Neil and Johanna's whole life is about mistrusting the government. It lied about the Vietnam War. Why wouldn't it lie about preparations for war now?"

Zachary turned his fork in his penne. "That's a real stretch, Maelle. Hard to believe the police would be intimidated. We only have this Rebecca's word for it that my father was involved in weapons testing. Why do you believe her?"

"Well, we both know something terrible happened. The fire, both our parents dead. Doesn't it make sense that if there were chemicals in the lab and your father was doing dreadful things to animals, then a fire could easily start if someone knocked something over? Rebecca said that FAR was going to free the poor animals, and my mother got in first."

Zachary regarded Maelle without hostility, vulnerability in his dark brown eyes.

"My question is, still, why? Why take it upon herself to break into Dad's lab and stop the research, when someone else would do this dirty work for her?"

"She didn't break in. She had a key card." Maelle tented her hands in front of her mouth, trying to think. The key card was a distraction, not really relevant. Or was it vital information, implying that Angela was on no interview? Did she have another purpose in wanting to catch David Kane by surprise?

"Look, talk to your mother, Zach. See if she remembers him talking about his work. Try to find out his political views. Maybe he thought whatever the government wanted to do to protect Americans was okay. Our parents died fifteen years ago, when the US started ramping up its military again after 9/11. People didn't question so much then, did they?"

"I don't remember. Your family certainly questioned everything. Hard to believe they would sell animals to my dad for the purpose of weapons testing. That's very different from research into cures."

"Then that's even more reason for you to question your mother, Zach."

"Oh, God. This is terrible." Zachary lowered his head. He said nothing for a few heartbeats. Then he pushed his plate of half-eaten pasta away. "This is a pretty damaging allegation. Can this Rebecca prove it? How did she know these experiments were about chemical weapons? Maybe I'll have to speak to the woman myself."

"You could. But why alert FAR to the fact that you're trying to defend your father? And why would Rebecca speak to you, anyway?"

"Did you have trouble getting her to talk?"

"After I said I wasn't writing a book or exposé or anything, she opened up."

"It's so hard to believe he would do this. My father—he was good to me. To think he would hurt animals like this—in order to hurt human beings—that violates his oath as a doctor. And his own principles. He must have had them."

"Yeah. At one time, perhaps. I hope Neil didn't know about your dad's, like, sideline."

Zachary looked up, like a kid who has just seen a way for another child to take the blame for an infraction. "You could ask him, Maelle."

"That's just it." Maelle's shoulders slumped. "I can't get to him these days. That filmmaker is always around. He ignores the rest of us."

"Yeah. Well, try to get him alone sometime. Maybe he'd like to get it off his chest."

"He doesn't know we've been looking into our parents' deaths. I doubt he even knows we're seeing each other. He certainly didn't recognize you when we came up to Joyous Woods together."

"So don't ask him about my dad and the chemical weapons. What would be the point? Just because we've been obsessed with it, knowing as much as we do now doesn't mean other people have to be dragged into it. They don't have to know at all."

"You're trying to say we should put this behind us?" Maelle's heart lifted. Then another thought tamped it down. He wanted her to give him a pass, to not face the reality of such a cruel father. Of course it wasn't his fault, what his father did. But then, Zachary had actually accused her mother of killing his father, as if she were a criminal. Who was the criminal now? She looked across at him and saw a face full of hurt.

"Can we?" he said, his voice scratchy.

"Do you want to?"

"It's big, what you just said. About what my father did. I need to go through Dad's papers. Mom never wanted me to, before, but with her condition as it is, I'll need to sort everything out anyway. I doubt he kept anything like this at home, but I could look."

"You do that." Maelle kept her voice even. A tumult of emotions somersaulted through her. Anger at Zachary, for being who he was, for being so attractive, for being involved in this impossibly complicated situation, made her sit back in her chair and pull together the edges of her coat self-protectively.

It hit her just then with certainty. Neil was not the key to the puzzle. Abby had the answer. Maelle did not want to reveal Abby's affair with his father to Zach. It would be painful for him, and part of her wanted to protect him. In a flash, she understood that Abby knew more than she let on. And family was family. She needed to protect the aunt who had always looked after her.

"Anything else?" Suddenly formal, Zachary pushed himself up from the table. "I need to get back to work. It's a long drive to the Pensinsula."

"It is a long drive. Let me know what you find." Her heart plummeted.

He looked hard at her as if trying to read her mind.

Maelle said, "I'll see what I can discover at my end. The sooner we can put all this to rest *and get on with our lives*," she added in an exaggerated tone, "the better." She rose, awkwardly hitting the chair with her leg in her hurry to find and pay the server, determined not to be in Zachary's debt. But when she heard him slap bills and coins on the table behind her, she turned to see him grab his coat from the back of the chair and head toward the door.

Chapter Thirty

Late the next afternoon, she barged into Abby's store. A customer was trying on a dress, and a couple more were fingering the racks. Up and down the metal bars they went, pushing the hangers along, pulling out items to try on.

"Abby, can we talk?"

"I'll be with you shortly, Maelle," she said. "Sorry. Why don't you go in back and make us some tea? I'll be with you as soon as we close."

Maelle edged her way to the break room where a few days before, she'd tried to feed a shaken Abby from the meager ingredients from the mini-fridge. She filled the kettle, turned it on, and hunted for tea bags. She found a few in a torn-open package. They were of the herbal type, and Maelle wanted caffeine. She'd have to wait. The room was still disordered, so she found paper towels to clean up, then placed the roll on the metal table.

In a few minutes Abby joined her, looking flustered.

"I've had a lot to do to put things back in order. Those FAR people created chaos here. Fortunately, customers who know me are still supportive. This will blow over."

Maelle pushed a cup and a teabag toward her, leaned back, and drummed her fingers on the table between them.

"Oh, what's up?" Abby said in a stricken voice.

"I'm sorry, Abbs, I've discovered something terrible about David Kane and what he was doing. But I think you might be able to tell me more."

"Oh, and what's that?" Abby's face tightened.

"I found the person who worked with Mom to uncover what Dr. Kane was doing. Her name is Rebecca. I remembered her from meetings at our apartment when I was little."

Abby dunked her teabag in her mug and laid it on a piece of paper towel.

"I tracked her down and met with her. She told me she'd become a lab assistant for David Kane. She got the job to spy for FAR. What he was doing was beyond cruel—he was experimenting with chemical weapons."

"Aghh." Abby put her head in her hands.

Maelle resisted putting out her hand to comfort her aunt. "So I told Zachary."

Abby's head shot up. "You didn't tell him anything about my affair with David, did you?"

"No. It's irrelevant."

For a second, Abby's posture eased, then she said, "But you're not finished, are you?"

"No. Because when Rebecca told me that FAR had planned their raid with my mother's full knowledge, I wondered, why did Mom take it upon herself to steal their thunder? Why did she put herself in danger? Why not let FAR do the job? What they planned would have been ugly, but it would have stopped his research."

"To warn him, maybe?" Abby hugged her arms around herself as if she were chilled.

"Because Mom didn't want FAR to hurt your

boyfriend?"

"She could have warned him with a phone call." Abby traced a spill of tea on the tabletop with her finger.

Maelle couldn't see her expression. "But I know how she was, Abbs. It's like she wanted to make some kind of a statement."

"Maybe. It was just like my sister to take everything so personally. You know, because she was the eldest and took the brunt of it when we were taken from our parents and given so little comfort and no unconditional love…" She stopped, suddenly. "I think Angie felt that somehow she needed to justify her existence."

"Justify?"

"Yes. Just being alive wasn't good enough for Angie. She had to prove herself, do some good."

"Don't we all feel that?"

"Oh, Maelle! No. Don't tell me you think that too. Just existing should be enough for a child to feel loved."

"Hard if you're an orphan."

Abby rolled her eyes. "I'm trying to explain, to make sense of it. With Angela, it was pathological. She saw everything in black and white. Good versus evil. She became fanatical."

"How come you're not?"

"Well, I don't know about that. I have my own problems." Abby gripped her tea mug. "You know, Angie was always jealous."

"Why? Because she had me to take care of and no one to help? Because she didn't have the freedom you had to take a lover?" Maelle could not help the bitterness in her voice.

"I see. This is all about you." Abby stabbed her teaspoon against the table.

"I'm sorry. I interrupted. You were saying Mom became a fanatic. Zachary said the same thing. He called these animal rights people *terrorists*. You're not saying that about my mother, are you?"

"Can we leave him out of this? Let's work toward our truth, not his. I'm saying Angie wanted to stop David Kane from being attacked by FAR. She wanted to reason with him, appeal to him. It was she who figured it out."

"What? Figured out what?"

Abby's face lost even more of its color. She held her mug so tight her fingers went white. "She noticed the bruises."

"Bruises?"

"David started to beat me." A whisper.

"Oh, Abby!" Maelle leaned forward over the table, reached for Abby's hand, and stroked as it gripped the mug for dear life. Abby relaxed her grasp. Maelle drew back her hand.

"He was a bully. Once we got close, I discovered things that shocked me. He didn't want to be just an ordinary doctor. He wanted to be famous, to discover something big. Get a top job, that kind of thing."

"Big ego?"

"You bet. I found out he'd do anything to get there, too. That morphed into doing anything to get his way. Soon he wanted to control everything, including me. That's when the abuse started. Then it got so anything could set him off. When he'd had a bad day, he'd come home and slap me around."

Zachary's kind face swam into Maelle's mind, that last hurt look. And this man had been his father?

"Why didn't you leave, Abbs?"

The laugh Abby tried fell flat. "Abused women aren't born, they evolve. They start off admiring a person's strength, their ambition, maybe. Their brilliance. And our upbringing made us believe, consciously or unconsciously, that we existed to be manipulated. That our wish for exclusive and unconditional love was not realistic, that we didn't deserve it." She stretched her neck, chin up, then down. "I'm just making excuses for myself, I know I am."

"No. It was not your fault. How could you get out of the situation?" Maelle pushed the mugs aside, needing space to absorb the information Abby was reeling off.

"Angie tried to help me. She wanted me to leave him, but it was so hard. I feel so complicit now. I stayed partly because he paid for everything, the rent and all, and I wasn't earning much money. I'd already abandoned that hippie philosophy of voluntary poverty."

Abby's eyes turned toward Maelle, pleading for understanding.

"Yeah, I know. I don't live the hippie life, either. Want a real career for myself."

Abby went on as if she had not been listening. "Angie tried to coax me into having more self-esteem. But I felt trapped. As much by my own weakness as anything else. By then I knew what David was doing in his lab, and after Angie wormed it out of me, she said she hated him. She said if he ever hurt me again, she'd ruin him. She urged me to get a restraining order. I didn't."

"Oh, Abby!"

"So I think, now, she just wanted to tell him to his face to stop hurting me."

"Again, why not do that during the day?"

"Simple, really. She couldn't risk anyone else being there. She wanted her conversation with David to be private."

"I guess that makes sense. Still doesn't explain the accident, though. The fire."

"Remember, we're not talking about two sane and rational people. David was obsessed. At first, it was with his research. Then it was with me and how he was going to earn enough money to leave his wife and son. That's probably why he took the army contract. Once he did that, he tossed out any chance of getting any awards for doing research that actually furthered the common good. So then he became angry at me, and the beatings got worse. That drove Angie into a frenzy."

"She was acting weird, wasn't she, at the time? I do remember that." Discomfort prickled Maelle's skin. These revelations needed to stop. "It's getting late, Abbs. Don't you need to go?" She started to rise.

"Wait. Sit back down, because there's something else you should know. Up at the commune, there were lots of drugs. All the adults smoked dope and dropped acid and acted crazy a lot of the time."

Maelle thumped back in her chair. "Not JoJo. She wouldn't."

"No. And I doubt Sally and Linda did, either. They wanted the farm to succeed, like Mom did. It wasn't a male-female thing, though. Lots of the women did drugs, including our caretakers."

"When you and the other kids were in the Children's House?"

"Oh, yes. I remember Melody and Starlight tripping, doing nutty things while they were supposed to be looking after us. I'm not saying our parents gave us drugs. But they were too busy to notice what these stupid teenagers in charge of us were doing. They gave us everything. Weed. Acid."

"LSD? That psychedelic drug that makes people see visions and nightmares?"

"That's right. A nightmare that went on and on. Faces, all contorted. Trapped in my mind, couldn't get out of it. Truly terrible, and flashbacks for years. It was a regular pharmacy up at Joyous Woods."

"Did this happen to all the kids?"

"It must have. Longer for Angie because she was the oldest. It really screwed her up. As long as she lived, she saw visions."

Maelle leaned close. "Do you think it made her crazy, Abby?"

"I don't know. But the drugs, all the combinations of drugs had to mess up her mind. She started having concentration problems when we went to school. So the school labeled her as ADHD, and my parents took her to the doctor."

"I thought the commune didn't believe in doctors."

"They just didn't have medical insurance. Used a lot of homegrown remedies, herbs and such. But they were worried about Angie. Maybe our grandparents paid for this doctor. Anyway, he prescribed a medication for ADHD. It's an amphetamine. It helped, so she took more. That can send a vulnerable person over the edge."

Maelle tried to take it all in. What Abby said explained some things, left others open questions. Could she ever find out the truth? Would it even matter?

It did. It mattered to her, and to Abby, and to Zachary as well. It should also matter to Johanna and Neil, but they'd chosen to push it from their minds.

And Abby had not answered the obvious question. Besides wanting to stop David Kane from hurting her sister, Angela's motive was also to stop the animals being killed. Maelle took a deep breath and risked it.

"So Mom went to the lab, with the key card, to barge in and confront him without warning. To tell him to lay off hurting you, or she would expose his work and encourage FAR to attack the lab, publicizing what he was doing."

Abby pulled on her hair, dragging a long tress down to her chin. "I guess. Yeah. Blackmail. That would be it."

"An exposé like that could have made Mom's career as a journalist, though. And freed animals from torture. I bet she took her digital camera, to get her own photos."

"Well, that would be been burned up, too. Oh…it's so terrible to think about it, a fire!" Abby's eyes filled. She hugged her arms around her body and hung her head toward the table.

"But she really wanted him to stop hurting you. That doesn't sound crazy thinking to me."

"I don't know. David wasn't rational. He may have come after me, tried to kill me, blamed me for getting his work stopped. Angie didn't think it all through. She acted impulsively, overlooked the risks. I don't think she was capable of thinking clearly. Look what happened, you left an orphan."

"But you could have stopped it all earlier, Abbs. You're the one who told my mother what David Kane was doing. And she told FAR. But if you knew, why didn't you tell Neil? Surely he would have stopped selling the rabbits to such a monster?"

"I did. I did tell him. He didn't believe me. Called me delusional. He actually said…" Abby yanked at her hair, pulled it as if to rip it out by its roots. "He actually told me not to worry my pretty little head about it. He told me he knew I was seeing David and it was fine by him even though he was much older than I was. You know how it was up there, Maelle. Exclusive partnerships were not the norm. Dad had no problem with David being married. He said he was fine with it because it was good for business."

Maelle could not speak for the raging storm in her heart.

Chapter Thirty-One

"Tell me what you remember, Abby." Pamela smiled encouragingly.

"What do you have in mind?"

"My documentary focuses on what became of the hippies. It's topical, nowadays. There's revived interest, because it's fifty years ago and many of those people are dying off. We're probably on another cliff, in terms of society. The country's divided, values have been turned upside down."

They sat in Abby's living room, camera trained on Abby's face. Maelle sat apart, waiting her turn. A vase held a graceful arrangement of leafy foliage and yellow and white chrysanthemums, which complemented the walls Abby had painted a light apple green. The Rookwood pottery and paintings on the walls gave an impression of calm. They couldn't override the thumping of Maelle's nervous heart.

"May I offer you a drink?" Abby said. "Isn't that what people always say in the movies when they begin an awkward conversation?"

"Oh, why not? Thank you. Let's get comfortable."

"I'll get it." Maelle bobbed up and went into the kitchen. She found a bottle of chardonnay and three glasses. As she came back into the living room, Abby was in full actress mode, striding around the room. Telling lies.

"I had a very happy childhood. With lots of people about all the time, we had fun, the other kids and I. The grown-ups were fun too—they laughed and played guitar, and we had sing-alongs, cookouts, and marshmallow roasts. It was great."

"Sounds like summer camp," Pamela cooed.

How much would Abby dare to give away? She'd broken through her carapace with the confidences of the other day. Would an experienced interviewer like Pamela see an opening there and take it?

But Abby was giving a sociology lecture. "The themes of separation and togetherness, they kind of underlined everything up there. We lived apart from mainstream society, and we lived together in a holistic system. So we had both, separateness and togetherness."

"Go on." Pamela's voice encouraged.

"About what?"

"How it was growing up on the commune. You're the only one who has any contact now with the original child members."

"Am I? Kevin's there."

"Kevin is there. I've talked to him, but he doesn't have much to say. I'm sure you'll be far more informative."

Abby handed a glass to Pamela, poured wine for both of them and for Maelle. "You're making it seem very important. What my parents did. Of course, they think it's important, but after I grew up, I always thought it was pure ego."

"Angry with them, are you?"

"Oh, no." Abby took her first sip of wine. "Though I do seem to be having a delayed adolescence." She sat and crossed her legs demurely.

Maelle sat straighter, alert. Abby should not confide this most intimate information with Pamela, an almost-total stranger. She shouldn't open this can of worms. Who knew what Pamela would do with the information?

Maelle sighed. As if a can of worms could be anything but good. Earthworms aerated the earth. Let it be opened up then, all the secrets. As Zachary had said when they first met, sunlight is the best disinfectant.

Pamela raised her glass. "Thank you. That's interesting, Abby. Would you call it a midlife crisis? I mean, a pre-midlife crisis in your case."

She looked down at her notes as if she had not been focusing on Abby's tight features with its little hemlines around the eyes. Today, Abby's tawny hair was pulled back in a ponytail, accentuating the contours of her face, every wrinkle obvious.

Abby rose from her chair haughtily, twirling as if she were a model, showing off her slender figure. Abby had chosen her clothes well—an orange jacket over a pair of slimming black trousers and black heels. To Maelle, she looked every inch the successful businesswoman, anathema to the hippie life.

Pamela signaled the cameraman to zoom in on Abby's face.

"Let's be clear," she said. "I'm not judging you or your parents or whomever you consider your family to be. America has a long history of utopian societies. But most of the stories about these utopias were told by the founders, not by the children who grew up in them. None of those societies survived past the first generation or two."

"No. That's wrong. The Shakers survived. The Amish. They live apart from society and share back-to-the-earth values."

"I thought your group was more iconoclastic? Everybody did their own thing without religion setting the tone?"

Maelle raised her eyes to Abby's face. Hadn't she told her the other day that the commune's children thought their parents were gods? Pagan deities, giving them life, then abandoning them without explanation. The talk at the Saturday meetings, all about love and feeling good and the smell of incense and weed. The ecstatic visions of LSD. Music. If that was not religious, what was it?

Abby sipped her wine. "I guess I didn't really question any of it till we went to school."

"Your family told me that was because there was no elementary school close by."

"That's true. When we were old enough, we were bused to a school which took in kids from outlying areas. There were other communes around at the time, so we weren't considered so weird."

"Let's talk about the Children's House."

Abby's lips tightened. "What do you want to know? Did they show it to you?"

"They did. An abandoned school. A building that could have been a dormitory."

Abby picked at a fingernail as Pamela went on.

"I understand it was based on the ideas of other pioneering societies. The kibbutzes of Israel. China, also, after the Revolution, sometimes arranged care of the children separately, so their parents could work."

Abby looked up. "My mother at least, had a

philosophy behind all this. She had a theory of bringing up children, believed she was doing the right thing. She wasn't like the others."

"No. She's not. That's not been my impression." Pamela consulted her notes. "Back then, how many children lived at the commune?"

"About twenty, I suppose, at any one time. Different ages."

"Neil wasn't much help to me on this subject. I understand you didn't call your parents Mom and Dad. You didn't live with them. The adults believed in sharing everything and in non-exclusive love. I'm just asking, it must have been confusing for a child."

"I wouldn't say confusing is the right word. If it's what you're used to, it's normal. Not that it was fun all the time."

Pamela cocked her head to one side, eyeing Abby.

"Your parents couldn't tell me how it felt for you, and they wouldn't say how it felt to be separated from their children. It's like I couldn't get that far with them."

Only the hum of the fridge in the kitchen stirred the sudden silence.

"The Children's House? How was it?" Pamela had to repeat the question.

Abby jogged her glass on her knee, sloshing the wine. Her eyes lost focus. "I remember being in a playpen. My mother picking me up. Then someone said something to her sharply, and she almost dropped me back down. She disappeared. I screamed and screamed."

"You must have just been a toddler."

"All the kids lived together, divided up by age.

Babies and toddlers in one room. When you were toilet trained, you went to another room to sleep, then the five- and six-year-olds were in another one. A different room for the older kids. My sister Angie was three years older than me."

Abby's eyes sought Maelle's, and Maelle remembered how Abby told her she'd cried and cried when they separated her from Angela.

Maelle pictured it. Cribs and cots all in a row. Angela trying to protect her little sister from others who hit her or snatched away their few toys. Communal meals. Little potty chairs, lined up, all the toddlers placed on them at once. A general kind of misery most of the time. No mother to kiss a scrape or a wounded feeling. And yet Johanna and Linda and Sally and all the other mothers lived right there on the commune. But they didn't have time for their own children.

Pamela had waited, giving Abby time. "Who looked after you?"

"One or two girls were assigned to each room. Teenagers, really." Abby bit her lip, as if she'd said too much already.

"Do you recall any names? Anyone I could trace or interview?"

"Melody. She was one. Patricia. Then Diamond and Starlight. Things got crazier, and people changed their names. Trying to escape their past, their own families."

"Is that why you never became a parent, Abby?"

Abby bristled. "What about you? We're about the same age, I think."

"Sorry. Didn't mean to offend. Some of us have our careers to think of, or never met the right person. I surely wasn't implying some deep psychological wound."

Abby gazed at Pamela as if seeing a crack in her glossy surface. "What's your story, Pamela? Why make a film about an era that's almost forgotten?"

"Not forgotten, at least by me. My father was a Vietnam vet."

"So he passed down to you his resentment at those who didn't serve?"

Pamela looked away. "Oh, it's more complicated than that, Abby. My father came to hate the government that sent him and his friends to die on the other side of the world. Our family suffered, too. My father had PTSD. He killed himself."

"Oh. I am sorry." Abby's face bloomed red. "Truly sorry."

Pamela looked at her lap. "So I know a little bit about fractured families. Families who don't fit into the norm."

"Yes. I guess you must."

The conversation stalled. Abby folded her hands over and over in her lap. Finally, she said, "My mother seems to think you want to make a film that speaks badly of us."

"Not true. I'm trying to be neutral. I'm a reporter. In film. Trying to tell a story, yes, but not a slanted one. I can't help how the world views hippies."

"Will you show how we lived, in a film without judgment or condescension? Can you promise me you won't cheapen it?"

Pamela's eyes went wide. A little line of wrinkles appeared above them on her forehead. "Try me," she said.

Pamela was the wrong person. Abby should stop speaking more truths. This was the Pamela who allegedly tried to seduce Neil. The barricades behind Abby's eyes came down. Yes, Abby was going to tell this woman her deepest secret. One of them, anyway.

Abby squared her shoulders, chest out. "I think when you're brought up to reject the outer world, you never learn how it operates. Mistrust breeds mistrust, and you learn not to expect a happy life. You learn not to expect love. That you don't deserve it."

She held up a silencing palm as Pamela opened her mouth to object. "And don't go on about getting comfort from religion, that a higher power is loving from afar. Because religion wasn't part of the Joyous Woods philosophy."

"That's what they told me. But I thought the Age of Aquarius was all about love."

Abby snorted. "That's their view. They all came from families that gave them plenty of affection, so they had the courage to go out on their own and do radical things. You can't do that if you have no confidence, don't believe you deserve anything. You know, I didn't even have a clean pair of jeans to wear to school the first day. And my shoes were patched. You can imagine how the kids made fun of me. Of us."

"Yeah. It's hard to be different. Believe me, I know."

"You know because of your own dad?"

"Yes." Pamela's voice was so quiet, her face pensive. She tipped her glass and finished her drink. Maelle poured her another.

Abby held out her own glass for more. "By then, some of the other families started to pull out from the commune. They moved into town, got real jobs. They got sick of being poor and could see their kids were going to have a hard time at an actual school. Those hippies grew up."

"Did you find school difficult?"

"It wasn't easy. The government puts out a curriculum for homeschoolers, but no one took responsibility for testing us. So when we went to real school, with real grades, it was okay if you were good at school, terrible if you had any trouble learning."

"And some of you did?"

"Same as everywhere. Kevin for example. But my sister, too. Angela was bullied and had some learning disabilities. The school practically forced our parents to let her be tested, said she needed special help. She was bright, but she had some trouble. I think she took some medicine for it, too."

"Medicine for academic difficulty? Give me some!" Pamela laughed.

"If only there were a magic pill." Abby smiled lopsidedly. "It was for attention deficit disorder. That's one of the things they said Angie had."

"Do you know where any of your school reports are? That might be helpful to get a picture of the kids and how they managed between home and school. I did ask them up at Joyous Woods, but they were not forthcoming."

"Can we call a halt here, please? I've told you what I know. Anyway, Pamela, it's all ancient history." Abby rose to clear the glasses.

"You seem to have done well. You own a clothing store, Woolley's?"

Maelle glanced up at Abby, saw her face tense.

Her chest tightened. Her aunt might offer to show Pamela the store. Not a good idea. A taped-up window would let the filmmaker know that Woolley's had been targeted by animal rights activists protesting the selling of fur. And reporters smell conflict. Pamela would pursue the story, and that could lead to questions about David Kane and Abby and her mother. She tapped her foot on the floor to warn Abby to be quiet.

Abby stopped, glasses held in midair. She wore a thin smile on her face as she pivoted to face the filmmaker. "Yes, I do. But you're making a film about the commune, not about me. You know, my parents and their friends were pioneers in organic farming. They had really innovative ideas and carried them out. They produce wonderful things to sell. It's not a high-income operation, but it has managed to support all of them."

"I understand the land is in danger of being sold."

"Is it?" Abby started toward the kitchen.

"Maybe that's good, if the money can support all of them in their old age." Pamela wasn't letting her go. "On the other hand, maybe what Joyous Woods has achieved is a precious thing and should be preserved."

"Preserved? When these old people get too old to work, what will happen?"

"Why not just sell it as a farm? Surely it could be managed by the younger generation. Get young interns, students, people who want to learn organic farming, to do the heavy lifting. Couldn't that work?"

Maelle broke in. "That's amazing! It's what I've been looking into as well. I don't want to see those trees and fields destroyed."

Pamela swiveled toward Maelle. "I see you care for Joyous Woods."

"I love it."

"Well, we can talk about your impressions next. If you have time."

"Maelle's a plant researcher. Of course she wants to save the farm." Abby's voice sounded muffled as she stacked glasses in the dishwasher.

"You don't, Abby? I do understand your mixed feelings from what you've told me. But a granddaughter will have a different perspective."

Abby returned to the living room, pulling at the bottom of her jacket with damp hands.

"Actually, I—we all are—a bit afraid of your perspective."

Pamela laughed. "Really? I found your father and his friends to be utterly charming. They tried to live by their principles. Threw out conventional ideas about partnering and child-rearing. And they did no better and no worse than most of us. Look at you, Abby, you're a success. You too, Maelle. The point is, they lived with intention. That's the narrative I see. So let them end the story with intention, too."

Maelle could not stop staring. Pamela had found Neil charming, but maybe that's as far as it went. Perhaps he reminded her of her own father in his good moments. She clearly hadn't liked Johanna much, but that could be because Johanna was a match for her own drive.

"I want to thank you, Abby, for being so gracious and candid about your life at Joyous Woods. Before we wind this up, I'd like one final long shot of your face."

Abby looked abashed. "If you must."

As the cameraman moved into position, Pamela gave a winning smile.

"You've talked quite a bit about how you found your childhood difficult. Mine was too. But it makes us creative, don't you think? Me with my documentaries, you with your fashion, your clothing store?"

Abby smiled back. "Well then, make your film. Show Joyous Woods at its best. Please show how our animals are loved and cared for. Do show the beautiful garments my mother creates, how she makes dyes from plants, knits angora from the rabbits and mohair from the goats. Wait here a minute."

She went into her bedroom and, a minute later, returned with a mohair jacket Johanna had made. Its soft pale-brown color, of stone mixed with fallen leaves, would suit Pamela. She folded it neatly and held it out to Pamela.

"I want you to have this," she said. "To remember Joyous Woods."

Chapter Thirty-Two

Maelle's work needed her attention. She'd now lost over a month in botched experiments, muddled thinking. The plants had stopped communicating. Perhaps they never had.

And yet. She sought out Heather and tried to talk it through.

"Don't you think communication is the essence of the universe? The ability to signal a need must be the basis of creation. Plants signal other creatures all the time. They're like salespeople, offering a freebie in return for a visit to the store."

Heather laughed. "That's right. Tasty nectar, come and get it! That's what a flower signals. They get dressed up, show off their colors. Look at me! And the bee zooms right in, bringing pollen from another flower. Bingo. Fertilization. Like a hookup, don't you think?"

"Then the bees who first find the food fly back to the hive and do their figure-eight dance to signal to their friends exactly where the flower grows." Maelle giggled, stepped off her stool, and made a few hula moves.

Heather gave Maelle a high five. "We don't have to actually speak to each other to give out information. Look at social media. Humans are attracted by the most potent nectar there is, the ability to communicate."

Maelle sat back on her stool. "Nature and commerce do have a lot in common."

Communication—so vital in the workings of the world. Why had there been blocks to communication among everyone associated with her mother's death? Herself and Zachary, Neil and the Circle, FAR, Rebecca, David Kane, and the secret rabbit operation.

Despite Angela's objections, making a living from selling animal products was not contrary to the commune's mission to live closer to the earth. And yet. They must have known—at least Neil must have known—that David Kane's experiments were too gruesome to contemplate.

She should confront Neil. She must confront him. Ask him what happened.

But she could not.

Neil's mood could be intense, upbeat, happy, or morose. His down days seemed more frequent these days, at least according to JoJo. Grief at his parents' passing, guilt at a life he now saw as wasted?

But who was she to judge or blame? Maybe Neil thought he'd lived a great life. Yet guilt must come into it somehow. He must feel some responsibility for his daughter's death. Perhaps guilt had made him so cold recently to JoJo, and so warm to Pamela, a new person, untainted by mutual history.

She doodled a figure eight on a pad, struggling to get back to work, musing on how a mathematical symbol is a form of communication in the natural world.

Her phone rang.

Zachary wasted no time on small talk. "Can I come over?"

She hesitated. "I'm really busy. Way behind." She had a split second to make a decision—to put him off or to give him another chance. She decided. "But if you come to the lab, we could talk for a bit."

"We do need to talk. Didn't you ask me to quiz my mother on…what you said the other day?"

"Yeah. I did. But maybe we should drop it. It's all too hard. You and I…"

"Is anyone else there?"

Maelle glanced at Heather, head bent to her microscope.

She sighed. "All right then. I can make sure we're alone, if you insist."

She gave him directions to the campus greenhouse, a favorite place of hers, calm, soothing, and quiet. She waited for him there, talking gently to the plants. It would be helpful if they could absorb any bad feelings, just as they breathed in carbon dioxide, poisonous to humans in large quantities. The glass enclosure oozed tropical warmth, the only sounds coming from periodic sprinklings. The air smelled oxygenated, with slight overtones of rot.

Maelle wandered along the rows. Suddenly, he was there in front of her, so handsome her heart jumped. Hair tousled, Adam's apple peeking above the unbuttoned collar of his shirt.

He gave her a quick hug, then stepped back. His shoes squelched on a water spill on the concrete floor.

"I'm apologizing. Seems what you told me is true. My mother didn't have all the details, but she did find some correspondence between Dad and the military. Hard to interpret, full of acronyms and allusions to things she didn't understand. So I did a little research.

It's true, Maelle. They conducted all kinds of bizarre experiments on animals, mostly to learn what happens to humans in war."

"As Rebecca claimed. Oh, Zachary, this is truly awful."

"Please don't interrupt. I need to get this out." He started pacing. "These experiments actually happened. They wrapped pigs in fire retardant blankets, then exploded IEDs next to them to see if the blankets prevented burns. They blew poison gas into their lungs, blistered their bodies. They submerged goats in deep tanks to see if they got the bends when they surfaced.

"I'm not saying my father did all that. But you're right. One of the experiments involved testing wound penetration so that they could figure out how to cure that wound. They put rats in boiling water, inducing a burn, then infected the burn to see how long it took the rats to die."

Maelle gasped. "How sickening."

"Yeah." He clutched the side of a plant table. "There was one experiment that explains the fire in the lab."

"Yes?"

"That experiment involved saturating the backs of rabbits with ethanol. Then they were set on fire. The idea was to measure the depth of burn and what it took to salvage the skin."

Maelle almost gagged. "What went wrong?"

"I think the experiment was so grisly my father decided to try it at night. Angela came across him doing this to the animals and interfered somehow. Ethanol is flammable, as you know. Some spark, we'll never know exactly what, set off the fire. The lab exploded, killing everyone and everything there."

Legs wobbly, Maelle found a wooden, slatted seat nearby and sat down. "So you think your theory is proved. That my mother was a fanatic and killed your dad from a political motive."

"Yes. Probably." He came to where she sat, stood over her.

A familiar fury gripped her chest. He was assuming something he couldn't know. "Yes, but she could have achieved the same thing by waiting till FAR invaded the lab. Wouldn't that have been more effective?"

"Possibly. But why does it matter now?"

"Because I can't bear the idea that my mother died for a cause. It makes me feel small and unimportant. I had no father. So if she risked her life and died I'd be an orphan. Why wasn't I more important than a philosophical or political belief? That's why it matters."

"Oh, Maelle, come here."

She didn't. She sat, facing him, the green plants witnessing, silently. "I can't accept that, Zach, because I believe there is another reason. My mother was behaving very erratically when she died. Her moods went up and down."

"You think she had a psychiatric diagnosis?"

She shrugged.

"And you're worried about inheriting that tendency?"

"Possibly."

"There could be other causes, you know."

"Tell me." She picked up a potted plant to hold. The leafy presence offered a barrier.

Zachary adopted a neutral tone, as if discussing a medical case. "I don't know exactly what happened up at Joyous Woods, but the communes were notorious for giving children drugs that only adults should take. LSD and so on. That can have an adverse effect on the developing brain."

"How?"

"It's controversial, but there's mounting evidence that teenagers who take mind-altering drugs alter their brain chemistry. So if they have a tendency to psychosis, they can develop a full-blown case."

Maelle's heart skipped over. Abby had implied as much.

"Let me tell you a story." Zachary walked up and down the aisle for a few steps and came back to sit down next to her. He took the little potted plant out of her hand, set it down, lifted her finger, and ran it along the scar that lined his neck. "You asked me about how I got this scar, and I told you that I turned to research rather than clinical practice when a patient attacked me."

His skin felt warm, familiar. How much she'd missed that sense of touch. "Yes. I remember. Must have been a terrible experience. But I guess it's a risk in your profession."

"It's rare, actually." He placed her hand back on the seat, gently, next to the plant. "This is what happened. The clinic had been super busy that day, and I was behind schedule. That always agitates patients. It was after five o'clock, and when I took a quick bathroom break, I peeked into the waiting room and saw it was still full of people."

"Reading those out-of-date magazines. Make anyone annoyed."

"Yeah. Well, when I called the next patient, he

shambled in, disheveled. I had not seen him before. I glanced at my notes and said, 'Sit down, Mr. Bray.' "

Maelle's skin vibrated. She breathed, "Mr. Bray?"

"You recognize the name. Good."

"Mr. Bray—Kyle—didn't sit down. He stared at me, first confused, then his face turned savage. Before I realized what he was doing, he pulled something from his pocket and lunged. I tried to protect myself with a chair, but I felt something slice my neck, blood spurt, and I fell. The noise must have alerted the nurses, and they rushed in and subdued Kyle Bray. I don't remember anything else. When I came to, in the hospital, I decided clinical practice was not for me."

"Kyle Bray. The patient was Kyle Bray." Maelle's voice was a whisper.

"When I was better, I dug into the patient's history. He was from the commune, Joyous Woods, and his parents were Sally and Curtis."

She shook her head. "So that's what happened to Kyle. Sally and Curtis never talk about him. But you connected him to Angela Becker and the commune!"

"Not immediately. I didn't see any connection. Both Kyle Bray and Angela Becker committed violent acts, and Bray at least is certified as schizophrenic. They both grew up at Joyous Woods. But I didn't know that then. I still didn't put it together—because the police report didn't say why Angela Becker was in the lab that night, and they didn't blame her for the accident."

"But you did." Maelle's voice trembled.

"Wait. At that time, I didn't link what my father was doing in his laboratory to the rabbits from Joyous Woods. I didn't connect the dots till I went up to the farm with you and saw the place."

"And you realized what, exactly?"

"It was then it dawned on me that *your mother* was the Angela Becker who had been in the lab that night. I recognized her from the photo album you showed me, and I'd always kept a newspaper clipping about the victims of the lab fire. So that's when I understood that she and Kyle were both violent. I wondered if they'd been given drugs as kids, since that often happened on these communes."

"So you weren't stalking me from the beginning."

"No. How could you think that?"

"I thought, maybe you were. That you befriended me—just to get information on what happened to your dad."

He turned his face upward, his mouth opened in dismay. He took a deep breath. "Your name, Woolley, meant nothing to me when we met. I knew my father used animals, probably rabbits in his research, but since his records were destroyed in the fire, I had no idea where he'd obtained them. As a kid, I'd gone to Joyous Woods but never thought to ask the name of the owner. It was a hippie compound as far as I was concerned. But when you took me on a tour of the place, the penny dropped."

"So because Kyle was crazy, you assume my mother acted crazy?"

"I'm not going to diagnose someone I never met, but you've described your mother having very labile moods. As you say your grandfather does. Possibly she had bipolar disorder. Of course she might have been simply acting out of an exaggerated sense of duty. To help animals. Whatever it was, she initiated the action, so I believe she started the fire."

"Go on." Chills went up and down her arms. He was still blaming her mother. "She must have had a very good reason to go there at night. To go alone. She must have known he was a vicious person."

Zachary recoiled. "Vicious? That's a bit much."

Maelle kicked at a pile of plastic pots stacked under her seat. "There had to be another cause. It's called revenge."

"Revenge?"

"Vengeance, then, if you like." She might burst if she didn't get this out. "Abby said it was because Angela was trying to protect her."

"Protect her? Why would that be?"

"My aunt Abby, Angela's sister, had an affair with your father, starting when she was about twenty. It went on for years." She hunched over, not looking at him.

"You're saying my father was having an affair with a hippie? No way." He gave a harsh laugh. "He was Mr. Preppy all his life."

"Don't generalize. We're not all smelly junkies. And Abby's hardly a hippie. Hated the lifestyle. She's a businesswoman."

"I'm sorry. You're not a hippie, Maelle." Zachary stood up, turned to survey the greenery around them, pivoted back to face her. His voice turned hard. "Anyway, if my father strayed, that's not your business, is it? Or even mine. That would be between my parents."

"Well, I'm sorry I had to bring it up. I didn't want to. The thing was, he manipulated her. He told her what to do, and he beat her up."

He folded his arms across his chest. "I don't

believe that."

She snapped her head up. "Why not? Someone who's cruel to animals can be cruel to people. David Kane hurt her! My mother saw the bruises, Abby said. He was emotionally as well as physically abusive, and she couldn't untangle herself from him. She couldn't get out of it."

Zachary stepped back. One step, two steps, three. Stared at Maelle. "God. So it was her. A kid knows something's not right. My mother did tell me—finally—when I pressed her. I asked her one day because it seemed strange to me she wasn't sad like I was when Dad died."

"She didn't say it was Abby your father was seeing?"

"No. I guess I was more perturbed that my mother seemed actually more lighthearted when he was gone."

"You mean she didn't miss him?"

"At some level, she must have been relieved. She kind of perked up. Went on to have a decent life, though a more financially constrained one."

"Abby told me that my mother started protecting her when they were little. See, they had to live in a special place they called the Children's House, and they had no adult supervision. Just a couple of older teenagers put in charge of the younger ones."

"Jesus. That's irresponsible."

"Johanna says the grown-ups had to work so hard, and with no money, they had to do something to keep the kids occupied while they worked the fields, did their crafting and cooking and whatever it was they did to survive.

"Anyway, Abby and Angela and Kyle and the

others were basically neglected. All kinds of sexual abuse went on at night in the Children's House, the boys forcing the girls, mostly. No one ever dared to report it, like kids who are bullied never dare to report that. Their parents wouldn't have believed them, anyway."

"So Abby grew up thinking she deserved to be abused."

"It seems that way."

"And your mother?"

"After she got pregnant with me, she may have believed she deserved to be dumped."

"What a mess."

Maelle dug her hands into the potted dirt around the plant she held, patting and smoothing. "Maybe that's why Mom loved animals so much, wanted to give them what she needed herself. She never thought she would be abandoning me when she tried to get them out of that lab. It just didn't occur to her."

"I see you've tried to make sense of it all."

"So now you *don't* think my mother was crazy?"

"Don't know. Do you think you believed that because it was easier to think she wasn't in control of her actions?"

Maelle bit her lip. Head games again. He'd turned the question back to her, wanting her to solve the riddle. She needed the truth. "I'm sure all the drugs they gave the kids didn't help. Not that I ever saw Mom toke up or even take a drink. But I was only little and can't really remember those kinds of details."

"If we're honest, Maelle, we'd have to say our families have a lot to atone for."

No. She could see no equivalence. For a minute,

she could not respond. Sprinklers sprayed gently over green leaves a few feet away. Finally, she found her voice. "Zachary, how about you think that through? I'm having a hard time letting this sink in, that you're related to an animal abuser and a man who beat up women. I don't believe you're like that. But you implied that my mother was a fanatic, and if she was not a fanatic, she might have been crazy. If not full-blown inherited crazy, then she got it from drugs."

"Maelle, stop."

"No. You're not willing to forgive my mother. You're not willing to see that however she acted, she acted with good in her heart."

"Is that how you see it?"

"Yes."

He stood back from her and nearly tripped over a curled hose peeking out from under a plant bench. "All right. You've just handed a shocking indictment of my father to me. I've just learned he used chemical weapons on defenseless animals. Then you accused him of infidelity and physically abusing your aunt. Giving it more thought is definitely in order. I really think I need to step back a little from this."

His face closed. "I'll see you." Zachary turned his back on her and strode out of the greenhouse.

Chapter Thirty-Three

"You look good, JoJo."

"Thank you, dear." Johanna pushed back a wisp of hair. "Look at Martha, though. Her face is as smooth as marble. How does she do it?"

Her granddaughter let that pass. As soon as she had arrived at Joyous Woods, Martha had removed her Hermes scarf, putting it carefully in her overnight bag, as she did so revealing rooster-like ropes of tendons at her neck.

Maelle brushed a speck of lint from Johanna's black mohair jacket, then searched her grandmother's top drawer for something to make her sparkle.

"Would you like to wear these pretty silver earrings?"

"These? My only earrings. Oh dear, sometimes I wonder…" Johanna adjusted the silver circles on her ears and drew her hair back in a chignon with an elastic band and a twist of the wrist.

Regret lay unspoken between them. This morning, Maelle and Johanna had seen Neil's sister emerge from the rental car, polished boots first, to reveal a well-kept figure in black trousers, silvery silk jacket, immaculate white shirt, and immovable hair. The scene emphasized the obvious; Johanna was poor and Martha was wealthy. Robert followed, and as soon as Neil's siblings were settled, Johanna excused herself and went to her room to hunt for dressier clothes, the soft mohair jacket, the long, pleated skirt she wore for special occasions.

"Come on, JoJo. You look great."

Maelle linked arms with her grandmother and came down to a room full of eager discussion. A fire roared in the brick hearth Neil had built years ago, contributing to the heat and noise. For Thanksgiving, Sally had decorated the great room of the pagoda house with sprays of dried flowers in her pretty pottery vases, and Linda had laid out wooden slabs with her cheeses and homemade bread, home-cured olives, and guacamole.

Curtis, who always loved a party, opened bottles, poured drinks. His bristly hair stood on end as he waved at Neil's brother, offering him a glass.

"Tell us, Robert, if this land is sold, what will happen to the commune?"

Robert took the drink with a grin and plunked himself in the most comfortable chair. "Is this an official meeting?"

"We might as well talk about it, don't you think? Get down to business before the festivities?"

"All right, if everyone agrees." Robert sipped greedily. Sitting beside him, Martha crossed her feet, lady-like, and looked serious.

Robert appointed himself the meeting's chair. "Neil, can you outline the economics of this farm?"

"Economics? Man, we don't do economics here. That's for you fat-cat accountants."

"Get real, Neil."

"Small farmers don't make a great living, Robert, if that's what you're getting at. I read the average is about twenty thousand a year."

"No one can live on that!" Martha almost choked

on an ice cube.

"We do feed ourselves off the land, see, and we built our own houses. No mortgages."

"Give me a rundown of how you do the numbers." Robert stirred an olive into his gin.

"I have some of it here." Ray retrieved from his shirt pocket a crumpled piece of paper from an exercise book. He listed some of their costs.

"Impressive, Ray, all this work you do. What's your income?"

"Cheese-making provides income. We breed and sell the goats, too. Castrate the male kids and sell them as pets and for meat. We rent out some of the goats to clear hillsides around here. Chickens provide eggs and meat, and the women here make pies, cakes, and bread to sell. Plus, the vegetable farm."

"I help with that." Kevin broke in.

"You do, Kev. It's great," Ray said.

Perhaps she was too close to the fire. Maelle backed away.

At the figures Ray provided, the farm would have to sell a hundred animals a year at least to break even, let alone make a profit from the cheese and yogurt. No way could Joyous Woods sell that number. And now the market for Johanna's mohair and angora creations had collapsed, at least as far as Woolley's store was concerned. She shot a look at Abby, and her aunt suddenly seemed to remember the oven needed her attention.

Robert appeared to be making calculations in his head.

Neil tossed back his drink. "Actually, Robert, you and Martha owe us for making this land livable. It would be wild hillside without the goats and far less valuable. If we clear-cut it, the hill would be prone to landslides in the rainy season. We always leave some trees, which stops erosion and fixes nitrogen in the soil. Goat and chicken manure fertilize the fields. That's what fuels the plants. See, circle of nature!"

Johanna beamed. "And that's not all. We mulch using waste wool from the goats as well. We keep angora goats for their fleeces. It's called mohair. Then I weave and knit it into jackets and sweaters Abby's always sold in her store." She frowned. "Actually, Abby's store was picketed the other day by animal activists. So she's going to take a break from stocking our products."

"Animal terrorists?" Martha shuddered.

Robert shook his head. "The term depends on your politics. I think they should be in prison, those people."

Her mother, deserving of prison? Hardly. Maelle gripped her glass, and the wine jiggled. All the communards were guilty. Not of terrorism. Not directly. But not one of them acknowledged their culpability in her mother's death.

The room went silent. Linda passed the cheese board, smiling brightly. Robert reached for a piece of brie. The tension fizzled like a balloon collapsing.

"Right. What about those chickens? Nearly ran one over when we arrived. Don't you keep them fenced in?" Robert settled back in his chair, munching.

"Free-range, Robert!" Curtis bellowed. "Most of the time they behave. Nancy or Myrtle might have got through the fence to explore. We'll round them all up about four o'clock so the night critters can't get them. 'Course if the girls persist in escaping, and they stop laying, they'll be dinner."

Martha blanched. "We're having turkey, today, I hope?"

"Don't worry," Curtis said. "From Perrys' farm down the road. The turkey you'll eat today led a lovely life while he had it. Trimmings courtesy of Joyous Farms. Our famous pumpkins and apples made into pies, thanks to the ladies here."

Robert's face relaxed. Appreciation, if not admiration, bloomed in his pale face, warming it to a soft beige.

"There's a good vintage we're bringing up from the cellar for dinner. Bartered it with our winery pals. Not that this gin's bad at all. Homemade." Curtis poured another for Robert. "Made with the berries of *Juniperus communis*. Grows wild a little north of here, so we propagated a few shoots to make a hedge. Not to be confused with *Juniperus californica*. Used to grow on our hills till the goats ate it all. Those berries are edible but not nice!"

"How do you know that?" Martha hesitated before sipping her drink. "How do I know I've got the right kind of berry in the gin?"

"Let's just chalk that up to bitter experience, Martha." Curtis grinned.

Sally picked up a swatch of conifer needles and berries laid artfully on the table as a centerpiece, stroked a berry. "This white fuzz on the berry is wild yeast. We use it to make a sourdough starter for our bread." She smiled wickedly.

Martha gripped the pearls at her throat.

Robert leaned toward Johanna's guacamole scooped a potato chip into it, wolfed it down, and reached for another. "Well, maybe I misjudged you. The fact that you don't create much profit has to be set against the tax deductions you get from all these expenses."

"Deductions?" Neil looked blank.

"Did you pay taxes?"

Johanna didn't wait for Neil to answer. "I don't think we earned enough to pay tax. Neil's parents took care of the real estate taxes."

"Did you not keep some of the funds back and put them aside for Social Security?"

"I don't know." Johanna twitched in her seat. "I didn't, anyway."

"You haven't saved anything, Johanna?"

"No. Everything I made went back into the communal fund. That's what we are, a commune." Johanna put her hand to her heart. "And we want to continue."

"Well, look, that's all very well. But you're getting on." Robert scratched his bald head. "So are we. You're not the deciders, here, I'm afraid. It seems kind of ridiculous for you all to insist that you can keep going. Especially when you could get enough money to live in comfort if we sell the land. California's desperately short of housing. We have the land. Why not put it to good use?"

Maelle jumped up. "No one here wants this land sold! It's sacrilege!"

Ray and Curtis shifted uncomfortably in their seats.

Robert continued, unperturbed. "Well, I'm not saying you haven't made a go of it. But you've all lived here, basically, for free, haven't contributed your share to the community, and now you want Martha and me to support you, like Neil's been supported all his life by our parents."

Neil scowled. "I wouldn't call it support."

"Really? Who paid the college fees for the children?"

"Angela and Abby attended community college." Neil's face began to redden.

"Maelle's doing her PhD. Must have had an undergraduate degree before that."

"True. Neil's parents paid for her education. We're grateful." Johanna smiled tentatively at Robert as Neil frowned.

Sally spoke up. "We had two children. We're artists. Sold our work. And yes, we set aside that money to pay for their college."

Robert persisted. "And now? Where is that money now?"

"What's left of it, we keep." Sally gave a defiant shake of her salt and pepper curls.

"I see."

Johanna went pale. She looked from one face to another, betrayal written all over her own.

Neil's eyes darted, searching for a friendly face. The others had turned to stone. He said, "You know, Robert, this is an unfair interrogation. The land our parents owned was given to us equally. We'll divide it three ways. You'll do what you want with your portion, and I'll work it out with my friends what to do with my share."

"Why does the land have to be sold at all?" Maelle interrupted. "These woods, the plants—don't they have any say in the matter?"

The visitors' heads swiveled. Martha appeared

surprised to see that her great-niece actually existed.

Maelle clenched her hands, holding them in a tight grip. "Apart from the fact that they provide food and oxygen for all species, I'm convinced that plants do actually talk to each other. It's been established they use chemical signaling to communicate with their own species."

Robert snorted.

She plowed on. "They communicate to preserve their sibling and offspring plants from attack." She paused for breath.

"Go on." Linda, sitting next to Maelle, nudged her gently. "Tell them."

"So what right do we humans have to destroy them? Plants deserve more respect. We eat them, and they provide wood and paper. They sequester carbon, they absorb carbon dioxide, and they breathe out oxygen. Every living thing on earth depends on plants."

"Okay, okay, that's enough, Maelle." Neil held up a palm.

Martha drummed her fingers on the arms of her chair. "So you're asking us to give up selling the land, which would give Neil and his friends enough money to live on without having to work themselves to death, because of some *trees*?"

"You're taking a short-sighted individual situation and solving it by creating a long-term problem." Maelle threw darts at Robert from her eyes. The communards sat there, staring. She felt a warm glow rise up her body. This was not like her. Never in her life had she confronted anybody, let alone a relative. She swallowed. "There must be a compromise somewhere. I've learned a little about land trusts. The property owner sells the state or a private land trust a conservation easement. That protects the land from development. It can be kept for agriculture or kept as forest or whatever. The land trust pays the owners for setting the land aside, but they still own it and can pass it to their heirs, so long as stays as farmland."

Abby came back into the room with a basket of bread rolls and laid them on the table. She stood there, listening.

Neil shook his head, as if trying to understand. "You mean we get paid to keep farming? That doesn't make sense."

"It works because the state wants to keep agricultural land in production. Or to keep natural woodlands from turning into shopping malls. The country needs to feed itself, and agricultural goods are a huge export, so it's in the government's interest to maintain farms."

"You say it's called a land trust?" Robert turned to his brother. "You could certainly do that with your share, Neil. But what about the hippies here? How are you going to spread the wealth? They took the risk with you, did the hard labor."

"JoJo told me that she didn't think Neil had any obligation to give her anything for the fifty years she's lived and worked here. They weren't married, you see," Maelle blurted.

Sally and Curtis, Ray and Linda and Kevin focused on the silverware. Linda surreptitiously slipped a fork from a place setting and rubbed its tarnish on a napkin. Neil glared at Maelle. Johanna, face scarlet, twisted her hands in her skirt, folding and refolding the material.

"What do you mean?" Martha swung her rigid hair,

her eyes sparking. "He most certainly does have an obligation! And not just to the mother of his children. To everyone here."

She addressed them. "You've all worked here like serfs, for years and years without a steady income, to make the land into a farm. I can see that you've made a difference with what you do. The gin was delicious, by the way, thank you."

"Thank you, Martha." Johanna leapt up, flapping her skirt as if she had a bee underneath her petticoats. "Yes, what about me?" She faced Neil. "You said you want to go off with Pamela!"

"I never said that."

"In that case, do I get my share? Plus any other money you've made?"

"What other money?"

"I know about the rabbits." She stood over Neil now, slumped in his chair, and spoke with gritted teeth. "The rabbits you sold to David Kane!"

A pin could drop. Linda and Sally stared at Johanna, while Martha looked about, lost. Maelle, Abby, Ray, and Curtis focused on the wooden floorboards.

"How do you know about that?" Neil said, finally.

"Angela told me." Johanna's voice trembled. "She said Abby knew all about it and told her. She said David Kane was doing bad things and had to be stopped."

Abby looked aghast. "He was doing medical research." She went over to her mother and held her wrist firmly.

Johanna flung the hand off, addressed herself to Neil. "But Angela hated that. Whatever he was doing."

Johanna's head shook, and one of her earrings fell to the floor.

"He paid us. Yes," Neil croaked.

"What did you do with the money?"

Maelle froze. Johanna had the wrong reaction. She should scream at Neil that the money he made helped kill their daughter. She should make him admit his remorse, say she was sorry too. Sorry for the way the children of Joyous Woods had been treated. Sorry that they'd all been such hypocrites, pretending not to need money, then taking it, hiding it, or spending it, and all the while knowing it came from an act of cruelty. Maelle wanted Johanna to say it, wanted to yell it herself. But she couldn't speak a word.

Curtis broke in. "The Circle divided it equally. We all set up bank accounts in town. That money has just been sitting there for fifteen years, earning interest. Not much interest, but it wasn't lost in the stock market, and it wasn't spent on useless junk."

"Oh, yes, the Circle." Johanna's voice curled with sarcasm. "When were you going to tell me, Neil?"

Neil's voiced muffled, as if he were under water. "We've done nothing with it. That money has been sitting there untouched. It seems tainted to me now. After Angela died, I just couldn't bring myself to think about it, even to acknowledge it."

Martha and Robert stared at their brother, confused. Neil looked from one to another, then to the floor, his hands curled into fists.

An icicle started to melt inside Maelle. So everyone had clammed up. All because Angela died. And now Neil had regrets. Knew that he'd been partly responsible. Maybe that explained his irascibility, his unpredictable moods.

Silence seemed to stretch on for a long time.

Finally, Martha broke it. "Can anybody tell me what you're talking about?" she said, again caressing her throat as if her pearls were too tight.

Maelle looked directly at Abby, held her gaze, then retrieved Johanna's earring from the floor and slipped it into her hand.

"I think," said Abby, "we need to eat. Can I have a hand to bring in the turkey?

Chapter Thirty-Four

Maelle itched to leave them. The turkey, browned and seasoned as it was, tasted bland, and she could not touch the pies. Johanna and Neil said very little during the meal, ate less, leaving it to the other communards to keep the conversation going. After dessert, Sally nudged Curtis. He winked, and as Maelle got up from the table, the sound of tinkling laughter followed her as Curtis passed the weed around. She could hear Martha say she hated the smell of tobacco but liked the herbal fragrance of pot and turned around to see Robert's shocked expression. Then Robert laughed and said if not now, when, carpe diem and all that. They'd all be occupied for a while.

Abby had slipped out of the big room with the excuse of clearing up. Maelle and Johanna followed to the kitchen. They filled the sink with hot water and liquid soap and left the scraped plates to soak. Abby called to someone to put away the remains of the turkey so the cat couldn't get it and propelled Johanna upstairs. Up into Johanna's aerie of a bedroom they went, Maelle following her aunt and her grandmother. Their feet stomped loudly because no one spoke till they entered the austere room with its view of fields and wooded ranges. Fog hung over the hills, curtained the woods and fields in a gray haze, and hugged the ground as the day darkened in the late afternoon.

Johanna switched on a lamp and sat heavily on the bed. She slipped off her shoes. Abby splayed herself on the only available chair, and Maelle, seeing no other place to locate herself, sat on the other side of Johanna's bed. Not near enough to touch her.

Abby spoke first. "Why, Mom, did you not tell Dad to stop selling the rabbits to David, if you knew Angie was against it?"

"He thought I didn't know. He kept it from us women."

"I know. Curtis and Ray told me that," Maelle said. "They all thought you had an emotional attachment to your rabbits. You wouldn't want any bred here to be hurt."

"They tried to hide it. The super-clean breeding facility. But they were only trying to help the commune financially. We needed that."

"You could have just asked Neil to stop!" Maelle's voice rose. "You knew when you came up here in the beginning, you were giving up the chance to earn money in the real world. And then, you let the guys get away with betraying their principles of love and kindness. All for money!"

"Why was it up to me? It was just one more thing Neil would blame me for. He was so touchy. Didn't like to be challenged. You know that." Johanna picked little bits of lint off her skirt, then pulled it tight around her knees.

"I asked Neil to stop." Abby punched a fist on the chair arm. "He said you all needed the money. You know how he is, Ma. His answer to everything is that the land is his and he can do what he wants. He told me the farm was scarcely getting by no matter how hard everyone worked and that he and Curtis and Ray had come up with this idea of selling the rabbits for medical research. The rabbits bred—well, like rabbits—so they created a never-ending supply. He said the business was supporting everyone, including Angie and Maelle. He said Angie didn't earn enough to support a child on her own."

Maelle hugged her knees with her left hand, drawing them up closer as Abby's words hit home. She, the unplanned child who messed up her mother's opportunities. With her right hand, she fingered the quilted coverlet patterned with little circles in different colors. She remembered Johanna working on that years ago. It had faded now.

"Did my mother ask you to intervene? To stop the Circle selling the rabbits to Dr. Kane?" her voice quavered.

Johanna's head drooped. "Angie came up to see me one day. She said that she was going to join that organization, FAR, and they would stop him. I told her they were terrorists, and she should stay away from them."

"It's true, JoJo. They were planning a raid. A FAR member who also worked as an assistant in Dr. Kane's lab admitted it. But Mom got in first. She must have accidentally caused an explosion."

"It's like she wanted to tell David to stop, personally. Otherwise, she just could have written an article and exposed him that way." Abby rubbed at a stain on the upholstery.

"But I asked her not to do that!" Johanna's voice cracked. "I said if she published a story on Kane's business, then FAR would be down all our throats.

They'd say all our products were tainted. Vile. People who buy organic food think about animal cruelty as well as their own health and climate change and all the rest of it. If we at Joyous Woods—a commune, for heaven's sake—were exposed as hypocrites, then the farm would be finished."

"Instead, my mother was finished." Maelle could not help the bitterness in her voice.

"We couldn't anticipate that!" Johanna twisted her hands together. "I've gone over and over it in my mind for years, trying to think what we could have done differently. You just can't anticipate consequences, Maelle. That's what you have to remember. You have to forgive. Every action has a reaction. A consequence you don't expect."

Abby sat up straighter. "The Children's House. That had a consequence. We kids all felt abandoned. You left us with teenagers who were stoned half the time. We couldn't protest, because you were too busy to notice!"

Johanna gripped the coverlet, bunching it up.

"Did you know about the drugs they gave us?"

Johanna held the bedclothes closer, so the pattern distorted. Her knuckles whitened.

Abby got to her feet, relentless. "I think the drugs sent Angie over the edge. Made her crazy. Made her reckless."

"She might have inherited that tendency from her father. You don't know."

Maelle's esophagus began a slow burn. She put a hand next to her mouth in case she threw up. "My mother was not crazy! I think that's just an excuse, to stop you all from taking responsibility. You, JoJo, and

340

Abby too. My mother did go into see David Kane deliberately. But she had reason to. She knew he was a cruel, vicious man, and she just had to stop him."

At last, she saw it clearly. Her fear and shame that her mother's mind was unhinged fell away. Her mother lost her life in a just cause. But she did not sacrifice it. Sacrifice was a knowing choice, and Angela Becker did not realize that tackling David Kane on the matter of chemical weapons and telling him to stop hurting her sister would lead to both their deaths.

Her aunt and grandmother gaped at her, astonished at her outburst. She saw they both believed her. Relief spilled down her tingling arms, the hardness within her melted. She loved her mother. Her mother had loved her.

"See, JoJo, Mom knew something about that animal testing that was much worse than you knew. David Kane tortured animals to test chemical weapons for the government."

Johanna's face turned pale, and her mouth flew open.

"He didn't! I don't believe that. Neil—and the others, they would never have sold rabbits to anyone who'd do that!"

"It's true, Mother." Abby wiped her cheek with the back of her hand. "That's what made Angie do what she did. She went to see David on her own, without witnesses, because she really didn't want FAR to do a public trashing of the place. That would have made Joyous Woods look like criminals for supplying the rabbits."

"Why didn't she tell me?" Johanna breathed heavily, had trouble speaking. "I could have...would

341

have told Neil to stop it."

"Maybe she did try to tell you?" Abby's voice held an edge.

"I don't know. I don't know. I know now I wouldn't listen to her, wouldn't listen to either of you girls when you complained. Angie wasn't really speaking to me much before she…went."

Abby and Maelle exchanged glances over Johanna's hunched body. She'd wrapped her arms around herself and was rocking backward and forward.

"It's unbelievable. Neil and the others, all those protests when we were students, against Vietnam, against soldiers using napalm and Agent Orange. Justifying our whole lives because we objected to that kind of cruelty."

Abby jumped up from her chair. "She tried, she tried to tell you," she said, her voice cracking. "And you just wouldn't listen to me, either, when I told you about the drugs Melody and the others gave us. And what the boys did to us in that dorm." She collapsed back in the chair and wiped her eyes. "It's hard to accept, all that hypocrisy. I've been so angry about it." Abby scraped the fabric of the chair arm again, pulling off a loose thread.

Maelle broke in. "Mom could have made her career by exposing David Kane's work. But protecting Abby and Joyous Woods was more important. So she just took it on herself to confront him."

"What does this have to do with Abby?" Johanna looked from her granddaughter to her daughter, who hung her head toward her knees.

"Maelle, I've felt so guilty." Abby's voice sounded clogged. "I was the one who kept on sleeping with

David Kane even after I knew what he was doing to the animals, even after he abused me, too."

"What?" Johanna's eyes filled. "He hurt you, too?"

"I just want you both to know that Zachary knew nothing about the chemical weapons." Maelle's chest hurt and hurt, like the flu was coming on. "He said he thought his father was testing medical drugs."

"Zachary, your friend, he knows?" Johanna turned her head toward Maelle, confused.

"He's David Kane's son. And when he recognized Joyous Woods, he put two and two together. But this whole thing has sort of ruined our relationship, for now, at least. Not to speak of ruining any chance that this family will accept him."

"Accept him as what?" Johanna said.

"I'm not sure. But as having a future with me, I guess."

Where were she and Zachary now? Would Zachary ever be able to work through his own confused feelings and guilt by association? If she'd never met Zachary, none of this would have come out. Unintended consequences, as Johanna said. But they had met, and the consequences had already happened.

A moan escaped from Johanna, and she was weeping, her shoulders heaving, making the bed move like a ship in heavy seas. Maelle got up on her knees and crawled over to her grandmother. She put her arms around her, and they rocked together for a few seconds. Then Johanna pulled up a corner of the quilt and wiped her eyes, and Maelle's too. When she put the textile down, Maelle noticed that one of the red circles seeped dye onto the white background. It reminded Maelle of the white rabbits spurting blood. She pushed the fabric

343

away and the quilt puddled on the floor. She forced her mind to the present and to the reality. Johanna's dyeing skills were imperfect. They were all of them flawed.

Chapter Thirty-Five

Pamela invited them all to a private screening of the movie before its release.

They gathered at Joyous Woods, Robert and Martha too. Sally and Linda had spruced up the party house, as they had begun to call the Brays' more spacious home. Ray and Curtis, even Neil, had spent a week or so of spare moments repairing all the chairs they could find on the commune. They brought them in from the pagoda house, from Linda and Ray's, and borrowed them from Perrys' farm, inviting the neighbors to come to the screening.

Years had passed since Johanna had seen a movie. She made an effort to look her best, a preemptive strike against the image of herself she anticipated on film. She retrieved from her closet her finest hand-knit cardigan, shimmering in deepest blue. She pulled her silver hair up in a bun, secured it with a silver clasp and matched that with her silver earrings. Her good black skirt and flat black shoes, not her usual boots, completed her ensemble. She buttoned and unbuttoned her cardigan. Which way would make her look thinner? Not that anyone would notice.

Abby came into the bedroom brandishing a handful of beauty products, face powder, blusher, and lipstick.

"I'll be blushing plenty when that film is shown," Johanna said, waving away the offer of glamour.

Abby laughed. "You look lovely, Mother." She held up a hand mirror to Johanna's face.

Johanna glanced at it, smoothed an eyebrow. "I don't know what you told that woman when she interviewed you. This whole thing makes me nervous."

"Well, we'll see, won't we?" Abby's smile lit up her sparkling eyes.

Johanna smiled back, a little shakily.

When they arrived at Curtis and Sally's, Neil was already there. He looked up as Johanna came in, and she saw in his eyes a spark of his old fondness for her. He came over and led her to a seat next to him. She sat down carefully. He'd chosen the finest sweater she'd ever knitted him, and she sensed his warmth seeping through it, making its way to her heart.

Pamela made a little speech, thanking the communards for letting her into their busy lives for a short time.

"I'll let the film speak for itself, and will answer any questions afterward," she said. "I set out to ask, 'What Became of the Hippies?' and it reflects my editorial viewpoint. But if I've made any errors of fact in the telling of the story, I'd appreciate a correction."

A shiver ran through Johanna. Neil tensed beside her. The thought came to her again as it had at the beginning of the film project. You invite someone to get to know you and you get to know them, and it's an equal relationship. But when you invite someone to write about you, or film you, and it's for public consumption, you invite them to judge you.

But her gaze was drawn to the screen, which Curtis had improvised by pinning to the wall one of his untouched canvases. As the audience waited, soft music played, and an image of a bucolic scene emerged. The barn, the dairy, the chicken yard, and the fields all appeared slowly, first from an angle so low the camera appeared to lick the landscape, then merging to a full screen image of the farm.

And the story began, Pamela's voiceover describing how Neil and his friends had left a seething Berkeley and moved up to the land his father had bought dirt cheap long before. Speculative land, to be held until the right time to sell.

Johanna shifted in her seat. Real estate development had made Neil's father rich. He foresaw Northern California ripe for shopping malls, hotels, and apartments. But Neil and his friends hated speculators. Pamela repeated this a couple of times. Still, the land sat there, remote, unfrequented, and they needed somewhere to hide from the draft board. So they took their girlfriends up there for a long weekend and never came back. The film wove its story deftly, from footage of the war in Vietnam—the black and white images adding more drama to the color shots of soldiers crouching in the jungle, bodies lined up on a road, children running in terror—to frenetic scenes in the United States. Huge protests of thousands of young people, police with shields facing off screaming students, the famous photo of a Kent State student keening over the body of a friend shot by riot police.

Johanna glanced at Maelle, who sat, riveted. She must have heard the story of course, but Johanna wondered how seeing its curated images made her feel. Neither Maelle's generation, nor Abby's, had ever had to face such choices. Even though the country had engaged in wars after Maelle was born, they had not torn at the heart of the nation in the way that the Vietnam War did, at least in her memory.

The film cut back to images of Joyous Woods as it looked when the communards first saw it. Quiet, wooded, and scrubby. A few farms, a gas station, a grocery store, a bar, a crossroads. Pamela must have gone to the county library and pulled these archival photos.

The next segment, supposedly of the commune's early days, stirred murmurs. Johanna recognized no one and nothing. Told that no Joyous Woods founders had owned a camera, Pamela had spliced in photos of other communes in the area. Johanna's hands started twitching. How dare she? Pamela had betrayed the commune by taking other people's stories and plastering them onto her narrative.

So Pamela had made a polemical film, not meant to show the truth. Scenes of wild parties, of long-haired individuals sitting in a circle listening to some kind of robed guru who beat a drum, intoning nonsense syllables. People lying stoned on the ground. Pictures of picnics, Frisbee playing, laughter, music. Then aerial footage of marijuana crops hidden in the woods. Those images must have come from newspaper archives. None of it related to Joyous Woods.

When was Pamela going to get to the part about their dedication to creating a working farm? Johanna began to jiggle her foot. She stopped short, because suddenly she saw herself on the screen. Recounting how she, Johanna, had gone to the library and checked out books on organic farming. How she'd told the others starvation loomed unless they learned to work the land. Her voice, telling the others that laboring work on other farms, fruit picking and foraging, even registering for food stamps, were all dead ends. They couldn't survive unless they took a more proactive approach. She'd forgotten she'd told Pamela all that. In this telling, Neil and the other men were nowhere to be seen.

Then, as music became more lyrical, the mood switched. Johanna saw a much younger Curtis putting the chicken coops together—they did have photos of that, she remembered now—and of herself in the pagoda house's kitchen. Neil wielding a saw. The film moved to the present day, showed how the women worked the vegetable garden, made cheese, kept the woodstove going all day, turning out pies, cakes, jam. The goats in the dairy. Showed the life of a hen. Eggs being picked out of the nesting box. A little speech about how a menopausal hen was headed for the stock pot. A graphic scene of a hen decapitation, the drawing and plucking and dismembering for the pot. A scene of them all enjoying a chicken dinner. Here, Johanna felt a little tingle of fear. Would Pamela go off on Angela's vegetarian beliefs?

But it seemed that Pamela had not understood that Angela's beliefs had any more significance than the other unconventional ideas holding sway on the commune. In fact, Pamela made no mention of Angela at all.

How clever they'd all been then, to pretend their tragedy had never happened.

Johanna crossed one leg over the other, moving away from Neil slightly, noticing the gap between his jeans and her skirt, a sudden cooling between them. Why had she not raised that terrible rabbit scheme with

Neil at the time? If she had objected, if she'd told Sally and Linda and they'd told the men to stop because Angie hated cruelty to animals, her daughter might be here today.

But then, the truth was, she never could confront Neil. Not just because this was habit, her irritation at him always suppressed and coming out in other ways, targeting other people rather than him because she just couldn't seem to contradict him directly. No, the real reason was that she knew the commune needed the money. She should have listened to Angela, instead of cutting her off when she had tried to tell her about the rabbit sales. She'd alienated her daughter completely. Look what had happened to Jasper and Kyle. Left the commune and never came back. But what happened to Angela was worse.

Far worse. It was a parent's worst nightmare, to lose a child.

But was Angela's rejection of her parents' values all their fault? Didn't it happen in every generation? And the commune had been tolerant. Just as Neil's parents succumbed to his wild scheme to elude the authorities and to live as a dope-smoking hippie, she'd let Angela soapbox them all about animals.

So, Angela, with her belief that animals deserved the respect that humans usually reserved for their own species, operated freely from her own ethical system. Her parents encouraged such independent thinking, and with hippie love and tolerance, never said they agreed or disagreed. The problem was they didn't listen either, they were so wrapped up in their own righteousness.

It was all so complicated, this issue of culpability and righteousness. She wiped the side of her face surreptitiously. Strange, how her eyes had developed a watery film. They'd all been so misguided. And they'd never acknowledged their own complicity. Love, peace, living in harmony with nature. What a crock. They'd been such hypocrites.

She blinked. Blinked again so her vision became clearer, and on the screen saw Ray and Sally explaining how they'd discovered their secret to efficient vegetable production by happenstance. They produced more, Ray was explaining, because they used hand tools only. They did not till the earth. They couldn't afford to buy a tractor, and had no means, nor the mechanical knowledge to repair it if they'd bought a secondhand one. "It was down to hard work with a hoe and broadfork," Ray said to the camera, scratching his bald head.

Curtis said, and here Johanna smiled, seeing Curtis make sure the camera went to him, "All the old-fashioned methods we had to use because we had no money are in fact being revived. It's called biodynamic farming. It's an old technology but the latest thing. Cutting edge, in fact. When you don't till the soil, you spare the roots and fungi working underground, and keep the carbon in the ground. Johanna here, she read all about it and made it happen, really."

So Pamela had understood, finally, what they were aiming for, what they had achieved on the farm. It was a viable organic farm and deserved respect. And the communards publicly paid their respect to her, Johanna, their true leader.

Not that she saw any evidence of her own handiwork anywhere in the film. Perhaps Pamela hadn't realized Johanna had sewed the upholstery on the wooden sofa on which she had settled herself, notebook in hand, that first day she'd come to the farm to interview them. Oh, here was a clip of Johanna knitting, and one of the angora rabbits being combed for its fleece. But no mention of the work of spinning the fleece into yarn, no shots of her making her wonderful dyes from the plants in the area. Sloppy work. Disregarding her contribution. Pamela's research was insufficient. Johanna folded her arms across her chest.

She scanned the audience, all intent on the screen, wondered if they, too, had noticed the slight. But no one caught her eye. More music, and the movie appeared to be winding down. Then, Pamela's voice, making an editorial comment.

"I came to Joyous Woods with preconceptions," she said. "I assumed the hippies had never moved on from the sixties and seventies. My own father, who had served in Vietnam, resented them, called them cowards for avoiding the nightmare he'd experienced. And I absorbed his attitude too, mixed with curiosity. Were they really so bad? So I came to find out for myself."

Johanna leaned forward. At last, Pamela's motives explained. Now she could understand the hostility she sensed that first day they'd met.

But Pamela had not finished. "What I found at Joyous Woods"—she smiled broadly—"was a group of friends who'd stayed together through poverty and hardship for almost fifty years, raised children, and now managed a farm that is as successful as any farm can be, given that it's not an easy way to make a living."

More shots of the landscape, seen with the sun setting through the trees, serene and lovely. Then the film cut to the kitchen of the pagoda house, where a stew bubbled on the stove while Linda took knives and forks to the table.

"While I was filming," Pamela went on, "I learned that the land would have to be sold because it was part of the estate of Neil's late parents. But I ask, does it have to go?"

A pause for effect. Then she said, "Do these old friends, vigorous still from a life lived mostly in the fresh air, a life of action, far removed from the sedentary, consumerist life that most Americans live today, do these people deserve to be thrown off the land that they've cherished for all these years?"

You could hear the collective sigh from the audience. Johanna relaxed. This was not at all the film she'd feared Pamela would make. She flicked a piece of lint of her skirt, unable to meet Neil's eye. She'd been wrong about him and Pamela too. Pamela clearly had admired him, whether or not she had flirted with him. Neil's natural flirtatiousness had aroused her jealousy. He couldn't help himself.

The screen faded to black. Silence filled the room for a minute as people took in that the movie had finished. Then someone clapped, and soon the room filled with the thrumming sound of applause. Relief inched its way down Johanna's body, and she stretched out her legs in front of her. There was nothing more to fear. The film had not mentioned the Children's House.

Pamela rose from her seat down the row, gesturing to the communards to come forward and take a bow. Johanna noticed she was wearing one of her own creations, a brown mohair jacket that complemented her hair. Where had that come from? Abby, who'd shunned her work lately, must have given it to her. Fury rose in her, and she resisted Neil as he pulled on her hand to help her up. She gave in, and as she stood, a cold breeze from the open window strengthened, bringing with it a metallic tang as the first raindrops hit the sill. Someone rushed to shut the window. A flash of lightning lit the sky, and a tremendous thunderclap rattled the building.

"Bring your chairs with you," Neil said. "Pamela will answer questions in the big house. Johanna and Linda and Sally have prepared great food for the reception."

Johanna thought she'd misheard. Neil had complimented her. She turned to thank him, but he was already picking up a chair.

Through the now pouring rain they all ran, folding chairs over heads for protection, and crowded into the great room of the pagoda house. Conviviality, delicious baked goods, drinks of all kinds filled the room. Gratitude swept through Johanna, and she hugged Sally, Linda, Maelle, and Abby over and over.

Outside the rain and thunder continued, a relief, assuring the farming community that the drought may have broken at last. It went on and on, competing in noise with the party. So it wasn't until people began to leave, reminding each other that the animals needed their evening care, that Johanna noticed that Neil was not in the room. She glanced around. He had not gone off with Pamela, still encircled with a group of questioners. The camera crew held cans of beer, laughing with other young people.

Ray and Curtis stood deep in conversation with Robert, and she went over. Robert's deep voice proclaimed the film's excellence; it was the best publicity they could have received, and could bolster the communards' case for a land trust, if that's what they really wanted.

"If that's what Neil wants," Johanna said. "But where is he?"

A sudden stomach-punch of dread hit her as noises came from a distance. Someone outside was shouting, then another panicked voice yelled for help. The noise came from the south side of the house. Johanna rushed toward it, followed by the rest of the group. Hard to see in the dark as she ran, Johanna made out people in a huddle, crouched over something on the ground.

A big fallen tree branch nearly tripped her. Under it, covered with blood and mud and pieces of the broken balcony, lay Neil.

Chapter Thirty-Six

As Maelle watched, Abby took three skeins of yarn from her mother's workbag and laid them on the big kitchen table.

"I know, Mother, you didn't understand what I mean about changing my business model. Here's a good example." She touched each skein in turn.

"What are you talking about?"

"They're all green, but not one matches the other."

Maelle said, "Why does that matter?"

"Because when you make your own plant-based dyes, you never get large enough batches of a consistent color to go mainstream. That's what I was getting at when I talked about moving to a different business model." She softened her voice. "My concern wasn't the quality of Mother's yarn colors; it was the quantity."

Maelle looked from her aunt to her grandmother. The older woman looked bewildered. Abby held notepad and pencil, and though Johanna had for the moment abandoned her knitting as the three sat around the farmhouse table, she appeared more intent on the cat weaving around her ankles.

"Garments I make are one of a kind, yet you want more." Johanna patted the cat. "Big quantity, you lose quality control."

"Not necessarily. It's about a more focused

strategy. Japanese indigo grows well in this climate. You know, the plant that makes that lovely blue dye? There's enough land here to grow *Persicaria tinctoria* in commercial quantities. It could be done by the biodynamic method. Harvesting the leaves three times a year can yield the five-thousand-pound minimum amount you'd need to create a commercial quantity of indigo dye."

Maelle nodded. "You've done your homework, Abbs."

"How does that affect me?" Johanna said.

"If I work with Maelle and the others to put together a research grant proposal, we might get what we need to keep Joyous Woods a viable organic farm, with dye plants a major crop. It's a huge potential market, with all those pairs of jeans dyed blue."

"You mean move from the spinning and weaving aspect?" Johanna reached for her workbag.

Energy shone from Abby's face. "Keep all that as a hobby, Mother. Teach it. I'm sure my idea can put the farm on a real business basis. Uncle Robert is going to help us put the acreage into a land trust. Hire young people to tend the fields. Really, it could work. Neil would have wanted that."

Johanna's face collapsed. She dabbed her eyes. "I think he would. He might have talked about Hawaii, but he couldn't imagine us living anywhere else. We can all stay here, keep on living on the farm?"

"Yes. That's exactly what I mean." Abby waved her arm toward the window, from which they could see Linda disappearing into the dairy. "Linda's already got a plan to train young people as artisan cheese makers. And Sally and Curtis want to stay here, to teach art as well as make it. You'll be taken care of, Mother."

Johanna's eyes filled. "If I'd been more patient with Neil, he wouldn't have suffered so. You, too, Abby. I should have paid more attention."

Maelle breathed deeply. After Neil's death, Robert had insisted on an autopsy. After all, no one had seen Neil go upstairs or knew why he'd stood on the rotting balcony in the pouring rain. The post-mortem delivered an answer. Neil had a brain tumor. His increasing moodiness, inability to concentrate or to make decisions, all came from a growing alien presence in his brain. With his death, Robert and Martha backed off their scheme to sell Joyous Woods to developers. There was plenty of inheritance left for them, and they seemed relieved to let the remaining communards work out a solution.

Maelle's work at the university had taken a temporary back seat as she became so energized about the fate of the farm. Now, seeing Abby taking charge, she smiled. It would be all right. Once she earned her degree, she might take a more active role in plant protection, using Joyous Woods as a laboratory.

She itched to get outside. Out the window, a toyon tree stood, watching. All of a sudden, a rustle, a squirrel's tail darted along a branch. She could swear that the tree winked at her. A berry dropped. Nature, surviving.

And Zachary. She still felt bruised after their last encounter. Yet the strange manner in which they were linked through their parents was a bond, too. No one else could share what they had experienced as kids, at the same time. No one else could have this peculiar history. He would come back to her when he was ready.

She was sure of it.

She'd write an email, that was it. An old-fashioned email, not a text. Ask how he was doing, how his work was going. Maybe they could meet for coffee.

Do it now, while her courage was up. She pulled her phone out of pocket and turned her mind off the conversation between Abby and her grandmother. With her experience of running a business, Abby could explain it all to the communards, who couldn't tell a legal document from a manifesto.

Maelle switched on her email program, and the screen opened up.

She was about to eliminate the unwanted spam when she saw a curious name. Harrison Bolt. Was this someone she'd met at a conference? Someone from the co-op she and Abby had talked to about growing dye plants commercially?

She took a risk and opened the email. And read.

Dear Maelle,

You will not know my name, nor will anyone at Joyous Woods. That's because I called myself Moonshine in those days. Youthful rebellion, I guess. I went to Joyous Woods on a whim, escaping a bad situation at home. I had no money. I was nineteen years old and had just dropped out of college. Angry young man, but also interested in an alternative lifestyle. That's when I met your mother, Angela.

I believe I must be your father. I just saw the movie about Joyous Woods. Recognized the farm, the name, the people in the pictures. Then I read in an article the filmmaker's interview with a young woman who had been born into the hippie community. You. I did the math. I spent a few weeks there a quarter century ago. I moved on because I needed to get back on my feet, earn some money, go back into college, and reconcile with my parents. Not that I didn't enjoy my time at Joyous Woods. I learned a lot there, about how to live cooperatively and unselfishly. I was the one who was selfish, just going off with no explanation. I had no idea Angela was pregnant. She wouldn't have known either till after I'd gone.

Anyway, Maelle, it seems you've done well, and I'm glad. I'll be surprised if you can forgive me for not being part of your life. But as I said, I had no idea. If you let me, I will make it up to you. My phone number is at the bottom of this page.

Sincerely,

Harrison

Maelle stared at the letter for a long time. She wondered if she should feel relief.

But she just felt numb.

She'd always grieved the lack of a father. A weird feeling of loss, even within the ethos of Joyous Woods, where blood ties seemed less important than in the outside world. Of course she should look up this Harrison Bolt, if only to get his medical history so that she could go safely into her own pregnancy.

Wait, where did that come from? Dare she hope, with Zachary? She couldn't imagine being with anyone else.

At least her father—if that's who he was—had done the right thing. He had contacted her.

But there was something missing here. A wrong tone.

She read the letter again.

The film had not mentioned Angela Becker at all.

When Pamela had been interviewing the communards, they must have clammed up about her death. Of course they had. It would have remained a buried subject if she had not met Zachary and felt that unbearable pressure to find out what had happened to her mother. So Harrison Bolt would have no idea that she had died.

She read the letter a third time. He never asked about Angela. He never once wondered, in all those lines of self-justification, how the mother of his child fared.

Maelle closed the phone. She breathed, long and deep. She would not send Zachary an email. She would call, then just get in the car and go and see him. No more muddled communication. The past was the past. It was time to forgive.

She looked around the room at the pagoda house. The old stove sent waves of warmth throughout the kitchen. She got up to fill the kettle. She'd make tea. The pantry beckoned, its strips of drying herbs and garlic hanging in the doorway, and she entered its dark depths. She found a large tin of cookies and brought it to the table.

Her grandmother sat at the table, staring blankly at a page of numbers Abby had put before her. Maelle bent her head to kiss the top of the gray hair. She wrapped her arms around the ample, ageing shoulders and nestled her face in Johanna's warm neck. The love that bloomed from her heart filled the room, encompassing them all.

A word about the author...

Margaret Ann Spence grew up on tales of her grandmother's childhood on a failing dairy farm and did learn to milk a cow. That's why she thinks it's easiest to live in the city. Born in Australia, she has lived in the United States since the age of twenty-three. At home in Phoenix, Arizona, she tends an unruly garden, cooks, writes, and enjoys her family.

Visit her at:

https://www.margaretannspence.com

Thank you for purchasing
this publication of The Wild Rose Press, Inc.

For questions or more information
contact us at
info@thewildrosepress.com.

The Wild Rose Press, Inc.
www.thewildrosepress.com

CPSIA information can be obtained
at www.ICGtesting.com
Printed in the USA
LVHW050311090221
678789LV00001B/32